"MR. AMBASSADOR!"

"What do you want?" Worf asked Kl'rt by way of greeting.

"Supervisor Vark needs to see you right away, sir."

"Regarding what?"

"I don't know that, sir, I only know that it's urgent."

Worf turned his back on Kl'rt. "I have an appointment that is more urgent. Tell Vark to make an appointment with Mr. Murphy."

"Sir, Supervisor Vark told me to fetch you and not come back without you. He'll kill me if I disobey."

Closing his eyes, Worf thought, *I do not have time for this*. He turned to face Kl'rt. "Then you will die, for I will not see Vark now."

Then he saw it.

Worf hesitated for only a moment, but that was apparently enough for Kl'rt, who removed the small weapon from under his shirt and fired it at Worf.

STAR TREK®
A Time for War, A Time for Peace

KEITH R.A. DeCANDIDO

Based on STAR TREK
and STAR TREK: THE NEXT GENERATION®
created by Gene Roddenberry,
STAR TREK: DEEP SPACE NINE®
created by Rick Berman & Michael Piller,
and STAR TREK: VOYAGER®
created by Rick Berman
& Michael Piller & Jeri Taylor

POCKET BOOKS
New York   London   Toronto   Sydney

This book is a work of fiction. Names, characters, places and incidents are products of the author's imagination or are used fictitiously. Any resemblance to actual events or locales or persons, living or dead, is entirely coincidental.

An *Original* Publication of POCKET BOOKS

POCKET BOOKS, a division of Simon & Schuster, Inc.
1230 Avenue of the Americas, New York, NY 10020

ISBN: 0-7434-9179-3

First Pocket Books printing October 2004

10 9 8 7 6 5 4 3 2 1

POCKET and colophon are registered trademarks of Simon & Schuster, Inc.

Cover by Zucca Design

Manufactured in the United States of America

For information regarding special discounts for bulk purchases, please contact Simon & Schuster Special Sales at 1-800-456-6798 or business@simonandschuster.com.

Dedicated with great affection and true sensawunda to the Mars Rovers Spirit *and* Opportunity, *which both landed on the red planet while I was working on this book, and to the wonderful explorers at NASA responsible for them. The pictures they sent inspired me all the more to keep writing about a future where we will travel among the stars.*

HISTORIAN'S NOTE

The bulk of this novel takes place in the weeks leading up to the feature film *Star Trek Nemesis*—a bit less than four years after "What You Leave Behind" (the final episode of *Star Trek: Deep Space Nine*), a bit less than two years after "Endgame" (the final episode of *Star Trek: Voyager*), and about one year after *A Time to Be Born* (the first book in this series). *Nemesis* takes place on Stardate 56844.9, which places it in late 2379 on the human calendar.

And after the strife of war begins the strife of peace.

—Carl Sandburg

Chapter 1
Qo'noS

SUNRISE ON QO'NOS had lost its appeal for Ambassador Worf.

There was a time, not so long ago, when the best part of his day was the very beginning, when he would enter his office in the Federation embassy and watch the sun blaze over the horizon through the huge picture window that took up most of the office's back wall. In the almost four years he had served as Federation ambassador to the Klingon Empire, the one part of his daily routine that he could count on enjoying was the spectacular view of the sun casting its fiery glow across the First City at the top of the day.

Recent events had dimmed that enthusiasm considerably. The actions of others less honorable had forced Worf into a position where he had to compromise himself in order to serve the greater good. The alternative was to allow an even greater evil, and he could not permit that to happen, regardless of the consequences.

It was a state of affairs that was all too familiar to the son of Mogh.

A little more than a month ago, he had used his position—as an ambassador, and as a member of the Klingon chancellor's House—to give his former crewmates on the *U.S.S. Enterprise* a weapon of sorts that they could use to prevent a Klingon Defense Force fleet from engaging in a suicidal attack on the planet Tezwa. Officially, no one could prove that he provided the *Enterprise* with the prefix codes that would disable the fleet; unofficially, it couldn't have been anyone else.

How many times? he asked himself. *How many times have I sacrificed my own honor to protect the unworthy? And how many times will I have to do it again?*

"It's supposed to be fairly hot today," came a voice from behind him.

Sighing, Worf turned around. Another part of the routine: his aide, Giancarlo Wu, would enter the office and make some offhand comment about the weather, thus signaling the start of the workday. Wearing his usual monochrome shirt, matching pants, and different-colored vest—today he went for red and green—Wu stood in the doorway to the office, reaching into the vest's pocket.

However, he did not pull out his padd, as Worf had expected—that padd was always either in Wu's hand or in his vest pocket, to the point that the ambassador honestly believed that his aide would suffer withdrawal symptoms if separated from it for any length of time. Instead, Wu removed an optical chip and walked it over to where Worf sat at his desk. "I think you'll want to see this first thing, sir. It was sent to you on a secure channel by T'Latrek."

After regarding the chip for a moment, Worf plugged it into the slot on the side of his terminal. Besides representing Vulcan on the Federation Council, T'Latrek served as the councillor for external affairs and was, in essence, Worf's superior.

The screen lit up with the logo of the Federation News Service. *Odd,* Worf thought. *Why would T'Latrek send me a news story?*

A female Pandrilite face replaced the logo. *"The top story is the surprise resignation of Federation President Min Zife. In a move that has shocked the entire quadrant, President Zife, his chief of staff, Koll Azernal, and Nelino Quafina, the secretary of military intelligence, have stepped down from office, effective immediately. This statement was issued across the Federation this morning."*

The image then cut to Zife sitting at his desk in the presidential office in Paris, his arms placed in front of him, resting on the large desk, which was currently empty of anything save the Bolian's blue-skinned hands. The flag of the Federation hung on a pole behind the president, in front of the huge window that provided a panorama of the City of Light that made Worf's own view of the First City pale in comparison. The Tour Eiffel was the only landmark in sight.

"It is with a sense of both regret and joy that I announce my resignation as president of the United Federation of Planets, as well as the resignation of Koll Azernal, my chief of staff, and Nelino Quafina, my military intelligence secretary. Regret because achieving this office has been the culmination of a lifetime of service to the Federation, and one that has been incredibly rewarding for my-

self and, I hope, for the Federation, particularly during the dark days of our war against the Dominion.

"Joy because I feel that this resignation is perhaps the greatest of those services that I can now give to the Federation. While my chief of staff and I were able to serve our nation well in war, we were, it seems, less suited for peace. As the war grows more distant in our past, it has become increasingly obvious that Koll and I need to step down for the good of the Federation. The model by which we survived during the war, and even during the first few months afterward, is no longer tenable as we and our allies attempt to bring a new era of peace.

"One of the truisms of sentient life throughout the galaxy is that different leadership is required for different circumstances. On Bolarus, one of our most revered historical figures is a monarch from a time before the planet was united, named Queen Vaq. She led the nation of Alnat to its most prosperous era after winning several consecutive wars. What most forget is that when Alnat became the greatest power on Bolarus, and all her enemies were defeated, Vaq was forced to abdicate, for without an enemy to fight, she led the nation to economic ruin.

"Unlike Vaq, I will not wait for a coup d'état to remove me from power. I was given a mandate from the people of the Federation—not once, but twice—to lead them through uneasy times, to make quick and difficult decisions for the greater good. Now, though, serving that mandate has proven more problematic. Quick and difficult decisions are not what is best for the Federation, nor for our allies. The time has come when I can best serve the people's mandate by stepping down, by allow-

ing the people to choose someone who can lead us in peace as effectively as I was able to in war.

"As per the Federation charter, an election will be held within the month. The Federation Council will continue to administrate on a pro tem basis until a new president has been elected.

"I thank you all very much for your support, your patience, and your understanding. Good-bye."

Back to the Pandrilite: *"The Federation Council made no comment regarding the resignations, but did release a statement: Councillor Ra'ch B'ullhy has been appointed president pro tempore, and the Council will be accepting petitions for presidential candidates immediately. The ballot containing the names of those who fit the criteria for candidacy will be announced by the Council one week from today. The election will be held at the end of the month.*

"At present, the front-runners for presidential candidacy include T'Latrek of Vulcan, the current councillor for external affairs, who has held that position for eight decades; Nan Bacco, the planetary governor of Cestus III; Fel Pagro, the chief special emissary for Ktar; and Admiral William Ross of Starfleet. Naturally, speculation is already running rampant as to what led President Zife and Chief of Staff Azernal to their decision at this particular juncture, especially with the next election less than a year away."

The screen reverted to the FNS logo, then went blank.

Worf leaned back in his large leather chair. "A—convincing fabrication."

"Sir?"

"Zife and Azernal's reasons for resigning begin and end with Tezwa."

"I suspected as much, sir. Still, the general public can't very well be aware of that, can they?"

Worf folded his arms. "No. This willing resignation is a far more palatable solution than admitting to secretly arming the Tezwans." If Martok or the Klingon High Council ever found out that the Federation president armed an enemy of the empire, it could lead to yet another abrogation of the Khitomer Accords, and possibly war between the Federation and the empire. Neither nation was in a position to wage a prolonged war against the other, and the collapse of their alliance would destabilize the Alpha Quadrant at a time when it could ill afford such a thing.

Yet another secret I must keep from a man I have called brother, Worf thought bitterly. "I sometimes regret the day I chose to enter the realm of politics," he muttered.

Wu tilted his head. "I should think that after all these years, sir, you'd be used to it."

Glowering at his aide, Worf said, "The time since I accepted the ambassadorship is hardly 'all these years.' "

"My apologies, sir, I thought you said you regretted entering the realm of politics. That happened when you entered the Great Hall thirteen years ago in order to defend your father against accusations that he aided the Romulans at Khitomer."

Worf's glower intensified. "Excuse me?"

Wu put his hands in his vest pockets. "You accepted discommendation in order to cover up the crimes of the House of Duras and preserve unity on the High Council, but kept your brother—a high-ranking officer in the Defense Force—shielded from the dishonor. When Gowron needed help during the civil war, you were then able to use Kurn's position to restore your House and keep House Duras from gaining power." He removed his hands from his pockets, taking the padd out with his right hand. "Each of the last two chancellors, not to mention the emperor himself, owe their positions directly to you. You've probably had more impact on the face of Klingon politics than any single person in the last twenty years. Your accepting the ambassadorship was simply the continuation of a process you'd begun long before."

The aide's words mirrored similar ones spoken to Worf by Ambassador Spock three years earlier on a shuttle trip to a diplomatic conference. He had dismissed them then as exaggeration. He was tempted to do so now, but hesitated. Neither Spock nor Wu were prone to such things. Indeed, Wu had always, at Worf's own insistence, been completely honest with the ambassador.

"This—analysis is your interpretation of what I have done over the years?" he finally asked.

Wu shrugged. "Not really—simply the facts as I and many others see them. I had always assumed that it was why you were given this position in the first place. You've always been an excellent politician, sir."

Although he had worked on Qo'noS and among Klingons for over a decade, Wu was still a human. For that reason alone, Worf let the insult pass. That, and he'd never find an aide as talented.

As was Wu's wont, he noticed that Worf was not pleased with the way the conversation was turning, and so stared down at his padd and changed the subject. "There was a personal message accompanying T'Latrek's transmission, sir. She wishes to assure you that she has no intention of running for president, any more than she has the other dozen times an election has occurred since she joined the Federation Council, and also that she will contact you with further instructions on how to present this new information to the High Council within the hour. This is useful, as the council has requested your presence in the Great Hall at high sun."

"Naturally." Worf felt a growl build in his throat, but he tamped it down.

"I took the liberty of clearing all your appointments for today, save one, so you would be free to speak to T'Latrek and the council. I assume that that particular business will preclude all others."

Worf rose from his chair. "You assume correctly." He started to pace the room, walking toward the window. "What is the appointment you did not clear?"

At this, Wu smiled. "The *Ya'Vang* was recalled to Qo'noS for maintenance yesterday, and its crew granted shore leave. Your son will be here in twenty minutes."

Once, Worf might have greeted that news with apprehension, even anger. Alexander was born to K'Ehleyr, Worf's first love. When K'Ehleyr was slain by Duras on the *Enterprise*-D, Worf had avenged her death in the proper manner, and also taken responsibility for their son. Alexander was raised alternately by Worf on the *Enterprise* and by Worf's human foster parents on Earth; neither solution proved tenable. Sergey and Helena Rozhenko did the best they could, but they were too old to raise yet another child, and Worf was simply unsuited to the role of father.

It was the Dominion War that gave Alexander purpose. He enlisted in the Defense Force, serving on several ships during the conflict. Though the youth would never be mistaken for a great warrior, he did eventually grow into a decent soldier.

In the years since the war, father and son had come to a certain peace, for which Worf was grateful. His failures with Alexander had always gnawed at him, made him feel as if he had betrayed K'Ehleyr in some way. She deserved better than that—as did their child. To make matters worse, the *Ya'Vang* had been at the forefront of the fleet that the Defense Force had sent to Tezwa. Though Worf's actions in stopping the fleet were primarily committed in order to preserve the peace and save Klingon lives, that he was able to rescue his son from a pointless death was never far from his thoughts.

The intercom on Worf's desk beeped. The voice of Damir Gorjanc, one of the embassy staff, spoke: *"Sir, you have a coded message from Earth."*

"That," Wu said, "will no doubt be T'Latrek."

"No doubt." To Gorjanc, Worf said, "Put it through."

Expecting the Vulcanoid features of T'Latrek, Worf was surprised to instead see the teal-hued face and horned head of another member of the Federation Council, one Worf had first met almost a decade earlier.

"Councillor Ra'ch. It is good to see you again."

"Likewise, Mr. Ambassador." Ra'ch B'ullhy, the former governor of Damiano, smiled. *"We've both come a long way since you saved my life at my inauguration."* Worf, then security chief of the *Enterprise,* had prevented an assassination attempt on Ra'ch's life when she

took office. *"You're an ambassador, and I'm the president pro tem."*

"Congratulations."

Ra'ch's face went sour. *"Easy for you to say—you're safe on Qo'noS. Believe me, I didn't want this. But since I'm stuck with the responsibility, I wanted to let you know how this needs to be presented to the High Council."*

Worf wondered if this was why Ra'ch rather than T'Latrek was making the call. While the notion that Vulcans never lied, much like the notion that Klingons never did, was more ideal than reality, that didn't change the fact that most Vulcans were uncomfortable with falsehood.

"I assume," he said dryly, "that the truth is to be avoided at all costs."

"Good assumption. As far as Chancellor Martok is concerned, this is a decision that both Zife and Azernal have been contemplating for quite a while, and they felt that the time was right to make the announcement."

"And if they ask why there were no indications of this—contemplation prior to now?"

"The fact that the president and his primary aide are about to resign is hardly something they want to spread around. The tightest possible security was kept on this to maintain stability and not jeopardize the president's ability to do his job."

Worf nodded. "He did not want to appear to be a lame duck."

Ra'ch frowned. *"I'm sorry?"*

Shaking his head, Worf said, "My apologies. It is a human metaphor, applying to someone in a position of power whose days in that position are known to be coming to an end."

"*Oh.*" Ra'ch was still frowning. "*I don't see what a maimed waterfowl has to do with that.*"

"It *is* a human metaphor. They are often abstruse."

"*True. Is there anything else you need to know, Mr. Ambassador?*"

There were, in fact, several things, but Worf had other sources he could call upon for them, ones less busy than the person temporarily serving as president of the largest governmental body in the quadrant. "No. I will be speaking before the council at high sun."

"*Good. I have every faith that you'll continue to serve the Federation with honor.*"

Worf wasn't entirely sure he had always done so up until now, but said only: "Thank you, Madam President."

Ra'ch winced. "*For Ho'nig's sake, don't* call me that. *I'm still a councillor, and I plan to stay one. Call the poor unfortunate who wins the election that—they're welcome to it. Now, if you'll excuse me, I have about a dozen other ambassadors to talk to.*" She smiled. "*It's good to see you again, Worf.*"

"Likewise, Councillor."

With that, the screen went blank.

Worf turned to Wu. "Have Bey write an official statement incorporating Councillor Ra'ch's comments. I wish to see it within the hour." Diplomacy included a great deal of written composition, which was not Worf's strong suit. He could write a Starfleet report that was the envy of other officers for its completeness and attention to detail, he could write decent verse if the poem's subject was sufficiently inspiring, but the language of the official statement from the ambassador's office continued to elude him. Thankfully, such skills were not required. Bey Toh had been a speechwriter for two first ministers of Bajor, and he joined the embassy staff shortly after that planet had joined the Federation. It hadn't taken him long to adapt Worf's particular style of address to the written word.

Making notes on his padd, Wu said, "Of course, sir. Anything else?"

"I assume the resolutions that you had for me yesterday are still needed by the end of the day?"

Wu smiled. "It's possible that they've fallen down the priority queue a bit with this morning's events, sir, but I haven't heard anything specific."

"Very well. I will review them while I wait for my son. Have someone send up some *gagh* from the galley."

Wu nodded. "Anything else?"

"That will be all."

"Very good, sir."

The aide took his leave. Worf turned back to the terminal and called up the resolutions he had mentioned. If nothing else, it was probably best to get them out of the way; with Zife resigning, there would be a great deal of new business that would require Worf's attention. In particular he was concerned about how some on the High Council might view the fact that there was a vacuum in the Federation's power structure, however temporary. There were many in the empire who believed that, with the Dominion War over, there was no longer a need for the Federation and the empire to remain allies, some who even believed that there should be a return to the days before Praxis, when the Federation was just one of a list of enemies the empire intended to crush under its heel.

Tezwa would only add strength to those radicals' positions.

As the Federation's representative in the empire, it was Worf's job to ensure that the empire remained a steadfast ally. His position as a member of the chancellor's House, and Martok's own strong feelings about the need for the Federation alliance, would make that job *easier,* but that did not make said job in any way *easy.*

At some point, his office chime rang. "Enter."

A young Klingon woman entered the room, carrying a tray. Worf glanced to see the vermicular creatures in the bowl that sat in the tray's center. Though the replicators could provide adequate sustenance when necessary, sometimes there was just no substitute for live *gagh.*

Worf did not recognize the steward. Since he prided himself on knowing the entire embassy staff by sight, he asked, "Who are you?"

The woman stood with her arms folded in front of her. "I am Karra." No mother, no House, which meant she was a commoner—hardly surprising, given her position as an embassy steward. Those of noble blood would not serve in such jobs, leaving them either to commoners or to *jeghpu'wI'*. "I began my employment here a week ago."

A statement that he was not aware of any changes in the kitchen staff died on Worf's lips. He usually left such minutiae to Wu, more so in the past few months. "Very well," he said. "You may leave."

Karra nodded and left the room.

Frowning, Worf called up the embassy staff records. Karra had indeed been hired seven days earlier. In fact, fifteen members of the kitchen staff had been hired in the last month. Those positions tended to have a high turnover, so it probably wasn't all that untoward—still, Worf made a mental note to speak with the head of personnel, a cantankerous old Klingon named Mag, about it after he got back from the Great Hall. If nothing else, that quick a staff turnover constituted a security concern, if not an out-and-out security risk.

The intercom beeped. It was Gorjanc again. *"Sir, your son has arrived. He's coming through security at the front gate now."*

Worf allowed himself a smile. *There will be time for security concerns and politics later.* "I am on my way."

He switched off his computer and proceeded to the narrow hallway outside his office. The embassy was shaped like an inverted pyramid, and Worf's office was located on the second floor, taking up the entirety of the south section of that level. The north section contained Wu's office and the embassy library, a narrow hallway between them, ending on the west side with a turbolift and on the east with an emergency stairwell. In the center of the hallway was a large desk, where Carl Murphy sat. The human handled Worf's in-embassy appointments.

As Worf nodded to Murphy on his way toward the turbolift, another steward ran up to him. Worf recognized him only because he had just seen the boy's personnel record. His name was Kl'rt, and he was hired only four days previously.

"Mr. Ambassador!"

"What do you want?" Worf asked by way of greeting.

"Supervisor Vark needs to see you right away, sir." Vark was the head of the kitchen staff.

"Regarding what?"

"I don't know that, sir, I only know that it's urgent."

Worf turned his back on Kl'rt. "I have an appointment that is more urgent. Tell Vark to make an appointment with Mr. Murphy."

"Sir, Supervisor Vark told me to fetch you and not come back without you. He'll kill me if I disobey."

Closing his eyes, Worf thought, *I do not have time for this.* He turned to face Kl'rt. "Then you will die, for I will not see Vark now."

Then he saw it.

All the stewards in the embassy wore the same two-piece white outfit, a simple shirt and pants. They were generally formfitting, though Kl'rt's was a bit loose on him. Too loose, in fact—the quartermaster was generally more competent at getting the sizes right.

Kl'rt's service record, which Worf had just been perusing, along with those of the other new arrivals to the kitchen staff, indicated no injuries or deformities of any kind. Such things were always listed in the records—for example, Vark's record noted that he was missing two fingers from his left hand, which happened either in glorious battle against the Kinshaya or after an accident in the kitchen of the House of K'mpec, depending on how drunk the kitchen staff supervisor was when he told the story.

Yet there was no indication in the records of the bulge Worf now saw on Kl'rt's right hip.

Worf hesitated for only a moment, but that was apparently enough for Kl'rt, who removed the small weapon from under his shirt and fired it at Worf. The life of a diplomat had done little to dull Worf's reflexes, and he was able to duck to the floor to avoid the weapons fire, which he recognized as being that of a Breen disruptor.

Murphy, to his credit, immediately pressed the panic button on his desk—one of many security procedures instituted by Worf. The panic button would alert the security forces throughout the embassy of a breach, and also set off an alarm throughout the building.

That alarm did not sound.

Worf reached into the pocket of his floor-length leather coat and pulled out a small Ferengi phaser and fired it on Kl'rt—

—just as Kl'rt turned his disruptor on Murphy.

Both men fell to the ground a moment later.

"QI'yaH," Worf cursed. He ran over to Murphy's desk. Worf had stunned Kl'rt—he would need to be questioned—but the human was quite dead. Carl Murphy was a good man who had served the Federation well. Worf swore that those responsible would pay for his life.

A quick check on Murphy's computer revealed that the security system was down, which tracked with the malfunctioning panic button. Worf then entered the code that only he had—indeed, that only he and Wu knew about—which would reactivate the security system.

The system obligingly came online a moment later. Before pushing the panic button a second time, Worf called up the views from the security recorders in the embassy. He needed intelligence before he proceeded further.

In every room, he saw people in the white shirt-and-pants outfits of kitchen stewards, armed with Breen disruptors, rounding up the embassy staff.

One member of security unholstered her Starfleet phaser and tried to fire it, only to have the weapon fail. In another part of the embassy, two more security personnel, armed with Klingon disruptors, did likewise, and their weapons also failed.

The perpetrators of this assault not only disabled security, but must have engaged a scattering field to neutralize any Federation or Klingon weapons. Worf offered silent thanks to Nog. The first Ferengi in Starfleet, the young lieutenant had given Worf the phaser as a going-away present when Worf departed Deep Space 9 to become ambassador. Nog had promised that it was immune to most known forms of tampering and might come in handy someday. *He was right.*

Growling deep in his throat, Worf examined the security monitors. As unthinkable as it may have seemed, the embassy was under siege and in imminent danger of being taken over.

Worf assumed that the fifteen new members of the kitchen staff were the primary instigators. The security monitors revealed that a dozen Klingons were herding the staff to the large meeting room at the center of the embassy's top floor. With Kl'rt down at his feet, that left three unaccounted for—*assuming that Vark is part of this.* Mag, the head of personnel, apparently was not, as he was one of the ones being walked at gunpoint to the meeting room.

So, Worf noticed, was Alexander, currently being brought to the stairwell on the ground level.

Then the screens all went blank again. *Whoever tampered with security is keeping an eye on those systems.* He attempted his personal reactivation code a second time, but it had no effect.

I will have to make do with the intelligence I have so far.

Running back into his office, Worf retrieved a tricorder and his Starfleet combadge from the drawer of his desk and shoved the former into his pocket. They functioned independently of the embassy systems and wouldn't be affected by the sabotage.

To his total lack of surprise, use of the combadge garnered no reply. *If they are capable of a scattering field to neutralize weapons and of deactivating embassy security, they are equally capable of blocking communications.* Still, he pocketed the combadge in case he might need it, and moved back out into the hallway.

"*Kl'rt, respond.*" Worf recognized the voice as that of Vark, coming from Kl'rt's prone form, indicating a communications device somewhere on the stunned steward's person. "*He isn't answering.*"

"*All right,*" said another voice that Worf did not recognize. "*Gitak, Akor, get to the second level and find out what happened to Kl'rt.*"

A third voice, that of Karra, spoke: "*Why send two people to stop a mere diplomat?*"

"*He's not a mere diplomat, he's a decorated warrior who served in Starfleet for fifteen years in security and strategic operations. He's the most dangerous person in this embassy.*"

Vark growled. "*Damn you, Rov, if you had waited until after Worf was gone like I suggested—*"

"Then we wouldn't have our most valuable hostage, would we?"

Worf wondered if Rov knew that they already had their most valuable hostage's son. If he didn't, he would soon; Vark knew Alexander from the latter's many visits.

The ambassador needed to get off this floor immediately.

Checking his tricorder, he saw that the only life signs in the building that weren't in the meeting room were the two on this level—his and Kl'rt's—and thirteen moving about the embassy.

This has been a very efficient operation. Worf knew he had to conceal himself in order to plan a counterattack. *Fortunately, I have the perfect place to go.*

Worf took a moment to find the com unit, which was in Kl'rt's ear. Worf inserted the device in his own ear.

Even as he did, Rov said, *"Close the channel, wait for Gitak and Akor to check in."* Then the device went dead.

Worf kept it in his ear in any case. *It might prove useful.*

The door to the stairwell opened to reveal two more Klingons. Worf snarled, leapt behind Murphy's desk, and fired his phaser, now set to kill. *I need only one prisoner.*

As he crouched behind the large metal desk, he heard the thump of a body falling to the floor, meaning his aim was true and he had only one foe to face.

Two disruptor blasts whined as they went over Worf's head. Then he heard a voice both in his ear and from across the room. The shrill report of the disruptor meant that Worf actually heard the Klingon's words more clearly over his stolen com unit.

"This is Akor. Kl'rt's down, and the ambassador's still here. He took out Gitak. I need backup."

"I'm sending B'Eko and Kralk."

Allowing himself the tiniest of smiles, Worf took out the tricorder even as another disruptor blast fired over his head, this one on a different trajectory. Akor was not staying in one place, keeping Worf pinned behind the desk while he moved closer. Worf would have given him credit for good tactics, save for his breaking radio silence. That meant Worf could use his tricorder to home in on the transmission.

A moment later, he'd done so, backtracking Akor's movements in order to predict where he'd be in a moment.

Disruptor shots continued to fire over his head, even as Worf crawled around to behind the desk, right under the chair on which Murphy's dead body sat. He aimed his Ferengi phaser through the legs of the chair at a spot just past the other side of the desk.

Five, four, three, two, one.

He fired just as Akor came into view. The shot only glanced his shoulder, unfortunately, and so Akor was able to return fire even as he fell backward. Fortunately for Worf, the shot hit harmlessly on the metal chair. The type of Breen disruptor the stewards were using affected only living tissue, doing no damage to inorganic objects.

Worf fired again, taking advantage of the larger target presented by Akor when he fell. This time, his aim was dead-on; Akor got off one shot that fired into the ceiling before he died.

"Akor, what happened?" Rov asked over the com unit. *"Akor!"*

Climbing up from behind the desk, Worf bent over to pick up Kl'rt's unconscious form and slung him over his shoulder in a firefighter's carry. Rov's voice continued to blare into his ear as the ambassador brought Kl'rt to the turbolift doors.

The embassy had only one turboshaft on the lower levels, though there were two turbolifts. As the structure widened in all directions, the shaft forked, providing passage on both the east and west walls from the sixth floor up. At this second level, however, there was just the one and, according to Worf's tricorder, both lifts were stopped at the top level and had been deactivated.

That suited Worf fine. He needed only the shaft, not the lift itself.

Utilizing the manual override, Worf pried the lift doors open, then picked Kl'rt back up. The shaft had emergency ladders inset into the walls on the three nondoor sides; Worf grunted from the weight of his prisoner as he clambered over to one of them and then started climbing down.

If one inspected the plans for the Federation embassy, one would see, besides the aboveground portions, an extensive basement level. If one had security clearance above a certain level, one could see a different set of plans, which included a subbasement that wasn't even accessible to all those who had clearance to know about it. Worf was among the latter.

However, there was a second subbasement that almost nobody knew about and wasn't on any plan of the building that existed. Worf suspected that the number of people who did know of it could be counted on the fingers of one hand.

The ambassador himself was aware of its existence only because of a family connection. A high-ranking member of Imperial Intelligence named Lorgh was a friend to Worf's now-defunct House, and had let Worf know of the secret bunker that had been placed beneath the embassy, under the control of people who seemed to be Starfleet Intelligence, but in fact had a much more shadowy agenda, and no oversight that Lorgh could determine. In order to aid Captain Picard at Tezwa, Worf had gone to that sub-subbasement to ask the commander working there for help. Shortly thereafter, the room was cleared out, with not even subatomic traces of the base that Worf had seen. It was just an empty room that nobody even knew about.

Which made it the ideal place for Worf to begin planning to take back the Federation embassy.

Chapter 2
U.S.S. Enterprise

"I THANK YOU all very much for your support, your patience, and your understanding. Good-bye."

After the recording of President Zife's resignation speech faded from the observation lounge's monitor screen, William Riker looked around the table to gauge the reactions of the *Enterprise* senior staff.

As it happened, they were virtually split down the middle. Captain Jean-Luc Picard and those to his left—Deanna Troi, Data, and Beverly Crusher—all looked impassive, or at least placid. On the other hand, the other two officers joining Riker, on the captain's right—Christine Vale and Geordi La Forge—looked like they were ready to jump out of their skin.

Vale was the first to speak, and she did so through clenched teeth. "Well, that was a remarkable pile of bullshit."

Riker couldn't help but agree with the security chief's blunt appraisal.

La Forge was fidgeting in his chair. "I can't believe we're letting them get away with that."

Data gave the chief engineer a quizzical look. "Did President Zife and Chief of Staff Azernal not agree to this resignation as a preferable alternative to exposing their secret arming of the Tezwans to the general public?"

The android's flat mode of speech was almost enough to make Riker grin. It had been a year since the events at the Rashanar battle site had, among other things, led to the removal of Data's emotion chip. Riker had finally, after seven years, gotten used to Data having emotions; now he had to readjust to the emotionless Data all over again. It had been slow going—but then, he'd had other things on his mind in the months since Rashanar.

"Maybe, Data—but I don't have to like it." La Forge leaned forward in his chair and continued fidgeting, as if desperate for something to do with his hands.

"I don't like it either, Geordi," Riker said, "and believe me, I've got more reason than anyone to be bitter about Tezwa." Unbidden, the rotted-food-and-fecal-matter smell of the pit on Tezwa returned. Kinchawn, the ousted Tezwan prime minister, and his resistance group kept him prisoner there for weeks. The stench had yet to entirely leave his nostrils; he was starting to wonder if it ever would. "But it's still the prudent course of action."

"And if there's one thing politicians are good at, it's being prudent," Vale said bitterly. "That doesn't change that what he said was bullshit."

Throughout, Picard had sat with his hand on his chin, seemingly staring at a point in the middle of the conference-room table. Riker was about to prompt the captain when he finally spoke. "Your opinion is noted, Lieutenant, however—it *was* the best solution to the problem. The alternative was a war with the Klingons."

"Oh, I'm not denying it, sir," Vale said quickly. "I'd just like to see a politician tell the truth once. Just, you know, for the novelty value."

Picard's hand fell from his chin and he tugged downward on his uniform jacket as he leaned back in his chair. "Sadly, Lieutenant, we live in an imperfect world."

Troi folded her arms in front of her. "What I'm more curious about is who's going to run."

Riker admired the ship's counselor—his *Imzadi* and now his fiancée—for her ability to change the subject. The mission to Tezwa had been a disaster and a tragedy, and dwelling on it did nobody any good. "I'm betting T'Latrek will finally run this time," he deadpanned.

Data cocked his head. "Given that Councillor T'Latrek has refused to run in any of the twelve presidential elections that she has had the opportunity to participate in, and given your own general success at gambling, Commander, I would have to assume that you are being facetious."

Emotions or not, he's still Data, Riker thought. "Once again, my friend, you have seen through my poker face."

"It would not be the first time, sir, as our last poker game would indicate."

Wincing at the month-old memory of losing an especially big pot to Data on an especially audacious bluff— one that had driven Crusher, La Forge, and Troi out—Riker said, "Good point. With any luck, I'll be in better shape tonight."

La Forge leaned back. "If Ross runs, he'll win it in a

cakewalk." Riker noted that his hands now lay unmoving on the chair's armrests. The counselor's subject change had had the desired effect.

"I consider that to be highly improbable, Mr. La Forge," Picard said dryly. "Admiral Ross is not a politician." The captain allowed himself the tiniest of smiles. "He's not that foolish. Actually, I would be most interested to see if Governor Bacco runs."

Riker nodded in agreement. One of the *Enterprise*'s assignments during the Dominion War was to attempt to enlist the Gorn to fight on the allies' side. Sadly, the *Enterprise* arrived just in time to get caught up in a coup d'état. However, once the crew managed their way out of it, the Gorn did aid in the war effort, thanks in part to some fine negotiating between their new leadership and Nan Bacco, the planetary governor of Cestus III, the Federation world closest to Gorn space.

"I don't know," Vale said. "There's a huge difference between running a planet and running the Federation."

"Depends on the planet." Riker turned to look at the security chief. "If this was just some ordinary Federation colony that hadn't changed much in two hundred years, that'd be one thing, but look at everything Cestus has gone through. They had a huge population explosion ten years ago when they took in a whole bunch of refugees from the Cardassian Demilitarized Zone, which required a massive shift in how the colony was run. Then they were attacked by the Gorn, then they had to rebuild both physically and diplomatically after that. Thanks to Governor Bacco, not only does the Federation have a treaty with the Gorn, but also with the

Metrons. I think everyone here knows how hard it is to negotiate with energy beings, much less get them to agree to diplomatic relations." Nods of agreement went around the table.

"Besides," Data added, "there is no comparable task in the galaxy to the magnitude of the duties handed by the Federation president. It is impossible to judge with any accuracy how someone who has never performed the task will do so without such a basis to make that comparison."

"In other words," La Forge said with a grin, "you won't know how they'll do it until they do it."

"I believe I said that, Geordi."

"Right—which is why I said, 'in other words.' "

Vale shook her head. "Still, it's a *really* limited sphere of influence. I mean, it's just one planet. I'd be more comfortable with someone like Fel Pagro. He's been all over the Federation, worked with dozens of different governments. For something like this, I'd rather have someone with a little more breadth."

"A jack-of-all-trades rather than an expert at but one, Lieutenant?" Picard asked.

Vale nodded. "Something like that, yes, sir."

"It sounds to me," Troi said, "that someone from Starfleet would be your ideal candidate. Which brings us back to Admiral Ross."

Grinning, Vale said, "Yeah, but the captain already said he wouldn't run, and the captain is *always* right."

Picard gave Vale a small nod. "Well said, Lieutenant."

"Not to change the subject from the lieutenant's sucking up, sir," Riker said with a wink to Vale, "but her point raises another one. Ever since Tezwa, we've been cooling our heels and making repairs here in the Xarantine system. What's going to happen to us?"

Picard frowned. "I'm not sure what you mean, Number One."

"It's been a year since Rashanar. We've been at the bottom of Starfleet's barrel for that entire time, and all we've done is solve a two-hundred-year-old mystery, make a historic first contact, and avert two major wars— one of those at considerable loss of life. I should think that would count for *something*."

"I believe, Number One, the true question you wish to ask is, what about *me*, since after all, I was the subject of Starfleet's investigation after Rashanar, not the *Enterprise*." Another smile. "Besides, *Captain*, don't you have concerns of your own?"

Riker refused to take the bait, regardless of the amount of pride he felt from finally taking on his first command. "Until I actually report to the *Titan*, Captain, I'm still your first officer."

"Indeed you are." Picard took a breath. "To answer your question, it's still to be determined. However, we are not the only Starfleet vessel in this particular quandary." The captain folded his hands on the table. "Along with the copy of President Zife's resignation, I received a communiqué from Admiral Nakamura. As many of you know, several Starfleet vessels have been the subject of inspection tours over the past few months. The *Enterprise* has now been added to the list."

Troi frowned. "What kind of inspection tour is this, exactly?"

"Apparently, the admiralty is concerned that some ships

may be having difficulties similar to those expressed by President Zife in his resignation speech. That four years after the fact, some vessels may not have made the adjustment back to peacetime service, especially those captains who achieved the rank during the war. It is, after all, far easier to fall off the horse than it is to get back on it."

La Forge shook his head. "What, they want to make sure that we bled according to regulations?"

Riker sighed. "Well, at least they're not just picking on us this time."

"True, Number One. The inspection team will be arriving in one week's time. All personnel are to be at their disposal for the duration of their stay."

"Do we at least know who's gonna be on the team?" La Forge asked.

Vale added, "Or how long their stay's duration's going to be?"

"The answer to both is no, I'm afraid," Picard said.

"Wonderful," Vale muttered.

"In any event, our orders are to remain on station here at Xarantine and complete repairing the battle damage we took at Tezwa until the team arrives."

"We'll be done long before then, Captain." La Forge spoke with his usual air of confidence.

"I'm glad to hear that, Mr. La Forge." Picard gazed at Riker. "After the inspection, we will be reporting back to Earth. And that, Will, is your cue."

Riker grinned. "The last few weeks have been a little too busy for Deanna and me to make proper wedding plans, but now that we're no longer fighting guerrilla wars and rotting in POW camps, we've had a bit of time to figure out what we want to do." Again, Riker had to attempt to banish thoughts of the Tezwan pit from his mind, forcing himself to focus on the fact that he and Troi had finally decided to get married back on Delta Sigma IV. "We just want to have a simple ceremony with a few friends. Obviously, everyone in this room is invited. I'm working on securing an area of Alaska in the Denali Mountains, near where I grew up."

La Forge shuddered a bit. "We're not gonna have to climb a mountain or anything to get there, are we?"

Riker looked at Troi. "What do you think, should we allow transporters and shuttles?"

Nodding with mock gravity, Troi said, "I believe that can be permitted, yes."

"You're in luck, Geordi."

"Good—after Tezwa, I've had enough of mountains to last a lifetime."

"Oh," Riker said, giving Troi a knowing glance, "there's one thing we need to take care of."

Picard frowned. "What is that, Number One?"

"Well, traditionally, in human weddings at least, the groom chooses a best man—someone close to him who can stand by his side as he takes the final step into matrimony." He turned to Picard. "I'd be honored if you'd take that role, Captain."

It was a rare thing indeed for Jean-Luc Picard to be flabbergasted. On those few occasions when he was, it generally lasted only a short time. Riker therefore always treasured those occasions when he could make it happen. For a full three seconds, Picard's eyes widened, his mouth fell open, his nostrils flared, and his hands fell to his sides. Riker could not recall the last time the captain looked quite so—well, undignified.

As was his wont, he recovered quickly. Straightening his uniform jacket—which was already straight—he said, "Thank you, Number One. I accept."

Data then spoke up. "Commander, may I ask a question?"

"Of course, Data," Riker said.

"Have you informed Counselor Troi's mother of this event?"

"I sent a message to her," Troi said. "She hasn't replied yet."

Riker frowned. "Why do you ask?"

"Based on observations over the fifteen years, six months, and twenty-two days since first encountering Lwaxana on the *Enterprise*-D, I am forced to conclude that she is likely to consider 'a simple ceremony with a few friends' to be inadequate for the counselor."

Picard regarded his first officer. "He has a point, Number One."

Putting up a hand, Riker said, "Deanna and I have already discussed this. It's *our* wedding, and we'll do what we want."

"Besides," Troi added, "my mother has been busy with the reconstruction of Betazed."

Another unpleasant memory, more distant but seared on his consciousness as much as the pit on Tezwa, came to Riker. This time it was sitting in this very conference room five years ago, getting the report from Admiral Masc of the Tenth Fleet that Betazed had fallen to the Dominion. One of the most lush and verdant planets in the Federation, it was also Troi's homeworld and the planet to which she traced half her heritage. Later on, they learned that the house Troi had grown up in was leveled, along with most of the capital city, by the Jem'Hadar and Cardassians. Lwaxana's valet Mr. Homn was killed. Lwaxana and her son Barin had survived, though, and soon Troi's mother was helping lead a resistance movement on the planet. Between that and the efforts of a five-ship task force led by the *Enterprise,* Betazed was liberated months later, but it did nothing to alleviate the black hole that had opened in Riker's stomach when he first heard Admiral Masc's report.

Whenever that memory surfaced—and it did so often, no matter how hard he tried to avoid it—Riker would attempt to overlay it with happier thoughts of his assignment to Betazed as a lieutenant, meeting Troi for the first time, and their blossoming relationship that was now, finally, twenty years later, culminating in marriage. Someday, he hoped, that attempt would actually work.

Troi added, "Not to mention raising little Barin."

"Not so little." Riker chuckled, once again grateful to his *Imzadi* for switching to a more pleasant topic. "That half-brother of yours is, what, six now?"

"Seven," Troi said.

"Right, seven, and he's already over a meter-and-a-half tall."

"The boy is half-Tavnian," Data said, "and they are, as a rule, a fairly tall race, by human standards."

Troi chuckled. "Which makes him even more of a handful. My mother's not as young as she used to be—"

"Who of us is?" Picard smiled wryly.

"—and she doesn't have the time or, probably, the energy

to organize a large wedding on top of her regular duties."

Data regarded Troi. "I believe your confidence may well be misplaced, Counselor."

"I can understand that, Data, but she's changed since the war. Really."

Riker leaned forward and, in a mock-conspiratorial tone, said, "You know what I think? I think he's just scared that he'll have to dance if it's a wedding your mother organizes."

La Forge and Vale both laughed at that. Data simply turned his golden-eyed gaze onto Riker. "Even if I were still equipped with such an emotion, Commander, I would have no fear in that regard. I still recall with perfect clarity the instruction in human dance that Dr. Crusher gave me twelve years, one month, eight days ago in preparation for the O'Brien wedding."

Turning his glance to Crusher, Riker said, "I guess we won't need the tutelage of the Dancing Doctor, then."

It was only when Crusher blinked twice, stared blankly at Riker for a moment, then quietly said, "I'm sorry, Will, what?" that the first officer realized that the doctor hadn't participated in any of the discussion that had gone on since they finished watching Zife's speech.

"Are you all right, Beverly?" Picard asked the question with evident concern.

Crusher shook her head, her red tresses waving with the movement. "I'm fine, Jean-Luc, really—I'm sorry, I just fell into a daze." She smiled gamely.

Riker didn't buy it for a minute. He knew that Dr. Yerbi Fandau was only a few weeks from retiring as head of Starfleet Medical, and he knew that the position was Crusher's if she wanted it. He also knew that the doctor had yet to formally accept the job. *If she doesn't give Fandau an answer soon, he's going to tap someone else.*

Vale looked quizzically at Riker. "The Dancing Doctor?"

Before Riker could reply, Crusher said, *"Don't ask."*

"Come now, Beverly." Picard had a twinkle in his eye as he spoke. "As I recall, you're a divine dancer."

"I would like to take this opportunity to reiterate," Data said with a glance to his left at Crusher, "that I have obeyed your wishes on the subject, and never referred to your past history in dance, Doctor."

"I know, Data," Crusher said with a sweet smile, then turned a frown on Riker. "I have my own theories on who unearthed that particular fact."

Riker grinned. "You shouldn't have left it in your service record where *anyone* could find it."

"We don't have a choice as to what gets put in those things, as a general rule. Kind of like medical records. Of course, sometimes facts can be altered—like the *real* cause of your broken arm on Elamin IX."

The blood drained from Riker's face. "Beverly . . ."

"What is she talking about?" Troi asked indignantly.

"Nothing," Riker said quickly.

Crusher smiled at Troi. "Nothing you need to worry about, Deanna. Besides, it'll all be in the file I prepare for the *Titan's* CMO."

Putting his head in his hands, Riker muttered, "Great. Just great."

Chuckling, La Forge said, "Why do I get the feeling this meeting is over?"

Picard stood up. "Dismissed."

Riker also rose, giving Crusher a pained look. For her

part, the doctor ignored it and left the observation lounge, followed by Troi, who gave Riker an annoyed look of her own before dashing out to catch up with Crusher. Data and La Forge followed Picard toward the bridge, leaving Riker and Vale in the observation lounge.

"Sir, can I ask a question?"

Riker looked down at Vale. Though petite, she was by no means small, and he had learned in the four years she'd served on the ship that she was also not to be trifled with. More than anyone else on the *Enterprise* crew, she had shined during the year since Rashanar, from spearheading two separate rescue operations at the Dokaalan colony, to aiding the local peacekeeping forces in their desperate attempt to maintain order on the increasingly chaotic Delta Sigma IV, to her expert work in coordinating ground movements under the worst possible circumstances during the Tezwa mission. She was also due for a well-deserved promotion to lieutenant commander, and he had not told her this only by dint of wanting the official approval from Starfleet to come through. In times past, he wouldn't have bothered to wait, as promotion recommendations from the *Enterprise* were generally rubber-stamped, but the cloud that Rashanar had cast on Jean-Luc Picard's judgment meant Riker could take nothing for granted.

Vale was staring at the floor, which surprised Riker, as she had always been the type to look one directly in the eyes.

He prompted, "Go ahead, Lieutenant."

"I was wondering, sir, if—" She finally looked up. "If there was room for one more at the poker table tonight."

Riker blinked. "I didn't know you played."

"Some, though it's been a while. Me and a bunch of my classmates at the Academy had a weekly game during our fourth year, and we used to have Texas Hold'em tournaments on the *O'Keefe.*"

"Well, you're more than welcome to join us any time. I'm surprised you didn't mention this sooner—especially since you were more than happy to take me up on that anbo-jytsu spar back at Delta Sigma."

At that, Vale smirked. "To be honest, sir, I didn't feel entirely comfortable asking to be dealt in. I always thought it was something you D guys did."

" 'D guys'?" Riker repeated with a frown.

"That's what Daniels called you. I talked to him after I got transferred over here."

Riker nodded. Daniels had served as the *Enterprise*-E's security chief from its maiden voyage until the end of the Dominion War, broken only by a six-month paternity leave, during which several other officers filled in. After the war, Daniels resigned his commission in order to be with his wife and raise their child on the Canopus Planet.

Vale continued. "It's nothing you do consciously, and only off duty, really, but you, the captain, Geordi, Deanna, Beverly, Data, Alyssa, Taurik—all of you who served on the *Enterprise*-D together—it's like you have you own clique. It's inevitable, from having served together for so long and doing all the things you did. Ambassador Worf's part of it, too—I noticed it especially when he came on board during the gateways mess. You guys all have your own code, almost. Daniels warned me about it when I came on, and he was right."

"Lieutenant—" Riker started, but Vale held up her hand.

"It's all right, Commander, really. Honestly, it makes perfect sense, and you guys *don't* do it consciously. It's not something that affects the work, either, which is why it really isn't that big a deal. Believe me, when I sound battle stations, I have *never* had the feeling that the captain would rather the ambassador was at tactical. But it's also why I never felt comfortable asking in on the poker game. Like I said, that always seemed to me like something the D guys did."

Thinking back over the seven years since they took the new *Sovereign*-class *Enterprise* out of drydock—a time frame that was almost as long as the interval they served on its *Galaxy*-class predecessor—Riker realized that the crew who came over from the previous ship did tend to cluster together off-duty. *There's a lesson in that,* Riker thought, filing it in his ever-growing mental folder of Things To Be Aware Of When I Have My Own Command.

"Well, on behalf of the D guys, Lieutenant, I apologize, and offer as penance a seat at our poker table tonight."

Vale grinned. This took Riker aback. Over four years, he'd seen her smile plenty of times, though it was often a vicious one, indeed one that frightened a security staff that didn't scare easily, not to mention whoever might be unfortunate enough to be on the other end of Vale's phaser. However, this was the first time he saw her let loose with a friendly grin. *I wonder if I'd have seen it more often if I ever opened up and let her in more.*

"I accept, sir," she said. "Thanks."

"You're welcome." As Vale moved toward the door leading to the bridge, Riker asked, "Lieutenant?"

She stopped and turned around. "Yes, sir?"

"What changed your mind?"

"Sir?"

"You said you weren't comfortable asking before. What changed to make you comfortable?"

Another grin. "Your promotion, sir. Once you're off on the *Titan,* they probably won't be having the weekly games on the *Enterprise* anymore, and I didn't want to miss my chance to beat the pants off you."

With that, she left.

This, Riker thought, *is gonna be fun.*

"The game," Data said, "is Murder. Seven-card stud, high hand splits with high spade in the hole, queen of spades up resets the game with a fresh ante, queen of spades in the hole is wild."

Riker tried to stifle a groan and failed. So did Troi and La Forge's attempts to do so. Picard simply let out a long breath through his teeth.

Vale, however, simply regarded the android—wearing his trademark green-tinted visor—with a penetrating stare. As usual for poker night, Riker kept the lights in the quarters he and Troi shared dimmed, aside from the big lamp hanging from the ceiling over the poker table. The directed light cast a shadow on Vale's face that made her already menacing stare all the nastier, and just at the moment Riker was glad for Data's sake that his emotion chip had been removed.

"You've *got* to be kidding me."

The security chief had, in fact, said that practically every time Data dealt, as the second officer had been favoring complex variations that often involved wild cards.

Riker allowed such things mainly because they helped vary the routine for their friendly game, but they were the sorts of things that would never be tolerated at serious professional tournaments.

Vale was apparently a purist, and Riker wished even more fervently that she'd gotten into the game sooner.

Data dealt the hand, and betting proceeded apace. Over the course of that and the next three betting rounds, no one got the queen of spades up, so the game was never reset. Riker was grateful, as whenever he had a good hand in this game, the queen almost invariably came up, and the redeal would provide him with a junk hand. This time, with one down card left to be dealt, he had a pair of tens showing, with the ten of spades in the hole. Three of a kind was a decent hand, and the ten of spades had a good chance of being the high spade in the hole as well, since the ace, king, and jack were showing in front of Picard, La Forge, and Troi, respectively. Data and Troi had both folded, and on this last bet, La Forge did likewise, leaving only Vale, Picard, and Riker.

Riker studied the table. The four cards Picard had showing included nothing useful beyond that ace of spades. Riker himself had the ace of hearts, and Data's now-folded hand had the ace of diamonds, so the best Picard could have was two aces—unless he had the queen of spades, a wild card, in the hole.

About a year prior to the destruction of the *Enterprise*-D, Picard joined the poker game for the first time, saying that he should have done so years earlier. Within an hour of playing at the table with him that evening, Riker agreed wholeheartedly, for one simple reason. Picard might have been the finest captain in the fleet. He might have been able to recover from experiences as brutal as Borg assimilation and Cardassian torture. He might have been perfectly at home amid the landmines of Klingon politics or the labyrinths of some ancient ruins,

But, his claims to have been "quite the card player" in his youth notwithstanding, Jean-Luc Picard was a very mediocre poker player.

It wasn't that he was particularly *bad* at it. He had a fine poker face—Riker found few "tells" in his facial expressions or gestures that he could use to his advantage—but he also wasn't particularly good at betting properly or judging the cards on the table beyond his own hand. As a result, he regularly stayed in long past the point where he should fold, and was often the first to run out of chips, mostly as a result of staying in too long with weak hands. He was better at draw games—where there were no cards showing to the other players, and so one relied on the ability to read people, at which Picard excelled—than stud games.

On this hand, Picard had been betting in his usual manner—not aggressively, but not passively, either. Unfortunately, that meant he either had the pair of aces, and he thought that was an improvement on Riker's pair of tens and Vale's pair of threes, or he had both the ace *and* the wild card in the hole, giving him three aces and a better hand than Riker's.

As for Vale, in addition to the pair of threes, she also had a six of hearts and a seven of clubs showing. It was possible she had a straight.

Only one way to find out, Riker said after Data gave

him an unnecessary reminder that the bet was his with the high hand showing.

"Check," Riker said. He wanted to see how Vale and Picard bet.

Vale, however, was no fool. "Check," she repeated.

Picard, predictably, put in two gray chips. "I bet twenty."

Not high enough to scare anyone out. Riker put in four gray chips. "Your twenty and up twenty."

Vale, her expression unreadable, put in four gray chips. "Call."

Picard's expression was just as unreadable as he did likewise.

Data dealt the final card down. Years of long practice kept Riker from reacting in the least to the fact that he got the eight of diamonds, which gave him a full house of tens over eights. His chances of winning the hand had just improved drastically.

He grabbed a white chip. "Fifty."

This time Picard raised an eyebrow, a mannerism he'd picked up after a particularly intense Vulcan mind-meld thirteen years earlier, and which was one of his few tells: it meant he wasn't sure how to bet.

Vale, however, didn't hesitate. "Call," she said, putting in a white chip of her own. This raised Riker's confidence: she didn't feel strong enough to raise, but felt that she could beat whatever he had alongside the tens.

After several moments' thought, Picard called as well.

The only time Riker ever allowed his face to relax when he played poker was after the final bet. This time he grinned as he turned over his hole cards. "Boat."

"You know," Troi said, "I still don't understand why a full house is called a 'boat.' "

"The etymology of the term, Counselor—" Data started, looked around the table, saw the annoyed looks most everyone was giving him, including Troi, and then continued with only minimal hesitation: "—is something we can discuss at a later date." Several people at the table chuckled, including Riker. "The commander has a full house, tens over eights, and also has the ten of spades."

Picard turned over his hole cards to reveal that he did have the other ace, as well as two kings, hearts and diamonds. Riker was not surprised, though he was disappointed that the captain was willing to part with his chips so easily. Riker would have beat the captain even if he still had three of a kind.

"Two pair for the captain, no spades in the hole." Data then looked at Vale. "Lieutenant?"

First Vale turned over the queen of spades. If nothing else, that entitled her to half the pot, since it was the highest spade in the hole.

Then she flipped over the four and five of hearts. Along with either of her threes, the six of hearts and the seven of clubs, it gave her a straight. Riker was now especially grateful for the eight he pulled on the last round, as the straight would have beaten his three tens.

"Straight flush for the lieutenant," Data said, and Riker's jaw fell.

What the hell?

Then he saw it.

Damn Data and his stupid variations anyhow. So focused was he on the queen of spades as the high spade that he momentarily forgot that it was also a wild card. Vale had the three through six of hearts, and could use the wild to substitute for the seven of that suit, thus giving her one of the best possible poker hands.

"Well played," Riker said glumly. "I'm surprised you didn't raise me."

"Nah," Vale said as she raked in her chips. "If I started going crazy with only a pair of threes showing, you would've known I had something good in the hole, which would've beat your three of a kind."

"I had a boat," Riker pointed out.

"You pulled that on the last card," Vale said confidently.

Frowning, and ignoring the giggles that were now emitting from the mouth of his fiancée, Riker asked, "How'd you know that?"

"You checked on the second-to-the-last bet. You never check when you have a hand better than a straight."

"Yes, I do!" Even as Riker said the words, he frantically thought back to the night's prior hands to see if that pattern had, indeed, emerged.

"Maybe you do generally, but you haven't tonight. You should be careful of that."

Again, Riker thought back over the night's hands—then stopped. *Dammit, she got me.* She was trying to psych him out—an obvious trick that he never used to fall for. "I can see I'm getting complacent in my old age."

"Well, it happens to the best of us, sir—stands to reason, it'd happen to you, too."

Riker snorted. "Watch it, Lieutenant. I'm still first officer on this ship for a little while longer, and it's very much within my power to have you keelhauling first thing in the morning."

"I'll keep that in mind, sir." Vale spoke in a mock-grave tone.

"See that you do," Riker said, barely managing to keep a straight face. He turned to La Forge. "Your deal."

Looking dolefully at his small pile of chips, then at the much larger pile in front of Vale, La Forge grabbed the cards and started shuffling. "The game is La Forge Takes the Pot. All my cards are wild, and nobody else is allowed to get a face card or an ace."

"I haven't played that one since the Academy," Vale said without missing a beat. "My roommate called it all the time."

"Playing against you, I believe it." La Forge shook his head.

"I'm glad you've joined us, Christine," Troi said. "It's good to shake things up a little."

"Agreed," Picard said.

"I was kinda hoping for a shakeup that would tilt some chips my way," La Forge said as he gave the cards a final shuffle, "but like the captain said before, it's an imperfect world." He placed the deck in front of Data, who cut it in half. Riker suspected that Data cut the deck right at twenty-six cards. "The game," La Forge said as he picked up the cut deck, "is five-card draw, jacks or better to open, trips or better to win."

Even as he dealt, the intercom beeped. *Bridge to Commander Riker.*

It was the soft voice of Lieutenant Wriede, the gamma-shift tactical officer. "Go ahead."

"*Sir, I have a message from Betazed for you and Counselor Troi. It's on a diplomatic channel, but it's marked personal.*"

Troi rolled her eyes. "I wonder who that could be."

"Stand by, Lieutenant," Riker said.

Picard stood up. "I believe that is our cue to leave."

"Damn," Vale said, also standing, "I was just getting warmed up."

"That's what we're afraid of," La Forge muttered.

Riker looked around in mild irritation. "You don't all have to go. This'll only take a minute. We'll sit out Geordi's hand and take it in the next room."

Picard turned to his second officer. "Data, in the fifteen years and however many months and days since we first met Lwaxana, what is the average duration of personal communications from her to this ship?"

Data opened his mouth to answer, but Troi interrupted. "Point taken, Captain. Come on, Will, let's get this over with."

Riker sighed as the four officers left the cabin. "Computer, full lights." As the room brightened, he said to Troi, "I don't see why this has to kill the game."

"Because the captain's right. No matter what she has to say, Mother will take three times as long as is necessary to say it. And if she finds out we're trying to cut her short just to get back to a poker game, she'll take even longer *and* we'll never hear the end of it." She smiled. "Besides, better we stop the game now before Christine *completely* humiliates you."

Drawing himself up, Riker said, "I was lulling her into a false sense of security."

"She didn't look very lulled to me."

"It was all part of my cunning plan. That's my story and I'm sticking to it."

She patted him on the shoulder. "The important thing is, *you* believe that."

"Damn right." He tapped his combadge as they both sat at the desk on the other side of the cabin's common room. "Patch it through, Mr. Wriede."

"Yes, sir."

The screen on the workstation in front of them lit up with the Starfleet logo, which then faded and was replaced by the smiling visage of Troi's mother. Lwaxana's face had considerably more lines than the last time Riker saw her, but her obsidian eyes looked more lively.

Another memory, now, this one of Lwaxana on Betazed when the *Enterprise* helped liberate the world. She was dressed in a battered, filthy one-piece outfit, her hair was unkempt and thinning, and her black eyes were rimmed with red. In many ways, Lwaxana's bedraggled state was the perfect metaphor for the devastation that the Dominion War wreaked on the Federation. In all the years Riker had known Lwaxana, she had never been disheveled, unkempt, or even rumpled.

More to the point, until that day on Betazed five years ago, he'd never seen her look *old*. Sick, yes. Comatose, once. Tired, many times. But never old.

Now she at least was more hale and hearty than she had been shortly after the war. Her dress was gaudy and well pressed, she was wearing one of her more subdued wigs, and of all the lines on her face, the deepest were the smile lines around her mouth. That bright smile had always been the second thing people noticed about Lwaxana.

"Little One, it's so good to see you! And you too, William, especially in light of the wonderful news you sent me! Congratulations to you both!"

The first thing people noticed, of course, was the voice, a remarkable instrument that could penetrate duranium—all the more impressive for a member of a telepathic species that generally used vocal communication only with offworlders and prepubescent children.

"It's good to see you too, Mother," Troi said.

"Very good," Riker added, and he even mostly meant it. "And thank you. How're things going on Betazed?"

"Quite well, I'm happy to say. The new housing development on the Emrin River was finally finished last week, and there's a lovely plaque dedicating it to the people who died during the occupation. Most of the structures have been rebuilt, and the ecological damage is being—well, repaired anyway. I don't think it can ever really be fixed, but we're doing our best."

"That's wonderful to hear, Mother," Troi said with a warm smile. Riker slipped his hand into hers. Betazed had been through so much during the war, it was good to hear that its recovery was proceeding well. "How is Barin?"

Lwaxana rolled her eyes. *"Oh, he's quite a handful. He's growing so fast, the clothes replicator can't keep up with him—and frankly, neither can I. The new valet—"*

"Mother," Troi cut in, "you haven't fired *another* valet, have you?"

"Now, Little One, stop playing personnel manager. I should think you had enough of that on that ship of yours without doing it in my house, too."

Troi closed her eyes. Riker squeezed her hand. Based on this latest news, Lwaxana had now gone through nine valets since the war. *And that's just the ones we found out about. Looks like Mr. Homn isn't as easy to replace as we'd thought.*

"In any case, I am so thrilled *to see that my precious girl is finally getting married. And to think, it only took me fifteen years to find the right man for you after that disaster with the Wyatt boy."*

Riker shuddered. His bride-to-be had once been betrothed to a human named Kevin Wyatt thanks to some arcane Betazoid ritual that Lwaxana, in a fit of lunacy, decided to impose on her daughter. That marriage had been avoided, a fact for which Riker was happy then, and downright grateful now.

"As I recall, Mother," Troi said with an impish grin, "you didn't find Will, *I* did."

"Yes, of course, Little One, whatever you say. The point is, you two are finally *doing what you should've done twenty years ago, and I couldn't possibly be happier. And you getting your own ship, too, William—that's marvelous!"*

"Thank you," Riker said. "The *Titan*'s a very good ship, it—"

"That's fine, dear, I'm sure it's wonderful, but what I really need to know is when Jean-Luc can get you two to Betazed."

Riker blinked. "I beg your pardon?"

"Well, naturally, you two will get married on Betazed. It won't take any time at all for me to set up the ceremony and put the guest list together. Of course, I'll have to bring the new valet up to speed, but—"

Angrily, Troi asked, "Mother didn't you *read* our message?"

"Of course, I did, Little One, how else would I have known about you two getting married and William getting to command the Giant?"

"It's the *Titan*," Troi said in a tight voice, "and if you know that, you should also know that we just want to have a simple ceremony on Earth."

"Well, you're certainly welcome to do that, too, if you want, Little One, but I don't much see the point when you're going to have an extravaganza on Betazed. After all, you are the Granddaughter of the Fifth House and Heir to the Sacred Chalice of Rixx."

Riker tried and probably failed to keep the sarcasm out of his voice. "And Heir to the Holy Rings of Betazed, don't forget that."

"No, dear," Lwaxana said in a patronizing tone, *"I'm the Heir to the Holy Rings of Betazed. If Deanna was the Heir, I'd be the Holder, like I am of the Sacred Chalice. Really, if you're going to marry into the family you're going to need to know these things."*

"Sorry," he muttered.

Troi blew out a breath. "Mother, do you really have time for this?"

"I'll make time, Little One. I've been waiting for this moment since you were a baby! Now that the happiest day of my life has finally arrived, do you really think I'm

just going to let you get married on some cold mountain on Earth?"

"That 'cold mountain' happens to be Will's home."

Riker could see this was getting out of hand, so he stepped in. "Deanna, maybe we should just—"

"Are you just going to let her belittle your home like that?"

"I'm not belittling anything, Deanna."

"Yes, you are, Mother, like you always belittle anything that you don't micromanage."

Oh God, Riker thought. *The last place in the universe I want to be is between these two if they start getting into it.*

And getting into it they were. *"How can you say that? After all I've done for you, after I gave you a home, raised you by myself, let you pursue your career . . ."*

"Intruded on my life at every opportunity, tried to force me to marry someone I'd never met, constantly matchmaking and making a fool of yourself in the name of making *me* happy . . ."

Lwaxana went on as if her daughter hadn't interrupted. *"And now—now you have the nerve to keep me from doing one last thing for you, something I've wanted for so long?"*

"We're not keeping you from anything, Mother. We want you to be there with us when we get married." She let go of Riker's hand and leaned forward into the small screen. "This is the happiest day of our lives too, Mother— can't you just be there for us and let us do it our way?"

"You can't even have a proper Betazoid wedding on Earth—especially not in Alaska. It'll be freezing!"

"Mother, that's enough!" Troi snapped.

Riker stared in horror at the expression on his fiancée's face. She looked furious, her black eyes blazing.

"Little One, this is what I've wanted for you for so long, and I don't see why—"

Speaking in a low, menacing tone that gave Riker a cold feeling in his gut, Troi said, "No, Mother, you don't see. You never did."

And with that, Troi cut off the communication, got up, and ran into the bedroom.

Riker blinked for several seconds, dumbfounded. Troi and her mother had argued before, certainly, but never like this. And Troi's anger was wholly out of proportion to what had just happened.

He followed her into the bedroom, and in a gentle voice, prompted, *"Imzadi?"*

Troi was lying facedown on their bed, her face half-buried in the pillow, muffling her voice. "Not now, Will, please, I want to be alone."

"Tough," he said, taking a seat on the edge of the bed. "We're in this together now, remember? Besides, after a blowup like that, you don't get to be alone without explaining yourself."

"It's nothing," Troi said, punctuating her words with a sniff. Then she rolled over, and Riker saw tears running down her cheek. "It's just the usual with my mother."

"No, Deanna, it isn't. And I'm not leaving this bed until you tell me what it is. We've been through too much for you to start holding back from me now."

She sat up. "I just want us to be happy, Will. Why can't she see that?"

"And why can't you see that I'll be just as happy with a major production on Betazed as I would be in Alaska?

Hell, we can go to Risa, to Qo'noS, to the Founders' homeworld, for all I care, as long as we're married at the end of it. After everything that's happened, all that matters is that you and I are together."

Troi nodded, even as more tears rolled down her cheek. "I know—I feel the same. It's just—"

Riker held Troi's hand in his. It felt oddly cool to the touch. "Deanna, I spent fifteen years trying and failing to figure out how to make my father happy. In the end, I never did figure it out, and he died without my knowing whether or not he was happy with me." He smiled ruefully. "Or if I was happy with him. But you still *have* your mother. So let's make *her* happy and have the wedding on Betazed."

Moments passed before Riker got the reaction he was hoping for: a smile from Troi. "We will. We'll call Mother back in the morning—give her some time to calm down first. If we try now, she won't answer just out of spite."

"Fair enough," Riker said, giving her a smile of his own.

The sound of William Riker's breathing was a comfort to Deanna Troi. The rhythmic inhaling and exhaling provided a certain steadiness to the external world that was woefully absent from her internal self. They'd lain beside each other, just being in each other's arms, for almost an hour before Riker finally dozed off.

Sleep, however, didn't come quite so easily to Troi.

She hadn't told the entire truth to Riker. Blowing up at her mother had precisely nothing to do with the wedding or Mother.

Minza.

Every time she closed her eyes, Troi saw the placid

face of the Tezwan general. Part of the deposed prime minister's resistance movement, the group that had abducted Riker, Minza had been captured by *Enterprise* security and brought to the ship, where Troi tried everything she could within Federation law to interrogate him.

No, to break him. To make him suffer. He knew where Will was being held, and he wouldn't tell me, and I wanted so much to just take that smarmy expression off his face, I wanted to rip his feathers out one by one . . .

Again the anger started to build, just as it had with Mother, just as it had with Minza. She remembered him leaning back, his arms folded behind his head, giving her that pitying expression, even as she tried—and failed— to break him by assaulting him with temperature changes, bright lights, and a cacophonous combination of both Klingon and human opera, combined with Data's near-monotone recitation of *The Mikado*. All he did was laugh at her, saying, "If this is your worst . . . I pity you."

She wanted so much to wipe that pity off his face.

Rising slowly from the bed, being careful not to disturb her fiancé's slumber, she padded into the next room. Regulating her breathing, which was speeding up at an alarming rate, she tried to tamp down the anger, quench the inferno that was building inside her.

How long will I have to do this?

She sat at the same desk where just a few hours ago she'd yelled at her mother for no good reason and contacted the bridge.

"*Wriede here.*"

"Falon, it's Deanna. Tell me—" She hesitated, then decided to vague things up a bit. "Are the *Amargosa, Repub-*

lic, and *Musashi* still in real-time communication range?"

"Let me check, Counselor." A pause. *"The* Republic *isn't, but the other two are. Why?"*

"Nothing you need to worry about," she said quickly. The last thing she wanted was to let the entire gamma-shift bridge crew know precisely what she was doing. "Thank you."

"No problem, Counselor."

She then put a private call through to Counselor Marlyn Del Cid on the *Amargosa.*

Moments later, a bleary-eyed Del Cid appeared on the viewer in front of her. Her long hair was uncombed and unkempt, and she was wearing only a nightshirt emblazoned with a large version of the Starfleet delta—she'd obviously been woken out of a sound sleep. *"Del Cid here."* Then she realized who it was. *"Deanna? What's wrong?"*

Troi hesitated. "I—I snapped at my mother tonight."

"Well, that's certainly a good reason to wake me out of a sound sleep," Del Cid said with a wry smile. *"After all, that sort of thing never happens between mothers and daughters."*

"It's not that—I just—" She sighed. "I'm sorry, I shouldn't have woken you for this."

Waving her hand in front of her face as if she was swatting an insect, Del Cid said, *"No, no, I should be the one apologizing. I just don't do well first thing after I wake up. I take it you don't normally snap at you mother?"*

She actually smiled at that, which was a relief, as Troi hadn't credited herself with that capability at present. "Actually, I do all the time, but not over something like this—and I never get *this* angry with her."

"Back to the anger, then?"

"Yes."

"Something to consider, Deanna. Those Federation laws that you were dancing on the edge of with Minza— the ones that kept you from torturing him, or even visiting any kind of cruel and unusual punishment on him?"

Troi frowned. "What about them?"

"The thought occurred to me that it's a natural instinct to want to inflict pain and suffering on someone who has done you wrong, or who was withholding critical information from you. If it wasn't, we wouldn't need those laws you had to abide by, would we? You said you felt poisoned, and maybe you were—but the point isn't that you wanted to beat Minza until he bled, the point is that you didn't."

Leaning back in her chair, Troi let out a long breath that she hadn't even realized she was holding. "You may be right."

Del Cid's bleary eyes twinkled a bit. *"Well, don't be too sure—it could just be the exhaustion talking. What does Will have to say?"*

Looking away from the viewer, Troi said, "I haven't talked to him about it."

Up until now, Del Cid had barely been able to keep her eyes open; at Troi's words, though, they widened considerably. *"Why not?"*

"I haven't—I didn't want to burden him with this."

"That's a particularly feeble excuse, Deanna."

Defensively, Troi said, "He's been through a lot, and—"

"So've you. You two are in this together now, remember? That's what marriage is supposed to be all about."

55

Troi closed her eyes for a moment, wincing inwardly at Del Cid's repetition of Riker's words from earlier. Then she opened them. "You're right."

"So instead of waking me out of a sound sleep, go wake him out of his. It'll be a lot easier for you to get past this if you've got him on your side. This is too deep in you to not share with him. If you don't, it'll come exploding out at the worst possible time—and you know that."

Again, Troi said, "You're right." She let out another breath. "Thank you, Marlyn."

"My pleasure. Really, Deanna, ignore my bitching and moaning—any time you need to talk, get in touch. I know how hard it is for us counselors to take our own advice, so I'm more than happy to give you the occasional kick in the rear."

Troi chuckled. "I'll be sure to remember that. Now go get some sleep."

"Gladly." Del Cid sounded thrilled at that very notion, and Troi felt a pang of regret.

I should never have called her—I should've gone straight to Will, she thought as she terminated the connection.

Getting up from the chair, she padded back into the bedroom. Reaching out with the mental link that the two of them had shared ever since their initial affair on Betazed all those years ago, Troi nudged Riker awake.

He rolled over, and looked at her with tired eyes. "Deanna? What is it?"

Sitting down next to him on the bed, putting a hand on his shoulder, she said, "Will—we need to talk."

Chapter 3
Earth

As Kant Jorel walked down the hallway toward the holocom, he riffled through the padds in his hand. "You sure we don't have a statement from Ross?"

His new assistant, an Andorian whose name he simply could not remember, said, "Permit me to use my telepathic powers to ascertain if the answer to that question has changed in the seventy-five seconds since last you asked it."

Kant, a middle-aged Bajoran man who had served as the Federation Council's liaison to the press for the past two and a half years, and gone through seven assistants in that time, grunted. "Being sarcastic won't get you very far in this job."

"Based on the sheer number of predecessors I've had, I'd say that nothing gets anyone very far in this job."

"Yeah, but that's only because I'm impossible to work with."

"That is what I heard."

Kant looked down at the padd on top of the bunch in his hand, which contained the official statement from the council that he was about to read to the members of the press. "The statement's been vetted by everyone who's supposed to vet it?"

The Andorian's antennae twitched. "I assume so."

Kant stopped walking and stared his assistant right in his blue-skinned face. At that moment, he remembered that he was called Zhres. "You're assuming, Zhres. That's bad. Assuming is what gets people killed."

"Councillor Ra'ch's aide told me that it was ready to be given to the press. Hence my assumption."

"Fine." He started walking again.

"Oh, by the way," Zhres said, "there's a new reporter in the room—a woman from the *Free Vulcan Gazette* named Annalisa Armitage."

Kant let out a long breath and prayed to the Prophets for guidance. "I was really hoping those lunatics had gone away."

"I take it the *Free Vulcan Gazette* is not a reputable journal?"

"Not remotely. For starters, not a single Vulcan is on its staff, and I would be stunned if there were any in its subscriber list."

"That's odd. I took a brief look at their latest issue, and they seem to advocate a very pro-Vulcan stance."

Kant scowled. "That's one way of looking at it. It started publication about three hundred years ago, right after the first contact between Vulcans and humans on Earth. A group of humans felt that Vulcans should rule the galaxy. They started the *FVG*, and it's kept going strong despite being officially repudiated by the Vulcan government, and being the laughingstock of pretty much everyone who doesn't subscribe to it, which is about ninety-nine-point-nine-nine percent of sentient life."

Zhres tilted his head in a way that Kant found especially annoying. "What's the basis of their argument?"

"What, why Vulcans should rule the galaxy?" Kant shrugged. "I guess because they're the only ones smart enough."

"It's a case that can be made."

Glowering at his assistant, Kant said, "I'm going to assume that was a joke."

"I thought assuming was bad."

"See, that's your second mistake. Your first was assuming. Your second was to believe that I'm someone who expects, desires, or needs you to *think*. Thinking just gets in the way of the work and irritates me. Kindly stop it."

Kant and Zhres reached the large doors that led to a small, empty room that was about to be full of people who weren't there.

Holographic technology had improved to the point that it could be married to communications technology. As a result, the days when Kant would be in the same room as the various members of the press assigned to cover the doings of the president and the council were long past. Instead, he scheduled his briefings, the press folk in question would activate their own holocoms, and their images would appear in this room, located in the same building as the council chambers in Paris.

The doors parted at their approach, revealing a room with the usual grid pattern on the walls indicating holo-

graphic emitters. As soon as they entered, the room activated, the computer altering the surroundings to one of a
pleasant, wood-paneled room, with a podium by the north
wall and plenty of floorspace in front of it. Kant preferred
it this way. He never understood why the press all got to
sit while he had to stand, so right after he took the job as
press liaison, he had all the chairs removed. With the ad-
vent of the holocom, that all changed, as the reporters
could present themselves however they wished—including at their seats—a change that Kant also found annoying.

Standing behind the podium and in front of the Federation flag that hung on the north wall, Kant asked, "They
ready?"

The technician that was hidden in some other room
where Kant couldn't get at him said, *"Yes, but Councillor Ra'ch's office specifically told me not to activate the
holocom until noon."*

Kant checked his chrono, which read 11.58. *Damn
literal-minded techies.*

He turned to Zhres. "Check with Starfleet again, see if
Ross has released any kind of statement."

Nodding, Zhres put a blue hand to his right ear, dis-
turbing his well-groomed, feathery white hair. Speaking
in a low voice, he asked to be put through to Starfleet
Command's press office.

An eternity later—though Kant's chrono insisted that
it was only thirty seconds—the answer came through the
Andorian's earpiece. "Nothing yet."

"Did they at least give some kind of estimate as to
when we'd get one?"

Zhres shook his head. "All they would say is that the admiral will make a statement when it's appropriate."

Kant rolled his eyes. *"Now* is when it's appropriate. Right after the council has declared him a candidate. Pagro and Bacco understood that, why the hell doesn't he?"

"Is that a rhetorical question? Because I'm afraid my telepathic abilities haven't improved in the last few minutes."

The technician cut off Kant's snide reply. *"Thirty seconds."*

"About time," Kant muttered.

Half a minute later, several figures appeared in the room in front of Kant. Some were humanoid, some not. (This was another major change with the holocom: It allowed those with different atmospheric needs to those of most humanoids to be in the room instead of in a separate area. While Kant agreed with the spirit, the actual result of more people in the room was something else he found annoying.) Some were of sufficiently acute resolution as to seem like they were right there in the room, others were laden with static and poor image quality. Some stood and some, to Kant's dismay, were seated. Some were also far enough away that there would be a time delay in their questions and responses, which Kant had gotten used to, but had no intention of ever liking.

When the figures blinked into existence, a cacophony of sound hit the room like a photon torpedo. Kant had grown accustomed to it; Zhres, though, winced. *I wonder if he'll get used to it. Probably won't last long enough to.* Kant took a certain pride in that.

The noise died down as soon as everyone realized

they were "on," so to speak, the more distant reporters taking longer thanks to the time delay. Kant began speaking as soon as the room was completely quiet.

"First I have a statement, then two announcements, then I'll take questions.

"Here's the statement: 'The Federation Council has examined all the petitions for presidential candidacy that have been submitted, and has chosen three who fit the criteria for consideration. An election will be held three weeks from today, with the votes to be tallied by an independent auditor and announced one week after that. The three candidates are: Ktarian Special Emissary Arafel Pagro, Cestus III Governor Nanietta Bacco, and Starfleet Admiral William Ross.' " Putting the padd with the statement aside, he then read from the one under it. "Both Special Emissary Pagro and Governor Bacco have agreed to run in the election. Special Emissary Pagro will be giving a press conference on the Golden Gate Bridge on Earth tomorrow, and Governor Bacco is en route to Earth for a press conference of her own at the Statue of Liberty, also tomorrow."

He then set aside that padd, and looked up. As soon as he did so, several voices blared at once. Before Kant could call on someone, a short human woman asked, "What about Councillor T'Latrek?"

Kant looked at her, pulled one of his padds, checked her face against the press list. *Yup, it's the new woman from the* FVG.

"Ms. Armitage, you've never been in here before, so let me fill you in on how we do things—I call on people who then ask a question. You do not barge in and get your question asked first by virtue of being ruder than everyone else. That's *my* job." He turned to a Trill woman. "Ozla?"

Ozla Graniv of *Seeker,* one of Trill's leading news-magazines, smiled sheepishly. "Actually, Jorel, I was also going to ask about T'Latrek."

Kant glowered at her. "Fine. For *you,* I'll answer it. T'Latrek's name was not submitted to the council for consideration." He turned to the reporter from the *Times.* "Edmund?"

"Has there been any further word from President Zife—sorry, *ex*-President Zife—on the subject of why he felt the need to resign now?"

"That ground was well covered in the resignation speech, I thought."

Edmund Atkinson smiled superciliously, as was his wont. "I didn't think so, and neither do my readers. He's three years into his second four-year term. What did he do that was so terrible that it required holding an election a year early?"

Kant sighed. "I would think that your readers would be grateful for a politician who realized his own short-comings and moved to address them. Maria?"

The squat human woman who covered the council for the high-gravity world of Pangea asked, "Does President Zife's resignation have anything to do with the horrific events at Tezwa, and is the Federation's alliance with the Klingon Empire in any danger of collapsing again, especially in light of the incident at the Federation embassy?"

"As I already said, the reasons for the resignation were covered in the speech. Given that this has been in the works for several months, it is unlikely that the tragedy of Tezwa had any impact one way or the other. As for your second question, relations with Chancellor Martok's government are as strong as ever. Regia?"

A human woman from the Federation News Service asked, "If this was in the works for months, why haven't we heard anything about it?"

At this, Kant smiled. "Do you really think the president would have been able to accomplish anything for the last few weeks if everyone knew he was resigning? Secrecy was necessary to allow him to continue to do the job properly until the time was right to announce the resignation."

He was about to call on another reporter, but Regia wasn't finished. "C'mon, Jorel, there are *always* leaks, but this came out of nowhere. Does the Zife administration really think that it's a good idea to suddenly announce a vacuum in power without giving anyone in the Federation time to adequately prepare for it?"

"You only think there are always leaks because we provide them periodically. Don't underestimate our ability to fool you guys." Some laughter went throughout the room. Kant then turned to one of the static-laden images, as much to get it out of the way as anything. "Regradnischrak?"

A two-second delay, then: "That's Regradnischrak," the reporter from *Sebrotnizskeapoierf* said. It always made that correction, even though Kant had never been able to determine the difference between Regradnischrak's pronunciation and Kant's own. It came from the rather distant world of Antares VIII or, as they called it, Grilasdixraksirvek. "Will any of the candidates be addressing the issue of alternative sources for faster-than-light travel, and will they be coming to Antares to speak to the issue?"

Kant sighed, having seen that one coming. Some Antarean scientists claimed they had come up with a new, more efficient way to travel faster than light that didn't come with the inherent risks of matter-antimatter annihilation. Kant knew this because *Sebrotnizskeapoierf* had taken up this cause célèbre, and so where once Regradnischrak would have asked substantive questions, now it just harped on this to the exclusion of all else. "You'd have to ask them." He gazed around the room to see if any of the other crackpots were in the room before going back to real news sources, saw none, and so called on a man from *Bolarus and You.* "Sovan?"

"Starfleet sources say Admiral Ross has said that he has no interest in running for high office. Does the council have a comment on that?"

"Someone submitted the admiral's name, though I can't say who, as such submissions are confidential. The council deemed him worthy of the honor. From this point, it's up to the admiral to decide if he's going to take them up on it, and if he says yes, it's up to the voters if they think it's a good idea. But, as you may have gathered from the fact that I *didn't* provide one, Admiral Ross has not yet made a statement accepting or declining candidacy. Kav?"

The stocky Tellarite cleared his throat. "Does the council have any comment on the rumor that the Ontailians are once again considering leaving the Federation?"

Again, Kant sighed. *Damned Tellarites.* "Kav, how long have you been covering the council for the Tellar News Service?"

"Seven years."

"Which means you've been here for the two and a half years that I've been running this particular room, right?"

"Of course."

"In all that time, have I *ever* passed on a comment from the council, the president, or any of their staff addressing a rumor?"

This got more laughs, though Kav was not among the amused. "Not to my knowledge, no."

"That answers your question, then. T'Nira?"

Before the Vulcan reporter could ask her question, Zhres handed him a padd. Its display simply contained the words ADMIRAL ROSS'S STATEMENT, with a glowing box next to it. He gave the Vulcan reporter an apologetic look as he applied his thumb to the box.

"Hang on, T'Nira, I was just handed a statement from Admiral Ross regarding his candidacy." At his thumb's touch, the display showed a short paragraph, which Kant read aloud. " 'While I am grateful to the council, and to those who submitted my name to them, for their implied confidence in my leadership abilities, I have no interest in running for public office at this juncture. I have every confidence that the new president, whoever it is, will lead the Federation to continued prosperity in this post-war age, and I look forward to working with him or her for the next four years. Starfleet Command has always shared a solid bond with the Federation government, and I look forward to keeping that bond as solid as ever.' " *Gotta remember to recommend that Ross get a better speechwriter.* He looked up. "T'Nira, your question?"

"President Zife was considering curtailing relief efforts to Cardassia. Is the council still considering that in light of President Zife's resignation?"

That had been covered in the briefing Ra'ch had given Kant half an hour earlier. "There are no plans to reduce humanitarian aid to Cardassian space. The Cardassians have suffered enough the last few years, and the Federation is not about to let their people starve just because their recovery has had a few setbacks. Vairo?"

"Yeah, I'm wonderin' about that 'solid bond' Ross mentioned. Is he includin' when Starfleet tricked President Jaresh-Inyo into declaring martial law on Earth seven years ago?"

Kant closed his eyes. "Hang on, let me use my telepathic powers to see what the admiral was thinking." He opened them. "Nope. Sorry, Vairo, left my telepathy in my other pants today. That's it, folks, next briefing's at 2100 tonight."

With those words, the room emptied of all save Kant and Zhres. That was the one thing Kant liked unreservedly about the holocom: the off switch.

As the two of them exited the room, the Andorian said, "You stole my telepathy joke."

Shrugging, Kant said, "I wouldn't call it stealing."

"Really?" His antennae quivered. "What would you call it."

Kant considered the point for half a second. "Okay, it *is* stealing, but I'm entitled."

"Oh?"

"I'm your boss, your every thought is mine to use as I will."

"Did you not say earlier that I was not supposed to think?"

"Now you're starting to understand." Kant smiled.

Again, the antennae quivered. "Understand what?"

"Why I'm impossible to work with."

The sound of a communication signal interrupted Governor Bacco's dream, for which she was eminently grateful. In eighty-seven years of life, it was only in the last four days that Nan Bacco started having weird dreams.

"Governor, it's time to wake up." The voice belonged to Nan's campaign manager and old friend, Esperanza Piñiero.

"The hell time is it?" she asked. Or, at least, that was what she tried to say, though it came out with fewer actual consonants.

However, Esperanza had long experience in deciphering Nan's morning voice. *"It's 0600, Governor."*

Nan blinked. "Esperanza, you mind telling me why the *hell* you're waking me up at this ungodly hour? Not that I mind all that much—I was having another one of those damn dreams."

"I'm sorry, ma'am, but you wanted to be awake when we came into orbit around Earth."

Nan rotated her body ninety degrees so her legs hung over the side of her bed. "Are we in orbit now?"

"Uh, no, ma'am, but we will be in an hour. I figured if I woke you now, there was a chance you'd actually be awake by the time we made orbit."

"Nobody likes a wiseass, Esperanza." Nan waited for

some energy to creep into her legs. Said energy was not forthcoming.

"So you keep telling me, ma'am."

"All right, all right, I'm getting up." Deciding to throw caution to the wind, Nan got out of bed despite the lack of energy and slowly stumbled her way in the general direction of the replicator. The yacht on which she rode, the *Palombo,* was at the disposal of Cestus III's governor, and included a rather large stateroom. "This room is too damn big."

"Ma'am?"

"The room. It's too big. This bed is farther from the replicator than any sane person should have to ambulate first thing in the morning, especially when her pain-in-the-ass campaign manager gets her up at 0600."

"It's my job to be a pain in the ass, ma'am."

"Explains why you're so goddamned good at it." She finally made it to the replicator. "Coffee, black, unsweetened." The replicator hummed and provided a large mug with the needed beverage. "And will you, for crying out loud, call me Nan? We're not on Cestus and it's not like I'm president or anything."

"We're hoping to change that, ma'am. Still having the dreams?"

Nan took a sip of her coffee, the feel of the hot liquid in her throat having a cascade effect on the cobwebs in her brain. Getting Esperanza not to be deferential was a hopeless cause, but that didn't stop her from trying. *She spent too much damn time in Starfleet is the problem.* "Yeah. It's ridiculous. Eleven years as governor, been through DMZ refugees, a major galactic war, and a Gorn invasion, and I sleep like a rock. I decide to run for president, and now I'm dreaming I'm sitting on the Gorn throne with a Metron glowing in front of me while two Vorta ask me if they can invade my planet. This is what happens when you move from the kiddie table, I guess."

"Probably, ma'am. The staff and I will be waiting for you in the lounge."

Nan took a final gulp of the remainder of the coffee. *Starting to feel almost lifelike.* "I'll be there in twenty minutes."

"Okay, ma'am. See you in half an hour."

"You know, Esperanza, one of these days I'm actually going to make it somewhere when I say I'm going to for the express purpose of pissing you off."

"Don't go to any trouble on my account, ma'am. See you soon. Out."

One shower and another cup of coffee later, Nan put on a brown suit and ran a brush through her paper-white hair. *Damn,* she thought, looking in the mirror at her wrinkled face, tanned from eight decades of exposure to Cestus's rays, *I got three more worry lines.* Esperanza would say she was seeing things, which was why she resolved not to share her recognition of these new wrinkles with her campaign manager.

Buoyed by the caffeine rush and the thought of visiting Earth for the first time in almost three years, Nan exited the stateroom—*still too damn big*—and walked the few meters across the *Palombo*'s middle deck to the lounge, arriving precisely half an hour after she told Esperanza she'd be there in twenty minutes. *Damn her, anyhow.*

The lounge was almost as big as her stateroom, which

Nan found ridiculous. *Someday I'll understand the human need to make everything bigger.*

Present were the "inner circle" of her campaign staff. Seated on the large couch, drinking tea from the service that they took with them everywhere, were her speechwriter and political advisor. The husband-and-wife team of Fred MacDougan and Ashanté Phiri looked nothing alike—he was tall, pale, and bald, she was short, dark, and wore waist-length braids—but regularly finished each other's sentences. How endearing that was depended entirely upon Nan's mood. Still, they were both excellent at their jobs, and had been part of Nan's team from her earliest days in politics on Cestus, when they were interns helping the campaign that got Nan elected as representative of Pike City's Fifth District. Nan was also the one who, after they'd been dancing around each other for ten years, told them both to stop being morons and get married already.

Standing at the replicator and removing a plate of donuts from its slot was the deputy campaign manager, Helga Fontaine, whom Esperanza insisted on hiring despite her being too young to have even hit puberty. In truth, she was thirty, but that still made her a toddler as far as Nan was concerned. Helga was talking with the transportation manager, a taciturn Triexian named Bral—if there was any more to her name, Nan had never been informed of it. Curled up in the chair perpendicular to the couch was the tall, lithe, furry form of M'Tesint, the Caitian whom Nan had hired as press liaison at the recommendation of Fred and Ashanté. Nan had to admit that she had done an excellent job so far, so much so that, if she lost, she was giving serious consideration to keeping M'Tesint on as her press liaison on Cestus. *Not that there's anything wrong with Piers, but there's nothing especially* right *with him, either.*

And sitting at the large chair on the far side of the room was the short, stocky form of Esperanza Piñiero, her raven hair tied back in a ponytail, wearing a severe outfit that might as well have been a Starfleet uniform, for all that it had no insignia. *You can take the woman out of Starfleet . . .* she thought, not for the first time. The outfit and tied-back hair served to harden what would otherwise have been a very soft face, as even all Piñiero's years in Starfleet couldn't put lines in her smooth olive skin.

"Remind me," Nan said without preamble as the doors whooshed shut behind her, "whose cockamamie idea *was* it for me to run for president?"

Esperanza smiled. "Yours, ma'am."

"No, it was my idea to run for president *next year* when the election is *supposed* to be held. I know *that* was my idea. I distinctly remember having it, and planning out an entire strategy that would involve months of campaigning. It's this whole thing where I get five minutes to run for office that I don't remember agreeing to."

Ashanté set her teacup down on the table in front of the couch. "Not like you had a choice. Hell, if you didn't jump on it now, it'd be four more years before you'd have another shot."

"And a lot can happen in four years," Fred added.

Helga smiled, the jelly filling from one of her donuts staining her teeth. "Yeah. For example, four years ago, Min Zife was sufficiently popular that he'd win reelection unopposed less than a year later. Today, he's resigning under dubious circumstances."

"What's dubious?" Ashanté asked. "Hell, I'm amazed he made it this long. Trill, the Ontailians—"

Fred picked it up. "—the holostrike, the Genesis wave—"

"—that Iconian con job," Ashanté continued, "the Selelvians."

"Which brings us nicely to the first order of business," Esperanza said.

That's why I keep her around, Nan thought with amusement as she ordered a third cup of coffee from the replicator and took a seat in the large chair on the opposite side of the room from her campaign manager. Helga took a seat next to Fred, while Bral remained standing. *Guess when you have three legs, being on your feet isn't so bad.*

Esperanza continued. "We're going to get hit with questions on everything Ashanté and Fred just mentioned. If, say, a planetary government is found to be mentally manipulating other Federation worlds the way the Selelvians did, how would President Bacco handle it?"

Nan rolled her eyes. "Oh, for pity's sake."

"Governor, it's something we'll have to face."

"And I suppose I can't just say, 'How the hell would I know?' "

M'Tesint bared her teeth. "You could, Governor, but that would significantly decrease your chances of being elected."

"Right, 'cause God forbid I should tell the truth."

"Gee, Governor," Fred said with a cockeyed grin, "I thought you'd been in politics long enough to know better."

"She does." Esperanza smiled at Nan. "She just hasn't had enough coffee yet."

"She's right," Fred said.

"What," M'Tesint asked, "about the coffee?"

Fred shook his head. "No, I mean when the questions do come, we need to be ready. We're supposed to have contingency plans."

"Like more thorough examinations of planets that apply for Federation membership," Ashanté said.

"We can throw the Evorans in their face," Fred added. "The Zife administration let them in during the war, and they turned out to have a huge anti-alien faction on-planet, one that almost succeeded in overthrowing the government."

"How does that help with something like the gateways crisis, though?" Helga asked. "There was no way to see that coming, and the Federation's response was pretty good, all things considered."

Ashanté snorted. "Tell that to all the people who got screwed by all those gateways opening at once."

M'Tesint straightened in her chair, stretching her already tall form even more so. "I believe we should make it clear that we won't handle anything rashly. If there's anything that characterized Zife's administration, it was haste. A lot of that was necessary because of the war, but the war's been over for four years. We can emphasize that we'll be cautious, that we won't, say, authorize the imprisoning of sentient beings without cause, as happened with some of the *Voyager* crew when they returned."

Helga shook her head. "I'm not sure cautious is the right way to go. I mean, no, we shouldn't come out in favor of some of the ludicrous things Zife signed off on, but we still need to be aggressive if we're going to impress people enough to win this." She turned to Nan. "I know you were being facetious, but to actually answer the question you asked when you came in, one of the reasons why it's best to run now, as opposed to next year or four years from now, is that your star is pretty bright right now. The treaty with the Metrons was *huge,* and it's made you a name people outside the Cestus system might actually recognize. But that recognition will only go so far. If we come across as too tentative or cautious, no one will pay any attention. Or worse, they'll think you're another Jaresh-Inyo."

Nan leaned forward. "First of all, what in hell makes you think I was being facetious before? And secondly, Jaresh-Inyo was a good person."

"Yes, but he let Starfleet fool him into declaring martial law. That killed his political career."

"And," Esperanza added, "paved the way for Zife to get elected. His leadership was a big reason why we won the war."

Helga smiled sweetly. "Not the best example to use, Esperanza, given how he wound up."

"Zife may not have been the right person to lead in a time of peace," Esperanza said, "but that doesn't change that he was very much the right person to lead us in war."

"The war's been over for almost four years now."

Nan angrily placed her mug down on the end table next to her. The ceramic on plastiform made a very satisfying clunk. "Anybody else want to mention that the war was four years ago? 'Cause I'm old and I don't retain facts all that well, so it's good to remind me every five minutes." She leaned back in her chair. "All right, fine, tell me this: How *would* I handle it if half the planets in the Federation suddenly decided to secede? Or if a bunch of energy creatures decided to turn us all into giant newts? I've got to admit, I'm pretty damn curious to know."

"Governor—" Esperanza started.

"If you'd asked me six years ago how I'd handle a big Gorn ship showing up in the system and blasting Pike City all to hell, I would've gotten a good laugh out of it and said, 'What a stupid question. We haven't heard hide nor scale from the Gorn in a hundred years, what makes you think they'll attack us *now?*' Truth is, any answer I give to a question like that is going to be crap, and anyone with half a brain is going to *know* it's crap, and frankly I don't want to be elected by a Federation with half a brain. Do I know how to handle a crisis? Hell, yes, I handled dozens of them. Do I know how I'll handle the next one? Hell, no. There's no blueprint for these kinds of things, and to pretend there is one is to just insult people's intelligence. We can send people through space at thousands of times the speed of light, we can speak instantaneously to people halfway across the galaxy, we can cure most of the ailments and diseases out there, but we still can't figure out how to predict the future, and until we do, questions like this are just a knuckleball in the dirt, and I'm not gonna swing at it."

The lounge was silent for several seconds.

Fred put down his teacup. "Works for me."

"I like it," Ashanté said.

Helga looked confused. "What's a knuckleball?"

Esperanza quickly said, "Baseball."

"Oh, okay."

Nan suppressed a chuckle as she dry-sipped from her now-empty coffee mug. *They make these damn things too small.* Getting up to get a fresh cup from the replicator, she added Helga's lack of baseball knowledge to the growing list of things she didn't especially like about her deputy campaign manager. True, Cestus III was one of the few planets in the galaxy that played the sport, though its growing popularity on that world was leading to revivals of the once-dead game elsewhere, but Nan saw that as a feeble excuse. "What's next?"

"Good news, actually," Esperanza said. "We found Bobby."

It took a great effort for Nan to keep from stumbling.

Nan Bacco married Roberto LaManna when she was twenty-two years old. Bobby was thirty-seven at the time, and she thought he was the most wonderful man in the galaxy. Four years later, he walked out on her only as a preemptive strike against her throwing him out. Nan had, it turned out, been the fourth woman the con artist had tricked into marrying him, but the first who had cottoned to him before he could make off with all her worldly possessions.

He had disappeared decades ago, with Nan's sole reminder of him the only one she truly wanted: their wonderful daughter Annabella, now living on Luna with her family.

"You're sure it's him?" Nan asked as she gingerly

took her seat, trying to keep her hands steady as they held the hot coffee. "Remember the last time?"

"It's definitely him," Esperanza said. "And he's definitely dead."

Nan blinked. "What?"

"He settled on Rigel VIII a few years back, opened a small tavern. Fairly popular place among the miners."

"How'd he die?"

"Natural causes."

Nodding, Nan turned to the others. "We're stopping at Rigel at some point. Bral, set it up."

The Triexian said, "Of course," even as Helga asked, "Are you sure that's a good idea?"

"I want to visit the grave—and, honestly, I want to make sure the son of a bitch is really dead."

"You shouldn't," Helga said. "Not before the election. The whole reason we tracked him down was to make sure he couldn't hurt the campaign."

"He can't hurt anything if he's dead," M'Tesint said.

"Oh yes he can. Even acknowledging his existence can hurt us." Helga started waving her arms around as she spoke. "Can you imagine what Pagro would do with the information that your husband—"

"*Ex*-husband," Nan said emphatically.

"Fine, ex-husband is a career criminal? If you go to his grave, you'll hand that to them on a silver platter. Worse, you'll make it look like you miss him, and they'll twist that."

Esperanza sighed. "She's right, Governor, we can't afford it."

Bastard finally died and I can't properly enjoy it, Nan

mused as she took a thoughtful sip of her coffee. "All right, we'll wait. But I want confirmation. See if you can get the Rigelians to exhume the body in secret or something. What's next?"

"We've got to start thinking about endorsements," Helga said.

Esperanza shook her head. "They'll come in due time."

"We don't *have* due time. The election's in only three weeks. If we were doing a normal campaign, I'd agree, but we can't afford to sit around and wait for people to decide they like us."

Nan smirked. "So I have to make people like me, is that it?"

"Actually, that isn't too far off, Governor." Helga removed a padd and a stylus from the pocket of her suit jacket. "We should start with the FNS."

M'Tesint's ears flattened. "No."

"They're the most reputable news service out there."

"Which is exactly why we shouldn't start with them. Or finish with them, or do anything in the middle with them. The only thing trying to curry their favor will accomplish is to guarantee that they'll endorse Pagro. They'll judge objectively who to endorse based on the platforms and past records, period. Trust me on this."

"But—"

Esperanza stared at Helga. "M'Tesint knows this stuff, Helga. Move on."

Helga looked like she wanted to say more but, to Nan's relief, she thought better of it. "We can write Starfleet off."

Nan frowned. "How come?"

Ashanté answered that one. "Once Ross dropped out,

Pagro's stranglehold on Starfleet was pretty much guaranteed. He's a special emissary, he knows most of the higher-ups."

Fred added, "And every time he goes somewhere it's with a Starfleet escort, and he's sure to spend the whole time making friends with the crew."

"Fine," Esperanza said. "Who else?"

Before Helga could answer, Nan said, "Wait a minute, I'm not so sure about this. You said we should seek endorsements, fine, I can give you one right now: Benjamin Sisko."

Helga blinked. *"The* Sisko?"

"Well, actually there are several," Fred said. "His son's written for the FNS, and his father has this *great* restaurant in New Orleans."

"Yeah, and his brother-in-law's the cleanup hitter for the Pioneers," Nan said. "I met Sisko at opening day last year. Gave me a wonderful holoprogram of the last World Series on Earth." Nan had played that program every spare moment she could—though such moments were few and far between—sitting in the stands with the other three hundred fans as the London Kings and the New York Yankees faced off in a dramatic seventh-game contest at Yankee Stadium. She had the box score memorized, but the thrill of seeing Buck Bokai's home run in the eleventh inning that eventually won the game had yet to diminish.

However, that excitement was as nothing compared with what Nan was seeing now in Helga's blue eyes. "This is *huge.* If we can get him, we can guarantee pretty much the entire Bajoran sector. He's a religious figure on Bajor, *and* he's the biggest war hero we've got."

Esperanza nodded. "He's also greatly respected in Starfleet. It's worth calling him."

"I'll put the call through to Bajor once we're done with today's meetings. What's next?"

Before anyone could speak, the intercom beeped. It was the *Palombo*'s shipmaster, a kindly old gentleman named Derek Fried, who had been running the *Palombo* for the last seven governors of Cestus III. *"Governor, we're entering standard orbit of Earth. You've got a whole lot of messages, and normally I wouldn't bother you with 'em, just send 'em to Ms. Piñiero, but there's one I get the feeling you're gonna wanna see. It's from Admiral Ross at Starfleet."*

Nan and Esperanza exchanged surprised glances. Helga's eyes went wide, and Fred almost spilled his tea.

"Ross wants to talk to *me?*" Nan asked.

"Well, you and Ms. Piñiero, ma'am, yes."

"What do you think?" Nan asked her campaign manager.

Esperanza smiled. "I think it's a fastball down the middle of the base."

Chuckling, Nan said, "Plate. The batters swing when they're standing at the plate. It's the other things they step on that are bases." She stood up. "Derek, call his office back, tell him we'll speak to him right away."

"Whatever you say, ma'am."

"If only *that* were true. Thanks, Derek."

Esperanza also rose. "This meeting's over for now. We've got the official statement at noon. Bral, you and M'Tesint go to the site, make sure everything's set up. Fred, you have the draft ready?"

Fred winced. "Half an hour?"

"Give me what you've got, at least."

"I'd really rather not."

Ashanté shuddered. "Don't do it, Esperanza—you take it now, he'll spend the next half hour worrying himself inside out instead of finishing it."

Esperanza sighed. "Fine, but don't forget, Klingon is spelled with a 'K,' all right?"

Nan laughed. "C'mon, let's go."

They proceeded back to the stateroom. As soon as the door to the lounge shut behind them, Nan asked, "You sure the Statue of Liberty's a good place to do this?"

"It's perfect. Your first big thing as governor was taking in all those DMZ refugees. What better place to formally announce your candidacy than a statue that says, 'Give me your tired, your sick, your teeming masses yearning to be free'?"

Nan smirked. "Actually, it's 'your tired, your *poor,* your *huddled* masses yearning to *breathe* free,' but we'll let that go."

"Being smart's your job, ma'am. I'm just here to make sure you remember to match your socks."

"So *that's* your job, I was starting to wonder," she said with a smile as they entered the stateroom. "By the way, I was only half kidding about exhuming Bobby's body before."

"Fine," Esperanza said, "we'll just exhume half the grave, then."

"You know, sometimes you can be incredibly funny. Then there's now."

"Yes, ma'am."

The bed had, of course, remade itself while she was gone. Setting her half-finished mug of coffee on the desk, Nan sat down and activated the workstation. Cestus III's emblem appeared on the screen, shortly thereafter replaced by that of Starfleet.

"I've got Admiral Ross," said Derek Fried over the intercom.

"Put him through."

The last time Nan had seen William Ross was three years earlier at the Council of Governors meeting on Pacifica, where he had been the guest speaker. That occasion was only a few months after the war. Back then, he looked exhausted, the years of fighting having worn him down. Now, though he had more gray in his hair and his jowls had grown more pronounced, he actually looked better. He no longer had the same level of responsibilities in the admiralty, and that seemed to suit him. *Well, he's earned it,* she thought.

"Good morning, Admiral," she said.

"Governor Bacco, it's good to see you again. You too, Commander Piñiero."

Esperanza smiled. "No one's called me that for three years, sir."

"And Starfleet is poorer for it, believe me."

Nan leaned forward. "I'm gonna assume you didn't call to chastise my campaign manager for her career choice, Admiral."

"No, Governor, I haven't. Several people in your campaign have put out feelers to various captains and admirals regarding possibly serving as advisors."

Shrugging, Nan said, "Several people in Special

Emissary Pagro's campaign have probably done the same thing. Pretty standard. Is that a problem?"

"Not as such, I was just wondering why none of those feelers has reached my *office."*

Rarely did Nan Bacco find herself speechless. When it did happen, though, it often wasn't for very long, so it took her only three seconds to say, "Well, until yesterday, we assumed you were one *of* the feelers. Are you saying, Admiral, that you'd be interested in an advisory position on my campaign staff?"

" 'Position' is too strong a word, but I would be honored if you'd allow me to serve as a consultant." He let out a long breath. *"It's been fairly obvious for some time that the Federation needs a change at the top. With all due deference to Special Emissary Pagro, he's not the change we need. I've seen what you've done on Cestus, and anyone who can actually convince the Metrons to sign a treaty is someone who I think deserves a chance at the highest office."*

Nan smiled. This was as big as Sisko—maybe bigger. *So much for writing off Starfleet.* "Admiral, I would be just as honored to have you available to be consulted, so assuming our respective honors can handle the pressure, I'd say we have us a deal."

"That's good to know, Governor. Oh, one thing—out of curiosity, how did *you get the Metrons to actually sign the treaty? They're energy beings, after all."*

Chuckling, Nan said, "Trade secret, Admiral."

Ross smiled. *"Fair enough. If you'd like, I can join you in New York this afternoon."*

"I'd like that very much, Admiral, thank you."

Esperanza added, "Have your people contact M'Tesint on our staff—she's handling the arrangements."

"I'll do that. Thank you both."

"Thank *you*, Admiral."

The screen went blank. Nan leaned back in her chair. All the coffee she'd drunk suddenly felt heavy and leaden in her stomach. "Son of a bitch."

"Ma'am?"

Nan looked up at Esperanza. "This is really happening, isn't it? I'm really seriously running for president?"

Esperanza looked down at her. "Er, yes, ma'am, you are."

She waved her arm in front of her face at Esperanza's worried tone. "I know what you're thinking, but the point is, it didn't seem like it was—I don't know, *real* until now. I mean, yes, we were making plans back on Cestus where it's safe, and it was just you, me, Fred, Ashanté, and the rest of them, but now . . ." She pointed at the now blank monitor. "Now William blessed Ross is telling me he thinks I can do this. I've only met the man once. I respect him, but I don't really *know* him, and now *he's* telling *me* that I should be president of the Federation. It's one thing for you to say it, you're supposed to be nice to me." She looked up at Esperanza. "About that, you should probably make more of an effort. I don't feel sufficient love coming from you."

"I'll be sure to work on that, ma'am."

Nan shook her head and chuckled. "Batting practice is over. Now it's a ballgame."

"What's that thing where you hit the ball over the wall in the back?"

"A home run?"

"Right. I think you just hit one of those."

Nan laughed. "Hell, Esperanza, that was a grand slam."

"That's where all the plates are full, right?"

"Bases are full, yeah."

"You said before it was plates."

"No, the batter's at the plate, the runners are at bases."

"How can they be at something if they're runners? Shouldn't they be running?"

Waving her finger in a manner depressingly similar to the way she used to wave it at Annabella when she was eleven years old, Nan said, "If you don't cut this out, I'm gonna force you to sit through that program Sisko gave me on a repeated loop."

Esperanza put up her hands. "Hey, I'm just trying to understand you better."

"Well stop it. I'm complex and contain multitudes. It is not for lesser minds such as yours to comprehend."

Smiling, Esperanza said, "Whatever you say, ma'am."

Nan headed to the door. "C'mon, let's go tell the others. I want to see Helga's eyes pop out of her head."

"Right behind you, ma'am."

Jas Abrik, retired Starfleet admiral, watched as the future president of the Federation stood before a small crowd and gave his statement of purpose. That statement was being sent out via subspace to every part of the Federation, and many places outside it.

Fel Pagro was an excellent public speaker, and Abrik had no doubt that his oratory would win the day. Governor Bacco had a certain regional charm about her, but that wouldn't help her on the galactic stage. When the council announced the candidates, Abrik had made a thorough study of Bacco's speeches over the years. The former admiral was born and raised on Trill, and had spent most of his ninety-seven years in the service of Starfleet, but he did not recognize most of Bacco's arcane references until a Vulcan staffer explained them. Apparently, some human game called baseball was played on Cestus III, and Bacco was a fan.

Obscure human sporting references were cute up to a point, and the woman was certainly no fool, but Abrik doubted her ability to adapt to the variety of circumstances one encountered every day on Earth. *Sure, over ten years she handled refugees and the Gorn attack and the war—but that's just one day's work when you get that nice office in Paris.*

No, Abrik backed winners, and that was why he'd accepted the job as Pagro's campaign manager.

Standing on the Golden Gate Bridge, which had been rebuilt after the Breen attack on Earth had all but destroyed it, Pagro spoke, his voice carrying out to the entire Federation:

"For two years, we fought a vicious, brutal war against the Dominion. It's easy to look back now and ask why we didn't try to negotiate with them, to live in harmony with them. But the name says it all: Dominion. They had no interest in living in peace, they just wanted to dominate us. We couldn't allow that to happen, so we fought them. The cost in lives was appalling, but ultimately worth it because the alternative was so much worse. Becoming part of the Dominion would've been no better than becoming part of the Borg collective—and the ashes of Cardassia Prime bear testimony to how the Dominion would treat those who dare to think for themselves or act of their own volition."

Abrik smiled. Jino Bustopha, the Efrosian woman writing Pagro's speeches, had done her usual good job. She'd been on Pagro's staff for years, and Pagro owed a lot of his popularity to her skills.

"But what we need to do is take it one step further. Our way of life is important to us—our freedoms, our ability to become the best that we are capable of becoming. It is the antithesis of what the Dominion stands for, and that's why we fought them—but we cannot afford to stop with the Dominion."

Checking his chronometer, Abrik saw that it was almost nine in the morning, which meant it was almost noon in New York. Pagro's speech would be over right about when Bacco started hers. Abrik had been hoping that Bacco could have made her speech first, but ultimately the decision came down to availability and travel times. Pagro was already on Earth, whereas Bacco wasn't arriving in the system until early this morning. It probably didn't matter much in the end, but the last speech always left the better impression.

Then again, he thought, *there'll be plenty of speeches.*

"It's long past time we stopped making excuses for our so-called allies. Fifteen years ago, we signed a treaty with the Cardassians, yet we let their oppression of the Bajorans continue. We aided them in their conflict with the Klingons only to have them turn and join the Dominion behind our backs. And look at the Klingons—they continue to conquer worlds, indeed they make such conquest policy. Yes, they're taking worlds in distant parts of space nowhere near Federation interests, but does that change what they're doing? Do we not fight for the rights of Bajorans, of the Children of San-Tarah, of the Brenlekki, and of all the others who do not have the freedoms we enjoy because it's convenient for us to be allied with their oppressors?"

Abrik certainly was grateful for the chance to right the many wrongs of the Zife administration. Their idiotic covert actions would serve only to hurt the Federation. Abrik left Starfleet because he couldn't stand the secrecy, the compromises that he was forced into for the so-called greater good. *What's the good of being a free and open society if we still have to hide like rats in the shadows?*

"We fought to preserve the Federation's way of life. Did the people who died on this bridge sacrifice their lives for nothing? I say, no. The people who died on this bridge died because they were free. If it's worth dying for, it's worth fighting for, and as president I will guarantee that those deaths will not be in vain and those freedoms will not go undefended. My name is Fel Pagro, and I'm running for president of the United Federation of Planets."

The crowd, a carefully picked group of Pagro supporters, had been cheering, building to a crescendo at the end that almost drowned out his final sentence. *That's not necessarily bad,* Abrik thought. *It's not like there's anyone here for whom the information in that sentence was news.* The only ones not cheering were the press, of course, because they were supposed to remain objective—or at least neutral. *That's fine, as long as they send out the whole speech.*

Waving to the still-cheering crowd, Pagro left the

podium he'd been standing behind and approached Abrik.

"Good work," Abrik said.

Pagro shrugged. "It was all right. I could've been stronger. I cut the bit on the holographic-rights issue. It didn't flow right. Jino'll probably be pissed."

They started walking toward the shuttle that was going to take them to their Earth campaign offices in Vancouver. "I'll talk to Jino. C'mon, we've got a staff meeting. We've got to see Bacco's speech."

Frowning, Pagro asked, "What for? She's just some governor who pulled a cute trick with some energy beings. Big deal. She's nothing. We need to focus on how we're going to—"

Abrik put a hand on Pagro's shoulder as they walked. "Fel, listen to me. Elections are volatile things. You of all people should know that. Until those votes are actually counted, you're not president yet, and it behooves you to be completely familiar with the one person who stands in your way."

"Please." Pagro rolled his eyes. "She's only in my way insofar as I have to step on her to get the presidency. We've already got the important endorsements lined up on the political side and the celebrity side, and Starfleet's pretty much in the bag. I'm telling you, Jas, now's the time to strike—we can finally make the Federation what it *needs* to be, what it was always intended to be. We can—"

"Fel," Abrik said as the shuttle door opened at their approach, "save the speeches for the people that need convincing. Let's get you elected first, then we'll take care of the rest of it."

Pagro made a dismissive gesture. "Fine, fine." He took a seat on the passenger couch.

Abrik got in next to him. *And then we can really get to work,* he thought. A retired admiral he might have been, but he still had contacts in Starfleet—and he knew what *really* happened on Tezwa. The Federation—and Starfleet in particular—had been making excuses for those Klingon animals for far too long. Azernal's mistake was in keeping everything under all that cloak-and-dagger nonsense so that it was impossible to expose the Klingons for the thugs they truly were.

To the pilot in the front of the shuttle, Abrik said, "Let's go. Oh, and give us the FNS on the viewer."

The small screen mounted on the back of the pilot's couch lit up with the logo of the Federation News Service, which then switched to the face of a female Pandrilite at an anchor desk.

"—gro's speech at the Golden Gate Bridge. Regia Maldonado's special report from Paris on the presidential candidates will be in half an hour, with commentary from former President Jaresh-Inyo, retired Starfleet admiral Norah Satie, and author Jacqueline Sharp. But first we now bring you live coverage of Governor Nan Bacco's candidacy statement from the Statue of Liberty in New York City."

The image switched to a podium in front of the five-hundred-year-old statue. Abrik looked down at one of his padds, wanting to go over some reports while listening to the speech.

"What the *hell*—?"

Abrik looked up at Pagro's words. "What is it?"

"What is Ross doing with *her?*"

"Ross?" Abrik looked at the viewer again. He saw Bacco standing at the podium, along with Commander Piñiero—like Abrik, retired Starfleet, though Abrik didn't really know the woman, and like him, the campaign manager—a Caitian Abrik didn't recognize, a couple of humans—

—and Admiral William Ross.

Son of a bitch.

"With Ross's support, Starfleet may not be the lock we thought it was."

"I *know* that, Jas," Pagro said through clenched teeth. "Fix this. I don't care what you have to offer Ross, but fix this. He's a goddamned war hero, if he throws his combadge in with her, we're screwed."

Abrik nodded. *Dammit.*

Chapter 4
Qo'noS

ALEXANDER HAD ALWAYS LOVED coming to the Federation embassy in the First City, which made being led into its conference room at gunpoint rather irritating.

"Sit down there, now." The Klingon dressed in white barked the order while waving a disruptor that Alexander didn't recognize, but one he knew wasn't Defense Force or Starfleet issue. Why the kitchen stewards were taking hostages was as yet unclear. Three other stewards were in the conference room when Alexander entered, all holding disruptors. They were also the only ones standing, except for Vark, the kitchen staff supervisor. Everyone else—most of the embassy staff, as far as Alexander could tell—was seated on the floor.

The spot where Alexander had been instructed to sit was also on the floor, next to Giancarlo Wu in the northwest corner of the room. Wu looked as calm and unflappable as ever, which made him unique among the human civilians in the room. The only other people not fidgeting or complaining or shifting uncomfortably or twitching nervously were the Klingons among the hostages and the three Starfleet security guards, who'd been put in the other three corners. Aside from them, Alexander was the only one in uniform.

Since there were more than three guards assigned to the embassy, Alexander had to assume that the remaining guards were either still at large or dead. He hoped for the former, but all things considered, the latter seemed more likely.

One of the stewards held his hand to his ear. "Akor, what happened? Akor!" He looked up. "I'm not getting anything. Everyone, switch to the alternate frequency."

The four stewards lifted the white jackets that were part of their uniforms and pressed controls on small devices they had at their waists. Alexander knew that such devices, like the disruptors, were *not* standard issue for the kitchen staff. Vark did the same, which meant he was in on this whole thing.

After making the adjustment, the Klingon spoke again. "Dohk, Gimor, get to the second floor, find out what happened."

Vark stepped forward. "Have Torvak reactivate the security system. Then we can track him."

"No. As long as the ambassador and that other security guard are at large, the embassy is *not* secure. Until it is, we cannot risk activating the system so either of them can use it against us."

One's still free. Good, Alexander thought. *With that one and Father still running around, there's a chance.*

Shaking his head, Vark said, "This isn't going as you promised, Rov."

Rov smiled. "No plan ever does. All that matters is the result."

"The result is that Worf and a Starfleet security guard are still free, and we don't know what happened to Kl'rt, Gitak, or Akor."

"First of all, we don't know for sure that the guard is alive—Krant said he might have hit her."

"And you believe him?" Vark sounded dubious.

Rov grinned. "No. But stranger things have been known to happen. As for Kl'rt, Gitak, and Akor, if they died, they did so in a noble cause. We *will* reclaim the empire, Vark—or is that no longer your goal?"

"Of *course* it's my goal! If it wasn't, I wouldn't give a *targ*'s ass for how you were running this operation."

"Good." Rov then put his hand to his ear. *"QI'yaH,"* he muttered. "All right, begin a coordinated search, top to bottom. Do not be fooled by the child's uniform the guard wears, nor by Worf's dishonorable actions—underestimating them will result only in defeat. Treat them like you would any other warrior you would stalk."

Alexander frowned. *Dishonorable actions? Father? What's he talking about?* Then again, these were obviously terrorists, possibly fanatics. They did not behave rationally. At that thought, Alexander almost smiled. *Mother would say there's no such thing as a rational Klingon.*

But Rov mentioned a noble cause. That meant he had taken the embassy with a specific purpose in mind. Alexander was determined to find out what it was.

"Worf may also have information," Vark said. "Kl'rt's body was not on the second floor."

Rov waved an arm. "He could've been vaporized."

"Gitak and Akor were killed *without* being vaporized," Vark said. "He probably took Kl'rt prisoner *and* has his communications unit."

"It does not *matter,*" Rov snapped. "Kl'rt would die before giving up anything, least of all to that honorless *petaQ*. And we have switched frequencies."

Again, Alexander suppressed a smile. He knew things that Rov and Vark obviously did not about Father: He killed only when he had to, and he had ways of finding things out if he needed to. If this Kl'rt's body was missing, it meant Father *did* have him as a prisoner.

"What if he discovers the new frequency? He is trained by Starfleet, and they are quite good at tinkering."

Rov scowled at Vark. Alexander could see the tension brimming in the younger man, and he wondered if a duel would break out right here. He sort of hoped one would, as it might provide a good distraction.

Unfortunately, Rov got himself under control and put his hand to his ear. "B'Urgan, run a systems check. Find Kl'rt's communications device." A pause. "You're sure it's *nowhere* in the embassy?" He looked at Vark. "Satisfied? Kl'rt probably destroyed the device. He's a *good* soldier."

"You'd better hope so," Vark muttered.

Again, Rov scowled. He moved closer to Vark. "Or *what?*"

"Or we will *all* die for nothing! I *told* you to wait until Worf was gone from the embassy, but you did not listen!"

"And *I* told *you* that we need him as a hostage!" Rov held up a hand before Vark could respond to that. "Enough! It is done. Speak of it again, and I *will* kill you, old man."

Vark said nothing.

Alexander tried to think of ways to exploit this rift between the two men who had violated his home—for that was how he thought of this place. Not long after he was born, Mother was appointed Federation ambassador to the Klingon Empire. They traveled a great deal, of course, but this was where they remained when on the Homeworld— in fact, it was the only place on the planet they ever went. Legally speaking, Alexander was truly never on Qo'noS until after he joined the Klingon Defense Force during the war. Prior to that, he'd been only at the embassy, which was Federation soil. Mother had always insisted on beaming directly to the embassy from whatever ship they were on, and they had taken an apartment within the embassy walls. Mother hadn't wanted Alexander exposed to "Klingon nonsense," at least not until, as she had put it, "you're old enough to make an informed decision about it."

Ever since Father was appointed to the very same position, Alexander had taken every opportunity to visit him here. Part of that was a desire to revisit the haunt of his infancy and youth, though the place had almost completely changed since he was a child. Still and all, despite having lived on the *Enterprise*-D, with his grandparents on Earth, and on the ships where he'd served in the Defense Force, he considered this embassy to be his first home.

But that was only part of it. For the first time in his life, he felt like he *had* a father. When Alexander first met Worf, he denied that he even had a son—his way of protecting Alexander from a dishonor he was suffering at the time—but after Mother died, he claimed the boy and tried to raise him. "Try" being the operative word. With the distance of time, Alexander could now objectively see that there were few people in this galaxy less suited to fatherhood than the son of Mogh. But his attempts to make Alexander into a warrior fell on the deaf ears of a boy who wanted to find his own path. After the *Enterprise*-D was destroyed and Father, Alexander, and some of Father's friends were caught up in a Romulan plot to overthrow the empire, Alexander went to Earth to live with Sergey and Helena Rozhenko, the humans who had raised Father after his own family was killed at Khitomer.

Oddly, the cry of the warrior did not come until after Alexander had been separated from Father for a number of years. Then he enlisted with the Defense Force, serving first on the *Korvak,* then the *Rotarran*—where he was reunited with Father—and finally the *Ya'Vang,* where he still served.

Except, of course, when he visited Father, whether here or on one of his assignments, as he had in the so-called Genesis sector a year and a half ago. He had even unofficially aided Father in some of his diplomatic duties.

Now it's time to help him out again. He needed to learn more about what was happening here.

Rov was now looking over the hostages. "My name is Rov, son of Pekdal. You are prisoners of *Klahb.* If our demands are met, you will all live, though you will probably not be able to remain in this embassy. If our demands are not met, you will all die unpleasant deaths."

Next to Alexander, Wu spoke. The aide had not moved, had barely blinked, for the entire time Alexander had been present. "And what would those demands be, Rov, son of Pekdal?" Wu's tone was one of respect, though not quite as deferential as Rov might have desired, in Alexander's opinion.

Smiling, Rov walked over to the northwest corner of the room. "I know you. You are Giancarlo Wu, the ambassador's senior attaché."

"That is correct. That also does not answer my question."

At that, Rov laughed. "You are brave, human." Rov then looked at Alexander. "I do *not* know you."

"I do." Alexander looked past Rov to see Vark actually smiling for the first time since Alexander had come in the meeting room. Indeed, Alexander was sure he'd never seen Vark smile at all before. "This is Alexander." He looked at Rov. "Son of *Worf.*"

That put a smile on Rov's face as well. "Really?"

"If you think capturing me will get you anything . . ." Alexander started.

"I *know* it has gained me another valuable hostage," Rov said. "That is all that matters." He put his hand to his ear. "B'Urgan, have you rigged the external—"

A voice came from the meeting-room doorway. "Yes, I have."

Alexander looked up to see a very attractive young woman, also dressed as a kitchen steward, holding a large communications unit of some kind. *I'm guessing this is how they're going to let the High Council know what their demands are.* Another steward, who was armed, walked in behind her.

"You're not gonna get away with this."

This time it was one of the embassy staff, a human named Gorjanc, who spoke.

Rov walked over to the human, who was sitting against the wall opposite Alexander, next to one of the Starfleet guards. "Did you say something, human?"

"I said you're not gonna get away with this."

"Perhaps. But you will not live to know."

With that, he fired upon Gorjanc with his disruptor, killing him instantly.

Alexander's most vivid memory of childhood was the day Mother died. Father held her in his arms, and screamed his grief to the heavens in what Alexander would later learn was the Klingon death ritual. Then Father asked Alexander if he had ever seen death, to which he replied in the negative. "Then look now," Father had said then, "and always remember."

He did. Twelve years later, the image of Mother dead on the floor of the VIP quarters on the *Enterprise*-D was still with him.

Now, Alexander knew that it was that memory more than anything that had held him back from being a warrior. Because he knew in his heart that, if he became a warrior, he would inflict deaths like the one that had been visited upon Mother. Worse, he would lead a life that would probably end with a death just like Mother's.

Once, when on the *Enterprise* holodeck with his father and the House of Mogh's *ghIntaq,* a man named K'mtar, Alexander was given a chance to kill a foe who was already down and defeated. He could not. Even now, as a soldier of the empire, though he was willing to kill in self-defense, and had done so both during the war and after it, he would not take a helpless life.

And those who did, the way Rov just had done, sickened him to his very core.

As Damir Gorjanc fell dead to the floor of the meeting room, Alexander swore a vow. *I'll make sure that you pay for what you've done, Rov, son of Pekdal.*

"Would anyone else like to speak?" Rov asked.

Silence greeted his request. Alexander noted that the humans who had been agitated were now sitting quietly, looking frightened out of their wits. They lived and worked on Qo'noS, but they were still not used to dealing with this side of Klingon life. The Klingons they did encounter were politicians and functionaries, not warriors, and so they were not accustomed to such naked brutality.

Alexander knew Rov's query was rhetorical, but he answered it anyhow. "I would."

One of the Starfleet guards shot Alexander a look that seemed to say, *Are you insane?* And perhaps he was, but Alexander knew that, as the son of the ambassador, he was too valuable to kill just yet. Besides which, the uniform he wore would accord him more respect than that which would be granted to a human or even to a Klingon civilian.

Rov walked over to him, aiming the disruptor between Alexander's eyes.

Alexander swallowed. *At least I hope I'm too valuable to kill.*

"And what do you wish to say?"

"I want to know what your demands are."

Lowering the disruptor, Rov said, "Then listen carefully, Alexander, son of Worf, and you will learn." Then Rov walked over to the unit that B'Urgan had brought in and touched a control. One of the telltales lit up. Satisfied that the machine was working, Rov nodded to B'Urgan and the man with her. They both nodded back and departed the conference room.

"My name is Rov, son of Pekdal, and I represent *Klahb*. I am sending you this message from the Federation Embassy on Qo'noS, which *Klahb* has taken possession of. Some of those within the embassy are dead; the rest are *Klahb*'s hostages. Whether or not those hostages join the ranks of the dead depends upon the actions of the Klingon High Council.

"We demand that the following actions be taken: That the lowlander Martok be removed from the chancellorship that he was falsely given by a conniving, honorless coward. That the alliance with the Federation be treated like the sham it is and abrogated. That the hologram impersonating Emperor Kahless be deactivated. And that we declare war on the Federation, and do not cease until the Federation is destroyed and the true Kahless returned to us from whatever Federation prison he's being held in."

It was all Alexander could do to keep from laughing out loud. *Hologram impersonating Kahless?* He had almost been willing to believe that Rov and Vark were championing a legitimate cause, right up until he got to that part of his demands.

"We do not expect any of these actions to be taken. The council would never admit that they have become the Federation's lapdogs, funneling instructions through their kingmaker Worf, who is now our hostage. They will not admit that thousands died at Tezwa in order to preserve Federation lies. And they certainly would not admit to the Federation replacing our beloved emperor with a photonic fake."

Alexander shuddered. The *Ya'Vang* had been assigned to the task force sent to avenge the six thousand who died at Tezwa, and Alexander had feared he would die that day. But from what he'd heard on the *Ya'Vang*, there was no complicity between the Federation and the empire over Tezwa—quite the opposite, in fact. The two nations almost went to war over what happened on that planet. *Obviously, Rov's relationship with reality is pretty strained.*

"I expect a response within three hours. If I do not receive one, I will destroy this entire structure. The members of *Klahb* are willing to die to save the empire, but I doubt the Federation will be amused by the wholesale slaughter of its embassy personnel *again*."

This time, Alexander simply shook his head. The embassy had been badly damaged and many of its personnel killed when Morjod attempted to overthrow Martok right after the war. *Now that I think about it, a lot of what Morjod was saying was the same thing Rov's saying now. And it was nuts four years ago, too.*

Rov touched the control again, and the telltale went dark. He then put his hand to his ear. "Has the ambassador or the guard been found?" A second later, his face contorted into a mask of rage. "Why *not? Find* them, or your journey to the afterlife will be a swift one indeed!"

Alexander felt something push into his hip. He turned to see Wu staring at him intently; it had been the aide's knee that he felt. Alexander stared back questioningly, not sure what it was Wu wanted him to do.

Then Wu mouthed the words *talk to him.* He mouthed them in English, so it was unlikely that Rov or any of the other Klingons would be able to discern the meaning.

At once, Alexander realized what Wu wanted. He needed to keep Rov talking, possibly continue to drive a wedge—or, rather, drive the existing wedge further—between Rov and Vark. As both a valuable hostage and the only Defense Force personnel among the hostages, Alexander was probably the one who stood the best chance of being able to speak without suffering the same fate as Gorjanc.

"What's happening next?" Alexander asked.

Shaking his head, Rov said, "You are as big a fool as your father. We wait."

"That isn't what I meant. I mean after the High Council tells you to—" He hesitated. There was no real Klingon equivalent for the human phrase "go to hell." After taking a breath, he amended his statement. "After they refuse your request, you're going to blow up the embassy, right?"

"That is what I said."

"So you'll die with everyone else?"

"Not quite. When we of *Klahb* die, we will be welcomed in *Sto-Vo-Kor*. The rest of you will wallow on the Barge of the Dead in *Gre'thor*."

Alexander had always been dubious about the whole Klingon afterlife notion, though he had always found it touching that Father dedicated a battle to his wife Jadzia after she died in the war to commend her soul to *Sto-Vo-Kor*. On those days when he actually believed, he wondered if Jadzia had found Mother in the Black Fleet, and if so, wondered how well they got along. He suspected they'd like each other.

However, that was not his concern at the moment. "Either way, you and your followers'll be dead."

"My 'followers,' as you call them, have pledged their

lives. Unlike these human weaklings," he spread his arms to take in the entire room, "they have no fear of death."

"Okay," Alexander said after pretending to consider the notion for a moment. "So then what?"

"What do you mean?" Rov sounded genuinely confused.

"I mean, then what? You'll be dead, your followers will be dead, all of us will be dead—and nothing will have changed. Martok will still be in power, the Federation will still be our allies, and—" *keep a straight face!* "—Kahless will still be a hologram."

"Perhaps. But the people will know the truth."

"How, by you letting yourselves get blown up? That doesn't prove anything."

Rov raised the disruptor again. "Be silent, son of Worf! Your value as a hostage decreases with each word you speak."

So much for that plan, he thought dolefully.

Turning his back on Alexander, Rov put his hand to his ear again. "Torvak, report." A pause. "Torvak, *report!*"

Vark shook his head. "That young *yIntagh* is probably listening to that wretched opera recording of his again."

"No doubt." Rov spoke in a menacingly low tone. "I will get a report from him personally. Keep an eye on the prisoners. B'Eko, with me."

With that, Rov departed, followed by the female steward.

Moments passed in silence before Wu said, "He's going to leave the embassy before it blows up. You know that, Vark."

What the hell is he playing at? Alexander wondered.

True, Wu knew Vark, but why was he so sure that Rov was going to leave his followers behind?

Vark turned to Wu and raised his own disruptor. "Silence, human!"

"Funny, you called me 'Giancarlo' this morning." This time, Wu smirked slightly.

"This morning, I had to pretend to be an employee of this embassy."

"There was no 'pretending' about it, Vark. You *are* an employee of this embassy—though, to be fair, your job prospects after today will probably be limited."

"I said, silence!"

One of the other humans whispered, "For Christ's sake, 'Carlo, shut the hell up!"

Ignoring this sage advice, Wu said, "You know I'm right, Vark. And so was Alexander. If he's trying to overthrow the High Council, he's not just going to blow himself up. He's a revolutionary, not a martyr. You and these other stewards are just his cannon fodder."

At once, Alexander saw that Wu was correct. Rov had never directly said that he was going to sacrifice his own life. Now that he looked back on the conversation, he hadn't even committed to killing any other member of *Klahb*.

But the uncertainty on Vark's face meant that, whatever Rov's true plans were, he hadn't shared them with the kitchen staff supervisor.

Let's hope that's a start, Alexander thought as he shifted position on the floor. Defense Force armor, whatever its benefits, was not designed for sitting comfortably on the floor, but he had the feeling he was going to be here awhile.

* * *

The last thing Kl'rt remembered before waking up in the empty room was killing the human.

His mission had been a simple one: to bring the traitor to the top-floor meeting room. Kl'rt considered it a great privilege to be given the honor of capturing the false one. True, Worf might have looked like a Klingon, he might have called himself "son of Mogh" as if he were a true Klingon, but Kl'rt knew better. It was like Rov told him: He was a traitor, the foulest of the foul. He was a *wam* serpent who had insinuated himself into the House of Martok, then helped that one-eyed coward remove Gowron from his rightful place as chancellor. And now what they did to the emperor whom Gowron had welcomed home was just despicable. . . .

But Rov would stop them, expose them for the *petaQ* they were, and Kl'rt would help him in whatever way he could.

That, at least, had been the plan.

B'Urgan had said that the device she'd fabricated would neutralize any Federation or Klingon weapons, which was why they were forced to use the weapons of the filthy Breen. But Kl'rt did not mind using them if it meant they would achieve their goal.

How, then, was I rendered unconscious?

Kl'rt remained still, but opened his eyes just enough to take in his surroundings. He was in a large windowless room. He was unbound, but lying up against one of the walls. The only distinguishing features of the room were the turbolift doors, currently open to an empty turboshaft, and the figure of Ambassador Worf standing near them. Kl'rt had memorized the embassy's floor-plans—including the classified subbasement—but nothing like this room was on those plans.

I will continue to feign unconsciousness until the time is right for me to strike. Rov had said all along that Worf was the most dangerous foe the empire had ever faced. Kl'rt had dismissed that as rhetorical hyperbole, but now he saw that Rov was correct. Somehow, without the use of standard weapons, he had rendered Kl'rt unconscious and brought him somewhere outside the embassy.

The traitor looked over at Kl'rt. "You are awake. Good. I require information."

How did he know—? Kl'rt put the thought out of his head. He knew, so Kl'rt would deal with it. "Where have you brought me?"

"I said *I* require information." Worf was, Kl'rt saw, studying a Starfleet tricorder, but now he closed it and walked toward Kl'rt. "I have no reason to provide you with any."

As soon as Worf was close enough, Kl'rt leapt to his feet and attacked. He had always been skilled at weaponless hand-to-hand combat—as a boy growing up on Mempa VIII, he'd always done well in brawls, and even wrestled professionally for a time, before he was expelled due to what the judges mistakenly deemed dishonorable behavior. The drugs he took in no way affected his performance; they simply allowed him to breathe more easily.

He therefore came at Worf secure in the knowledge that he could take a diplomat with little trouble.

A second later, he was sprawled on the floor, wondering why his entire face hurt.

"You will not move until I say you can," Worf said.

"Now speak—where is the device that is blocking use of weapons?"

"I will die before I tell you anything, traitor!"

The ambassador tilted his head. "That is the second time you have labeled me a traitor. Why?"

This question Kl'rt would happily answer. "You have been a puppet of the Federation all your life, and through you, the Federation has controlled the empire."

"Really?"

Kl'rt spit on the empty floor. "Do not attempt to deny it! First you had K'mpec killed and then framed Duras for the crime, paving the way for your first puppet, Gowron. But he was too strong for you—he found Kahless, made him emperor, and then would not listen to your Federation lies when he invaded Cardassia or during the Dominion War! So you had *him* killed and installed your one-eyed fool. Now you have stolen the emperor from us!"

"The emperor remains on his throne where he belongs. Your words are the ramblings of a deranged *toDSaH.*"

At that, Kl'rt laughed. "I do not expect you to admit it. But your days are numbered, traitor. We will expose your perfidy, and your blood and that of your slime devil of a chancellor will paint the streets of the First City!"

"And how will this goal be accomplished?"

Kl'rt folded his arms. "I will speak no more to you, traitor. As I said, I will die before I tell *you* anything."

"Of course. That is the way of all cowards."

"You *dare* call *me* coward?" Kl'rt leaned forward, but did not get up. He did not know how, exactly, Worf managed to knock him to the ground before—he had moved that fast—but he wasn't ready to risk it again.

"No dare is required—I simply speak the truth. Dying for your cause is easy. It requires no effort on your part, no sacrifice. You simply sit there and spit like a rabid *targ* and wait for me to kill you. No, the true act of bravery is to live for your cause—and to suffer for it."

"What do you mean?"

Worf reached into his pocket and pulled out what looked like a small weapon. "This weapon has three settings—stun, kill, and burn. The kill setting is fixed, but the others have levels. Different species have different tolerances for what will stun them, and the amount of power required to burn something will vary depending on the target." He pushed two buttons on the weapon, based on the beeps Kl'rt heard. "It is now set on light burn. Your embassy record indicates that you are left-handed. I will therefore fire on your right arm if you do not answer my question. That will leave you with a one-centimeter hole in your arm. If you continue to be uncooperative, I will fire on your left arm, and your capacity as a warrior will be greatly diminished. After that, I will proceed to your feet."

"You lie. You are a Federation diplomat—you won't torture me. You are soft and weak and have no taste for blood."

"Don't I?"

Something in the ambassador's tone made Kl'rt hesitate. That, and the pain he still felt in his face, most of which was now localized in his jaw and right cheek.

But it did not matter. "Do your worst, traitor. Rov is no fool. I could tell you nothing even if I wished to. I do not have the information you seek. If there is a device such as that you asked of, I have not been informed of its location. And even if I had been, I would *never* reveal it to *you*. It does not matter if you slice off my arms and legs, if you leave me suffering for all eternity, if you cast me onto the Barge of the Dead yourself, I will say nothing!"

Kl'rt stared directly into the traitor's brown eyes, refusing to give in, refusing even to blink. *I will not let you down, Rov. I believe in our cause, and will die for it—or, if the traitor will resort to such tactics, I will suffer for it, too.*

Finally, Worf looked away. "I believe you."

That caused Kl'rt to blink in surprise. "What?"

"However, your response is no longer relevant. I already have all the information I need. Rov has just broadcast his demands to the Great Hall. In addition, I have the positions of all of your fellow terrorists."

Only then did Kl'rt realize *why* Worf had looked away from Kl'rt's gaze. It was not a show of cowardice or of defeat. The ambassador was simply showing Kl'rt that he was now wearing the earpiece that had been assigned to Kl'rt. *No! How could I have been so stupid?*

"At first, I thought I would require your intelligence, as Rov had changed frequencies when they discovered that your body was not among the corpses on the second floor. However, a few minutes ago, my tricorder was able to determine the frequency, and I have heard everything Rov has said."

In the brief time that Kl'rt had served at the embassy, he had never once seen the ambassador smile. Indeed, his lack of true passion was one of many things that branded him as a false Klingon.

Now, though, Kl'rt saw Worf smile. It wasn't an especially broad one. His lips just curled upward a bit. Still, based on his usual, that was the equivalent of a wide grin, and it was the first thing Kl'rt had seen since waking up in this room that truly scared him.

"I therefore have no further use for you."

Fully expecting to be shot, Kl'rt was surprised to see Worf pocket the phaser. "What are you doing?"

"I am leaving. I must take back the embassy."

Again, Kl'rt laughed. "By yourself?"

"Yes."

"You really *are* a fool."

"I have little choice. The empire will not negotiate with terrorists, and no aid from the Federation can possibly arrive in time. Even if it could, I doubt that Martok would allow Starfleet to take any unilateral action without his approval. He will destroy the embassy and all those inside it before allowing himself to be extorted by bloodworms such as yourself."

Shaking his head, Kl'rt said, "You will not succeed."

"You would be wise to hope that I do, Kl'rt, son of Krul. For my success is the only hope for your rescue." He pointed to the open lift doors and the shaft beyond it. "That turboshaft is the only means in or out of this room. Only two people in the empire know of this room's existence—three, including you—and I am the only one of those two who knows that you are here. If I am successful, I will come back for you. If I am not, you will live out your days in this room. There are no weapons here, nothing with which you will be able to take your own life, nor is there any food or water—you will be forced to waste away like an old woman, and then stumble your way to *Gre'thor* like the honorless *petaQ* you truly are."

With that, Worf turned and entered the turboshaft.

Panic slicing into his chest, Kl'rt leapt to his feet once more and ran for the doors, trying to stop Worf from shutting them.

He reached the entryway just as the doors slammed shut with a most resounding thud.

Placing the tips of his fingers at the seam of the two doors, Kl'rt attempted to pry them apart, but he could not gain purchase.

He felt around for something on his person that he could use to wedge between the doors, but he carried no blade, and Worf had taken his disruptor and his communications device.

Looking around the room, Kl'rt saw nothing but blank walls and an empty floor. There didn't even appear to be a mote of dust.

This is worse than torture, and reveals you as lower than the Lubbockian slime devil we all thought you to be, Worf. You should pray that I die down here, for if I live, I will not rest until you are dead at my feet.

The sounds of Kl'rt pounding on the turbolift doors faded as Worf climbed back up the shaft away from the sub-subbasement. In order to implement his plan of attack, he needed to be far away from the sensor-resistant walls of the lower floor. Though the space had been cleared of everything—even the interior walls—whatever was in the walls, floor, and ceiling that kept the secret room literally off the radar still interfered with tricorder readings. He needed to be able to screen out specific life-forms if his plan was to work.

Once he reached the fifth floor, just under where the shaft forked into a second shaft for the east side of the building, he paused, hooked his right arm around one of the ladder's rungs, and removed the tricorder from his pocket with his left hand.

From what he'd overheard on *Klahb*'s communications channel, one of the Starfleet security guards assigned to the embassy was also still at large. Worf needed to locate that guard first.

He screened out the conference room from the tricorder's scan. That was the last place he could go right now; all the hostages were there, and it was the most heavily defended room. *I need to engage in guerrilla tactics to win this battle,* he thought, *and that means avoiding the heart until all the extremities have been cut off and are bleeding.*

Once that was done, he scanned for life-forms in the rest of the embassy. The first thing he noted was that the subbasement was clear. That space Worf knew about, not because he was ambassador but because his position as head of strategic operations for the Bajoran sector and later as fleet liaison between Starfleet and the Defense Force during the war gave him clearance to be aware of the floor's existence. Worf wasn't surprised to see that it was empty, as it explained the faces among the hostages he saw that he didn't recognize, but he was disheartened, as it meant that Vark and Rov had found out about the subbasement's existence, which pointed to a leak in security.

Then again, this entire operation points to a leak in security. One that I intend to plug.

In addition to housing several top-secret operations

and data, the subbasement was also where the embassy's main computer was kept. That meant that whoever had locked out the security system—based on what Worf had overheard, that was someone named Torvak—was doing so remotely. *That provides one option on how to disengage the security lockout.*

The other life-forms he detected were two Klingons moving on the third floor, two more moving on the fifth—and rapidly approaching Worf's position—and another two on the seventh. *Probably roving patrols trying to find myself and the guard.* Three more Klingons were stationary on the eighth floor, two on the west side of the floor, the third on the east.

Rov's voice sounded on the comm. *"Torvak, report."* A pause, then: *"Torvak, report!"*

A moment later, two more Klingons "appeared" moving toward the emergency ladder access on the top floor. *It seems Rov and another of his people will be getting Torvak's report in person.*

The only other life-form Worf read was that of a human, inside one of the guest bedrooms on the sixth floor. Assuming that was the missing guard, he or she was in no immediate danger, leaving Worf to go after the two most valuable members of *Klahb,* who were about to be in the same place: Rov, the ringleader, and Torvak, the one who had disabled the security system.

He put the tricorder back in his pocket and unhooked his arm from the rung. Just as he got into position to continue his upward climb, the doors to the fifth-floor turbolift bay on the wall perpendicular to him started to part. Worf muttered a curse as he fumbled for his Ferengi phaser.

Two beams from Breen disruptors shot out from between the doors as they opened. One harmlessly hit the
center of the shaft. The other was off-center, and struck a
glancing blow on Worf's left elbow. The entire arm went
numb and fell to his side, his fingers hanging loose, and
the phaser tumbling out of his grip and falling down the
shaft, making a clattering noise as it went.

This, Worf thought, *is not good.*

The doors opened three-quarters of the way to reveal
two Klingons in stewards' outfits.

Using his legs and right arm to propel him, Worf leapt
from his perch on the turboshaft ladder right at the pair
of them. He had no particular plan in mind; it was a des-
peration move, borne of the hope that they weren't expecting quite this kind of frontal assault.

Even as Worf flew through the air toward them, one of
them shouted, "It's hi—" with the final consonant cut off
by the impact of an ambassadorial chest with his face.
Worf and both Klingons tumbled to the floor.

There was no art to Worf's attack, nor in the melee
that followed. Worf simply flailed with his one good arm
and both legs in an attempt to do damage to his oppo-
nents. One of them managed to punch Worf in the gut,
but neither of them were able to do much beyond that. At
one point, one of them dropped his disruptor. As he bent
to pick it up, Worf kicked him in the face, which sent
him stumbling backward.

A second later, that Klingon's screams echoed into the
walls, and faded as he fell down the turboshaft he'd
fallen into after Worf's kick.

His companion scrambled to his feet and stood at the

open doorway. "Pek! Pek! You *petaQ,* you killed him! I'll—"

Whatever it was he was going to do was left unsaid, as a shot from the disruptor the late Pek had dropped caught him square in the chest, and he fell to the floor, dead.

Worf, still lying on the floor, but now holding Pek's weapon, let out a long breath. He got to his feet, using the disruptor's stock to balance himself in lieu of his now-useless left arm. Once upright, he holstered the disruptor into his belt, then reached down and grabbed the other disruptor. *Even if I can't fire both at once, better to have a backup,* he thought, angered at the loss of the Ferengi phaser. Few things disheartened a warrior more than losing a good weapon, and the phaser had proven an excellent one.

"Vark, I'm on my way back." That was Rov again. Tucking the disruptor under his left shoulder, Worf awkwardly reached into his left pocket with his right hand to pull out the tricorder. *"Dohk, Gimor, report."*

"Nothing on three. We're moving up to four."

Worf examined the readings, and saw that the human remained in place, one Klingon was now climbing the emergency stairway back up to the tenth floor—presumably Rov. Four Klingons were now on the eighth floor, leading Worf to assume that B'Eko had been left behind to protect Torvak. *A wise precaution.*

"Krant, Mukk?"

Worf moved quickly, kicking the Klingon's body so it too fell down the shaft. If Rov was getting reports, the lack of reply on this floor would lead someone to investigate. Finding no bodies would delay action more than finding a single one, and give Worf more time.

"Nothing on seven yet."

"Larq, Pek?"

Silence greeted Rov's request. With both disruptors holstered in his belt, Worf awkwardly climbed over to the ladder with one arm. At once, he realized he couldn't close the door behind him, as he needed his only good arm to hang on to the ladder.

"Larq, Pek, report!"

Unfortunately, Worf had to use the shaft—the *Klahb* people were using the emergency stairs, and now he especially needed to minimize confrontations that weren't on his own terms.

"Dohk, Gimor, move up to five, find out what's happened to Larq and Pek."

"They probably shot each other," either Dohk or Gimor said, and the other laughed.

"Do it!" Rov yelled at a volume that threatened to puncture Worf's eardrum.

"We're on our way."

Then he thought of something. He hooked his arm into a rung, then unholstered one of the disruptors. If his memory was correct, this disruptor also had a burn setting. Gazing at the display, he saw that he was right. Thumbing the indicator to that setting, he then aimed it at the manual-override box to the right of the doorway.

The first shot missed; the second did not, melting the metal covering of the box and the circuitry inside.

However, all it did was open the doors the rest of the way. Worf sighed, but he knew it to be a sensible security procedure. If the manual override was damaged or sabotaged, it was usually because someone didn't want the doors to be opened. The logical default in the system would be to open the doors if the override was, say, melted by a Breen disruptor.

On the other hand, he thought, *now I will be able to access the other floors without sacrificing my hold on the ladder.*

He climbed the rest of the way to the sixth floor, then did the same thing with that door's manual override, with the same result.

This time, Worf's leap from the shaft ladder to the open doorway was smoother, since he didn't have two Klingons blocking the way.

Worf stood and took his bearings. Even if the tricorder hadn't told him that the human was on this floor, the distinctly human blood trail would have given it away. The ambassador followed it to one of the doors. This floor contained a dozen residential suites used by both embassy staff and guests, and the human had chosen the largest guest quarters, generally reserved for visiting dignitaries. The rooms were massive and luxurious—necessary, as the Klingon notion of luxury was viewed as insultingly uncomfortable by most visiting dignitaries—and the human had wisely chosen the one that had the most places to hide.

He double-checked the tricorder—then blinked and checked it again.

The human life reading was gone.

Now he ran to the large suite. The doors opened at his approach—privacy locks were part of the security system and were disengaged when that system went down—and he ran in, following the blood trail.

It led to a lavishly appointed bedroom whose deep white pile carpet was marred by the familiar stain of human blood. The crimson path took Worf to the bathroom, where he found the corpse of a human woman lying in the sonic shower stall. He recognized her as Miriam Masekela, the chief of the Starfleet security contingent at the embassy. Her trail of blood was created by a nasty wound in her chest. *One of the Klingons must have been using the burn setting.* He was amazed she stayed alive as long as she did, and swore that her death would not go unavenged.

"Rov, we're on five, but I see neither Larq nor Pek. However, the lift door is open. I am guessing that they fell down the shaft."

Rov snorted in Worf's ear. *"That would not surprise me. Keep searching. Until you find their bodies, assume nothing."*

Another Klingon voice spoke. *"I do not like this, Rov. That's five the ambassador has killed—"*

Again, Rov shouted. *"I do not care what you do or do not like, Dohk! Continue the search!"*

Worf took out his tricorder. Without Masekela's aid, he needed to find some other way to even the odds. His plan was to take out Torvak and his guard on the eighth floor, something that would have been considerably easier with Masekela's help.

Since I do not have brute force at my disposal, I shall have to use guile.

* * *

Alexander was starting to get nervous at the quiet. The conference room had been silent save for people breathing for several minutes after Rov reentered the room. Vark and the woman who was guarding the hostages looked at their leader, waiting for some kind of sign from him as to what to do next.

Just as Wu shoved his knee into Alexander's back again, prompting Alexander to consider saying something to break the silence, Rov put his hand to his ear. After a moment, he said, "That would not surprise me. Keep searching. Until you find their bodies, assume nothing." After a momentary pause, Rov's face contorted into one of fury, and he screamed, "I do not care what you do or do not like, Dohk! Continue the search!" Rov shook his head. "I'm surrounded by fools!"

Some idiot then said, "Isn't that the kind of thing that starts from the top?"

To Alexander's shock, he himself was that idiot. *What am I doing?*

Then he shot a quick glance at Wu, who gave him an encouraging nod.

All right, if I'm going to piss him off, I may as well do it right. "What did you think you were going to accomplish, anyhow?"

Rov again pointed his disruptor at Alexander's head. "Be silent!"

"Why? You can't kill me because I'm a valuable hostage, remember?"

"Not *that* valuable," Rov said through clenched teeth.

"Then shoot me or answer my question." *He's gonna shoot me, take it easy, don't let him rile you, you're a soldier, dammit.* "How do you think taking the Federation embassy is going to affect empire policy?"

At that, Rov laughed and spread his arms as if to take in the entire room, which had the fortuitous side effect of moving the disruptor muzzle's path of fire away from Alexander's head. "Because *this* is where empire policy is made! It is where policy has been made since Praxis was destroyed! Since that dark day, we have become an empire of weaklings, dependent on others to keep us strong— well, no more! Today, our dependence on the Federation is ended as if it never was! As it never should have been!"

He really is nuts. "You realize that if the empire hadn't allied with the Federation after Praxis, there wouldn't *be* a Klingon Empire now."

Rov snorted. "If you believe propaganda."

"I don't believe propaganda, but I do believe facts. I've read the accounts of the time, and I've seen the scientific surveys done *by Klingons* of the Homeworld after Praxis was destroyed. I also know how reliant the empire was on that moon for most of our industrial production." Alexander was only stretching the truth a bit; the surveys he saw were Federation ones, and all of what he saw was in a history class taken on the *Enterprise* as a boy. *Let's hear it for a human education.* "And if we weren't allied with the Federation, do you really think we would've won the Dominion War? Why do you think the Founders went to so much trouble to break the alliance?"

Rov once again aimed the disruptor at Alexander. "We needed no one's help to win the war!"

"Oh yeah we did. Trust me, I was there, I know what

it was like to go up against the Jem'Hadar and the Cardassians *and* the Breen." Then a thought occurred to Alexander. "But then, you should know that. You all fought in the war, didn't you?"

"Of course," Vark said.

"I did, proudly," the woman added.

Rov said nothing.

Alexander gazed at the *Klahb* leader. "You didn't fight, did you?"

Through clenched teeth, Rov said, "I was not permitted to join the Defense Force."

"What do you mean?" the woman asked, no longer pointing her disruptor at the hostages, but staring at Rov with a seriously angry expression.

"That's crazy," Alexander said. "The Defense Force will let *anybody* in." He smiled. "I mean, they took *me,* so they'll obviously allow anyone." Then the light dawned. "You mean they wouldn't take you as an officer."

"I was not going to go into battle as a *bekk* like some kind of commoner animal or weak-willed bloodworm. I am a warrior! I should have been—"

"You didn't fight in the war?" Vark asked.

"*I* was a *bekk,* Rov," the woman said.

Vark grabbed Rov by the arm. "You ask us to follow you into battle, into death, yet you refused the call of battle when the empire needed you?"

Rov backhanded Vark, causing the older Klingon to fall to the floor in front of Alexander and Wu. "The empire needs me *now,* you senile old imbecile! And I am providing—"

"What?" Alexander asked. "Entertainment? Because

that's all you are. Kahless as a hologram? Do you really think anyone will take you seriously? I'm sure the main reason why the High Council hasn't gotten back to you is because they're laughing so hard—especially if they looked up your service record." Alexander grinned. "Well, your lack of service record, anyhow. Look, I may not be the greatest Klingon in the galaxy, but even I know better than to expect anyone to take me seriously if I won't even fight for the empire in times of war."

"I said be *silent* or I will—"

"Rov!"

It took Alexander a moment to realize that the voice that had called Rov's name was coming from Vark's ear. The old man lay insensate on the floor, but his com unit was still functioning, and now Alexander could hear what came through the earpiece.

"What?!" Rov screamed.

"We've finished this floor. There is no sign of the ambassador or the guard. Should we move down to seven?"

"That would be pointless."

Alexander's heart sang—he knew that voice. *Father!*

"Who is this?" Rov asked.

"I am Worf, son of Mogh, Federation ambassador."

Rov laughed. "Of course you are. I should have known that you'd find the new frequency. In fact, one of my advisors warned me that you would do such a thing." Rov looked down at Vark's prone form. "Perhaps I should have paid more attention to him."

"Perhaps. You should be aware that Chief Masekela and I have killed several of your people already. It is only a matter of time before we take back the embassy."

"You are a fool, Ambassador."

"This is the only chance you will get to surrender the embassy to me."

"I will *never* surrender to the likes of *you,* Ambassador. You, who have done everything you can to destroy the empire! You, who have—"

"Your rhetoric bores me, Rov. Surrender or die. Those are your choices."

Rov laughed. "You can do *nothing* to me, son of Mogh. You *are* nothing." Then he switched his com unit off. "Karra," he said to the woman, "grab Krant and Mukk and take them to the subbasement. Either Worf or the guard must be there attempting to regain computer access. Go!"

Karra hesitated.

"I will not lead you astray, Karra. You believe in our cause as much as I do."

"I believe in this cause," Karra said, "because *you* convinced me it was a true one. No longer am I quite so convinced. I will go and find the ambassador for you, but this is *not* over, Rov." With that, she left.

Switching the com unit back on as Karra ran out the door, Rov said, "Do your worst, Ambassador. Soon you will be dead, as will the traitor Martok. The hologram of Kahless will be deactivated, and your treachery will be revealed for all the empire to see!"

"Rov, I think I hear something."

Alexander frowned. That was a female voice.

"Worf may be approaching your position, B'Eko— switch to the alternate frequency."

"We're on the alternate frequency," B'Eko said.

It was all Alexander could do to keep from laughing.

Then he looked over at Gorjanc's body, and the urge to laugh left him.

"Damn you, woman, just be ready for that Starfleet woman or the ambassador to attack. B'Eko?" Silence. "B'Eko!?"

Vark started to stir.

"Damn you—"

Vark sat up. "No, Rov, damn *you!*" He aimed his disruptor at the *Klahb* leader.

Unfortunately, Rov was too fast for him, and he fired his own weapon. Vark fell back to the floor, his own shot firing harmlessly into the ceiling as he collapsed, dead.

Turning away as if Vark were unimportant—*and to him,* Alexander thought bitterly, *he probably isn't, any more than Gorjanc was*—Rov put his hand back to his ear. "B'Eko, *respond,* damn you! Torvak, can you hear me?"

Then the lights went out.

Emergency lights came on a moment later.

Then a green gas started to waft into the room.

Anesthezine gas. Alexander recognized it from his days on the *Enterprise.* The Federation wouldn't allow any fatal security measures in their embassy. The gas, though, would take care of everyone in the building. *Including,* he thought as he started to grow drowsy, *me.*

The last thing Alexander heard before falling unconscious was Rov screaming. The last thing he saw was Giancarlo Wu smiling.

Chapter 5
Earth

MONTGOMERY SCOTT had yet to grow tired of the view.

For as long as the building had been in existence, the commissary at Starfleet Command headquarters on Earth had a spectacular view of the San Francisco skyline. The first time Scotty came here was when he was an Academy cadet. The reason for a cadet getting to dine in the Command commissary was long since forgotten, but even now, well over a hundred years later, Scotty still marveled at the sight of San Francisco's skyline. Over here, the restored Golden Gate Bridge. Over there, the Romanova Building, named after the mayor who spearheaded the rebuilding of the city following the disastrous earthquake in 2109. In the center, DeLaGuardia Tower, built shortly after the forming of the Federation. On top of Telegraph Hill, the World War III Memorial, built on the remains of the Coit Tower after the latter was destroyed during that conflict. To the right, the sprawling complex of Starfleet Academy.

Of course, it helps that I was out of commission for

seventy-five years. He chuckled to himself at the memory of waking up in the transporter room of the *Jenolen,* seemingly moments after he and Ensign Franklin—the last survivors of the ship's crash into a Dyson Sphere—had rigged the transporter to keep them alive in the buffer until a rescue came. That rescue did come—over seven decades later, and too late to save poor Franklin.

For Scotty, who'd been on the road to retirement, it was a new lease on life, and he'd taken it with gusto. In the decade since his "revival," he'd traveled the galaxy from Risa to Romulus, seen things he'd never imagined possible, helped out some old friends, and even aided in Starfleet's horrendous battle against the Dominion.

It was during the war that he became the liaison between the Starfleet Corps of Engineers and the admiralty. The job was ideally suited to Scotty, who had made a career out of navigating the dual landmines of command necessity and engineering possibility. Where once he would have considered an administrative post to be the equivalent of death, his recent years of gallivanting around the galaxy served to remind him why he thought retirement was a good idea in the first place: He wasn't getting any younger. These days, he was content to work with the S.C.E., doling out mission assignments, and keeping the brass off their backs so they could do their jobs. *Perhaps it doesn't have the excitement of the old days, but these bones aren't up to quite that level anymore. Let the children have their day in the sun.*

"Admiring the view?" came a familiar voice from behind him.

Scotty smiled. The old engineer wasn't at the commissary today on S.C.E. business, but rather to meet with the man who'd just entered: Admiral William Ross, the one who'd offered him the S.C.E. post in the first place.

"Aye," Scotty said. "Never fails to take my breath away."

Ross chuckled. "It's funny. It wasn't until after the Breen attack that I ever even noticed it. I saw it, of course, but never really thought anything about it. Then I saw what the Breen did to the city—to the Golden Gate . . ." He took a breath. "Well, let's just say I've come to appreciate the reminder it provides of what we've got—and what we could lose."

"I know what you mean, Admiral. I spent the Breen attack stuck with Admiral McCoy in a broken-down runabout on a Bakrii repair facility without a clue as to whether or not the bloody planet was still in one piece. Leonard and I almost went mad with the not knowin'."

Nodding, Ross said, "I was on Deep Space 9 when the news came in. It took all my self-control not to commandeer a ship back home, believe me." He sighed. "Well, you didn't ask me to lunch to reminisce about the war or talk about the view. Shall we?"

"Aye, we shall."

The two officers proceeded to the replicators, ordered their respective lunches—for Scotty, a *fehrgit* chop, wild rice, and Irish breakfast tea; for Ross, *hasperat,* a Cajun salad, and *raktajino*—then proceeded to an empty table. Along the way, both nodded hello to assorted officers they knew, though Ross's salutations far outnumbered Scotty's. That only made sense, given Ross's position as the head of Starfleet forces during the war. He was arguably the most popular person in Starfleet, which was no doubt why he had been deemed a viable presidential candidate.

Scotty indicated the *hasperat* with a nod of his head. "What is that, exactly, Admiral?"

"A Bajoran delicacy. You can blame Captain Sisko for getting me addicted to it." Ross smiled. "Have a taste."

Nothing ventured, nothing gained, Scotty thought as he scooped up some of the food into his fork. Gingerly, he tasted it.

"Not bad," said as diplomatically as he could, then quickly gulped down as much of his hot tea as he could stand.

"It's an acquired taste."

" 'Twould seem I haven't acquired it, then." He swallowed, which only made the taste linger. "I'll stick with this, I think."

"Fair enough."

Scotty took a bite of his chop, the replicated alien meat doing much to alleviate the stain on his taste buds left by the *hasperat*—not to mention the awful stench of that Klingon sewer water they called coffee. Even after ten years in the twenty-fourth century, even after the Dominion War, even after having been present for the writing and signing of the Khitomer Accords, Scotty still had trouble wrapping his mind around the idea of the Klingon Empire as a Federation ally. "You made quite the impression the other day, throwin' your hat in with that governor woman."

" 'That governor woman' is quite impressive in her own right. She negotiated a treaty with both the Gorns and the Metrons." Ross smiled. "You more than anyone should appreciate that accomplishment, since you were there for first contact with both of them."

"As far as I'm concerned, they can both go hang. I

cannot say what's worse, what the Gorn did to Cestus III or what the Metrons did to the *Enterprise.*" He sighed. "Still, I suppose 'tis better to be at peace. I'm sure she'll make a fine president, should she win, especially as you've chosen not to run."

"I don't want the job. And I wanted to support someone who wouldn't force me to—" Ross hesitated. "I just don't want to get into that level of decision making anymore. I've had my share of that. At this point, I'm content to live out my career as a simple bureaucrat."

Scotty barked a laugh. " 'Tis nothing simple about that, as you well know, Admiral. Still, I don't blame you for turnin' down the nomination, though I have to confess, I don't follow politics overmuch."

"You're better off. Besides, I'm sure the politics of dealing with bureaucrats like me is more than enough for you." Ross smiled again as he scooped more *hasperat* into his mouth.

"Aye, that it is."

After swallowing his food, Ross said, "Scotty, we could spend all day making small talk, or you can get to the point of this lunch. I don't mean to be rude, but I've got an afternoon full of meetings here, and then an evening full of them with Governor Bacco's staff in Venezia."

Scotty nodded as he chewed his meat. Ross was a busy man, and it was only Scotty's own reputation that allowed him to carve out the time to have this lunch. "I understand that Admiral Nakamura has added the *Enterprise* to the inspection list."

"Yes." Ross's voice contained a slight note of annoyance. "Honestly, I think that Nakamura concocted the entire inspection tour as an excuse to give Picard a thorough going-over, and waited until now to put them on the list to cover his tracks. Not," he added quickly, "that I think the tours are a bad idea. The transition to peace has been a difficult one, and in light of what happened with Zife and Azernal being forced to resign—well, let's just say it's for the best."

Recognizing the look on Ross's face—that of someone who'd said more than he should—Scotty didn't ask him to pursue the matter, though this was the first that he'd heard anything about the president and chief of staff being *forced* to resign. Still, between that and the sentence Ross didn't finish earlier, Scotty was starting to wonder just what exactly went on in the upper reaches of the Federation government over the past few months. However, he'd been in Starfleet long enough to know that things were classified for a reason. Not always a *good* reason, mind, but still for *a* reason.

"I'd like to ask you a favor, William."

That got Ross's attention. Scotty rarely referred to a superior officer by anything other than rank, even when that officer was a friend, as Ross had become over the years. Hell, he and James T. Kirk had been through life and death and everything in between back in the day, and he could count on the fingers of one hand the number of times he'd called him "Jim."

"Scotty, I think it's safe to say that the universe owes you several dozen favors, and I know for a fact that I do. For one thing, you've done a better job keeping the S.C.E. running than anyone has in a hundred years. Name it."

"Nakamura hasn't finished putting the *Enterprise*'s

inspection team together—there's still one slot open, and it's to inspect the ship's mechanical efficiency. I'd like to be on it."

Ross frowned. "You don't need me for that. Just put in the request to Admiral Nakamura."

Blowing out a breath through his teeth, Scotty said, "Nay, that will not be—ah, prudent." At Ross's questioning glance, Scotty elaborated. "Last year, after that incident at Rashanar, Nakamura told me to send an S.C.E. team to 'evaluate' Commander Data. In the end, he ordered the lad to remove his emotion chip. I—well, protested. A bit." He smirked. "A great deal, in fact. I believe I called his parentage into question, and informed him that if he wanted my people to perform an act that was in violation of everything the Federation stood for, he could perform an act of his own—one somewhat anatomically impossible for a human."

Ross had picked up his *raktajino* to drink, but set it down again as he burst out laughing. After a moment, he caught his breath. "Captain Scott, for the record, I would like to say that I'm appalled that you would speak in such a way to a superior officer."

Forcing himself to sound contrite, Scotty said, "Aye, sir, as well you should be."

Grinning, he added, "Off the record, I wish I'd been there to see it. Admiral Nakamura and I haven't seen eye-to-eye about any number of things over the years, particularly with regards to Rashanar and the *Enterprise*." He took a breath. "So, you want me to recommend you for the team?"

Scotty nodded as he swallowed his rice.

The admiral took a sip of his *raktajino*. "Well, you're certainly qualified, and I don't have a problem with recommending you in principle—but the tour's supposed to take several weeks. I really don't want to lose you from the S.C.E. for that long. Is there any particular reason why?"

Placing his fork down and folding his hands on the table, Scotty said, "Because, Admiral, I've seen who else is on the team."

Ross shrugged. "So've I. They're all qualified personnel."

"In the abstract, aye, they are." Scotty hesitated and brushed the end of his mustache with his right hand. "Do you play cards, Admiral? Are you familiar with the phrase 'stacked deck'?"

Leaning back in his chair, Ross fixed Scotty with the most serious expression he'd used since entering the commissary. "I'm familiar with the term. How does it apply here?"

"The leader of the team, Captain Wai-Lin Go."

"She's got an impeccable record," Ross said defensively.

"Aye, but are you aware that she went to the Academy with Captain Leeden?"

Ross straightened up. "No, I wasn't."

"They've been close friends for thirty years. After they graduated, they shared a house on Prince Edward Island until Captain Go got married. Since the official story has Captain Picard at least partly responsible for Captain Leeden's death at Rashanar—"

Holding up a hand, Ross said, "I see your point. What about the others?"

"Nakamura assigned Dr. Toby Russell to inspect the

medical staff. She's a fine doctor, I'm sure, but she also butted heads with Dr. Crusher about a decade back over a medical procedure. *They've* not seen eye-to-eye about a blessed thing in the time since, including some rather nasty spats in the literature."

At this, Ross smiled. "Since when do you read medical journals?"

Scotty shuddered. "I don't, *believe* me, but Leonard keeps babblin' on about this nonsense. He's taken a shine to Crusher—worked with her a few times—and so every time she publishes, I hear about it."

"I'll bet. So this Russell is her archnemesis?" Ross asked with a smirk.

"I'd not go *that* far, but she's not the prime candidate for an objective opinion. Which brings us to Sabin Genestra."

"He's evaluating personnel and security. I can't believe you'd have a problem with *him*. He's served as the aide to half a dozen admirals, all of whom have had nothing but praise for him."

"Seven admirals in total—including Norah Satie. He worked for her when Captain Picard disgraced her."

Ross folded his arms. "Would you mind telling me how you got all this information?"

" 'Tis all in the records."

"Yes, but only if you look hard for it."

Scotty again grabbed the end of his mustache. "You're not the only one who does not trust Nakamura's motives, Admiral. I had my suspicions from the minute I saw the memo that announced the *Enterprise*'s inspection, and so I did a wee bit of research."

Shaking his head, Ross said, "I think you may not be

giving Captain Go, Dr. Russell, or Mr. Genestra enough credit."

"Perhaps. But I cannot believe it's a coincidence that three of the positions on the team are occupied by people who might have personal dislikes for members of the senior staff." Feeling a bit parched, Scotty took a sip of his tea. The now-lukewarm liquid soothed his throat. "I owe Picard and La Forge and Crusher and the rest of the people on that ship a lot. If not for them, I'd still be trapped in the *Jenolen* transporter buffer—or worse, my pattern would've degraded. And I think, after the way they took it on the chin after Rashanar, that they deserve a fair shake in this inspection tour, and that means that there should be at least one person on that team who doesn't have an agenda *against* those good people."

Rather than answer right away, Ross picked up his fork and sampled his Cajun salad. After chewing on it for several seconds, he swallowed and said, "I don't get it. The replicator has been programmed with the exact recipe that Captain Sisko gave me for this, yet it never tastes as good as when he or his father make it. You're an engineer, can you explain why?"

Scotty smiled, recognizing the stalling tactic and going along with it. "My sister, rest her soul, was a sculptor. A fine fine artist, she was. Could bring the clay to life. I remember when we were teenagers, I told her I could build a machine that would make a figurine that would look just like one of hers, but do it in half the time."

"And did you?"

Chuckling at the memory, Scotty said, "Oh aye, I made the machine. We both made small figures of our da. Both looked like him, but hers *felt* like him. I got the size of his nose right, but she got that look on his face he always had whenever we did somethin' wrong. 'Twas that day I realized the difference between art and science—and that my way lay toward the latter." He chuckled. "Replicators are science, Admiral, and cooking, as I'm sure your Captain Sisko would tell you, is most definitely an art."

"That he would." Ross put the fork down. "I'll talk to Admiral Nakamura, tell him I'm recommending you for the *Enterprise* inspection team. Assuming he approves—and I'll make *sure* he does—consider yourself on temporary reassignment from the S.C.E. for the duration of the inspection."

Grinning, Scotty speared the last bit of meat on his plate. "Thank you very much, sir."

Chapter 6
Qo'noS

ON THE DAY PRESIDENT ZIFE RESIGNED, Ambassador Worf was injured while risking his life in order to liberate the Federation embassy from the terrorists who had taken it over.

The subsequent two weeks made him nostalgic for that day.

Once he subdued Torvak and his guard—a task made easier by Worf's loaded conversation with Rov, which sent the *Klahb* leader into a panic—and was able to reactivate the security system, ending the siege of the embassy was simple work. Once he rendered everyone unconscious, he retrieved Kl'rt, the bodies of the other two Klingons, and his Ferengi phaser from the subsubbasement, taking the time to stun Kl'rt first. It was a laborious process with only one functioning arm, but necessary—Worf wasn't prepared to share the intelligence about the lower floor with anyone just yet.

Unfortunately, in the confusion following the flooding

of the embassy interior with anesthezine gas, Rov managed to escape.

After the tiresome recovery of Kl'rt and the others from down below, Worf had to deal with the more tiresome aftermath of the seizing of the embassy. First he had to let the High Council and the Federation know that all was safe. Then he had to argue with the Defense Force commander who had been about to take the embassy by force when Worf sounded the all-clear—he almost attacked Federation soil without Federation authorization, in direct violation of the Khitomer Accords. Then he had to deal with jurisdictional issues regarding the disposition of the surviving captured *Klahb* members, finally agreeing to let the empire prosecute them, but with a Federation representative present during all proceedings, a task Worf delegated to Wu. (The magistrate assigned to the case laughed derisively at this, assuming a human would not be able to handle observing Klingon interrogations, but Wu had seen worse in over a decade of service at the embassy on Qo'noS and Worf was not concerned.)

Delegating that task was necessary, as Worf had been recalled to Earth to give a full report to the council, which was understandably concerned at the embassy being taken over on the very day that the president resigned.

In addition, Worf felt it important to provide in-person condolences to the families of Carl Murphy, Damir Gorjanc, and the security personnel who were killed.

Now, a fortnight later, he was at last returning to Qo'noS aboard the *U.S.S. Sugihara,* eager to meet with the High Council to finally have the discussion he was supposed to have regarding Zife's resignation.

The door chime to his guest cabin sounded. "Enter," he said, and the doors parted to reveal Captain Janna Demitrijian.

"Am I intruding, Mr. Ambassador?"

In fact, Worf had been working on some overdue paper-work that had backed up in the last two weeks, and he rel-ished the opportunity to take a break from it. "Not at all."

"We've entered the Klingon home system—we'll be in orbit of Qo'noS in twenty minutes. I thought you'd want to be prepared."

Worf nodded, and got up from the desk at which he'd been working. "Good."

Demitrijian hesitated. Worf, realizing that she had some-thing else to say—if she hadn't, she would have simply used the intercom from the bridge to inform him of their ETA—prompted her. "What do you wish to ask, Captain?"

"Mr. Ambassador, to be blunt, I want to know if this is the last chance I'll get to cross the Klingon border freely."

Walking over to the nightstand in order to pack the few personal items he'd brought with him into his duffel, Worf said, "I do not know what you mean."

"Yeah, you do. Let's face it, Fel Pagro has a pretty good chance of winning the election, and you must have heard his speeches. If he is elected, the alliance is in se-rious jeopardy. Even if he isn't, you and I both know that Tezwa was a nasty piece of work, and that new am-bassador the High Council appointed is the textbook definition of 'hawk.' Klingon loonies taking over the embassy isn't helping, either. So I'm asking you, since you know Klingon politics as well as anyone: Is the al-liance in jeopardy?"

By way of stalling, Worf packed his wedding photo with the late Jadzia Dax and the photo of him and Alexander taken on the *Enterprise*-D, when his son was much younger and Worf was a Starfleet lieutenant.

The fact of the matter was, he did not have a good answer to give Demitrijian. Before Tezwa, there would have been no doubt in Worf's mind that the Federation-Klingon alliance was as strong as it ever was, but the time since had served as a reminder that it was never all that strong to begin with.

Choosing his words carefully—a skill with which he had had a great deal of practice in these past four years—Worf said, "I will do everything that I am able to do to keep the alliance strong, Captain. I can tell you no more than that."

Demitrijian shook her head, her black hair bouncing with the motion. "Figures—never expect a straight answer from a politician."

Worf reacted as if he'd been slapped.

The captain apparently noticed this. "No offense was intended, Mr. Ambassador. I'm just—concerned, is all. Before the Dominion War, the alliance was the only thing that was maintaining galactic peace. During the war, it was the only reason why we won. Now—I don't know what to think. The Romulans and the Breen have gone quiet, and every time that damn Bajoran wormhole opens, I'm expecting a fleet of Jem'Hadar ships to come through and start the war all over again." She looked at Worf with deep black eyes that suddenly reminded Worf of Deanna Troi's. "I joined Starfleet to maintain peace in the Federation, not to wage its wars." Before Worf could say anything in reply, Demitrijian held up a hand. "I'm sorry, I'm philosophizing." She grinned. "Comes with the big chair, it seems."

"So I have observed."

At that, Demitrijian laughed. "I'll bet. You've probably been ferried on a lot of different ships over the years."

Blinking, Worf said, "I was referring to my time in Starfleet. I served as an officer on the *Aldrin*, the *Enterprise*, and at Deep Space 9 for fifteen years before I was appointed ambassador."

It was Demitrijian's turn to blink. "Really? I didn't know that. Hmp. Well, maybe there's hope for the alliance after all, then." She straightened, her face growing more serious. "Sorry to have taken your time, Mr. Ambassador. I hope you've enjoyed your stay on my ship."

Worf inclined his head.

After the captain took her leave, Worf finished packing, considering her words. Worf had met Special Emissary Pagro a few times, and had no doubt that he would make a fine president. But, Captain Demitrijian's assumption to the contrary, Worf had not heard any of Pagro's speeches as a candidate, having been far too busy the past fortnight with problems of his own. *If he is advocating breaking the alliance, I will need to know about it. If nothing else, I suspect someone on the High Council will question me about it this afternoon.*

"Computer," he said, grabbing a padd, "copy all of the public speeches by Governor Nan Bacco and Special Emissary Fel Pagro since they were declared presidential candidates to this padd."

"Working." A moment, then: *"Transfer complete."*

By the time the *Sugihara* entered orbit, Worf had only

had time to view the two candidates' initial speeches, but it was enough. Pagro wasn't just questioning the alliance, he all but said he would dissolve it unless the Klingons changed their ways. *That,* he thought, *will never happen.* Either Pagro was a complete fool, or he was a warmonger, because the only possible outcome of his proposed agenda would be war between the Federation and the empire.

Wu greeted him when he beamed to the embassy grounds, which had been fully repaired, with yet another upgrade to the security system. As they walked through security at the front gate and thence to the turbolift, Worf paid only partial attention to the lengthy list of items he had to deal with after the meeting, but one thing Wu said grabbed his attention: "The members of *Klahb* all turned on each other. Each was happy to sacrifice the others, and they all were happy to sacrifice Rov. Alexander did his work well."

It was the mention of his son in particular that drew his notice. As they exited the turbolift to the second-floor landing, he asked, "What did Alexander do?"

After Wu explained how Alexander was able to sow seeds of discontent among the *Klahb* members, Worf beamed with paternal pride. He had barely had any time to speak with Alexander in the chaos that followed the embassy takeover, and so had known none of this.

"Make a note for me to contact Alexander on the *Ya'Vang* to thank him."

"That won't be necessary, sir. He has remained in the First City—the High Council requested he be detached to the investigation, since he was the only Defense Force soldier present."

Worf nodded. "In that case, I will wish to speak with him after I meet with the council."

Wu made a note on his padd. "Very good, sir. There is one other thing, I'm afraid, and it cannot wait."

If Wu said it could not wait, then it could not. Worf inclined his head, indicating that he should proceed.

"Carl and Damir were both killed, and three other people resigned after the attack. Starfleet has sent replacements for the guards who were killed, but we're still horribly short-staffed, and the aftermath of the attack has left us with little opportunity to search for replacements. In addition, you have to approve any new hires."

"That task I will delegate to you," Worf said, with a glance at Carl Murphy's now-unoccupied desk.

"Thank you, sir, but that only solves part of the problem. We need at the very least to bring in temporary help to handle some of the more menial tasks, which are lying fallow and threatening to cause difficulties down the line."

"Do so," Worf said. "I will also see if there is anyone I can convince to work here."

Wu smiled. "That would be appreciated, sir. Is there anything else?"

"No."

"Very good, sir." Wu took his leave.

After placing his duffel in the office, Worf then left the embassy and walked to the Great Hall, which was only a short distance away. Councillor Ra'ch's words to him from two weeks ago had been buried in the back of his mind, but he recalled them—and the other words spoken to him by the Federation Council a few days ago—now.

The first time Worf set foot in the council chamber of

the Great Hall was thirteen years earlier, when he challenged the High Council's ruling that Captain Mogh, son of Worf, of the Klingon Defense Force was a traitor to the empire. The council had declared him guilty of consorting with the Romulans in the destruction of the Khitomer outpost, at which thousands of Klingons died—including Mogh and his mate Kaasin. Their six-year-old son Worf, named for Mogh's father, barely survived, and was raised by humans on Gault and Earth. Although Worf's challenge was valid, he was forced, for political reasons, to withdraw it, and accept discommendation from the empire.

The last time he was in the chamber was six weeks ago, when he was trying to convince Martok to let the Klingon fleet heading to Tezwa be under the command of Jean-Luc Picard and the *Enterprise.* Then, too, Worf's actions were driven as much by political expediency as by honor.

That would seem to be the story of my life, he thought bitterly.

In between those occasions, the Great Hall had been destroyed by the traitor Morjod and rebuilt. As with every other time the hall had been damaged or destroyed over the centuries, the new hall was built as close to the previous one as possible. So, while the actual room was not the same one in which he had challenged the council's judgment against his father, it looked just like the dark high-ceilinged space with directed light casting long shadows. The strongest light shone on the large raised metal throne that sat under the trefoil emblem of the empire, in which sat Martok.

This time, Worf was addressing the entire council for the first time since before Tezwa. Though the dim lighting made it difficult to make out the features of the councillors, the ambassador could sense the tension in the room. No one was thrilled to see Worf here these days.

Martok sat on the edge of his chair. Unlike K'mpec, who was chancellor a decade and a half earlier, Martok was not at all comfortable in the seat of power. He had always been one who preferred to be moving—a literal man of action—and he obviously hated being stuck in that chair for any length of time.

"So," the chancellor said, "it would seem that the Federation has lost its leader."

"Yes," Worf said, and proceeded to give the cover story Ra'ch had provided.

As predicted, Martok asked why there was no warning of this, and Worf gave the planned answer. It was as if they were performing an opera, long rehearsed.

"And now, your people will choose a new leader by drawing lots." Martok shook his head. "Madness. Elevation in status comes from the judgment of your peers and your betters, not your lessers. It is an insane system."

"The Federation government has worked successfully for centuries." Worf bemusedly realized that he'd used similar words to justify Klingon traditions to humans over the years.

One of the councillors spoke. "And if Fel Pagro should win the accolades of your people and be granted power—what then?" Worf finally placed the voice as belonging to Qolka. "Will they insist upon our becoming as weak as the Federation?"

"No one is proposing that!" This was another councillor, whom Worf did not recognize.

"Pagro is," Qolka said.

Worf said quickly, "Pagro is not president yet."

A third councillor, whom Worf recognized instantly, said, "And if he is, Mr. Ambassador? Can you, as representative of the Federation to the empire, guarantee that the Khitomer Accords will not be abrogated?"

Worf turned to the speaker. "I can make no such guarantee, Councillor Kopek, as you well know. None of us may predict the future." He paused. The comforting lie he told Captain Demitrijian would not work on the High Council. "I will give you my word on this: As long as I am ambassador, the alliance will stand."

Kopek smiled, and Worf felt as if the temperature in the chamber had dropped. "And we all know that the son of Mogh is a man of his word."

Qolka snorted. "All that means is that he will resign if the Federation withdraws from the Accords."

Several other councillors spoke in response, but Worf ignored them. He was more concerned with Kopek.

In exchange for not revealing Kopek's dishonorable secrets to the High Council, Kopek provided Worf with the prefix codes for the fleet en route to Tezwa. Worf had dealt anonymously with Kopek, disguising himself physically and electronically, but the councillor knew precisely who had blackmailed him.

Worf had kept his word not to reveal Kopek's despicable actions to the council—or to the public. Not for the first time, he wondered if that had been such a good idea.

"Enough!" At Martok's interjection, the council grew

silent. "I am willing to accept Worf's assurances." He gazed with his good eye upon Worf. "For now. But rest assured, Mr. Ambassador, if Pagro does ascend to power, this conversation will be revisited."

"Of course, Chancellor."

"Now then, there is other, more important business. You might recall that the *Klahb* terrorists who took over the embassy claimed that I was your puppet, that the High Council took its orders from the Federation, and that Kahless had been replaced by a Federation hologram."

"Yes," Worf said, wondering why Martok was telling him what he already knew.

"Based on your report, as well as that of the rest of your staff, these were assumed to be lies."

"They *are* lies."

Martok hesitated.

Worf closed his eyes. *No.*

"Summon Emperor Kahless!" Martok cried, and one of the guards ran out of the room.

A moment later, the emperor entered, escorted by the guard. He looked much the same as ever he did: short, stocky, with a crest that was less refined than the crests of most modern Klingons, befitting the era from which he came.

Or, more accurately, the era from which the being he was cloned from came. The person who appeared before Worf on Boreth a decade earlier was a clone of the original Kahless, educated with the knowledge of Kahless from the sacred texts and the oral traditions of the Klingon people, and trumpeted as the prophesied return of the man from whom most Klingons derived their notions of honor, duty, and spirituality. Although the truth of his laboratory-grown nature did come out, many people still embraced the clone as the rightful heir to Kahless's legacy, and so Worf proposed to then-Chancellor Gowron that he be installed as emperor. Political power in the empire had long since migrated to the High Council, to the point where the office of emperor was dissolved, but Kahless took it now as a spiritual position.

Shortly after the Dominion War ended, Kahless had been instrumental in the fight against Morjod and the restoration of Martok to the chancellorship, after which he disappeared for several months. However, he did eventually return, and had continued in his appointed task as a guide to Klingon honor and glory for the past several years.

"Greetings, Worf," Kahless said in his scratchy baritone.

In response, Worf bowed his head. "Excellency. It is good to see you again."

Martok snorted. "You need not bow your head to this one, Worf." The chancellor nodded to the guard, who pressed a button on a device on his wrist.

Kahless disappeared. A small device fell to the floor of the chamber with a hollow thunk.

The guard bent down to pick up the device, and Worf realized with a start that he recognized it from a year-old intelligence briefing. *A mobile emitter.*

Worf turned on Martok. "Rov was correct?"

In a low, dangerous voice, Martok said, "Yes."

"How long has this been going on?"

Again, Martok hesitated. "We do not know."

It seems the tension in this room is not all directed at me, Worf realized.

Qolka said, "According to Imperial Intelligence, this is a Federation device."

Worf said nothing. The briefing, which also mentioned that the Starfleet Corps of Engineers had been working on reverse-engineering the emitter for a few years now, made it clear that the information contained in it was to remain within the Federation.

"Or," Martok continued, "more accurately, a device the Federation scavenged. It was brought back from the Delta Quadrant by a Starfleet vessel that was stranded there for seven years."

At once, Worf realized that his worst fear—that Kahless had never returned from his walkabout following the war, and had been a hologram all the time since—would not be realized. Kahless had returned after only a few months. The exchange of flesh and blood for photons had to have happened in the slightly less than two years since *Voyager*'s return to the Alpha Quadrant.

He also realized that Martok's original statement was, in an odd sort of way, accurate. The mobile emitter *was* Federation technology, albeit from a possible future, representatives of whom were encountered several times by *Voyager* during their Delta Quadrant sojourn. However, there was no point getting into that with Martok. Even if he could speak of it to the High Council, he preferred to avoid discussions of time travel, as they invariably gave him a headache.

Another councillor, this one a young warrior named Grevaq, spoke. "The chancellor does not wish to ask this question, Mr. Ambassador, so I will. Is—"

"Be *silent!*" Martok stood up as his words echoed off

the chamber's walls. "Do not presume to speak for me, Grevaq!"

"My apologies, Chancellor, but—"

"I said be *silent!*"

Grevaq stepped back, actually looking abashed.

"Worf, you know what I must ask you. Is the Federation responsible for replacing Kahless with a hologram?"

"Of course not."

No longer abashed, Grevaq asked, "And do you expect us to believe this?"

Turning toward the young councillor, Worf said, "The Federation would never attempt to destabilize another nation in that way."

Another councillor spoke. "Did not the disease that afflicted the Founders of the Dominion originate with the Federation? I would think that would qualify as attempting to destabilize another nation."

"We were at war with the Dominion. The empire is the Federation's ally."

"For the moment, yes," the councillor said. "I have to wonder if that is the case any longer. The Federation attempted to undermine our just actions against Tezwa's aggression. The Federation president now speaks of breaking the alliance."

"He is not president yet," Worf said, wondering if the councillor was being deliberately obtuse. "At the moment, there is no president."

"Ah, so there is a vacuum of power. How, then, are we to trust that what you say is true? You have just admitted that there is no authority."

"The Federation Council continues to govern the Federation, and they have authorized nothing like this."

"What about Starfleet?" Qolka then asked. "They have taken rogue action against the wishes of the council before. I seem to recall an attempted coup by an admiral named Leyton several years ago."

This is getting ridiculous, Worf thought. "That was an isolated incident."

"Enough!" Martok said before Qolka could reply to that. "For now, Ambassador, we will take you at your word. However, this still leaves the question of what happened to the emperor."

"The hologram did not provide its origins?"

Martok shook his head. "It was well programmed—it is not even aware that it *is* a hologram." Retaking his seat, Martok continued. "Even if you are correct, and your government had nothing to do with this, that still leaves us with a hologram for an emperor—a feat accomplished by technology that only exists in the Federation."

Before Worf could reply to that, a young Klingon burst into the room. "Chancellor! We have found Rov!"

Again, Martok stood. "Where?"

"The fifth planet in the Pheben system. He is broadcasting a message to the entire empire."

Several grunts came from around the chamber. Martok asked, "What forces are in the Pheben system now?"

The youth said, "Captain Tavana's fleet is on maneuvers in that system."

"Instruct them to destroy the source of that transmission."

"Yes, Chancellor. It will take some time for the captain to reach the planet. If you wish, we can pipe Rov's transmission in here while we wait."

"Do so."

The young man mumbled into a communicator on his wrist. A moment later, a screen located over the main entrance to the chamber lit up with the trefoil emblem, then switched to an image of Rov.

"—*ederation will no longer be able to control us like* jatyIn *possessing the dead. I tell you now, people of the empire, that Kahless has been taken from us! The Federation has stolen away our emperor and put a soulless collection of photons in his place! They do not wish*—"

Clenching a fist, Martok asked, "Why has this not been jammed?"

The youth shook his head. "The transmission is broadbased and complex. We have had only limited success in jamming it."

"—*ou to rise up! To remove the commoner puppet Martok and his puppet master Worf! To ta*—"

Qolka stepped forward. "Chancellor, this changes *everything.*"

Silently, Worf agreed. As long as Rov's claims were known only to the High Council and the embassy staff, the situation could remain controlled. But a public declaration like this would outrage the general populace. *Most would believe it to be foolishness, as I did—but enough won't to be problematic.*

"—*ire must be strong! It is we who will rule the galaxy—not the Romulans, not the Dominion, and certainly not the Federation! We sha*—"

The youth spoke. "Captain Tavana is entering orbit of the planet now."

Worf felt the need to speak. "It is possible that Pheben V is only a relay station—or is only the source of a previously made recording."

Martok nodded, conceding the point. "Perhaps, my friend, perhaps—but for now I am more concerned with ending the transmission."

"*—en we shall take the traitors and rip out their hearts with their own* d'k tahg*s as we—*"

The transmission went dead.

"Captain Tavana has fired upon the only energy source on Pheben V," the youth said.

Several cheers went up around the chamber. Worf noticed that Martok was not among those doing so.

When those cheers died down, Martok sat in his throne and spoke in a low, rumbling voice. "I expect a *full* report on how that transmission was able to penetrate our security and why it was impossible to fully jam it."

Now sounding a bit scared, the youth said, *"Yes,* Chancellor. You will have the report within the hour." With that, he left the chamber.

Martok turned his one-eyed gaze on Worf. "It would seem, Ambassador, that your word is no longer sufficient. Before, we could treat this matter internally within the council, but now that the public—and the Defense Force—is aware of Rov's accusations, we must take more overt action."

"Must we?" Grevaq asked. "We can condemn Rov as a terrorist and an agitator."

"And we will prove our words, how?" Martok pointed

to the spot where the false Kahless had stood. "Shall we put *that* before the people and proclaim it emperor? This council will *not* spin lies in order to spare ourselves inconvenience."

No one spoke in objection to that, which gave Worf a proud feeling. He had been responsible for Martok's ascension to chancellor, on the assumption that he would bring honor back to the High Council. Statements like that, and the complete lack of objection to its sentiments, proved to Worf once again that he had made the right choice.

Turning back to Worf, Martok said, "You will return to your government and tell them that the Klingon Empire wishes the formal written assurance of whoever's in charge that the Federation is not responsible for abducting our emperor. And—" For the third time today, Martok hesitated, which also marked the third time in recent memory that Martok had done so in Worf's presence. "And, assuming they make such an assurance, tell them that the empire requests the Federation's assistance in finding Kahless and restoring him to us."

Worf nodded, wondering if he could justify doing this by subspace.

No, he thought, *this will need to be done in person. Even on a secure channel, we cannot risk confirming the replacement of Kahless with a hologram over a com line. Rov has already proven himself capable of circumventing security measures and having access to classified intelligence.*

Which meant that he had to turn right around and go back to Earth.

Wu's earlier words came back to him, both regarding

the staffing situation at the embassy and about his son's performance during the crisis.

"Chancellor, I must make a request."

"Yes?"

"My son is currently assigned to the investigation into *Klahb*. When those duties are concluded, I would like him to be temporarily assigned to Mr. Wu at the embassy. We are short-staffed since the *Klahb* takeover, and his assistance would be—useful."

For the first time since Worf entered the Great Hall, Martok smiled. "Very well, my friend. It shall be done."

Worf inclined his head. "If there is no other business, I will arrange for a return to Earth." He wondered if the *Sugihara* was still nearby. At the very least, it might be able to bring him to Starbase 24, and he could more easily find transport back to Earth from there.

As he left the chamber, he felt the eyes of many of the councillors drilling into his back. Worf wondered how many of them believed as Rov did, that the Federation was responsible for Kahless's fate. He also wondered how many of *those* believed that Worf himself was responsible.

Chapter 7
U.S.S. Enterprise

PICARD HAD JUST settled down with his backlog of archeological journals when the door chime sounded.

He came very close to not answering. The week since Captain Go and her inspection team's arrival had been grueling. Truth be told, the entire last year had been grueling, and Picard was hoping that, on this night at least, he would be able to relax. The recent issues of the various journals to which he subscribed to feed his amateur's interest in archeology had been piling up over the past six months, and tonight when he came off duty he was bound and determined to finally catch up. The days of questioning and of Go's team interfering with his people's work had worn thin, and Picard longed for an evening where he could lose himself in the ruins on Myrmidon or the artifacts of the Tkon Empire or the recent discoveries in the B'Hala excavation on Bajor. Better that than listening to a team of so-called experts second-guessing his command decisions.

We all had our fill of that after Rashanar, he thought bitterly.

Still and all, whoever rang the door chime would not have done so without reason. *At least I hope they haven't.* "Come," he said.

The doors parted to reveal the tall form of William Riker. Upon seeing that Picard was wearing civilian clothes and sitting in a relaxed position on his sofa, Riker's face fell. "I'm sorry, sir, if this is a bad time—"

"Not at all, Number One, please, come in."

"I'll only be a minute, sir, I just wanted to give you the news."

Picard raised an eyebrow and indicated the chair perpendicular to the sofa. "Oh?"

Riker took the offered seat, sitting comfortably with left leg crossed over right. "There's been a lot of communication back and forth between the *Enterprise* and Betazed."

"Yes," Picard said with mock gravity, "I've been reading Lieutenant Vale's reports on communications traffic." He smiled. "Or should I say Lieutenant *Commander* Vale's reports."

Riker returned the smile. "She's quite happy about the promotion, sir. I wasn't sure if it was appropriate to have the usual promotion ritual, given the inspection team . . ."

Growing serious, Picard said, "Probably not, Number One. Anything that can be interpreted as frivolous should probably be avoided for the time being—though I suspect that Captain Scott, at least, would appreciate it."

Letting out a breath, Riker nodded. "You're probably right—on both counts. Anyhow, Deanna and her mother have been talking. Or, rather, Lwaxana's been talking, and Deanna's been listening."

"Not an unusual state of affairs."

"No," Riker said emphatically. "But—well, we've decided to have the wedding on Betazed." He chuckled. "Actually, we decided that a couple weeks ago, but it took a while for Deanna to get that through to Lwaxana. She's been playing the injured mother role after Deanna hung up on her after the poker game."

That surprised Picard. "Really?"

Quickly, Riker said, "It's a long story. Anyhow, it's all settled now, so with your permission, I'd like to set a course there, and engage as soon as the inspection tour is finished."

Picard wondered what the story was behind Troi's actions toward her mother, but trusted that if it was important, Riker would share it. Aloud, he simply said, "That could be another week at least, Will."

Chuckling, Riker said, "It'll take Lwaxana that long to get everything together, if not longer."

"Mm." Picard rubbed his chin. "It will, I assume, be a proper Betazoid ceremony?"

"Yup." Riker adopted a grave tone. "A very open people, the Betazoids."

"You may want to add an extra warning to Ambassador Worf."

"Only if I get to tell him in real time." Riker grinned. "I want to see the look on his face."

"Understandable. Was that all?"

Riker hesitated. "I also wanted to talk to you about the *Titan*."

"What about her?"

"Well, not the ship so much as her personnel." He uncrossed his legs. "I have several positions to fill—including first officer."

Picard nodded, understanding. "You wish to choose from among the *Enterprise* crew?"

"Yes, sir. That is—only if you don't object. The senior staff is already coming apart at the seams with me and Deanna leaving, and Beverly going off to Starfleet Medical."

"*If* she's going." Picard regretted the words as soon as he said them, if only for the slight bitterness he detected in his own tone of voice. The truth was, when Dr. Yerbi Fandau informed the captain that he was making a formal offer to Crusher to take his job as head of Starfleet Medical when he retired, Picard felt as if he'd been punched in the gut. To make matters worse, Crusher waited months before discussing it with Picard—though she had talked it over with other members of the crew. However, that did give him an advantage when she did finally talk to him about it at the end of the Tezwa mission. Mentally prepared, he had been able to say the supportive words that she needed to hear as opposed to the selfish answer he wanted to give.

If Riker noticed Picard's bitterness, he gave no indication of it. "So—*do* you object, Captain?"

Picard had, in fact, been anticipating Riker's request, giving the matter some thought ever since Admiral Janeway told him that she planned to offer Riker the *Titan*. Initially, his desire for Riker to have the best personnel available warred with his own desire to keep the *Enterprise* crew together. But he soon realized that the latter was pointless wish-fulfillment. He had been extraordinarily lucky in his career as a shipmaster to keep his senior staffs in place for longer than usual—both on the *Stargazer* and the two *Enterprise*s—but all good things had to come to an end eventually, and he would not be so churlish as to deny Riker the chance to start off his captaincy without restriction.

"Not at all—with one exception. Mr. Data is off limits. He's long overdue for a first officer's position, and I want to keep him on the *Enterprise*."

"Well, I can't argue with that." Riker stood up. "Thank you, Captain. I'll leave you to your reading."

"Very well, Number One." He smiled. "Sorry—*Captain*."

As he moved toward the door, Riker said, "Like I said two weeks ago, Captain, I'm still your first officer." The doors parted at his approach; he stopped and turned. "Oh, that reminds me, the first debate between Pagro and Bacco is tonight—Data's having it piped into Ten-Forward, if you're interested."

This time Picard had no problem with the bitterness in his voice. "I've had my fill of politics and politicians, Number One. I'll watch the recordings of the speeches and interviews next week when we're closer to the election."

"Fair enough. Good night, sir."

"Good night."

As the door closed on Riker, Picard picked up the padd he'd set aside and reactivated the display. *Now,* he thought, *do I read about B'Hala, Myrmidon, or the Tkon Empire? So many choices . . .*

Before he could make that decision, the intercom

beeped, followed by the airy voice of Captain Wai-Lin Go. *"Go to Picard."*

Picard leaned his head back and gazed to the ceiling in supplication. Sadly, the ceiling was not forthcoming with any aid or comfort. Finally he said, "Picard here."

"I have some questions for you regarding your personnel."

Several possible replies were considered and rejected by Picard over the course of half a second. Go was probably fully aware of the fact that he had just gone off duty. Picard, on the other hand, was aware of how important this inspection tour was—not so much for him, but for the rest of the crew. In all honesty, Picard couldn't give a damn what Starfleet Command thought of him, nor did he much care about what he personally had to suffer in order for the Federation to keep face with the Ontailians after Rashanar. He did the right thing, and was willing to face whatever consequences that action precipitated.

But he cared very much about his crew, and they had been unfairly tarnished by his own pseudo-disgrace at Rashanar. The only way it would end was if they passed this inspection with flying colors. That was why he had told Captain Go that he would available at any time to speak to her.

It would seem she took me at my word.

"Shall we meet in my ready room in ten minutes, Captain?"

"That would be acceptable, yes. Go out."

Picard rose from the couch, grateful she'd acquiesced to the ten minutes. That gave him time to change into uniform. Somehow, he didn't imagine that Go would be receptive to having so official a conversation with a person in civilian clothes.

As he removed his shirt, he wondered if the other shoe would drop regarding Go's friendship with Jill Leeden. The destruction of Leeden's ship, the *U.S.S. Juno,* was the primary reason for Picard's censure, and while Picard would not expect a Starfleet captain of Go's experience to let personal concerns get in the way of a professional evaluation, he also knew that Go had to be at least initially biased against Picard because of his connection to her friend's death.

The question is whether or not she has overcome that bias to give the Enterprise *a fair hearing,* he thought as he fastened his uniform's jacket and then pulled it down to straighten it. To date, Go had provided no indication one way or the other in her demeanor. Picard hoped that was a good sign.

Exiting his quarters, he proceeded briskly to a turbolift. The doors parted to reveal two officers, both wearing the gold of operations. They were, Picard noted, holding hands, but unclasped them as soon as they saw the captain. After a moment, Picard placed them—the large, dark-skinned, broad-shouldered man was Lieutenant Aaron Studdard from security, and the short, lithe woman was Ensign Anh Hoang from engineering.

"Captain!" Studdard said, straightening.

"As you were." Picard entered the lift and said, "Bridge" as the doors closed behind him.

The lift proceeded up a few decks before stopping at deck four. As the two officers moved past Picard to exit, the captain said, "I understand the view of the gas giant from the forward section of deck four is quite spectacular."

Hoang smiled sheepishly, and Studdard's mouth opened and closed. "Uh, we'd heard that, too," the security officer finally said.

Picard smiled. "Enjoy it."

In a soft voice, Hoang said, "We will, sir, thank you."

The lift doors closed and took Picard the rest of the way to the bridge. It did the captain's heart proud to see the young people under his command finding happiness amidst all the tragedy they'd gone through of late.

Nodding to Data in the command chair, Picard proceeded to the ready room. His many decades of service, which included more than a fair share of diplomatic experience, made it easy for Picard to put on his game face, as it were, presenting a pleasant affect for the benefit of his audience.

Go was waiting in one of the ready room's guest chairs, engrossed in one of her padds. Several other padds sat on the other guest chair.

Looking up, she said, "Thank you for coming, Captain."

"Not at all." Picard moved over to the replicator. "I did, after all, promise to be available to you at any time. May I get you anything?"

Shaking her head, Go said, "No thank you."

"Tea, Earl Grey, hot."

The replicator glowed and the steaming beverage materialized before Picard with a soft hum. Gingerly holding the hot ceramic cup by its handle, Picard took his seat opposite Go. "How can I be of service?"

"I've been going over the personnel movements on the *Enterprise* over the past year. There've been over a score of transfer requests and resignations, all of whom are from junior officers in the top tenth percentile on their evaluation reports. In the meantime, your replacement crew have all been officers who generally scored considerably lower on their evaluation reports before arriving here."

Picard tried to keep his voice even. "There were only two resignations."

"Yes, Lieutenants Peart and Perim both resigned their commissions after Tezwa. Both of them were top-flight officers, and both of them squandered good careers by quitting Starfleet. I have to wonder what happened to make them want to go."

"I believe, Captain," Picard said tightly, the pleasant affect now struggling to maintain itself, "that a casual perusal of the Federation News Service reports on Tezwa would provide some enlightenment in that regard. After what they'd been through, the lieutenants wanted to begin their lives anew away from Starfleet." *What's noteworthy,* Picard thought, *is that they were the only ones to resign.*

"Very well, but what about Crain, Nybakken, Johanssen, Bdgralsik, Kawasaki—"

Now the pleasant affect was shattered, and Picard interrupted in a more imperious tone than it was perhaps politic to use with the head of an inspection tour. "Lieutenant Bdgralsik and Ensign Kawasaki did not transfer. Neither did Ensign Malak, nor did Lieutenant Hsu."

Go regarded Picard with a maddeningly placid expression. "It isn't whether or not they transferred, Captain—it's that they asked in the first place. And then there are the replacements: Ensign Fillion, who washed out of special ops training; Ensign Hoang, who has had several notations by counselors regarding poor socialization in her file; Technician Nafir, a disciplinary problem; Chief Petschauer, who has more reprimands than this ship has decks; Ensign Studdard, whose jacket indicates that he'll never advance in security; Lieu—"

"Yes, enough, Captain." Picard sighed, paused to take a sip of his tea. The beverage burned his tongue, which only added to his irritation. He set the cup back down on his desk. "I am aware that there were several—defections, for lack of a better term, following the incident at Rashanar. However, I believe that we can both agree that such is to be expected after the *Enterprise* endured such a public—" He hesitated.

Showing the most emotion since he met her, Go smirked slightly. "Humiliation?"

"That is one word for it, I suppose." Picard thought about Hoang and Studdard, both on Go's list of "substandard" officers, both of whom had performed excellently at Delta Sigma IV. He recalled glowing reports from both La Forge and Vale following that mission, and the fact that they were seeing each other belied the "poor socialization" Go cited. "However, Captain, I think that your inspection of this ship would be best served by paying less attention to the service records of my crew *before* they arrived, and on what they've done since then."

Go gathered her padds, then rose from her seat. "This is *my* inspection tour, Captain, not yours. And you can rest assured that *all* the records on this ship are subject to my perusal."

Without another word, she departed the ready room.

* * *

Beverly Crusher took the Hippocratic oath very seriously. She had lived her life by its tenets, to work to benefit the sick, to keep them from harm and injustice, and to keep all matters between doctor and patient confidential.

Right now, that devotion to medicine in general and to the oath in particular was the only thing that was keeping Crusher from hitting Dr. Toby Russell.

Russell was that most unholy of combinations: a brilliant researcher and a dreadful physician. Had she been content to remain in the lab, Crusher probably would have never crossed her path except as a name on a few monographs. But because she was a practicing neurospecialist, and because she was well regarded in that field, Crusher had called her in eleven years earlier when Worf—then the chief of security of the *Enterprise*-D— had suffered a severe spinal injury. Worf's Klingon pride would not allow him to accept traditional therapies that would grant him only limited mobility. Russell proposed a radical, and very risky, treatment that would mean full recovery—or death. The latter option came very close to being the result, but Worf did pull through, and Russell was vindicated.

Still, Crusher had reported her ethics violations—both with Worf and with her unorthodox treatment of a civilian the *Enterprise* rescued from the *U.S.S. Denver* who died—to Starfleet Medical. Russell had received a reprimand, but Crusher's hoped-for revoking of Russell's medical license never came. At the time, she'd chalked it up to the success of her genitronic procedure on Worf.

More than a decade later, after the two of them had disagreed both in print and once at a medical conference on Trill, Russell was now assigned to evaluate the medical practices on the *Enterprise*.

That irresponsible medical hack is going to evaluate me. That's just too rich.

Sitting now in her office, reading over the latest progress reports from Dr. Wasdin on Delta Sigma IV—which were very encouraging—Crusher tried to ignore Russell when she entered. Sadly, that would not make her go away.

Russell had let her blond hair grow to neck length, and there were several more lines in her face, but otherwise she looked exactly the same. She even still favored the Atrean suits with the flared "wings" on the bottom of the shirt over a Starfleet uniform, just as she had a decade earlier. Her long-fingered hands were holding a padd tightly to her chest, almost as if it would protect her.

Just at that moment, it occurred to Crusher that, should she accept Fandau's offer to head up Starfleet Medical, she would be in a position to start proceedings against Russell that would possibly lead to her license being revoked.

Cheered by this thought, Crusher, in as pleasant a voice as she could muster—which wasn't especially pleasant, really—asked, "What can I do for you, Doctor?"

Russell pursed her lips. "Well, whatever you do next for me will be the first thing you've done for me since I arrived."

"Hasn't Dr. Tropp given you everything you've asked for?"

"Yes, he has."

"Good. I'm sorry I haven't been able to speak with you," she lied, "but I've been very busy with other duties."

Taking a seat in one of the guest chairs, Russell said,

"Be that as it may, there are some questions I need to ask you."

"I *really* don't have time to talk to you right now, Doctor."

"Come on, Beverly, you can call me Toby."

I don't believe it—she's still trying to be friends with me. When Russell first set foot on the *Enterprise,* she complimented Crusher on an obscure paper she'd written, something Crusher recognized instantly as a feeble attempt at sucking up, which she found distasteful. Russell did nothing in the days that followed to wash away that distaste. "Very well, *Toby*—it certainly is better than actually referring to you as a doctor, which frankly, I'd prefer wasn't the case."

"It's been eleven years, Beverly. I would think you'd be over your resentment."

Crusher felt her jaw drop. "Resentment? I don't *resent* you, Toby. That would require my thinking highly of your abilities. You're right, it *has* been eleven years, and you haven't changed a bit—you still take shortcuts in an attempt to get instant gratification that saves you the trouble of doing the real work required in research, and never mind who might die."

Russell regarded Crusher coldly. "That's a lovely speech, Beverly, but you're ignoring the fact that my procedure worked."

"On Worf, yes, it did work—barely, and only because of the unique nature of Klingon physiology."

"That doesn't change the fact that it was a tremendous medical breakthrough."

Crusher nodded emphatically. "Yes, Toby, it was. Tell

me, what kind of progress have you made since then? I haven't seen a single thing about genitronics since the initial wave of articles after Worf's operation. Why is that, I wonder?"

In a tight voice, Russell said, "We're not here to discuss my medical practice, Beverly—we're here to discuss yours."

Picking up her padd, Crusher looked down at its display. "As I said, I don't have time to talk with you right now."

Gazing at the top of the desk, Russell looked at the padd. "Reading the latest from Delta Sigma IV, I see. We're in luck—that's exactly what I wanted to talk to you about."

"Dr. Tropp can surely answer—"

"No, Beverly, he surely can't. The primary work done to cure the Bader and the Dorset from the effects of the liscom gas was done by you, not by Dr. Tropp, and in order to complete my report to Captain Go I need to know what *you,* as chief medical officer, did during that mission."

Trying very hard not to clench her teeth, Crusher said, "All the information you need is in my log reports."

"Yes, but I'd like your verbal account."

"It won't sound any different from the logs." Crusher knew she was just being stubborn at this point.

"Indulge me."

She smiled sweetly. "Do I have a choice?"

"Yes. You can talk to me now, or you can refuse, and I'll go to Captain Go, who'll order you to comply—probably with Captain Picard standing next to her." Russell leaned back in her chair. "Come on, Beverly, it's not like it matters that much. Yerbi's position is yours if you want it, so it's not like a report on one starship will have any effect on your future. Just tell me about what happened on Delta Sigma and that'll be that."

I suppose it was too much to hope that she wouldn't know about the job offer. Not that there was any realistic chance of the medical grapevine *not* knowing about it by now, truth be told.

Letting out a long breath, Crusher set down the padd. "Fine. After settling on Delta Sigma IV, the Bader and the Dorset found that they were able to live in peace, even though the two species were at war everywhere else in the galaxy that they met. They also started suffering from significantly shorter life spans. Starfleet Medical determined that a gas native to the planet was affecting their cells' ability to regenerate, and that they'd die within a few generations if a cure wasn't found. Unfortunately, the liscom didn't just lower their life expectancies—it also worked as a pacifying drug. With the drug removed, both species' natural aggressiveness started to reassert itself. It didn't take long for the planet to devolve into chaos."

Russell nodded. "So you and your staff devised a treatment that would negate the liscom's effects on their life span, but also put them back in the pacified state?"

"Yes. We—"

"You chose a shortcut in an attempt to get instant gratification. I'm sure it saved you the trouble of doing any real work necessary for research." She stood up. "Thank you, Beverly, this has been most enlightening."

For two seconds, Crusher stared at Russell in openmouthed stupefaction.

Then she closed her mouth and shook her head. "Not bad."

"I beg your pardon?" Russell was moving toward the exit, but stopped to find out what Crusher meant.

Crusher stood up, not wanting to be in a position where she looked up at Russell. "Not bad at all. If you ever give up medicine—well, I'll dance a jig, for one thing, but you'll also have a career in rhetoric available to you. That was a very nice job of turning my argument against me. I'm sure you intended it to sting, and for a moment there, it did. You wanted the high and mighty Beverly Crusher to see that she's no better than the mean and nasty Toby Russell whom she so unfairly condemns. There's only one problem." Crusher placed her hands flat against her desk, mainly to keep her from balling them into fists. "I argued against the procedure, but Captain Picard ordered me to implement it anyhow. And do you know why?"

"It was expedient?" Russell asked, a bit snidely.

"No—because it saved lives. People were being killed on the surface—an entire population with no conception of how to cope with violent emotions suddenly found itself feeling passions it had no capacity to process. We needed a quick and dirty solution to keep Delta Sigma IV from going up in flames. And that, Toby, is the difference between you and me. I know that my solution wasn't the best, but that it was the only one possible under the circumstances, and I will go to my deathbed wondering if I could have done something that might have helped the Bader and the Dorset more. Now then," she said, sitting back down at her desk and retrieving the padd with Wasdin's report, "is there anything else, or can I get back to running my sickbay?"

Russell's lips formed a very small line perpendicular

to her nose. Crusher hadn't seen her this nonplussed since relieving her of duty after the *Denver* civilian died. "That's all for now, Beverly—but I do have more questions that *only* the chief medical officer can answer."

"I'll bet you do."

Without another word, Russell turned and left sickbay.

Whistling a happy tune, Crusher went back to reading the report.

Sabin Genestra looked up at the door two seconds before it parted to allow Christine Vale to enter the observation lounge.

The middle-aged Betazoid had been using the room as his base of operations during the inspection tour. Unlike Captain Scott and Dr. Russell, whose concerns were with a particular physical part of the ship, Genestra's focus related to personnel and security, which could just as easily be conducted from the relative comfort of this room. It was a space in which his interview subjects felt relaxed yet alert—familiar due to its typical use as a meeting place, but also associated with one's duties aboard ship.

Genestra would have decorated the room differently, had he any say in the matter. He had no use for the model ships that bracketed the viewscreen on one wall— but then, Genestra had never understood the almost fetishistic affection some had for spacefaring vessels. They were tools, nothing more, and the specifics of their look or design was of very little importance, as far as Genestra was concerned. It was for that reason that he sat on the side of the table facing the viewport to the stars. At present, that view included the sixth planet of the Xarantine system, a gas giant, which Genestra found preferable to the toy ships behind him.

Of course, he could have chosen to sit at the head of the table, but that would imply that he held a position equal to that of Captain Picard, which would put his interview subjects on the defensive. No, better to make them feel they were on an equal footing with him.

He telepathically felt Vale's approach, and so called up her service record on his padd and greeted her as she walked in.

"Thank you for coming to see me, Lieutenant—or should I say, *Commander.*" Genestra, of course, had not forgotten her promotion, but he wanted to gauge her reaction to his self-correction.

Predictably she beamed with a certain pride. It was the nature of that pride that concerned Genestra.

"It's not like I had a choice," she said. "Captain told us to be at your disposal while you were here."

"And you always follow orders, don't you, Commander?"

Vale pulled out the chair opposite Genestra's and sat in it. The gas giant framed her head like a halo. "Yes, I do, Mr. Genestra. I also recognize transparent interrogation techniques designed to get a rise out of me."

The self-satisfaction at the mention of her promotion faded, replaced with a general resentment that Genestra recognized from his previous interviews with Vale—indeed, with most of the crew, but it was more intense in the security chief for some reason.

"I wish to speak with you about your promotion, actually."

Suspicion. Confusion. "What does my promotion have to do with your inspection?"

"It's a security concern, Commander. You see, ever since your promotion, I've been detecting a sense of pride—and, more to the point, a sense of self-justification and vindication."

Anger. Vale leaned forward in her chair. "Okay, *now* you're getting a rise out of me. What the hell are you doing poking around in my head?"

"I'm not *poking*, Commander." Genestra was appalled at the suggestion. He gave her a small smile. "Believe me, I would not have been able to work for the admiralty all these years if I had shown any proclivity for such things."

"Oh, I don't know, I've met some admirals in my time who'd love having someone around who could do that."

Genestra frowned. "Such as who?"

"Nobody who's still in Starfleet," Vale said, but Genestra saw a very clear image of Admiral Nakamura in her thoughts.

He sighed. For all his life, Genestra had worked not to pry into people's minds beyond the simplest surface thoughts—nothing that couldn't be inferred from speech or body language by someone who was well enough trained. He saw himself as a supplement, nothing more. To even read as much as the impression of Nakamura in Vale's mind meant that the thought was so prominent as to be impossible to screen out.

"We're getting off topic."

"No we're not," Vale said, "we're talking about you reading my mind."

"I'm not reading your mind," Genestra said firmly. "As

I said, I am basing this on impressions I've received. If I was simply reading your mind, as you accuse, I would not have any need to interview you, I'd simply report my findings to Captain Go. But I do not have findings, Commander, I have impressions. Now I can confirm my suspicions based on these impressions one of two ways. One is to in fact read your mind, which I most emphatically will *not* do. The other is to question you. So here we are."

Resignation. Vale leaned back, setting her hands in her lap. "Fine. Question me. What about feeling proud and justified and vindicated raises red flags?"

"It's the vindication more than anything, Commander—it's almost as if you feel you've gotten away with doing something wrong."

More anger. "I haven't 'gotten away' with anything."

"But you do feel that you've done something wrong." Genestra deliberately did not phrase it as a question.

"What the hell's that supposed to mean?"

"I should think that would be obvious, especially considering the losses your security division has taken over the past year." He consulted his padd. "At the Dokaalan colony you lost a few guards in rescue operations, then a few more at Delta Sigma IV, and the figure skyrocketed at Tezwa."

Her rage seethed and festered. "Mr. Genestra, we've covered all this."

"We've covered the facts, but what interests me now is what's behind those facts." He set the padd down. "Commander, do you feel that you could have done something different to prevent the deaths of Aiken, Razka, Melorr, Jeloq, Nikros, Fillion, Maxson, Carmo—"

Now the anger grew white-hot. Vale stood. "What the

hell kind of a question is that? And I do *not* need you to list their names, thank you, I'm *fully* aware of who and how many people died on my watch."

"Sit down, Commander."

"No, sir, I think I'll stand, because right now I'd rather look down on you." She all but kicked the chair back and started pacing on her side of the table. "You want to know if I could've done something different to save all of them. And I asked you what the hell kind of a question that was, which, I admit, was dumb, because I know *exactly* what kind of a question it was."

Genestra folded his hands together. *Now,* he thought, *we're getting somewhere.* "What kind would that be, Commander?"

"The one I ask myself every single damn day. And you know what the answer is?"

"What?"

"I have no clue. But I also know something else: Each one of them died doing their duty. Aiken was so fresh out of the Academy he was practically still putting his cadet uniform on in the morning. Razka'd been in Starfleet for well over a hundred years. I will bet you anything you care to name that if you told either one of them ahead of time that they'd die defending the ship and the Federation, neither the rookie nor the veteran would have changed a thing, because *that's what they signed up for.*" She stopped pacing and put her hands on the back of the chair, her body now blocking the view of the gas giant. "I'm sorry they're gone, and I wish there was *some* way to bring them back, but they died because they were good at their jobs. They died saving lives or attempting to save lives. I'm proud to have had each and every one of them on my team, and I will *not* let you use their deaths as an interrogation tool."

The anger had, over the course of Vale's diatribe, slowly transformed to righteous indignation. "A bit late for that, Commander."

She frowned. "What?"

"That will be all," Genestra said, wiping the display on the padd. "Thank you for your time."

Confusion. "Hang on a second—"

Genestra smiled at her. "Commander, my concern wasn't over the guilt you felt about the deaths on your staff over the past year. The guilt is to be expected—in fact, if you hadn't felt it, I'd be a lot more concerned. But what did worry me was whether or not that guilt was in any danger of overwhelming your ability to do the job, particularly in light of your promotion. Some who receive a reward after so many people under their command didn't make it find themselves crippled by the guilt. I think, however, that we've proven that not to be the case."

Embarrassment. "Which you accomplished by using a transparent interrogation technique to get a rise out of me."

"Something like that, yes."

Vale shook her head. "You're a real bastard, you know that?"

"So I've been told, Commander." He gazed at the time stamp on his padd. "Now if you'll excuse me, my next appointment will be here any moment."

As it happened, that next appointment was five minutes late, to Genestra's annoyance. But then, Genestra had come to expect that sort of thing from Captain Scott. History was not Genestra's strong suit, so he had no idea if punctuality was something that Starfleet simply did not encourage in the twenty-third century, but it was certainly a concept alien to Montgomery Scott.

When he finally did arrive, Genestra said without preamble, "You're late."

Resentment. "Do not take such a tone with me, Mr. Genestra. We're colleagues on this endeavor. You're not my superior—in *any* sense, truth be known."

Genestra ignored the rebuke, as he'd been ignoring Scott's general disdain for the rest of the inspection staff for the past week, and called up Scott's most recent report on the display. "I've been reading over your report, and I'm appalled that you haven't mentioned Commander La Forge's gross violations of procedure."

"What're you talkin' about?"

Scott remained standing, so Genestra rose and held the display for Scott to see. "Hiring a *Ferengi* to ferry parts around the sector? Bypassing the quartermaster entirely for—"

"I'm aware of Mr. La Forge's solution to the *Enterprise*'s supply issues."

Genestra was amazed at Scott's lack of concern. "And you didn't feel this warranted a reprimand?"

Amazement. Confusion. "Of course not. On the contrary, I'm applaudin' his initiative."

"You must be joking," Genestra said, even though he knew Scott had no humorous intent. "This is a gross violation of standard procedure, and—"

"Mr. Genestra, do you know what standard procedure

is?" Scott's mind was now awash in pity, and it only made the patronizing tone he took more infuriating to Genestra.

"Of course I do, it's—"

"It's the procedure you follow when things are goin' normal. I think we can both agree, can we not, that things out here are a wee bit off from normal. Since the war, Starfleet's supply lines have been stretched thinner'n syntheholic scotch. On top of that, since that foolishness at Rashanar, the *Enterprise* has not been Starfleet's top priority when it comes to resupply."

Genestra could not deny the truth of Scott's words. "But to involve a Ferengi—"

"Who better? We're hardly at war with 'em, and if there's one thing a Ferengi can do right, it's scrounge." Scott grinned, and Genestra felt an odd combination of appreciation and affection. "Situations like this call for creative solutions, Mr. Genestra—and you'd know that if you'd had any time in the field instead of spendin' your career hemmin' admirals' trousers."

"Captain Scott—"

Irritation and dismissal. "If that'll be all, Mr. Genestra, I promised to have dinner with Mr. La Forge and Mr. Data—and I'll thank you to keep your nose *out* of my area of this inspection."

Without another word, Scott turned on his heel and left the observation lounge.

Genestra sighed. He supposed that Scott did have a point, but he still should have noted the improper procedure in his report. It was Captain Go's place to decide the propriety of Commander La Forge's actions as head of the inspection team; their job as inspectors was to bring *all* data to her attention.

Perhaps the chain of command was also lax in the twenty-third century.

With another sigh, Genestra sat down at the table and started compiling his latest report on Commander Vale.

"Come," said Riker's voice from the other side of the door to his quarters.

In response to the keyword, the door slid aside. La Forge looked in to see the distinctive biosignature of William Riker seated comfortably in the large chair in the common room, just a couple of meters from the poker table. Riker had been reading a padd, which he set aside as La Forge entered the cabin. "Geordi. Thanks for coming."

"What can I do for you, Commander?"

"Quite a bit, actually." Riker indicated the couch perpendicular to his chair, and La Forge sat down in it. "I'm not taking you away from anything, am I?"

"I'm supposed to be meeting Scotty and Data in Ten-Forward for dinner, but I can cancel, if—"

"No, that won't be necessary. This'll only take a minute." Riker chuckled. "I envy you, you know."

"How so?"

"You've got Scotty checking you over. We should all be so lucky."

La Forge let out a breath. "Yeah, I wasn't exactly doing cartwheels when I saw Genestra again. After what he did to poor Simon . . ." Simon Tarses had been a medical technician on the *Enterprise* when Admiral Satie's search for a Romulan spy got out of control. It was

Genestra who interrogated Tarses, revealing in front of the entire crew that Tarses was one-quarter Romulan, not part-Vulcan as he'd said on his Starfleet application. Tarses recovered from the experience, thankfully, as wiser heads prevailed over Satie's irrational judgment. He went on to attend Starfleet Medical and, last La Forge heard, was serving as a doctor on Deep Space 9.

"I know," Riker said. "And Beverly's chewing nails over Russell's presence."

"I haven't come across Captain Go—what's she like?"

Riker hesitated, then: "Not the friendliest person I've ever met. She makes Worf look chirpy."

Wincing, La Forge said, "That bad, huh?"

"Worse."

Grinning, La Forge said, "Well, I'll just count my blessings down in engineering."

"As well you should. Like I said, Scotty's an ideal inspector."

"*Oh* yeah—if nothing else, he's been in my shoes plenty of times before."

It had been good to see Scotty again. Their first meeting, back when they rescued the old captain from the *Jenolen*'s transporter, had not started out well. La Forge viewed the time-displaced engineer as an intruder in his engine room, serving mostly to keep La Forge from getting any work done with his inability to adjust to the technological changes during the seventy-five years he was away. Years later, Scotty would confess to La Forge over drinks that, had someone behaved like that in Scotty's engine room on his *Enterprise,* "I would not have been nearly so patient as you were with me." This led Scotty into one of his stories about the old days on the *Enterprise,* when they hooked up the M-5 computer—or, as he called it, "some useless pile'a junk"—to the ship's engines, with tragic results.

"Geordi—how'd you like a different pair of shoes?"

La Forge frowned and looked at Riker. Based on what his optical implants were telling him, Riker's heart rate was up a bit. *Like he's a little nervous about something. Then again, the man* is *getting married and getting his own command.* "What do you mean, Commander?"

"I've got an opening for first officer on the *Titan.* I'd like you to fill it, if you're interested."

La Forge was suddenly very grateful Riker had asked him to sit down, because he probably would have had trouble keeping his footing if he was still upright. He stared at Riker for several seconds. Now that he'd asked the question, the commander's heart rate had gone back to normal. *But that's okay, 'cause mine just shot through the roof.*

"First officer?"

Riker held up both hands. "I don't need an answer right away—in fact, I don't want one. I want you to think about it."

"Sir, I don't know if I'm—"

"Geordi, don't tell me you're not ready," Riker interrupted before La Forge could say the words. "You're *past* ready. Look at the good people who've come out of your engine room—Sonya Gomez, Reg Barclay, Miles O'Brien, Robin Lefler, Emma Bartel, Raisa Danilova, Taurik. It all speaks to good leadership, and that's what I want in my first officer."

La Forge did not often find himself speechless, and in

fact his mouth did attempt to form words, but his brain had, as far as he could tell, short-circuited.

Riker leaned forward. "Think about it, that's all I ask. If you refuse, I understand completely—but you *are* my first choice, Geordi. Let me know when you decide." Leaning back, Riker picked the padd back up. "Now, if you'll excuse me, I've got to go over the fifth draft of the guest list for the wedding." He squinted, as if trying to remember something. "Or maybe it's the sixth. Hell, I've lost track. I swear, though, we're going to have half the Federation attending this thing."

Finally, La Forge managed to get his mouth to move. "Thanks, Commander, I—uh—I guess I have a lot to think about." He stood up and moved toward the door slowly, still not trusting his body to respond properly to ordinary stimulus. *First officer?*

After he departed Riker's quarters, La Forge tapped his combadge. "La Forge to Data."

"Go ahead," said the android's voice a moment later.

"Data, I'm gonna have to beg off dinner. Apologize to Scotty for me, but—well, something's come up."

"Is there anything I can do to assist, Geordi?"

As ever, La Forge was grateful for his best friend's presence. "Eventually, probably, yeah, but for right now—I gotta deal with this alone."

"Very well. I will convey your regrets to Captain Scott."

"Thanks, Data. La Forge out."

So much for counting my blessings in engineering. . . .

Chapter 8
Earth

"A HOLOGRAM?"

Worf was back on Earth and in the heart of Paris, sitting in Councillor Ra'ch's office. Although she still served as president pro tem, Ra'ch steadfastly refused to use the presidential office on the top floor of the building. Unlike that of the president, councillors' places of work on Earth were small and practical. However, while T'Latrek—the councillor whose office Worf most often visited when on Earth—displayed no personal items or decoration of any kind, Ra'ch's office was filled with them, from the painting of the sunset over Damiano's capital city of Iaron on the side wall to holographic representations of her mate and all three of her parents on her desk.

"Yes, Councillor," Worf said. "I have seen the hologram with my own eyes, as well as the mobile emitter that powered it."

"Mobile—Oh for Ho'nig's sake, the Klingons got their hands on *that?*"

"The *Klingons* did not—whoever replaced Kahless did. In fact, there is great concern on the High Council that this is a Federation plot."

"You're not serious."

Worf simply looked at her.

"Sorry, forgot who I was talking to."

"The terrorists who seized the embassy did so in part because they believed the Federation kidnapped the emperor and replaced him with a hologram that was programmed to advocate a Federation agenda."

Ra'ch put her head in her hands, her fingers splaying around the horn that protruded from the center of her forehead. "This is all we need right now." She looked up. "What does the High Council want?"

"Several things. The first is a written assurance from you and the council that this is *not* a Federation plot."

Ra'ch shrugged. "Since it's true, that ought to be easy enough. Honestly, I doubt the idea would have occurred to any of us."

"A similar assurance from the admiralty would be prudent as well. Many on the council believe that Starfleet is the true power of the Federation."

"Really?" Ra'ch's lips twisted into a frown. Then her face softened. "Actually, I can kind of see why they might think that. Fine, I'll talk with Nakamura tomorrow. What else?"

"The High Council would also like the Federation's aid in attempting to locate Kahless. The Defense Force will share what information it has regarding the emperor's whereabouts." *What little information there is,* he thought dolefully.

"Of course, we'll be happy to help." She smiled. "I suspect that will cause more goodwill than the written assurances, but we'll do both. The last thing we want to do right now is kill the alliance."

"That leads me to the council's final request."

Ra'ch's face fell. "Uh-oh."

"There is—concern among some members of the council that the Federation intends to dissolve the Khitomer Accords."

"Based on what?" Ra'ch asked, straightening.

"Special Emissary Pagro has—"

"Fel Pagro's a presidential *candidate* making speeches to try to get himself elected!"

"You and I are aware of this, Councillor, but Chancellor Martok and the others do not understand that distinction. As far as they can see, the person most likely to rule the Federation is calling for Klingons to change their ways or face war."

"Yeah, I can see how they'd think *that,* too. Damn cultural relativism, anyway." Ra'ch set her hands down on the desk, and stared at the hologram of her mate. Then she regarded Worf with a determined expression. "Mr. Ambassador, I need you to return to the empire and talk to the members of the High Council. Assure them that the Federation hasn't abrogated the Khitomer Accords once over the last eighty years, which is more than the Klingons can say. For that matter, their embassies have never been attacked by Federation citizens, either. There may be problems between our peoples, but they are ones that can be dealt with diplomatically. We have no designs on their emperor or their territory. The alliance was our best hope for victory during the war and is our best hope for a prolonged peace in the wake of it."

Relief washed over Worf. This was exactly how he hoped this conversation would go. "Very well. It will also enable me to see which of those on the council will use this as an excuse."

Ra'ch tilted her head slightly. "An excuse for what?"

Worf hesitated. "There are some on the High Council who feel that an alliance with the Federation is—inappropriate. That the Federation, like any other governmental body that is *not* the Klingon Empire, should merely be the next on the list of what to conquer."

"Joy." Ra'ch rose from her seat. "Well, I hope your powers of persuasion are as good as I've heard, Mr. Ambassador."

Getting up from the guest chair, Worf said, "We shall see."

"I'll have the official statements from both the council and Starfleet Command by tomorrow."

"Good. I will return to Qo'noS as soon as they are delivered to me." Giving Ra'ch a small bow, Worf said, "Thank you, Councillor."

"You're welcome, Worf. Do well for us, please."

"I have always endeavored to do so."

With that, he departed, his business for the Federation completed. He headed to the nearest transporter station, intent on beaming to the Rozhenkos' house in Minsk. Since he was on Earth until at least the following day, he was going to take advantage of the opportunity to spend time with his foster parents. *I have not had Mother's* rokeg *blood pie in far too long. Nor,* he added to himself with the tiniest of smiles, *her* latkes.

The musty smell of old buildings and canal water assaulted Esperanza Piñiero's nostrils as she materialized outside Bacco campaign headquarters on Earth, located in the city of Venezia. United Earth government regulations stipulated that transporters were not allowed within any building designated a landmark, and almost the entirety of the Italian city was so designated. To compensate, transporter stations were constructed all over the walkways that snaked around and over the canals.

Helga Fontaine had chosen the site for their campaign headquarters, and Piñiero was still of two minds about it. It was a lovely place, no doubt about it. In many ways, the city had not changed in a thousand years, and it had a medieval beauty that no modern architecture that Piñiero knew of could match.

But that beauty could be very distracting, and the last thing a three-week campaign could afford was distractions. *It's going to be enough of a challenge to win this thing. Hell, it's gonna be damn near impossible to win this thing.*

She walked the few meters to the headquarters entrance, which was an old-fashioned door that had to be opened by hand. *More of that landmark foolishness,* Piñiero thought. *I should've overridden Helga on this. We need to be looking at the future, and all this place does is romanticize the past. The past is Min Zife and Koll Azernal. The past is Jaresh-Inyo letting Starfleet make an ass of him. If we're going to win, it has to be by embracing the future.*

Then she caught it.

It had been late evening in San Francisco when she left there moments ago, but dawn was just arriving in Italy. The sun started to peek out over the horizon, bathing the ancient buildings in a beatific molten butter glow. The canal water bounced the light in all directions, looking like a pile of scattered gemstones.

Piñiero just stopped and stared at the pure glory of daylight shining on millennia-old stonework. Again, she inhaled, feeling the sea air waft into her nostrils, admiring it rather than viewing it as an intrusion the way she dismissed the smell when she first beamed in.

That's why we're here, she realized. *Because the Federation is a thing of beauty, and we need to preserve it the way the government has worked to preserve this most magnificent city.*

Opening the door, she thought, *How the hell am I going to explain this to her?*

At least the governor was still on ship's time from their trip through the Rigel colonies, so it was late afternoon for her. There would be no worries about waiting for the caffeine to kick in. The time changes mattered little to Piñiero, whose Starfleet career took her to so many planets that her internal clock had given up the ghost by the time she made lieutenant. But Nan Bacco still had trouble with ship lag.

Even as Piñiero made her way through the lobby area—which was empty of all save the security guard at this early hour—she wondered if she should even share this latest news. *Maybe she'll be better off not knowing. If we lose, this knowledge can only . . .*

She shook the thought off. *What is it Fred keeps saying? We've got to act as if we've already won. If the vot-*

ers see a lack of confidence, they won't have any reason to be confident in us.

She could hear Bacco's voice in her office before she turned the corner to face the open doorway. "Look, Piers, I shouldn't have to explain this to you. Talk to Lieutenant Governor Gari, she'll be able to handle everything. That's her job."

"But Governor, she is the one who told me to confirm with you."

Bacco ran her left hand through the curls of her paper-white hair just as Piñiero entered the office. Bacco, who was standing behind her desk and looking down at the com unit on her cluttered desk, glanced up at the sound of her footfalls and waved her in with her right hand. "Piers, I'm confirming it now. You got that?"

"Yes, ma'am, that was all I needed."

"Good for you. Bacco out." She angrily stabbed at the com unit's control panel, cutting off the image of Piers Renault, the governor's press liaison. "I don't know who's worse, Piers or Gari. Neither one of 'em seems to be able to go to the bathroom unless I sign off on it."

"If they do ask, I'd say let them."

"It'd be a welcome change for Piers." Bacco chuckled as she sat in her chair and indicated that Piñiero should take the guest chair. "So how'd that thing go in San Francisco? What was it, a reception?"

"A birthday party for Admiral Nechayev. I served with her on the *U.S.S. Gorkon.*"

Frowning, Bacco said, "There's a *U.S.S. Gorkon?*"

Piñiero nodded.

"Wasn't Gorkon a Klingon chancellor?"

"Yes, but he was the one who was instrumental in getting the Khitomer—"

Bacco waved her hand back and forth across her face. "Yeah, I *know* who he is, I'm just wondering why Starfleet named a ship after him."

"Because he—"

"—was instrumental in getting the Khitomer Accords moving, and Starfleet'll name a ship after any damn thing. Don't the Klingons have a ship named after him?"

"Yeah, they do."

"That must get confusing as hell." Bacco grabbed a coffee mug, moved to sip from it, and discovered that it was empty. She got up and went to the replicator in the side wall. "Fine. So how was the party?"

"Not bad. I talked to some people. Ross's support is definitely helping."

"Coffee, black, unsweetened." The replicator hummed. "You want anything?"

Piñiero shook her head. "Look, Governor, you and I need to have a conversation."

"As opposed to what we're doing right now?"

"I mean about something specific."

Bacco took a sip from her coffee, then sat back down. "Is the conversation going to get more interesting? Because, I have to tell you, so far, you're boring the living hell out of me."

Piñiero hesitated. "The thing is—I'm not sure we *should* be having this conversation."

"That makes two of us. Can you make up your mind in the next thirty seconds or so? I've got about four hundred calls to make—calls, I might add, that *you* said I should make while we were on Earth and before the debate tonight, so—"

"I had an interesting conversation with Admiral Upton."

"Was it more interesting than this one?"

Nodding emphatically, Piñiero said, "Oh yeah, it was. See, Upton was working with Azernal on a few projects, and he had some interesting things to say to me."

"Like what?"

Piñiero started to talk, then stopped. "How familiar are you with Tezwa?"

Bacco frowned, though a moment, then said, "Independent world near the Klingon border. They just had a rather bloody change in power."

"Prime Minister Kinchawn threatened the Klingon colony of Qi'Vol. He eventually abdicated, then led an unsuccessful coup until Starfleet—barely—contained the situation."

"Right, I got all this from FNS."

Piñiero fidgeted, then stopped herself.

"Esperanza, what's wrong? You don't fidget."

Damn, but that woman knows me too well. "Everyone assumed that Kinchawn's threat against the Klingons was the last act of a madman who needed to be removed from power—right up until he used Federation pulse cannons on the *Enterprise* and its Klingon escort. The *Enterprise* assumed that they were stolen and sold on the black market by the Orions." Piñiero started to fidget again, and finally sat on her hands. "What Upton told me was that—" She took a breath. "Governor—Upton told me that Azernal armed the Tezwans with those cannons *through* the Orions."

Bacco stood up. "What!?"

"Governor—"

"You mean to tell me that the chief of staff of the Federation president armed an entire planet run by a nutcase—and nobody *knew* about it?"

Piñiero sighed. "Governor, if you'll let me—"

"Wait a minute." Bacco waved her arms again. She got a look on her face that Piñiero recognized. It was when she was working her way through something. "Who is this Upton person, anyhow?"

"Cultural affairs, he—"

Bacco snorted. "Cultural affairs. Which means, in real terms, he's as much of a nobody as an admiral can be and still wear that ugly uniform. And if *he* knows about this . . ." She shook her head. "Dammit all, Starfleet knew about this, too. And hushed it up." Slamming her hand on the desk, she asked, "What the hell kind of government are these jackasses running?"

"Governor—"

Her eyes widened. "Oh no." She looked at Piñiero. "That's why Zife and Azernal really resigned, isn't it?"

Slowly, Piñiero nodded.

"This is insane. Hell, at this point, I'm not sure I *want* the damn job."

"Governor, there's more."

Bacco finally sat back down. "I'm an old woman, Esperanza. Please keep that in mind before you put any more strain on me."

At that, Piñiero actually smirked. "It won't be any worse than all that coffee you drink."

To Piñiero's relief, the smirk was returned. "Good point. All right, what's the other thing?"

"If Upton knows, then there's a good chance that Abrik knows. Which means—"

Rolling her eyes, Bacco said, "Which means Pagro knows, too."

"Or he will soon enough." Piñiero sighed. "Public opinion is pretty divided on the Klingons right now. The war was recent enough for a lot of people to be happy with the alliance, but far enough away that people are wondering what the upside is—especially after Tezwa. Pagro's counting on that. I'm worried that, if he can't bully the Klingons his way, he'll force their hand by revealing that the old administration armed the Tezwans."

"Which is a treaty violation that'll give the Klingons all the excuse they need to go to war. Again."

"And if we win, then Abrik can still reveal it, and cut us off at the knees before you have a chance to settle in." Piñiero let out a long breath. "So we're pretty much screwed, ma'am. Unless—"

She let the word hang. *I don't want to suggest this. Come on, Governor, make the leap, figure it out so I don't have to suggest it.*

Bacco gulped down the rest of her coffee. "You're suggesting we leak it."

"I'm not suggesting any such thing," Piñiero said almost truthfully. "But it is an option."

"Don't play semantics with me, Esperanza, you're not as good at it as I am."

Piñiero smiled wryly. "That's certainly true, ma'am."

Bacco got up from her chair and wandered over to the small window that looked out on the Grand Canal. The meeting room upstairs had a nicer view, and Piñiero had expected Bacco to choose it for her office, but Bacco thought it was better to have meetings with a beautiful view so, as she put it, "I'd have something to stare at once you people start boring me to tears." For her office, she wanted as few distractions as possible.

Patiently, Piñiero waited. She knew that Bacco would make her decision in due time. Piñiero herself had given all the advice she could give, and her best bet at this point was to shut up and wait for her.

"No. Not yet, anyhow." She turned around and looked straight at Piñiero. "I don't want to use this unless we're desperate, and we won't be there for at least another week yet."

Letting out a breath she hadn't realized she was holding, Piñiero said, "That's probably prudent."

"How the hell did I get here?" Bacco asked as she retook her seat.

Piñiero frowned. "Ma'am?"

"How did I get to the point where my level of prudency has a direct impact on whether or not the Federation goes to war?"

"Part of the job, ma'am."

"I don't even *have* the damn job yet." She grabbed the coffee mug, again forgetting she'd finished it. "Dammit all, we need bigger mugs."

"So you keep saying, ma'am."

Once again going to the replicator, Bacco said, "I've got two more questions for you, Esperanza. One, you sure you don't want something?"

A sudden wave of thirst came over Piñiero. *Now that*

I've finally talked to her about this, I'm parched. "Actually, I'd love a raspberry tea—iced."

"Coffee, black, unsweetened and tea, raspberry, iced." The replicator hummed to life, and the two beverages appeared in the slot, steam rising from the coffee mug.

The heavenly aroma of raspberry caressed Piñiero's nose as she took the chilled glass from Bacco's hands. *Jewel of the Adriatic be damned, I'll take this smell over a canal any day.*

After taking a quick gulp of the cool, soothing liquid, Piñiero asked, "What's the other question?"

"Why did Upton share this with you? I mean, I don't know all that many admirals, certainly not as many as you do, but the impression I get is that this isn't the kind of thing they usually blab about."

Piñiero shifted uncomfortably. "No, ma'am." To her surprise, Piñiero found herself embarrassed by this part, and was as reluctant to divulge it as she had been the intelligence.

"So why the hell'd he tell *you?*"

"I'd really rather not say, ma'am."

Bacco grinned. "Okay, if I didn't want to know before, I for *damn* sure want to know now."

Piñiero sighed. Bacco wasn't going to let this go—in fact, she'd hound Piñiero for days on end until she learned the truth, and the last thing either of them needed was this kind of irrelevant distraction, especially with the first debate tonight and the election a week away.

"He was hitting on me."

Bacco was just about to take a sip of her coffee, but she managed to stop herself before she sputtered, narrowly averting a big mess on the desk. "You're joking."

Her mouth twisting into a scowl, Piñiero said, "It's not like the phenomenon is unheard of, Governor."

"I know, but still—"

"The admiral's an old man, still single, and even though he's got the rank, he's basically a glorified bureaucrat. And, well—" She sipped her iced tea, then sighed. "He's not the most attractive man I've ever met, either. I can see why he'd try to impress someone he was interested in with all the wonderful secrets he was in on by way of puffing himself up. He was, you know, trying to swing for the walls."

As expected, that got a rise out of Bacco. Piñiero had to admit to getting a sadistic kick out of the reaction her deliberate malapropisms got out of the governor. In this case, it also served to alleviate her irritation over having to reveal that she got major intel like this from a sad old admiral trying to pick her up.

"Fences, dammit, not walls. If you don't stop misusing the baseball metaphors, I swear, I'm going to have you beaten." Bacco sighed. "Well, I guess if he's desperate enough, he'd hit on you, yeah."

Piñiero smiled thinly. "We can't all be as beautiful as you, ma'am."

"Damn right." She took a sip of coffee. "Millions of years of evolution, and we still act like fools when we think sex might be involved. What a species." She set down her coffee mug. "Okay, who do I have to talk to next?"

There were few things that Jas Abrik missed about Starfleet, but one of them was the ability to just ask the computer where someone was and be told their precise location.

Unfortunately, the Diplomatic Corps did not equip their ambassadors with combadges, so Abrik had to use more mundane means to track down Ambassador Worf. And he had to do it quickly. The *U.S.S. Crazy Horse* was scheduled to take Worf back to Qo'noS within the hour, and Abrik needed to speak with him before he left—but he hadn't actually reported to the ship yet.

Abrik had already tried the ambassador's foster parents in Minsk, his only family on planet. Nor was Worf at the Launching Pad or any of the other nearby bars. Finally, some ensign or other told him that he'd seen the ambassador heading for the VIP lounge at Starfleet Headquarters.

Sure enough, the massive form of the Federation ambassador to the Klingon Empire was seated in one of the chairs that dotted the dark-red-carpeted floor of the VIP lounge. Only a few other people were present—two Starfleet, the others in civilian clothes—and Abrik recognized none of them. All of them, however, were engaged in the same activity: watching the first debate between Fel Pagro and Nan Bacco.

Abrik should have been at that debate, being held in the Collins Amphitheatre on Luna, but his need to speak to Worf before he departed was great, and at this point there was nothing that Abrik could really do for Pagro. For these two hours, at least, he and Bacco were both wholly on their own.

Bacco was speaking as Abrik entered the lounge. "—alk to the Romulans unless they actually come to the table, and they haven't shown much interest in that since

*that Watraii business a couple years ago. Remember,
these are the same people who closed their borders for
over fifty years. If they don't want to talk, they don't
want to talk, and there are limits as to what can be accomplished. Speaking for myself, I was hoping for more
after our cooperation during the war, but I wasn't really
expecting anything other than what we got."*

Abrik shook his head at the completely truthful but
wholly uninspired answer. *Nail her, Fel.*

*"Special Emissary Pagro, you have one minute for re-
buttal."*

Pagro gave the audience—and the camera recording
the event—his most pleasant smile. *"It's easy to say,
'They won't come to the table.' That saves you the trouble
of having to do any work, and shifting the blame. But the
Romulans are an enemy of the Federation, and have been
for as long as there's been a Federation. In fact, they've
been an enemy of anyone who isn't the Romulan Empire
for as long as they've existed as a political entity. They
only helped us during the war out of self-interest, and
that self-interest is also keeping them from talking to us
now. Lifting the trade embargo was good for people who
want to drink Romulan ale without guilt, but it's not really doing us any good right now. Furthermore, we can't
afford to sit around and wait for our enemies to make the
first move. That's what leads to things like Wolf 359—or
the Gorn attack on Cestus III during the war."*

Now Abrik grinned. That was the perfect retort, and
based on the brief look on Bacco's face before she got
herself under control, it hit close to home. *That's my guy,*
he thought proudly.

Satisfied that his candidate was wiping the floor with his opponent, Abrik approached the man he'd been looking for. "Ambassador Worf?"

Worf looked up at the prompt. "Yes?"

"I don't think we've met. I'm Jas Abrik—I'm running Special Emissary Pagro's campaign. May we speak a moment?"

"I will be departing for the *Crazy Horse* in ten minutes. Be brief."

Love that Klingon bluntness, Abrik thought as he sat in the chair that was sitting at a forty-five-degree angle to the ambassador's own seat. "There's something you need to know, Mr. Ambassador, something that the council probably didn't tell you, and probably never will."

"And that is?"

Most of the diplomats Abrik had encountered in his life—including the one whose campaign he was currently managing—had open, friendly demeanors, and always gave the impression that they were ready to talk. Even the ones from less—there was no other word for it—refined species, like the Tellarites or the Klingons, tended to be somewhat open and welcomed discussion.

Worf, however, fixed Abrik with a stare that didn't say, *I wish to have a conversation with you.* Instead, it said, *Speak quickly and I might not kill you for daring to intrude upon my life.* Abrik found it at once refreshing and more than a little intimidating.

"Are you aware of what happened on Tezwa?"

"Yes."

Abrik smiled. "Mr. Ambassador, I know for a fact that that is an incorrect response, because I know something you do not: those pulse cannons that wiped out the Klingon fleet and almost did the same to the *Enterprise?*"

"What of them?"

If Worf had any emotional reaction to Abrik's comments, or his statements regarding Worf's former shipmates, he kept it very well hidden. *He'd have made a decent Vulcan, if not for that air of brutality he carries around.* "They weren't stolen from Starfleet. They were provided—by Koll Azernal."

Worf leaned back in his chair. "An interesting theory."

"It isn't a theory," Abrik snapped. "It is, however, a secret, one that we cannot afford to keep."

"Had Azernal done what you accuse him of doing, Mr. Abrik—the Federation would be in violation of the Khitomer Accords. The likely next step would be war."

"Not necessarily."

Worf gave him the stare again.

"Hear me out," Abrik said, holding up a hand. "The Federation was founded on the principles of truth and freedom. The alliance with the Klingons isn't based on lies—in fact, it came about thanks to the exposure of lies on the part of a Klingon general, a Starfleet admiral, and—"

"I am aware of the history surrounding the Khitomer Accords."

Abrik leaned forward. "Then you should also be aware that the longer we keep this secret, the worse it will be when it comes out. And it *will* come out, Mr. Ambassador, sooner or later. It always does. Perhaps we'll be fortunate and it'll come out at a time when it'll have no effect on our people, but we can't count on that. It's better to reveal it and own up to it."

The stare intensified. "Do you intend to reveal this information?"

Sighing, Abrik said, "Not yet. The situation is too volatile, and we don't even have any leadership in place. But if it becomes necessary—"

"You mean if Special Emissary Pagro loses the election next week."

Abrik cursed the ambassador his perspicacity. "That is one option, but—"

"You have not told him, have you?"

Repeating those curses, Abrik said, "No. But I will if—"

"Ambassador Worf, please report to transporter station nine. Ambassador Worf to transporter station nine."

Worf stood up. "This conversation is over. I will take your words into consideration when I return to the empire in order to convince the members of the High Council that the Federation is an honorable ally."

Klingons were not known for their facility with sarcasm; Abrik chalked Worf's expert use of it to his years living in the Federation. "I thought you'd understand. The truth about the Khitomer massacre came out, after all."

"When the time was right, yes," Worf said. "I do not think that time is now for Tezwa, nor do I see what you have gained in sharing that intelligence."

I was hoping to gain an ally after the election, Abrik thought glumly. *That seems to have backfired rather spectacularly.* Worf was probably the person in the galaxy best qualified to do his job, and Abrik was hoping that this confidence sharing would have the added benefit of guaranteeing that he would continue in the role once Pagro was elected.

Abrik said none of these things, however. Instead, he simply stood up, reached out a hand, and said, "Thank you for your time, Mr. Ambassador."

Worf returned the handshake, but said nothing as he departed the lounge.

"Dammit," Abrik muttered.

Then he looked over at the viewscreen. Pagro was talking.

"—lem with determining the needs of the rehabilitation efforts is that it's an answer that will vary. The rebuilding efforts that have fallen by the wayside since the war do need to be addressed, but we won't be able to please everyone. I have confidence that I, at least, will be able to navigate those requests with a proper notion of resource allocation. I'm sure Governor Bacco will make all kinds of promises in that down-home style of hers about what she's done in the past, and she'll probably throw in a baseball reference while she's at it. But promises don't feed the sehlat."

Several members of the audience had laughed at various points, which heartened Abrik, as it meant the room was responding to him. Abrik had caught bits and pieces of the debate during his search for the ambassador, in addition to the segment he watched when entering the lounge, and with each question Pagro had grown more confident as Bacco's answers had gotten more generic. The special emissary was used to the formal structure of the debate, and adjusting to the needs of the people he was dealing with at the moment. Bacco, as a longtime governor, was more accustomed to being the one in charge directing matters, which made her an excellent public speaker, but hamstrung her here. Both skills were, of course, of great use once one took office, but the flexibility was needed to reach that office in the first place.

"*Governor Bacco, you have one minute for rebuttal.*"

Bacco looked over at Pagro. Up until now, she had looked polite and reserved and kindly. Now, though, something was different, and Abrik wasn't entirely sure he liked it.

"*It's funny, I could've sworn this was going to be a civil debate. I mean, yeah, I was expecting a few cheap shots—and I'll definitely give you points for the Cestus III jab. That was—to use one of those baseball references you seem to like so much—a fastball you blew right by me.*" She turned to the audience. "*But to take that kind of patronizing tone about my understanding of the realities of resource allocation is, to borrow from another sport for a minute, hitting below the belt. If my grandson talked to me like that, I'd wash his mouth out. It's also bunk. Believe me, Special Emissary, I know from resource allocation. You see, back about ten years ago, a bunch of diplomats just like you decided it would be a good idea to give a bunch of Federation colonies to the Cardassians. I'm sure it looked great at the negotiating table, but the hard reality was that a lot of people had to leave their homes. About a quarter million of those wound up on Cestus III. Getting a twenty-five percent population increase all at once on a colony that has had a below-average population curve for a hundred years will tell you everything you need to know about resource allocation. So, Special Emissary, to use one of my down-home-style phrases, don't teach this grandmother how to suck eggs.*"

The room erupted into spontaneous applause. Abrik felt his stomach shrivel up. Looking back, he realized that Pagro had pushed a little too far.

However, recalling what the next question would be, Abrik breathed a sigh of relief. *Ozla's going to ask about the Klingons. Fel will nail this one.*

Abrik walked over to the replicator in the far corner as he heard the moderator say, *"The next question for Governor Bacco is from Ozla Graniv of* Seeker. *The question is: Governor, how do you respond to Special Emissary Pagro's insistence that the Klingon Empire change its ways in order to preserve the alliance?"*

Bacco shook her head and smiled. *"You know it's funny, I would've thought that a diplomat of Special Emissary Pagro's standing would know better than to think that change can be effected at phaser-point. And make no mistake, that's what we're talking about here, because what he's proposing is to* threaten *the Klingons. Thing is, change doesn't come from threats—especially within the Klingon Empire. It also doesn't come quickly, when you're talking about societal norms that have been in place for thousands of years, unless there's some kind of catastrophe associated with it. But you know what's funny? Since the Khitomer Accords, the rate at which the Klingon Empire has conquered other worlds has decreased by seventy-five percent. Even if you slice out the first fifty years after the Accords, when the destruction of Praxis left the empire in pretty lousy shape, it's still a sixty percent decrease. More humane medical practices are slowly becoming the norm within the empire, as well. Now, those statistics may not seem like much for ninety years' work, but it's a start, and it's one that'll have long-term benefits that won't start another war—because that's what we're talking about here. Special Emissary Pagro's threat will only serve to get more good people killed in a conflict that neither side should have to fight.*" She turned to look at Pagro. "*Frankly, sir, I've had enough of war, and I don't see what's to be gained by putting us in a position to fight another one. It's, to put it mildly, a very bad allocation of our resources.*"

More applause. Abrik found himself no longer interested in drinking the *allira* punch he'd gotten from the replicator, and he set it down on a side table. *I have got to stop underestimating that woman. Get it back, Fel, get it back.*

"*Special Emissary Pagro, you have one minute for rebuttal.*"

Pagro's lips were pursed. After a two-second pause, he finally spoke in a much tighter voice than he'd been using up until now. "*The Klingons conquer people. I don't know how much more clear I can make that. They subjugate people to their whims, and make them into second-class citizens, almost slaves. Worse, their citizens feel free to attack our embassy. We cannot countenance an ally that engages in this kind of behavior, as it violates everything we stand for.*"

Abrik put his head in his hands. Pagro sounded petulant and annoyed, and he was giving his stock answer, not responding directly to what Bacco said.

He got up and left the VIP lounge, unable to stand watching this anymore. *I should be able to catch the next moon shuttle. I need to be there for Fel when this is over and see what we can do to fix this.* Even as he walked down the corridor, he started formulating possible plans of action—including, much as he hated to do it, taking the low road and starting character attacks. Bacco didn't have very many skeletons in her closet, but she did have a now-deceased ex-husband who was a career criminal. In fact, their marriage was part of one of his cons, from what Abrik had been able to piece together. It wasn't something that would matter much if Bacco were an ordinary citizen, but the leader of the Federation could not afford to be someone whose judgment was so poor as to fall prey to a grifter.

That, at least, is the spin we'll put on it, if we go that route. He had hoped to avoid such a measure, but the latest FNS polls showed Bacco gaining ground, and Abrik suspected that this debate was only going to close the gap further.

Chapter 9
U.S.S. Enterprise

WHEN DATA RECEIVED the summons from the computer to the observation lounge, he had assumed that he would be speaking to Sabin Genestra, as he had been conducting ninety-two-point-seven-eight percent of his interviews in that space, with the lone exceptional case being when he interviewed Lieutenant T'Eama in the security office on deck four.

He was therefore surprised to see that Captain Go was waiting for him in the lounge rather than Genestra. Unlike Genestra, Go had established no pattern for her interviews, having conducted them on the bridge, in the captain's ready room, in engineering, in Ten-Forward, in the gymnasium, and in the quarters of some of the interviewees. This was her first time conducting an interview in this location, and he amended his analysis of the captain's pattern appropriately.

In another deviation from the norm, Go had arranged her hair in a bun at the back of her head. During the six days and four hours she'd spent on the *Enterprise,* Go had kept her hair—which was seven centimeters longer than it was in the most recent image of her in her service record—tied in a simple ponytail. Data wondered what the occasion was for the change in styling. He had observed that some humans were mercurial in their follicle arranging—Troi's mother came to mind as an obvious example, as did Dr. Crusher—but Go had seemed consistent with the ponytail. However, as such a query did not fall within the purview of the inspection tour, and Go was not numbered among Data's friends, he did not feel it was appropriate to ask the question.

Data also noted that Go was sitting at the head of the table, in the seat that was generally occupied by Captain Picard. For his interviews, Genestra had sat on the side facing the viewport. From his extensive studies of human psychology, commenced after his dream program activated, Data deduced that, where Genestra wished to put his interview subjects at ease by speaking to them as equals, Go preferred to make it clear from her seat that she was the person in authority.

On Data's entrance, Go looked up from the padd she was perusing. "Ah, Mr. Data. Come in, sit down."

Data pulled out the chair that was perpendicular to Go's and sat in it. "How may I be of service, Captain?"

"I have a few questions for you, Commander." Go's face indicated confusion. "But I'm not sure how to phrase the first one."

"What is the source of your difficulty?"

Go shook her head. "Well, normally, if an officer underwent a medical procedure equivalent to the removal of your emotion chip last year, I'd ask them how they were feeling—but that doesn't really apply, does it?"

"Not as such, no."

Now Go frowned. "What do you mean, 'as such'?"

"Although I no longer experience actual emotions, I still retain the memory of the emotions I felt when I was equipped with the chip. I am therefore conversant with them, and can liken them to the state of affairs in which I find myself."

Nodding, Go said, "Interesting." She made several notes on her padd. "Do you think removing the chip has diminished your capacities as a Starfleet officer? I ask this mainly in light of the fact that you're about to become first officer of this ship. You're one year away from what was literally an emotionally crippling procedure. Do you think that will affect your ability to perform as first officer of the *Enterprise?*"

Data had, in fact, given this a great deal of thought in the eleven months, two weeks, five days, three hours, and ten minutes since the Starfleet Corps of Engineers removed his emotion chip. "I do not believe that it will. The lack of an emotion chip did not factor into my ability to function as a Starfleet officer prior to its installation."

"Yes, but you had never had emotions then. Now you've lost them. Before, you didn't know what you were missing."

"True. However, my positronic net is capable of functioning at peak efficiency with the addition or removal of data. In addition, my dream program was activated before the emotion chip was installed. It did not impair my ability to perform my duties. In fact, on Stardate 47226, the program proved beneficial in identifying an alien presence aboard the *Enterprise*-D."

Go made several more notes. "What if you decide to have the chip replaced? That option is available to you in the future, if you're willing—"

"I am aware of the stipulations regarding possible re-instatement of the chip, Captain. However, I do not believe that it will be necessary."

Blinking several times in rapid succession, Go set the padd down and stared at Data. "Really? Why not? Don't you want the feelings back?"

"When the chip was first removed, I proceeded on the assumption that someday I would be able to reclaim what I had lost. However, in the time since that removal, I have had an opportunity to compare my development before installing the chip with my development since. In sentient life, emotions are shaped by experiences, by response to stimulus. For example, human children learn love and affection from the love and affection given them by their parents. I too have learned to adjust my program to react to certain stimuli. When Commander Riker's father died, I did not feel the same emotional grief that I felt when shipmates died in combat during the Dominion War. However, I do have a sense of loss regarding Kyle Riker—one that has also been present when others close to me have died, including my father, Noonien Soong, my grandfather, Ira Graves, and Lieutenant Tasha Yar."

Picking up the padd, Go made some more notes. "Interesting. So you're saying that you can fake the emotions."

"I do not believe I am 'faking' anything, Captain. I have been close friends with Commander La Forge since he first reported aboard the *Enterprise*-D. While it is true that there is no feeling associated with Geordi, I do continue to seek out his company off-duty, continue to be solicitous of his well-being, continue to be concerned for his welfare, and continue to be available for him when a friend is needed, as he has been for me. When he and another crew member were believed killed on Stardate 45902, I organized a funeral service for them based on what I felt their wishes would be. I believe that these actions are entirely consistent with human friendship."

Go grabbed another padd and tapped instructions into it. Then she held it up for him to see. "Do you recognize this?"

The image on the padd was that of the bridge of a *Nebula*-class starship. The captain's chair was located in the center, with various consoles arranged in a circle around it. Data was moving toward the command chair, with assorted red- and gold-uniformed officers at the other positions, and Lieutenant Commander Christopher Hobson standing to Data's left. "It is the bridge recording of the *U.S.S. Sutherland* from Stardate 45022.1. I was in command as part of a blockade to prevent Romulan aid from entering Klingon space to aid Lursa and B'Etor in their conflict with Chancellor Gowron."

"Yes. This is the part that interests me." Go touched a control, and the playback commenced.

Data took his seat in the captain's chair. Hobson moved closer to Data, now standing one point three meters to Data's left.

"Sir." Hobson paused. *"The fleet's been ordered to Gamma Eridon."*

Data turned to face Hobson. *"The tachyon signatures will not last long. By the time the fleet is deployed, it will be too late. Begin to reconfigure the sensors to detect ionized particle traces."* With the last sentence, Data turned back toward the main viewer.

"The entire area's been flooded with tachyon particles—we'll never be able to find what we're looking for!"

"I am aware of the difficulties." Data turned back to look at Hobson. *"Please bring the phasers back online."*

"That will flood three decks with radiation." Hobson had yet to move to carry out any of Data's orders.

Data continued to face forward. *"We will initiate radiation protocol when necessary."*

"You don't give a damn about the people whose lives you're throwing away! We're not just machines—"

Now Data's head turned sharply toward Hobson, his face changing expression for the first time since the playback began. Data's features took on a more stern aspect, one that he had seen Captain Picard utilize under similar circumstances. *"Mr. Hobson! You will carry out my orders, or I will relieve you of duty."*

A pause, then Hobson finally said, *"Yes, sir."* Then Hobson moved toward the starboard console.

The playback perfectly matched Data's own memory of the event.

Go stopped it. "You snapped at Lieutenant Commander Hobson."

"Yes. Mr. Hobson was questioning my orders and obstructing our attempts to expose the cloaked Romulan ships. I have observed that in similar situations, the commanding officers under whom I have served will often speak in that tone in order to make their displeasure clear and to goad their subordinates into action."

"Yes, but didn't those commanding officers do so out of frustration and anger?"

Data considered the point. "I did not feel anger, but my efforts to expose the Romulan fleet were being frustrated."

Go curled half her mouth in a smirk. "Now you're piddling over semantics."

"The choice of the word 'frustration' was yours, Captain."

"True." Go picked up her other padd and made more notes. "You've given me a great deal more food for thought than I was expecting from this interview, Mr. Data. However, for what it's worth, you've made it clear to me at least that you're going to make a fine first officer."

"Thank you, Captain."

Go stared at him. "Okay, that sounded like a prideful expression of gratitude. But you don't feel pride."

"I do, however, recognize the praise for what it is."

Before Data could continue the thought, Go said, "And you tailored your reaction to how you've observed others reacting to similar praise?"

"Yes."

Shaking her head, Go said, "You remind me of my daughter. My husband and I always make it a point to be polite around her. She's growing up to be the most well-mannered child in her class. Response to stimulus." She made some more notes on her padd. "I have a few more questions regarding your recent missions, and Captain Picard's performance during them."

Data tilted his head. "Should these questions not be asked of Captain Picard?"

"They have been—or they will be. But I'm interested in your take on them, especially if you're going to be Picard's first officer."

Unable to deny the logic of Go's thesis, Data said, "Very well."

"At the Dokaalan colony, Picard made a decision to beam twenty-seven people onto the ship despite the fact that transporters were not deemed safe for humanoid transport given the ambient radiation. Those twenty-seven people died in transport."

"That is correct."

"Do you think he made the right choice?"

"I do not believe that the captain had another choice."

Again, Go smirked. "There's always another choice, Mr. Data."

"In this particular instance, Captain, the only other choice was to do nothing. Among the many observations I have made over the course of my Starfleet career is that doing nothing is rarely the right choice. It was not the right choice in this instance. Had the captain not acted, those twenty-seven people would have died from exposure to a vacuum. By attempting to transport them, he was giving them a chance to survive."

"But they lost that chance."

"Yes. Captain Picard once said to me that it is possible to do everything correctly and still lose. That was the case on Dokaal."

Go made some more notes. "On Delta Sigma IV, Captain Picard had the option to declare martial law and take over from the planet's ruling council. Do you think he should have done so?"

"The option was never discussed." Data spoke truthfully. Jean-Luc Picard was not a person who would even consider such an action, based on Data's observations of him over the fifteen years, eight months, and four days since they met on the *Enterprise*-D.

"Really?" Go made a few more notes. "Why do you think that was?"

"Had the captain done so, it would not have changed any of the rescue and repair activities that *Enterprise* personnel were engaged in on the planet. The Bader and Dorset were already viewing Starfleet's presence with hostility. Had we, in essence, usurped their government, that would have only, to coin a phrase, made a bad situation worse without giving us any concomitant advantage."

Go made more notes on the padd, then set it down and picked up another one. "Very well, Mr. Data, thank you for your time. That will be all."

"Thank you, Captain." Data rose from the chair to return to the bridge. He still had four hours, two minutes, and seven seconds left on watch, and Lieutenant Commander Vale had wanted to run a security drill before alpha shift ended. As second officer, it behooved Data to be present to supervise the drill and aid Vale in the evaluation of it.

Before departing, he realized a discrepancy in Captain Go's questioning. He stopped, turned, and asked, "Captain?"

"Yes, Mr. Data?" Go did not look up from her padd.

"You questioned me about the two missions that occurred after Rashanar. I am curious as to why you did not question me about Rashanar itself, especially as it was based on my word that Captain Picard accepted the existence of the so-called demon ship."

Now Go looked up. "That's not your concern, Mr. Data. My job is to ask you people questions. I'm under no obligation to answer yours. You're dismissed."

Recognizing the commanding tone, Data turned and took his leave.

"First officer, you say?"

La Forge stared at Scotty from across the table in Ten-Forward. The old engineer was drinking scotch, of course—Scotty seemed to live on the stuff—while La Forge nursed a synthale. He had just informed Scotty of Riker's offer from the day before. The question of whether or not to say yes had kept La Forge from getting a decent night's sleep and from focusing properly during alpha shift. On the one hand, he was flattered and excited. He'd known Riker on and off since they were at the Academy, and they served together briefly on the *Hood* before coming to the *Enterprise*-D. There hadn't been a significant period of time in the last sixteen years when La Forge wasn't serving under Riker. Not accepting the post would put an end to that association.

Not that that was a good enough reason. If he just went by friendship, leaving the *Enterprise* would mean being separated from Data, who was remaining on the *Enterprise* to take Riker's place. La Forge didn't relish that possibility, but he didn't want to judge a professional decision on such personal criteria.

Normally this kind of dilemma would drive him to

Troi's office or to talk to Data—but, since he had Scotty here anyhow, he decided to go to him for advice for the simple reason that, unlike anyone else on the ship, he knew what it was like to be the chief engineer of a ship called *Enterprise.* In fact, like La Forge, he'd run the engine room of two different vessels with that proud name.

Scotty took a sip of his scotch. "I must say, Geordi, that's quite the feather in your cap."

"But?" La Forge prompted Scotty, as that word had been implied in his tone.

"Well, you *do* know what you'd be leavin' behind, don't you?"

"Well, yeah." La Forge studied his synthale, using his ocular implants to view the ebb and flow of the molecules that made up the beverage. "I mean, aside from Commander—*Captain* Riker and Deanna, I'd be leaving all my friends behind here." He smiled. "Unless he plans to poach a few more people. But still—"

Scotty shook his head. "That's not what I mean, lad. You'd be leavin' behind the engine room."

"I've been running the engine room for fourteen years, Scotty. Maybe it's time to move on."

"Tch." Scotty picked up his glass and started swirling the drink around in the clear, square-sided glass. "I fail to see the virtues of movin' on from somethin' you love. Remember what I told you way back when, right before I buggered off in that shuttle you lent me?"

La Forge smiled, remembering the words clearly. "That being the chief engineer of a starship is the best time of my life."

"Aye, it is," Scotty said, a smile of his own peeking out

from his mustache. "And fourteen years? 'Tis but a drop in the bottle. I was chief engineer of the *Enterprise* for two decades, and her successor for another seven. And in retrospect, choosin' to retire after they decommissioned the *Enterprise*-A was not the smartest move I ever made."

Chuckling, La Forge said, "Well, it was good for the rest of us. I mean, if you hadn't retired, you wouldn't have been on the *Jenolen* and been here all this time giving us the benefit of your wisdom."

"Quite true, lad, quite true." Scotty sipped some more scotch. Actually, the word "sip" was misleading—it was closer to a gulp. La Forge, who was able to discern the precise composition of the drink, had no idea how Scotty could even swallow a little of it at a time, much less the amount he did imbibe. *Maybe his liver's made of duranium.*

He took a sip of his own ale, and then regarded Scotty. "The thing is—I *do* like running engineering. I've got no complaints about that, but—" He blew out a long breath, puffing his cheeks. "I've always thought about having my own ship someday, and that's not gonna happen if I stay where I am."

Scotty looked at La Forge as though he had sprouted a second head. "Laddie—you *have* your own ship! We're sittin' in it! Oh, aye, Captain Picard *technically* has command of the thing, but you and I both know better, do we not?"

"I know what you mean, Scotty, but it's still not the same thing."

"Believe me, lad, I know it isn't." Now Scotty's look grew grave. " 'Tis far far worse." He set the scotch glass down. "Do you know what five words I dreaded most from Captain Kirk back in the day? 'Mr. Scott, you have the conn.' "

La Forge frowned. "That's six words."

Scotty sighed dramatically. "I'm an old man, Geordi, you cannot expect me to be able to count."

"Right, because doing math isn't a skill an engineer really needs," La Forge said with a smile.

"Are you gonna sass me, lad, or are you gonna listen to my sage advice?"

La Forge held up his hands. "Sorry. Really, I just—" He hesitated, unable to find the right words. *Been doing that a lot the last twenty-four hours.*

"I understand, Geordi, truly. Which is why I'm tryin' to tell you this story. Now, where was I?"

" 'Mr. Scott, you have the conn.' "

"Aye." He drank down the last of his scotch, then signaled for another. "The captain was fond of leading away teams—we called them landing parties back then—and since Mr. Spock doubled as first officer and science officer—"

La Forge's eyes widened. "You're kidding!"

"Oh aye, he did both. Did 'em both well, too."

Shaking his head with amazement, La Forge said, "I'm intimidated enough by the idea of being first officer on the *Titan* without adding a second duty to it—and the *Enterprise* had, what, three hundred people?"

"Four hundred, actually. Quite the man, Mr. Spock."

"He'd have to be." La Forge couldn't imagine that. The first officer was the one who more or less ran the day-to-day of the ship. To add the responsibilities of science officer to that . . . *Spock must never have slept.* "Anyhow, so you were put in charge a lot?"

"Aye. 'Twas captain's discretion who to make third-in-command—sometimes 'twas I, sometimes 'twas Mr. Sulu. And I've got to tell you, whenever it was me, the butterflies were reproducin' like mad in my stomach."

For La Forge's part, he wondered how the chief engineer contrived to be part of the chain of command, which was not standard procedure. On the other hand, neither was having your first officer pull double duty in the sciences. *Kirk obviously did things his own way back then. And hey, it's not like you can argue with the results.*

Before La Forge could comment on this, Ten-Forward's steward, a young man named Jordan, came over with a fresh glass of scotch. "Here you go, Captain. Anything for you, Commander?"

"I'm fine, thanks."

After Jordan departed, Scotty said while staring into the amber liquid he'd been given: "The worst was Eminiar VII. They were havin' a war with another planet, Vendikar—except they didn't fight the war in a traditional way."

A memory poked at La Forge. "I remember reading something about this at the Academy. They fought by computer, right?"

Scotty nodded sadly. "Aye, they did. The computer would do battle simulations, and assign casualties. Those people would then report to 'elimination chambers.' The problem started when they declared the *Enterprise* a casualty. Naturally, Captain Kirk refused to report to any bloody elimination chamber. He was down on the planet with Spock and a team—and he gave me General Order 24."

La Forge nearly dropped his synthale glass—that order was to destroy the surface of a planet. Then he recalled his long-ago Academy reading. "But Kirk and some ambassador stopped them in time, right?"

"Ambassador Robert Fox, aye." Scotty's face twisted into an unpleasant smile. "There were times when I would've been glad to have that one report to the elimination chamber—but," he continued, his face softening, " 'twas not to be. But you can imagine, can you not, Geordi, what it was like to sit on the bridge of the ship and being told I had to be responsible for the destruction of an entire world? I'm an engineer—I put things together and make them work better. What the captain was askin' me to do . . ." His voice, which was as strained as La Forge had ever heard it in the ten years he'd known Scotty, trailed off.

However, La Forge was not thinking of Eminiar VII, he was thinking of events more recent than that—ones that predated his promotion to chief engineer of the *Enterprise*-D. Specifically when he was conn officer and put in command of the ship at Minos. Riker led an away team to the surface that also included Data, but when the first officer was incapacitated, Picard beamed down, leaving La Forge in charge of the bridge. It turned out to be a rather brutal trial by fire, as La Forge found himself under attack, both by an automated weapon trying to destroy the *Enterprise* and by the chief engineer, a self-righteous prig named Logan, who tried to convince La Forge to cede command to his higher-ranking self when the attack started. Logan was one of four chief engineers, each one worse than the last, that the *Enterprise* went through before Picard promoted La Forge.

Like Scotty at Eminiar, La Forge was faced with difficult command decisions, though his were related to protecting the *Enterprise* and keeping its civilian population safe. But unlike Scotty, La Forge felt nothing but pride over what he accomplished at Minos. He numbered it among his proudest hours in Starfleet.

Which doesn't make the decision any easier.

"Do you see what I'm gettin' at, lad?"

La Forge started at Scotty's words, having lost himself in thought. "Uh, yeah, yeah, I do. But still—" He sighed, finished off his synthale, and got up. "I don't know. Look, Scotty, I appreciate the advice—really, I do. I guess I just need to think about it some more."

"You do that, lad," Scotty said gently. "But remember one important thing, Geordi: If you do say yes, that's it. There'll be no goin' back."

"Yeah. That's what makes it so hard to say yes *and* so hard to say no." He shook his head. "Thanks again. I'll see you later."

"A hologram?"

Picard held a steaming mug of Earl Grey tea in one hand and its saucer in the other as he said those words to Admiral Kathryn Janeway. The admiral's face was framed within the small screen on the desk of Picard's ready room.

"That's right. Apparently, someone got their hands on a mobile emitter," Janeway said bitterly. She had been the one to bring that technology to the Federation, thanks to a time-traveling adventure she had while her ship, the *U.S.S. Voyager,* was in the Delta Quadrant. *"We don't know who replaced Emperor Kahless with a hologram or why, but we do need to find him."*

"What is it you wish the *Enterprise* to do?" Picard asked, setting the tea down on his desk.

"Well, originally nothing, but Ambassador Worf strongly recommended that you be assigned to aid in the search."

Picard beamed inwardly. Although he had nothing but praise for the work Christine Vale had been doing for the past four years, there were times when Picard missed Worf's presence on the bridge. It was good to see that, even in his new career, he was solicitous of his former shipmates. "That is generous of the ambassador."

Janeway smiled conspiratorially. *"Honestly, Jean-Luc, it just gave some of us an excuse to give you the assignment. You aren't completely out of the doghouse yet, but you're pretty damn close—and there are a lot more people on your side. Even Upton was grudgingly admitting that you hadn't entirely lost it yet."*

"How nice to hear," Picard said dryly. Upton had been the one to assign the *Enterprise* to the powder keg that Delta Sigma IV had become, and Picard's impression had been that the admiral had not expected the *Enterprise* to perform at all well.

"We've assigned two dozen ships to search several sectors that match some sightings of Kahless during a particular time period, as well as places he liked to visit in the past. This is in addition to the searches the Klingons are making."

Since the *Enterprise* was still in the Xarantine system, which was a stone's throw from Klingon space, Picard assumed that they would be getting a sector of their own to search.

However, Janeway surprised him. *"But that's not what*

we're looking for from you. You were in command of the ship on the scene when Kahless 'returned' on Boreth ten years ago, and several members of your crew have interacted with Kahless."

Picard winced. "Kathryn, 'interacted' is a rather generous term. Worf was the only one who spent significant amounts of time with him."

"I realize that, Jean-Luc, but even that minimal interaction puts you one up on the rest of us. Plus, Will served on a Klingon ship, you served as K'mpec's arbiter of succession, Data's the best analyst in the Federation, and most of you served with a Klingon for eight years. You're the closest we've got to a proper Klingon think tank, and that's what we need. I'm forwarding all the intelligence the Klingons gave us, plus what little our people have been able to figure out so far. I'm also giving you everything on the mobile emitter, including our own attempts to reverse-engineer it, both on Voyager *and by the S.C.E. since we got back."* Janeway gave Picard a rather mischievous smile. *"Actually, since* before *we got back. From what I understand, they were trying to rebuild the thing just based on the log reports we were sending through Project* Voyager."

"From what I've seen of the S.C.E., that doesn't surprise me." Picard sipped his tea. "And what are we to do with this embarrassment of riches?"

"Sift through it. Analyze it. Look for a pattern. See if you can figure out where Kahless is." The mischievous smile was now gone, replaced by a stern look. *"Jean-Luc, we've got to do this right. There's a good chance that the next president is going to be calling for a war*

with the Klingons, and between Kahless's disappearance, the embassy seizure, and Tezwa, we may have that war without any push from Fel Pagro. Restoring Kahless to the empire would go a long way toward easing tensions."

"I agree. We will, of course, get right on it." He paused. "What of the inspection team?"

"Their work isn't finished." The smile came back. *"Consider this assignment part of the inspection. They can see you in action."*

"Kathryn, I'm not sure that's entirely wise. Captain Go's team has been rather disruptive to the ship's routine. While we're holding station here, that's less of an issue, but—"

"Don't worry, Jean-Luc. Even as we speak, Captain Go is being cut new orders to continue observation and evaluation, but not to interfere with the operation of the ship. Interviews will be optional and limited to off-duty time."

"Grand. Thank you, Kathryn. These past few weeks— months—" He leaned his head back. The bones in his neck snapped lightly. "In truth, this past *year* has been unduly strained. This crew deserves better."

She nodded. *"My pleasure, Jean-Luc. And I agree completely. You people have done excellent service for Starfleet and the Federation, and you deserve better than this. That's why I've been pushing for your assignment to improve, and it's why I made sure to hold the* Titan *for Will when he was captured on Tezwa."* With a warm smile, she said, *"If there's one thing I learned flying through the Delta Quadrant for seven years, it's that patience pays off eventually."*

"Indeed."

"One other thing, Jean-Luc," Kathryn said in a quiet tone.

Picard set his tea down and leaned forward, resting his arm on the desk. "Yes?"

"Be on the lookout for Klingon ships. A few Defense Force vessels have taken it upon themselves to fire on Starfleet ships—revenge for 'stealing' Kahless. Chancellor Martok has promised that those ship captains will be dealt with, but there may be more like that around. Watch your back."

"We shall. Thank you again. I will keep you apprised as to our progress."

"I'm looking forward to your reports, Jean-Luc. Starfleet out."

Picard switched off his screen, grabbed his teacup, and sipped its now-lukewarm contents. Though the mission was, on the face of it, a simple one, it carried huge potential. The Klingon-Federation alliance had been the cornerstone of the relative peace the galaxy had enjoyed for most of the past century—and most of the exceptions to that peace were either beyond the scope of that alliance or caused by the Dominion, and the latter was primarily defeated in the end because the two powers were united.

He tapped his combadge. "Picard to bridge."

"Data here, sir."

"Data, we should be receiving several files from Starfleet Command."

"Yes, sir, we are, in code and on a secured channel."

"Have Commander Vale decode the files, then I want all senior staff to review them for a meeting at—" He checked his chronometer, then added three hours to the time it gave. "—1700 hours."

"Aye, sir."

Chapter 10
Qo'noS

"I WAS NOT AWARE that the ambassador _had_ an heir," Councillor Qolka said as Alexander entered his office, "much less that he was a soldier of the empire. And now his lackey as well?"

Alexander did not take the bait, but instead simply stood opposite Qolka, in the spot where guest chairs would be in the Federation. Klingon officials saw no reason for their guests to be comfortable—and even if they did, the chairs would be metal slabs of some kind. _I'd just as soon stand,_ Alexander thought.

Aloud, he said, "I've been temporarily assigned to the embassy until they can restaff after the attack last month."

Qolka sat behind his desk, grabbing one of five mugs that sat on the table. Though Alexander's olfactory senses were not as sharp as most Klingons'—and given most Klingon smells, he was more than happy to have inherited a weak nose from the human quarter of his heritage—he could definitely make out one _warnog,_ one *raktajino,* and one prune juice. The latter had become a popular import item in recent years. *I wonder,* Alexander thought with amusement, *if Qolka's aware that it was my father who started that trend.*

The mug Qolka gulped from had one of the two unidentifiable drinks—though Alexander could see that it was green, based on the bit that spilled into Qolka's gray beard. After setting it down, he regarded Alexander. "Why has a Defense Force *bekk* been assigned to the *Federation* embassy? Or is it solely because you're the ambassador's whelp?"

Again, Alexander did not take the bait. "I'm also a Federation citizen, sir. In fact, I was born there. But I also lived in the embassy when I was a child before my mother died."

Qolka squinted at Alexander, looking like he was making some kind of deduction. Then his eyes widened again and he grinned. "You're Ambassador K'Ehleyr's boy, aren't you?"

Alexander smiled. "Yes, sir."

"She was quite a woman. Only Federation ambassador I could stand being near for more than five minutes, including your father." Qolka laughed. "And she and Worf actually mated? It is a strange universe."

"I've noticed that, sir. If we can get to the business at hand . . ."

"That Wu person said you wished to speak with me about the Federation alliance."

"Yes, sir." Alexander paused to take a breath. "The Federation Council's concerned about the state of the alliance."

"Really?" Qolka grabbed another mug—Alexander was pretty sure this was the *warnog*—and held it near his mouth. "Then they should have allowed us to deal with Tezwa ourselves."

"Sir, I assume you've read the reports from Tezwa."

Qolka shrugged. "My aides have. What of it?"

"You're aware, aren't you, sir, that it was the crew of the *Enterprise*—which was the only ship to survive the Tezwans' first attack on the fleet—who were able to destroy the Tezwan weapons. If they hadn't, the second fleet that went in—a fleet which I was part of, by the way, on the *Ya'Vang*—wouldn't have survived."

"Of course they were able to destroy the weapons— they were *Federation* cannons that the Tezwans stole from Starfleet. Which is what I'd expect from a collection of weaklings. The Federation's concept of security is pathetic." Now he drank from the mug. Slamming it down after guzzling its contents, he said, "With each day, I see less and less reason to continue to be allied with a body of fools. And now your own leader calls for *us* to change *our* ways in order to be worthy of remaining aligned with you." He laughed. "It is even *more* pathetic. If anything, the Federation should change its ways."

Based on the lengthy meeting he had with Father and Wu the previous day, Alexander had expected something like this, so his answer was ready. "Fel Pagro isn't the leader of anything, Councillor. He's just a man trying to get elected. There are plenty of people in the Federation who think the way he does, and he's hoping there's enough of them that they'll vote for him."

"This is supposed to put me at ease?" Qolka asked with a snort. He picked up the prune juice mug.

"No, but this is: Pagro's losing ground. The Federation News Service takes regular polls, and with each one, the number of people who say they're gonna vote for Pagro goes down. His opponent—"

"—is a female," Qolka said dismissively.

Alexander gritted his teeth. "So was my mother, Councillor."

Smiling, Qolka said, "Which is why I could stand being in her presence. Your mother was quite the comely one."

Resisting the great urge to respond with violence—mostly because he knew Qolka would stuff him headfirst into one of the drink mugs if he tried—Alexander instead said, "Well, Governor Bacco has negotiated treaties with the Gorn and the Metrons."

That seemed to surprise Qolka. "Really? A female did that?"

"Yes, sir." Alexander let out a breath. Klingons generally respected the Gorn, as much as they respected anyone, and they had a healthy regard for advanced beings like the Metrons, owing mostly to the empire's experiences with the Organians a century earlier. "And she's come out in favor of keeping the alliance strong."

"That merely proves she knows that we will crush the Federation if we do go to war."

"Really? You sure of that? Since the war, the Federation's been rebuilding its fleet, and it's getting stronger every day. In that same four-year period, the empire's lost ships at battles from San-Tarah to Tezwa, against the Elabrej, the Kinshaya, the Kreel—you really think you can win a war against the Federation?" Before Qolka could answer, Alexander pressed his advantage. "Look at the shape the empire was in before the Khitomer Accords were signed. Soldiers were dying by the thousands in battles with the Federation, the Romulans, the Kinshaya, the Tholians. Whole planets were starving to death. Planetary resources were next to nonexistent. A moon blew up—one lousy moon—and it would've destroyed the empire if the Federation hadn't helped out."

"That is ancient history—" Qolka started, but Alexander interrupted, hoping it wasn't a mistake to do so.

"But it leads to current history. Nobody in the empire's starving, and they haven't been since Chancellor Kravokh's day. We've got replicator technology, we've got access to resources that we *never* had before the treaty. Our ships have stronger shields, better sensors, and quantum torpedoes because of the alliance." He pointed to the mug Qolka still held. "You're drinking that prune juice because of the alliance. Why do you want to give that up? Why do you want to go back to the way things were?" Alexander paused a moment, then went for what he hoped was the killer ending to the rant he'd been practicing all morning. "When the Federation was the empire's enemy, the empire was weak and cowardly. Since the alliance, the empire has just gotten stronger. You don't win battles by retreating, Councillor."

Qolka started to drink his prune juice, then set it down. "Truly you are a man of two worlds, Alexander, son of Worf—you talk like a human, but you speak as a warrior." He smiled. "Tell your father that I will continue to support the alliance—for the time being."

Alexander blinked. *That was too easy.* "Just like that?"

"I did say 'for the time being,' did I not?"

Nodding, Alexander said, "Yeah, you did."

"When you speak to your father, be also sure to tell him that I expect not to be given reasons to change my mind." Grinning lasciviously, he added, "And tell him I admire his taste in women."

Again, Alexander gritted his teeth. "I'll do that, sir. Thank you."

With that, he left Qolka's office. He checked the time, and saw that he had only a half hour until his next appointment, with Councillor Grevaq. *This may not be as exciting as serving on the* Ya'Vang, *he thought, but I gotta say I'm liking this. I feel like I'm doing something good. I'm helping the Federation and the empire—and I'm helping Father.*

Thinking back to the less-pleasant parts of his conversation with Qolka, he nonetheless got a warm feeling inside. *And in a way, I'm helping Mother, too. I think she'd be proud of what I did today.*

"Ah, Ambassador Worf. Once again you grace the Great Hall with your presence."

His stomachs rumbling with nausea, Worf stepped into Councillor Kopek's office. Unlike most of the other members of the High Council, who decorated their chambers sparsely if at all, Kopek made his as lavish as possible, from the Betazoid water sculpture to the *targhDIr* furniture to the crystal sconces for the candles that provided illumination. A Danqo tapestry decorated the wall behind his desk, and a J'lang sculpture of Aktuh embracing Melota sat on one end of his desk. He had replaced the functional duranium doors with Terran redwood ones, covered the ceiling with Vulcan paper tiles and the floor with black marble, and added wholly unnecessary pillars of obsidian.

Kopek walked over to the small table on which he kept an assortment of liquids in crystal pitchers. "Can I interest you in a drink, Ambassador? I have prune juice straight from Earth."

Under any other circumstances, Worf would welcome the refreshing beverage, but Worf was ever mindful of the Klingon aphorism *Drink not with the enemy.* And, despite the purpose of his visit, Kopek was most definitely the enemy. He had opposed Martok from the moment he took his seat on the council, three years earlier, and an enemy of Martok's was, by definition, an enemy of Worf's.

But for now, I need to cultivate him as an ally of the Federation ambassador, he reminded himself.

"Thank you, but no," Worf said, "I will not be here long."

"Are you sure?"

"Quite sure. I would speak to you about the Federation alliance."

Pouring himself an amber liquid that looked like no Klingon beverage—but looked a lot like Saurian brandy, a drink Worf had always found rather bland—Kopek said, "Suit yourself." He brought the glass—not a traditional Klingon mug, but rather a clear glass, decorated with the empire trefoil—with him to his desk and sat in a chair that was upholstered with Terran leather. "What about the Federation alliance would you like to speak of?"

"The Federation has expressed concern that the High Council will attempt to sway Martok in the direction of breaking the alliance."

Kopek laughed. "Of course they have. So you come to me because you know that I am an opponent of Martok and all he stands for. And that is as it should be—commoners do not belong in the Great Hall. As a scion of a noble House, you should be aware of that." With a look of mock-realization, he added, "Oh but wait—your father's House was dissolved by Gowron, was it not? A pity. Still, the rule of men belongs to those of *noble* blood; it is not a place for laborers from the lowlands."

It was all Worf could do to restrain himself from saying, *No, that place is your bed.* "Regardless of his origins, the chancellor feels that the empire's alliance—"

"The alliance is a sham, and it does me no good. The Ferengi have a saying—" He chuckled. "In fact, they have an entire book of sayings, but the one I like best is the one about how war is good for business. Peace with the Federation means nothing. War with the Federation means new ship construction, it means a rise in the sale of difficult-to-obtain goods, it means a rise in weapons sales across the galaxy. It means I profit, and, as an added bonus, it strikes another blow into Martok's lowborn heart." Kopek downed his brandy in one gulp by way of punctuating his statement.

Worf's mouth twisted in annoyance. He had expected no less from Kopek, but he had to make the effort. "Very well. Thank you for your time."

Even as Worf turned to leave, Kopek continued speaking. "I do wish to thank you, Ambassador. You've done me a great service."

Worf stopped, but did not turn around. "How is that?"

"Oh, I know you can't admit it—and those toys you

used to disguise yourself were quite impressive—but we both know who it was who traded a data rod for my access code. By the way, I've changed the code, so don't think that will do you any good in the future. That rod, however, has been a great boon. I had no idea that I.I. knew that much about me. It has enabled me to strengthen my own position, and eliminate several enemies I did not even know I had."

The nausea in Worf's stomachs increased. Kopek had mentioned ship construction in his litany of potential benefits from a Federation-Klingon war, but the dossier Worf had been provided on Kopek said nothing about shipbuilding being among his many concerns. *No doubt one of those enemies did,* Worf thought angrily, *and those concerns now belong to the House of Kopek.*

Kopek stood and walked back to the drinks table. "Oh, one more thing, Ambassador. A mutual acquaintance of mine is here. He wishes to give you his regards."

At that, Worf turned around, just in time to see the door to the antechamber open. During the Tezwa crisis, when Worf had broken into these very same chambers and rendered both Kopek and his aide-de-camp unconscious, he had placed both their prone forms in that antechamber.

Now, it was Kl'rt who leapt from the now-open doors, firing a disruptor.

Worf ducked behind one of the pillars. Kl'rt's shot was wild, as he fired before he could take proper aim, and so the blast only grazed Worf's shoulder. It didn't even make it through to the skin, although his cassock was badly singed.

"Now you will die the death you deserve, traitor!" Kl'rt cried.

Reaching into his pocket, Worf pulled out his own phaser and fired back.

Kl'rt fell to the floor, dead, even as his disruptor fired into the ceiling, damaging the Vulcan tiles.

Kopek smiled. "Well done, Ambassador!"

Coming out from behind the pillar, blood boiling in his veins, Worf growled and asked, "What was *he* doing here? He should be dead!" According to the report he'd read upon his return to Qo'noS, all the members of *Klahb*—except for Rov, whose body was predictably not retrieved at Pheben V—were executed.

"And he is dead," Kopek said, pointing at the body. "See?"

Worf squinted, and reined in his temper. Tempting as it was—justified as it would be under the circumstances—killing Kopek would do him no good.

Then, even as he calmed down, his mind worked through the true meaning of Kopek having Kl'rt hiding in his closet, as well as the still-unanswered question as to how a group of kitchen stewards were able to so easily take over the Federation embassy.

"You," he said.

"What about me?" Kopek asked, trying and failing to sound innocent.

"You were behind *Klahb*. Only someone with the High Council's resources could have given them the information they needed to neutralize weaponry and take over the security system."

Laughing, Kopek said, "Of course. As I said, war is

good for business. All the pieces were on the game board. There was the disaster at Tezwa. That tiresome clone of Kahless had been replaced by a Federation hologram. And there I was, with a clean slate, as it were, thanks to a fool of a diplomat who labored under the delusion that I.I.'s file on me was fair payment for so ephemeral a piece of data as an access code."

Though it did not seem so from Kopek's perspective, the trade *was* a fair one, because the one thing Kopek did not factor in was time. Worf had a limited window of opportunity in which to act. He could not afford to think about the long-term consequences of what was, of necessity, a short-term solution. *Now,* he thought bitterly, *those consequences return to haunt me.*

Kopek went on. "With my newfound freedom to maneuver, it was child's play to start the game by providing *Klahb* with the means to take over the Federation embassy. No matter what the outcome—and I have to give you credit, Ambassador, I did not expect you to so readily resolve the situation all on your own—it would send our respective governments further down the road to war, especially with Special Emissary Pagro's leadership a distinct possibility."

Recalling his conversation on Earth with Jas Abrik, Worf thought angrily, *Pagro will make your desires reality more quickly than you realize.* Whenever there was a change in leadership in the Federation, all ambassadors traditionally handed in their resignations, to allow the new president the option to select new ones. Those the administration wished to keep in place would be reinstated right away. After talking with Abrik, Worf had decided that, should Pagro be elected, his resignation would be permanent, and this conversation with Kopek was only reinforcing that decision.

Aloud, Worf asked with surprise, "You admit this freely?"

Kopek poured himself some more brandy. "Why shouldn't I? The truth will never leave these chambers. The only way for it to do so would be for you to admit publicly that you provided the codes that enabled Picard to disable Captain Krogan's fleet at Tezwa—and you're not prepared to do that, are you?"

No, but it might be worth it just to bring you down. Again, Worf had to restrain himself from speaking the words.

Instead, he pointed to Kl'rt's body. "What of him?"

"If you check the magistrate's records, you will find that Kl'rt escaped imprisonment prior to execution and is at large. Somehow, he broke into my chambers and waited until the arrival of the Federation ambassador—against whom he had sworn revenge during his trial—before attacking both of us. Luckily, the quick-thinking ambassador was able to subdue him, thus striking a blow for justice."

Again, Worf growled. "And had Kl'rt succeeded in killing me, you would have then killed him yourself, avenging my death, and making yourself a hero of the empire—even putting Martok in your debt."

"I am *so* glad you appreciate the intricacies of my plan. Either way, I win. But then, victory is not difficult when my enemy—in this case, you—makes it *so* easy on me." Again, he swallowed all his brandy in one gulp. "Is there anything else I can do for you today, Ambassador?"

"You have done quite enough, Councillor." With that, Worf turned his back on Kopek. The insult was probably lost on the honorless *petaQ*, but under the circumstances, an insult was all Worf could really give him.

This is what it has come to, he thought as he left Kopek's derisive laughter behind. *I have kept my word to a* yIntagh *who does not deserve or appreciate it, and it has driven the Federation and the empire closer to war.* The immediate need to preserve the peace at Tezwa was fulfilled, but Worf now had to wonder if his effort to achieve peace only served to make it easier for war to come later.

Worf had deliberately saved Kopek for last on his list of councillors to visit this day, so he returned to the embassy. Until this last visit, the trip had been more or less successful. Unsurprisingly, the hardliners had not changed their position, but Worf had been able to convince the more moderate councillors to support the alliance. He wondered how Alexander did.

Upon arriving at the embassy, he was greeted in the lobby by Wu. "How did it go, sir?" He looked at the singed material on the shoulder of Worf's cassock. "Or should I even ask?"

"It went quite well, despite the damage to my clothing," Worf said, not wishing to dwell on Kopek. He filled Wu in on his progress.

"That's good to hear, sir." They entered the turbolift, which accelerated up to the second floor. "You'll be happy to know that Alexander was able to obtain the support of Grevaq, Mortran, and Qolka."

Worf shot Wu a look of surprise at that last name, even as the lift came to a halt. "Qolka?"

"Yes, sir." They exited the turbolift as the doors opened. "He seemed quite pleased with himself."

"As well he should."

"If I may say so, sir—if there is a way to make his assignment to the embassy permanent, you should attempt to find it. He has a knack for this sort of work."

Worf had been thinking much the same thing—indeed, he had entertained such thoughts as far back as the mission to Aluwna two years earlier, when Alexander had resolved a dispute. "Perhaps" was all he would say out loud. "Are there any other matters that need my immediate attention?"

As expected, Wu ascertained from Worf's phrasing that right now he wanted to deal with diplomatic matters only if absolutely necessary. "Nothing that can't wait until morning, sir."

"Good." He removed his cassock and tossed it to the floor of his office. "I will require a new cassock. Make sure all the decorations are transferred. I shall be in the gymnasium." The embassy gym was equipped with holoemitters that could generate sparring partners, and at the moment Worf felt the need to hit something very hard.

Chapter 11
U.S.S. Enterprise

"A HOLOGRAM?"

Picard regarded his first officer with surprise. The captain had specifically requested that everyone read the material Starfleet had sent them before this meeting, so the fact that Kahless had been replaced with a hologram should not have come as a shock. Riker and Troi were seated in the two chairs to Picard's immediate right, both looking rather strained. Next to them was Vale, who kept fingering the hollow pip on her collar—Picard expected her to be doing so unconsciously for at least another month; he certainly had done so every time he was promoted, though it had been over four decades since his last one. Data, La Forge, and Crusher had the seats opposite those three. At the other end of the table sat Go, quietly making notes on her padd. Picard found he was glad she was observing his crew in action. *If she's going to evaluate us, let her do so when we're actually on a mission, doing what we do best.*

"Yes, Number One, a hologram. It *was* in the mission briefing."

Riker closed his eyes. Next to him, Troi looked guilty. Suddenly, Picard understood.

"I'm sorry, sir, but Deanna and I have been a bit—preoccupied," Riker said, confirming Picard's suspicions. "Lwaxana's changed the plan."

"Again," Troi added through clenched teeth.

Squeezing his fiancée's hand, Riker said, "It's no excuse, sir, I'm sorry."

Picard held up a hand. "It's quite all right, Will. Under other circumstances, I might be less lenient, but I think almost everyone in this room is aware of what a force of nature the counselor's mother is. Suffice it to say, the Klingons' spiritual leader was replaced an indeterminate time ago by a hologram using technology that, as far as we know, is only available in the Federation." He turned to his second officer. "Mr. Data?"

Data proceeded to give an overview of the history of the mobile emitter, a piece of futuristic technology that *Voyager* had acquired during its first of several encounters with a twenty-ninth-century Federation captain named Braxton. According to Starfleet records, the *U.S.S. Excalibur* also encountered Braxton, some five years earlier in Sector 221-G. The android concluded: "It is unknown how this technology made its way to Klingon space."

Picard nodded. "Thank you, Data. Our job is to try to deduce where Kahless might be."

Riker asked, "Has anybody made any kind of ransom demand, or claimed to have taken him?"

Shaking her head, Vale said, "No, which makes it pretty damn hard to narrow the search parameters."

"We have to at least consider the possibility," Troi said, "that the emperor is dead."

"It could even be natural," Crusher said. "When I examined Kahless ten years ago, he didn't have any of the markers of the standard cloning techniques—but there are plenty of techniques that don't leave any kind of trace behind."

Picard frowned. "What are you getting at, Doctor?"

Crusher shrugged. "It's quite possible that the clone the Klingons made doesn't have much of a shelf life. And before you ask, I've already put in a request to have the records of the cloning sent over, but the High Council claims not to have them." Her tone dubious, she added, "The records were supposedly destroyed during an attack on Boreth four years ago."

La Forge shot Crusher a look. "They didn't keep backups?"

Another shrug. "If they did, they're not telling us about it. And all the people involved in Kahless's creation are dead." She snorted. "Do you know there's a song about the arrival of Kahless at Boreth? Of all the people besides Kahless named in that song, the only ones still alive are me and Worf."

Vale's eyes went wide. "*You're* part of a Klingon song? How'd you manage that?"

"I did the genetic test Gowron requested to prove that he was truly Kahless."

Shaking her head, Vale said, "It's amazing the things you find out. Four years I've been on this ship, and it's only in the last month that I find out that you dance and you got put in a Klingon song."

Crusher smiled. "I'm a woman of many talents, Christine."

"Bringing this back to the original topic," Picard said, folding his hands in front of himself, "it would seem that we have to assume Kahless is still alive. And speed is of the essence. Some ships that were en route to Tezwa to aid in their resupply were harassed by a pair of birds-of-prey. It's the third case of Klingon ships taking an aggressive posture with Starfleet vessels, complete with accusations of the Federation kidnapping their emperor. In one of those cases, another Klingon ship came to the Starfleet vessel's aid, but that does not change the fact that some Klingon captains are taking it upon themselves to retaliate."

Data then spoke up. "Sir, we are proceeding on the assumption that Kahless was replaced against his will, are we not?"

"Of course, Data. How else would we proceed?"

"In addition to perusing the files sent by Starfleet Command, I have also read everything in Starfleet's records and in the Klingon Information Net regarding Emperor Kahless in the time since Ambassador Worf discovered him on Boreth nine years, eleven months, twelve days ago. Those files have led me to a hypothesis."

Giving his second officer a small smile, Picard said, "I don't doubt it. Proceed, Mr. Data."

"The attack on Boreth that Dr. Crusher mentioned was the conclusion of a coup d'état against Chancellor Martok led publicly by a man named Morjod, but masterminded by a woman named Gothmara. Martok was able to regain the chancellorship and killed both Gothmara and Morjod, with the aid of several Klingons, among them Worf and Emperor Kahless. However, during that attack on Boreth, Kahless disappeared. He came back several months later, having gone on what humans would term a walkabout."

Riker asked, "Is it possible that the Kahless who came back was the hologram?"

"Doubtful, sir," Data said, "as his reappearance pre-dated *Voyager*'s return to the Alpha Quadrant by one year, four months, and seven days." Data turned back to Picard. "Sir, I believe it is possible that Kahless himself chose to depart, and left the hologram behind."

Vale sounded incredulous as she asked, "Why would he do that?"

Turning to face the security chief, Data said, "Although the emperor is a biological match for the original Kahless, his personality and memories all came from the stories about Kahless, both oral and written. Therefore he is a literal creation of myth and fables."

Troi nodded in what seemed to be understanding, for which Picard was grateful, because he himself wasn't seeing it. "You think," Troi said, "that he's playing out a story—with a lesson of some sort at the end of it?"

"Yes, Counselor, I am."

Picard thought back to when Kahless appeared on Boreth, and then came on board the *Enterprise*-D. *He spent most of his time telling stories—no, fables. His every sentence was spoken as an aphorism.* Aloud, he said, "Let us assume you are correct, Data—how do you suggest we proceed?"

"Based on all the stories relating to Kahless that have

become part of Klingon lore, I believe the one that is most relevant to this discussion is the story of the promise."

Riker nodded. "When Kahless said he'd return."

"Uh," La Forge said, "my Klingon history's a little rusty."

"Mine, too," Vale said.

Data folded his hands in front of himself; Picard smiled at the gesture that matched Picard's own.

"After uniting the Klingon people," Data said, "Kahless claimed that his work was done and he gathered his belongings and prepared to depart the First City. When the Klingon people entreated him to stay, claiming that they needed him, Kahless said, 'You are Klingons. You need no one but yourselves. I will go now to *Sto-Vo-Kor,* but I promise one day I will return.' Kahless then pointed to the star that orbits Boreth and said, 'Look for me there, on that point of light.' "

Riker asked, "You don't think he's returned to Boreth, do you?"

Before Data could answer, Picard said, "That was the first place the Klingons looked. However, according to the report from Commander Logt, who is in charge of the emperor's personal guard on Boreth, they did not know he was a hologram." The report made no mention of Logt's current status, but Picard would not have been surprised to learn that the commander had been killed for her inefficiency. *Such a waste,* he thought. There was much about the Klingon culture he admired, but their casual use of death as a disciplinary tool was not one of those things.

Looking at Data, Troi asked, "So what are you suggesting, Data?"

At that, Data rose and walked to the viewscreen that took up the wall opposite the window. The android touched a control, and the screen lit up with a star map. "Kahless's promise occurred approximately fifteen centuries ago. I instructed the computer to account for stellar drift during that time, and to approximate which star would be at the same point in the night sky over the First City today that Boreth was one thousand five hundred years ago."

Picard watched as the image on the screen showed the Klingons' home system on the right-hand side of the graphic, with Boreth on the left. Some of the stars located near them were also indicated, such as No'Mat, Alhena, and Gamma Eridon.

"Because the exact date of Kahless's departure is unknown," Data said, touching another control, "a precise match was not possible." The image enlarged, with Qo'noS remaining on the right, but with the left-hand side expanding past the Klingon border and showing two more suns. "However, two stars in Federation space might qualify: Davlos and Cygnet. Either one could be in the same spot in the night sky now as Boreth's home sun was in Kahless's time."

Smiling, Riker said, "It's certainly worth a shot."

"Agreed." Picard sat up and straightened his uniform jacket. "Set a course for the Davlos system, Number One, maximum warp. Commander Vale, inform Admiral Janeway at Starfleet Command of our heading."

Both Riker and Vale said, "Yes, sir," as everyone save the two captains headed for the bridge.

To Data's retreating form, Picard said, "Well done, Mr. Data."

Stopping and turning, Data said, "Thank you, sir."

A moment later, only Picard and Go were left in the observation lounge.

Go, still seated, looked up at Picard. "That's quite an officer you have there."

"If you mean Mr. Data, I was already aware of that, Captain. It's why I was willing to trust his judgment at Rashanar. If only those at Starfleet Command were able to do so a year ago, we might not even need you here today."

"Quite possibly, yes." Go looked up at Picard. "Captain, you've been nothing but professional during this inspection, and you've been completely cooperative, but there's been an undercurrent of annoyance every time you and I have spoken. What you just said made that more of an overcurrent. I take it you have a problem with my presence here?"

Picard hadn't wanted to say anything, but Go had asked a direct question, and he *did* promise to answer all her questions. So he decided to put all his cards on the table. "You personally? No, though I question the wisdom of your being assigned to this tour. The stated purpose of this inspection is to assure Starfleet Command that officers who fought in a war can adjust to a time of peace. But I was a Starfleet captain for decades prior to the war, and my staff have proven themselves time and again in both war *and* peace. The *Enterprise* would not, on the face of it, appear to fall within purview of this tour."

Go tapped the side of her padd for several seconds before responding. "If I had been given this assignment a year ago, I'd agree with your assessment that I was unfit for it. It's a good thing you and I didn't meet then, Captain, because I don't think I would want to be held responsible for my actions. Jill Leeden was my best friend. She was maid of honor at my wedding. I read the eulogy at her brother's funeral. We've been through hell and back together, and when they told me that you were responsible for her death . . ." Go trailed off.

Picard found himself remembering the first time he met Benjamin Sisko a decade earlier at Deep Space 9. Sisko had lost his wife in the battle at Wolf 359, a battle that was directed by Picard when he had been assimilated by the Borg and made into the creature Locutus. Although Sisko did eventually forgive Picard, the waves of hatred emanating off the younger man at that first meeting had hit Picard like a slap. He imagined that, had he encountered Wai-Lin Go a year ago, the situation would have been similar.

And I doubt I would've been able to entirely blame Go any more than I blamed Sisko.

Go finally spoke again. "I take this uniform very seriously, Captain. When I'm asked to do a job, I do it. Admiral Nakamura instructed me to lead an inspection of the *Enterprise* and to evaluate the performance of the ship and its crew since Rashanar." She took a breath. "You're right to question my placement here. The admiral knows damn well how close Jill and I were, and I'm willing to bet he was counting on that. But I do my job, Captain, and I can assure you that my personal feelings will not get in the way of my evaluation."

With that, Go stood up.

Picard stared at her for a moment, then said, "Captain, if I may ask—why haven't you questioned me or anyone else about Rashanar itself?"

"Several reasons," Go said. "For one thing, that ground was pretty well covered in the inquiry after the fact. For another, I'm not sure I could maintain the professional objectivity I'm so proud of if I delved into that." Then Go favored Picard with a small smile. "And my orders from the admiral were to evaluate the *Enterprise*'s performance *since* Rashanar. When I'm asked to do a job, I do it, and Rashanar does not fall within purview of this tour."

At once, Picard was both annoyed and relieved. The former because he had allowed himself to jump to conclusions about this woman before she even came on board, based in part on the way the admiralty had treated him after Rashanar. The latter because those conclusions were obviously unfounded. "Thank you, Captain."

"You're welcome, Captain. Now, if you'll excuse me, I have a report to write—and you have an emperor to find." With that, Go turned and took her leave.

Smiling, Picard went to the other door and returned to the bridge.

In the beginning, Riker and Troi's wedding was to be a ceremony in the chapel in the capital city. Since it was where they had first met, it had a symbolism that appealed to both Lwaxana and to the couple.

Then the guest list grew to a number that the chapel simply could not accommodate, so the venue was changed to the spacious grounds behind Lwaxana's new house.

Then she decided that the grounds weren't spacious enough, so she reserved a park near Lake Cataria.

Then she realized that the weather this time of year was such that an outdoor wedding was impractical, so she reserved Amick Hall. Named after one of the Betazoids who died in the fight to drive the Dominion off the planet during the war, it was built on the site of Byram Hall, the place where Lwaxana and Ian Troi were married, which was destroyed when the Dominion took Betazed.

Then she added a hundred *more* names to the guest list, and even Amick Hall was no longer large enough, so she altered the day's events so that there would be a before-wedding party on Lake Cataria, with the actual wedding—with a different list of guests—to be held at Amick Hall.

Now, two hours after the *Enterprise* left the Davlos system, Riker was ready to commit an act of matricide. *All right, she isn't even my mother-in-law yet. What do you call it when you murder your fiancée's mom?* The endless amendments to the ceremony were getting beyond tiresome.

He had tried to lose himself in the mission, but there was no joy there, either. Davlos proved an easy system to eliminate as Kahless's location, as it had no Class-M worlds. Three planets were inhabited, but all the sentient life was located within easily scanned atmospheric domes. The only Klingon they found was a patron in a bar on Davlos VI, and he turned out to be the supervisor of an independent mining team.

As the *Enterprise* warped its way to the Cygnet system, Vale looked down at her status board and then at Riker and Troi. "Commander, you and Counselor Troi have *another* mess—"

Before Vale could even finish, Troi said, "Not my mother *again?*" Her voice sounded to Riker like a plaintive wail.

"Afraid so, Counselor. I'm really sorry."

"It's not your fault," Troi said with a sigh.

"Oh, I know it isn't," Vale said. "I'm sorry because I had 1700 in the pool."

Picard turned to look back at Vale. "A pool?"

Suddenly nervous, Vale said, "Uh, yes, sir. Captain Scott put up a bottle of single-barrel scotch as the prize. I think Ensign Hoang was the one who picked 1640."

"I see." Picard turned back around with a neutral expression on his face.

I'm glad somebody's *getting some entertainment out of this,* Riker thought. He wished he'd known about the pool, as he might well have chosen 1640 hours, and right now he really felt like he could use a good stiff drink. *On the other hand, maybe Hoang can use it on her next date with Studdard.*

Turning to his left, he asked, "Captain, can we use your ready room?" To Riker's chagrin, his voice sounded strained and irritated, the very qualities he was trying to keep out of it.

"Of course, Number One."

"Thank you." Looking over at Vale as he and Troi rose, Riker said, "Pipe it in there, Commander."

"Yes, sir."

As soon as the doors closed behind them, Troi turned to Riker and said, "You're upset."

"I'm gonna go out on a limb and assume you didn't need your empathy to pick up on that one."

She smirked. "Good guess. Look, Will, I know my mother is micromanaging this thing, but it's very important to her—"

"Deanna, I had no problem with having your mother run the ceremony on Betazed—when it was just a few dozen people in the chapel where we met. But this is getting out of control. This is supposed to be *our* wedding, not her look-my-daughter's-finally-getting-married party."

"I'm sorry you feel that way, William."

Oh, damn, Riker thought, looking over to see that the viewer on Picard's desk had raised out of its slot. *Of course, I told Vale to pipe it in here, so of course the channel's already open. I'm an idiot.*

Troi had the same stricken look on her face that Riker imagined was on his own. However, she recovered quickly, touched the control that rotated the viewer so they could see it from the two guest chairs, in which they each sat. "Mother, he has a point. I understand how important this is for you, but—"

"But enough is enough," Riker said.

"Will . . ." Troi said with an undercurrent of menace, but Riker refused to be intimidated.

"Of all the unmitigated gall—"

At that, Riker stood up, putting a hand to his chest. "You're saying *I* have unmitigated gall? This is my *wedding.* This is the most important day of my life. I watched my father step into a disruptor blast meant for me and then die in my arms. I sat in a pit on Tezwa that was less than two meters long for *weeks,* with my hands and ankles bound. The *only* thing that got me through those things was knowing that I'd be with Deanna at the end of it. So yeah, I have the unmitigated gall to tell you to go to hell, Lwaxana. We are getting married on Earth in Alaska in the Denali Mountains. You and whoever your valet-du-jour is are welcome to join us."

"How dare you speak to me that way! I am a Daughter of the Fif—"

"I don't care if you're a Daughter of the American Revolution or a member of the Order of the *Bat'leth*," Riker snapped. "That's what we're doing."

Troi snapped right back, "Will, that's enough!"

"You—"

"You too, Mother," Troi said, whirling on the viewer. "Both of you calm down."

"Little One, I'm the picture of calm. It's William who's not being—"

"You're *both* behaving like idiots, and I'm not going to stand for it anymore."

Riker, who was still standing, looked down at Troi. "Deanna, that's not fair, I—"

"Not fair? You're the one who just unilaterally decided we were getting married in Alaska. Were you planning to consult me on this decision?"

Abashed, Riker sat back down and put his hand on Troi's. "Deanna, I thought that's what you—"

"No, you didn't—think, that is." She turned to the viewer. "And as for *you*, Mother, I'm amazed you didn't simply invite the entire population of the Federation and have done with it. You haven't been thinking either—or, rather, you have been, but only about yourself."

"Little One, that's hardly fair. I just want what's best for you."

Glowering at the viewer, Riker said, "So do I."

Troi smiled sweetly. "Good. Then here's what we're

going to do. Will, you're going to reserve the spot in the Denali Mountains."

"But Deanna, I—"

"Thank you," Riker interrupted, feeling triumphant.

"As for you, Mother, you're going to continue making arrangements on Betazed."

Riker's triumphant feeling fled. "What?"

"What?" Lwaxana parroted. *"Deanna, I—I don't understand."*

"Simple—we're going to have two ceremonies. It's a common enough practice in mixed marriages. First we'll get married on Earth, and then we'll do it again on Betazed."

Riker blinked. He opened his mouth, then closed it, then opened it again, then closed it again. He blinked a few more times. Finally, he managed to say, "Why didn't I think of that?"

"Don't be so hard on yourself, dear—I didn't think of it, either." Lwaxana spoke in as close to a contrite tone as she was ever likely to adopt. *"Can you both accept the apologies of an old woman who let herself get carried away?"*

Troi smiled so widely, her perfect cheekbones crinkled up to her lovely black eyes. "There's nothing to apologize for, Mother. You were simply being you."

"Well, who better?" Lwaxana also smiled. *"The funny thing is, the reason why I called is to say that I wanted to add an after-ceremony party at the house, just for close family and friends, plus a few people I forgot about that need to go on the guest list, and so—"*

Riker grabbed Troi's hand and squeezed it. "Lwaxana, do whatever you need to do. We'll just show up, strip, and get married."

Lwaxana let out what sounded like a sigh of content-ment. *"Of course, Little Ones. I'll see you in a few weeks on Betazed, then."*

"Of that, you can rest assured, Mother."

With that, Lwaxana signed off.

Riker stared at Troi. "So is she gonna start calling *me* 'Little One' now?"

"Apparently."

Shaking his head, Riker stood up, pulling Troi into a hug. "So I get to go from Number One to Little One—both from people shorter than me."

"You'll live." She looked up at him. "You know, when I said I needed help getting past my anger at Minza, I didn't mean for you to get angry instead of me."

Riker laughed. "Yeah, sorry about that. I guess I just let your mother get to me. I just can't believe we didn't think of doing two ceremonies sooner."

"I can. We just wanted to keep things simple—two cere-monies belie that, as does what Mother is doing." She smiled, and Riker felt his heart melt, as it always did when she favored him with the expression. "But it doesn't mat-ter. Like you said, as long as we're married at the end of it, I don't care how we do it—or how many times we do it."

Rather than respond verbally, Riker kissed her pas-sionately.

When they broke the kiss several joyous eternities later, Troi stroked his beard and said in a small voice, "Yuck."

"I'm *not* shaving the beard again, Deanna."

Troi shrugged. "That's your choice—just as it's mine to say, 'yuck.' "

"Suit yourself, Counselor." He broke their embrace

and indicated the ready-room door. "Shall we get back to the business of finding lost emperors?"

"After you, Little One," she said with a smirk.

The red-hued river flowed down from the distant mountain, its current splashing regularly against the black rocks.

When he first came to this world, he had heard about the crimson rivers, and he had assumed that they would look like blood, but they didn't. This one in particular looked more like a ruby given liquid form.

As he stood before the mighty river, the yellow grass staining his boots, he marveled at the natural beauty, which, he was told by the natives, had remained unchanged for countless millennia.

He had memories of standing near a similar river by a volcano, at which he forged a mighty weapon. But that memory was false, implanted within his mind by those who would use him for their own ends.

For a time, he was content to let them do so, for his own desires matched theirs. *Was it because they programmed those desires into me? Perhaps. But ultimately, it did not matter. I did what I was compelled to do, and I was happy to do it.*

Reaching into the large satchel he had carried with him to the riverbank, he pulled out the easel, canvas, paints, and brushes. His landscapes had improved in recent weeks—indeed, they hardly could have gotten worse. Those who made him did not feel the need to provide him with any artistic ability, but he *was* a living creature, capable of learning and adapting. After several false starts, and dozens of truly abysmal landscapes, he finally was getting the hang of painting. It was a most soothing and—now that he was actually starting to approach competent—satisfying way to pass the time.

The process fascinated him. He began with an empty canvas. Initially, the process was laborious and irritating. The smell of the fresh paint overpowered the natural scents beyond. Worse, there was always the vexing process of where to start: the river? the large tree to the right? the smaller one to the left? the sun? the mountain? the sky? the grass? the *fortra* bush? Then there was the matter of color, finding the right blends of the too-bright red and the black to capture the look of the river, and also mixing the red with the yellow to properly illustrate the sunlight.

With each stroke, he became more confident. With each portion of the landscape complete, he felt more satisfied. This day was different from all the others. The lack of clouds meant the sun was brighter than usual; the river flowed more intensely thanks to the warmer weather melting the snow on the mountain; and this was the one day a year that *fortra* flowers went into full bloom. He did not know if he had enough colors in his palette to properly do the flowers justice.

But he would try. This was a day he wished to preserve.

He dabbed the last of the red-mixed-with-black on the lower-left-hand corner of the canvas, finally completing the river. Although he was not altogether happy with the way he rendered the water splashing on the rocks, he was mostly satisfied with how it looked.

The question before him now was what to do next, the tree or the flowers. The flowers were a bit intimidating, as they had several colors in a small space. But then, the challenge was part of the fun.

Before he could make the decision, however, he heard the sound of a transporter effect—specifically a Federation one.

How disappointing.

He turned around to see three figures in Starfleet uniforms. He recognized two of them as William Riker and the android named Data. The third was a woman he did not know. All three were armed, but they had their phasers holstered.

"Emperor Kahless?" Riker said as he approached him.

"That is the name I generally answer to, yes."

"And it's really you?"

"Yes, I am truly the clone of Kahless, the one who was created on Boreth and placed on the throne. And I am *not* a hologram, unlike the person who has occupied the throne these past six months."

Cautiously, Riker said, "So you know about that."

"Of course. I was the one who, with the help of some friends, created the hologram."

"Friends?" Riker asked.

"Yes. I am sure that Imperial Intelligence will go to great lengths to try to determine who those friends are. But being an emperor does not merely buy friendship— it buys discreet friendship."

"I see," Riker said, though he clearly didn't. "If you don't mind my asking—what're you doing *here?*"

Kahless smiled. "I am doing whatever I want, Commander. It is a very welcome change."

Chapter 12
Qo'noS

MARTOK, SON OF URTHOG, did not consider himself to be of a sadistic bent. Yes, he would and could kill without hesitation or mercy, but only in battle or on the hunt. He never did so simply for the pleasure of inflicting violence.

Now, however, he strongly felt the urge to inflict pain on whichever being, sentient or otherwise, presented itself as he stood behind the desk of his personal chambers in the Great Hall. Also present, standing around his office, were Worf, Worf's son, Picard, Picard's first and second officers, and the focal point of Martok's rage, the real Kahless. Or, rather, the real clone of Kahless. *With so many copies of copies, it's a wonder I don't go mad. At least this one is flesh and blood.*

When he'd received the communiqué from the *Enterprise* that they'd found Kahless, and that the deception was of the emperor's own doing, the chancellor abandoned his original plan of welcoming him home in front of the entire High Council. He would confront Kahless personally before dealing with him in an open council session. He also asked Picard and his seniormost officers to beam down with Kahless; Picard, in turn, insisted that the Federation ambassador be present, a condition which Martok naturally had no difficulties with.

Glowering at the emperor with his one good eye, Martok channeled all his rage, all his anger, all his frustration into one word, spoken in a low, rumbling voice: "Why?"

"That is a complex question you ask, Martok. It is at the heart—"

Wincing and waving his arm in front of his face, Martok said, "Do *not* ply me with your tiresome aphorisms! It is not a complex question, it is a simple one. *Why* did you replace yourself with a hologram and go to Cygnet IV to pick flowers?"

Picard's android spoke up. "Actually, Kahless was painting landscapes when the away team made contact with him."

"Thank you, Commander," Martok said witheringly, and marveled at Picard's patience for not having this babbling creature disassembled.

Kahless said, "My reason was simple, Martok. I replaced myself with a holographic duplicate to see how long it would take you to notice."

It became all the more difficult for Martok to restrain himself. Bile rose in his throat from the fury, tasting of that morning's *jInjoq* bread. "This was a *game* to you? Our nations are on the brink of *war* because of your foolishness!"

"If that were so, I would offer my life up in exchange for dishonoring you and the empire with my actions— but it is not so, and you are fully aware of this fact."

Kahless started to pace Martok's chambers, indicating Picard and his first officer with one hand. "I have spoken at length with Captain Picard and Commander Riker. They have informed me of the planet Tezwa, and of the seizing of the Federation embassy. *Those* are the events that have led to this state of affairs, *not* my deception."

Worf said, "And yet, at least one of those events occurred *because* of you." At the questioning glances of the others in the room, including Martok, Worf added, "The members of the terrorist group who seized the embassy did so in part because they obtained the knowledge that you had been replaced with a hologram."

"Perhaps. But it no longer matters, for the point has been proven."

Baring his teeth, Martok asked, "And what point might *that* be?"

"That my time has ended." Kahless turned to look at Worf. "When I first appeared before you on Boreth," he said, then turned to Picard and added, "and rode on your ship, I was told many times of how decadent the empire had become, and how I was desperately needed. And, after I became emperor, I saw that those words were true. The empire was divided by petty concerns and strayed from the path of honor." He looked back at Martok. "But that was ten years ago. Few things in this life are sureties, but one thing that never changes is that things will change."

Martok felt a growl build in his throat. "Another of your tiresome aphorisms."

"Actually," the android said, "that particular tiresome aphorism was not originally from Kahless, but from the

Andorian philosopher Chasinthrof zh'Mai, from her book *New Sun, Old Sun.*"

This time, Martok felt less of an urge to rip the android to pieces. "Interesting. You've expanded your repertory of idiotic truisms, then, Excellency?"

"The point, Martok, is that the empire of today is not the same empire that was in sufficient disarray to lead Koroth and the others on Boreth to have me created. We have fought a great war against a mighty enemy and emerged triumphant. We have defeated all those who would oppose the path to honor, from Gothmara and Morjod to the Elabrej. We have restored the Sword of Kahless to its rightful place and the Order of the *Bat'leth* to its rightful purpose." He looked at the others. "And we have a chancellor who does not put politics before honor." Regarding Martok once more, he said, "If you wish a truism, Martok, then here is one: I am no longer necessary."

Worf stepped forward. "Kahless, with all due respect, your work is not done."

Reaching up to put a hand on the ambassador's shoulder, the emperor said, "Worf, my good friend, I could live a thousand lifetimes, and the work for which I was created would not be finished." Again, staring at Martok, Kahless said, "But our people needed a spiritual leader because the political power was in the hands of creatures to whom honor was at best a convenience, to be used or not at whim. Now, though, the High Council leads the way to honor, it leads the way to glory—and I am not needed."

"Not needed?" Martok's shout echoed off the walls of his chambers. "The alliance with the Federation is hanging by a thread. I have acquired more enemies on the

High Council than I thought was possible to accumulate in four years. I have been forced to appoint a Federation ambassador who wants war almost as much as that special emissary who is attempting to win the Federation presidency. The—"

Kahless chuckled. Martok cut off his diatribe and had to use all his willpower to keep himself from strangling the emperor right there. *If all these witnesses were not here, willpower might not be enough.*

In a low voice, Martok slowly asked, "What is so funny?"

"You speak of *politics,* Martok. There will *always* be politics. But I was needed because politics had become more important than honor, and I think that even you must admit that that is no longer the case."

Picard said, "Such things are cyclical, Emperor."

"All things are cyclical, Captain. And if that cycle comes around to a point where I am needed again, then so be it."

Silence then blanketed the office. Emotions roiled within Martok's gut. His throat had gone dry, and he was desperate for a mug of bloodwine, but he could not drink now without offering the same to his guests, and he did not have a sufficient quantity for the task.

While the chancellor was flattered that Kahless considered him a strong enough leader that he made the emperor's own function irrelevant, he did not appreciate being lied to or being a puppet in someone else's game. He had enough of those feelings during the final days of the war. Gowron's egotistical need to dishonor Martok as a means of dimming the latter's popularity dictated his tactics against the Dominion, leading Worf to challenge him and install Martok as chancellor when he was victorious. Even now, four years later, he sometimes felt like a puppet on other people's strings—the very thing Rov and his *Klahb* fools accused him of being.

Now Kahless was doing it again.

It was Riker who broke the silence. "What will you do now, Emperor?"

"My intention, Commander, is to return to the glade where you came upon me." He smiled. "I have not yet completed the landscape."

"That's it?" Riker asked. "Just go back, and leave the empire without their emperor?"

"Millennia ago, the original Kahless united the Klingon people. When that work was done, he gathered his belongings and went to the edge of the city to depart. The people pleaded, saying they needed Kahless. But he said—"

" 'You are Klingons. You need no one but yourselves.' " Martok, Worf, and even Alexander said the words. It was from the Story of the Promise, a tale every Klingon was told practically from birth. Martok had few memories of his very difficult childhood that he could truly call happy, but one such was when his father told him many stories of Kahless on their first hunt together in the Ketha Lowlands. The hunting itself was poor, and the weather awful, but he still recalled old Urthog telling him stories all the night long, ending with the Story of the Promise.

"Those words," Kahless said, "are as true today as when they were first spoken. Kahless left you then, and you flourished. I will leave you now, and I have no doubt that you will still flourish."

Snarling, Martok asked, "And what are we to tell the

people? I will not lie to them, but we *cannot* tell them the truth."

Picard said, "The wisest move, Chancellor, would be to do neither. Condemn Rov and his terrorists as madmen, but neither confirm nor deny that Kahless has been a hologram for six months."

"I will also address the people one final time," Kahless said. "I will tell them what I have just told you—that it is time for me to once again leave our people. If I am needed again, I will return." He grinned. "Or perhaps the true Kahless will."

Martok shook his head. "I hope you are correct, Excellency."

"Hope is the first step on the road to victory."

"That," the android said, "*is* one of Kahless's tiresome aphorisms."

Unable to stop himself, Martok burst out laughing. "Indeed it is, Commander, indeed it is. Very well, Excellency, if that is truly what you wish, it shall be done. You will address the people immediately—I will have no more accusations against our allies, nor will I let the empire be governed by rumor and supposition. You will participate in the *vIt 'Iw tay.*"

Picard and Riker both frowned. The former said, "I'm not familiar with that ritual."

Before Martok could explain, the android said, "The *vIt 'Iw tay* is a ceremony whereby a being whose biological origins are in doubt is cut by at least six different warriors with their respective *d'k tahg*s in order to prove that the being is truly a Klingon. The ritual was created by the High Council shortly after Imperial Intelligence began surgically altering deep-cover agents to infiltrate the empire's enemies. The council at the time feared that the tactic might be used against them, and so created the *vIt 'Iw tay.*"

Riker smirked. "I'll bet that ritual was popular after we made contact with the Dominion."

Martok licked his teeth. "No Founders were discovered that way, though many who were accused of being changelings were forced to participate." Unbidden, the memories of being captured by the Dominion and put in a prison camp while a shapeshifting slime devil took his place as Gowron's chief of staff returned to Martok. Shaking them off, he turned back to Kahless. "You will do this in open council with myself, three councillors, Captain Wovogh, and a commoner whom we will choose at random." Wovogh was the first officer to one of the captains who fired upon the Starfleet supply ships near Tezwa. That captain was put to death for his effrontery and Wovogh promoted; Martok felt it important to have someone from one of the ships that believed the Federation had taken their emperor participate in the *vIt 'Iw tay.*

Nodding, Kahless said, "Of course."

"Good." Martok was about to declare the meeting ended when Alexander stepped forward.

"Excellency, can I ask you something—please?"

"Of course, Alexander. Questions are, after all, the beginning of wisdom."

Yet another aphorism, Martok thought, shaking his head, stunned that the android hadn't provided a full citation for it.

"Actually, it's the same question the chancellor asked before: Why?"

"I gave my reasons for what I did." Kahless sounded confused, which matched Martok's own feelings. *Wasn't the boy paying attention?*

"No, sir, you gave *some* reasons—and they're good ones, and I'm sure it's the best way to sell this to the people. But I want to know the *real* reason." He pointed to his chest. "The one in here."

Kahless threw his head back and laughed. "As ever, the son is but a smaller version of the father. Like him, Alexander, you use your words to cut directly into the heart without need for a blade."

Worf said, "So there *is* another reason."

"Yes, Worf, there is."

This, Martok thought, *should be interesting.*

"I have grown weary of doing what I am supposed to do. I have served my purpose, and I have done my duty. Now is the time for me to be selfish. Now is the time for me to find my own path, not the path that the clonemakers of Boreth mapped out in my genetic structure. As I told Commander Riker on Cygnet IV, it is time I did what *I* wanted."

Alexander grinned. "That's kind of what I thought."

"If we are quite finished baring our souls," Martok said impatiently, "it is time we restored a bit of order to the empire."

"Indeed it is, Chancellor," Picard said. "With your permission, we'll remain in orbit of Qo'noS until the emperor has concluded his business here. Then we shall take him wherever he wishes to go."

Martok considered the captain's words. "Your offer is

appreciated, Captain, and you may remain in orbit as long as you wish—but I think it would be best if a Defense Force vessel bring the emperor to his new home."

"Why not both?" Alexander asked.

Martok frowned. "I do not understand."

"My son is correct," Worf said. "It would be a more potent symbol if both the *Enterprise* and a Klingon ship—preferably a *Chancellor*-class vessel—escort Kahless together, as a sign of unity between our people."

Unable to find a good argument against the suggestion, Martok said, "Very well. I believe the *Ditagh* is within the system. I will have Captain Vikagh report here immediately."

"Grand," Picard said.

Martok moved around from behind his desk toward the door. "Let us proceed, then."

"It is the end of an era, Martok," Kahless said, "but the beginning of a greater one, I think."

Shaking his head as he approached the door, Martok said, "Somehow, Excellency, I knew you would not let this meeting end without one final aphorism."

Chapter 13
Sarona VIII

ESPERANZA PIÑIERO SAT nursing a cobalt soda in the Blue Parrot Café, wondering if Jas Abrik was actually going to show up.

The election had begun, a laborious process involving the entirety of the Federation—all the worlds, stations, and spacefaring vessels that were part of it. The sheer number of votes to be tabulated over interstellar distances, as well as the complicated oversight, meant it would take a week for all the votes to be tallied, counted, verified, and announced.

From this point forward, both the Bacco and Pagro campaigns, which had worked tirelessly for the past three weeks, had nothing to do but wait.

And speculate. We're doing plenty of that.

The governor's last campaign stop had been on Pacifica, and she was now en route back to Cestus III to await the results and probably to get some sleep. Piñiero hoped that said sleep would finally be free of dreams.

She knew that Bacco's restless nights were due primarily to the stress of the campaign, and she hoped that next week, regardless of whether she was the new president or the old governor, the dreams would abate. *She deserves better than that after all she's accomplished.*

Abrik had said that he would meet with her here on the eighth planet in the Sarona system at 1500 hours, but that was half an hour ago. She had never met the man during the time when they both were in Starfleet, but from what she knew of him, he was always punctual. *Let's face it, Esperanza, if he's this late, it means he probably isn't coming.*

Her seat was near the door. Its location notwithstanding, it was one of the more private booths in the place, thanks to the café's peculiar architecture. The Blue Parrot was built in the shape of the Saronan emblem, which was a dodecahedron that was vaguely crescent-shaped. In practical terms, it gave the place a labyrinthine feel, but it was one that made it ideal for private conversations.

Assuming, of course, that the other half of that conversation deigns to turn up.

Even if the architecture hadn't favored privacy, the booth would have served Piñiero's purpose nicely, as the midafternoon crowd was sparse—it was late for lunch and early for dinner. The Blue Parrot generally catered to visitors to the nearby conference center, but there were no events there at the moment.

She finished off her soda, and started debating the merits of ordering another versus giving up and leaving when she heard the familiar whine of a transporter, meaning someone was arriving via the station in the lobby.

To her surprise and relief, Jas Abrik then entered the main part of the café.

"Sorry I'm late," the old Trill said as he sat down in the booth opposite Piñiero. "The transport I was taking here got diverted."

"Not a problem," Piñiero said, glad to see that Abrik's reputation remained unscathed.

A Saronan server approached. "What may I bring you?"

Holding up her empty glass, Piñiero said, "Another cobalt soda, please."

"An *allira* punch, if you've got it," Abrik said.

Bowing, the Saronan said, "Of course." She took Piñiero's glass and departed.

"Thanks for coming, Admiral."

Abrik made a dismissive noise. "Please don't call me 'Admiral,' Commander. I *left* Starfleet."

Smiling sweetly, Piñiero said, "Then don't call me 'Commander,' since I haven't been one for three years."

"Can we get to the point, please?" Abrik shifted uncomfortably in his seat.

He doesn't want to be here, Piñiero thought. *I wonder why he bothered to show up, then.* "You have access to the same polling data I do, so you know that there's a pretty good chance that Nan Bacco's going to be the next president."

Abrik snapped, "In your dreams, *Commander.* The votes haven't been tallied yet."

"You're right, they haven't. But the FNS's exit polls are predicting that the governor will be the winner. Do you know when the last time the FNS's exit polls made a wrong prediction was?"

Frowning, Abrik said, "No, actually."

"Neither do I. That's because such a time doesn't exist. They've *never* not called an election at this stage."

"There's a first time for everything."

Piñiero nodded. "True. After all, this was the first time that a Federation president resigned without warning. And you and I both know the real reason for that resignation, don't we?"

Abrik stared at Piñiero for several seconds. For her part, Piñiero held her breath. She wasn't entirely sure that Abrik knew the truth about Zife and Azernal arming the Tezwans, but she couldn't believe that Abrik—a longtime admiral whose departure from Starfleet was more recent than her own—couldn't have found out something that Piñiero herself could learn, even if her own method of obtaining the information was a direct result of Admiral Upton's libido.

The Saronan returned with their drinks, which gave Abrik a few moments to compose an answer. *And,* Piñiero thought, *he's definitely composing an answer. His eyes are darting back and forth like crazy.* She took a sip of her cobalt soda, the electric tingle of the blue-hued drink tickling her tongue.

After the Saronan left and Abrik took a swig of his punch, he finally said, "Assuming I know what you're talking about—"

Paydirt, Piñiero thought. Nobody started a sentence like that unless they really did know what you were talking about. "You do, *Admiral,* so don't insult my intelligence by pretending you don't. Regardless of who wins, you're going to reveal what you know about Tezwa."

"Not if I don't have to. But the Klingons *have* to be

stopped, and we can't call ourselves a truly free society if we're going to let this kind of thing go on. Yes, it'll give the Federation a black eye, but it'll be worth it to—"

"Start another war?" At Piñiero's words, Abrik recoiled as if she'd hit him. Pressing her advantage, she continued: "Because that's what's going to happen if you let this out. The Klingons will—quite justifiably, I might add—go supernova on us."

Glaring at her, Abrik said, "So, what—I'm supposed to sit on this?"

"You have for this long, and I think that's because you know damn well that this is way too incendiary to let out."

Abrik clenched his fists. Piñiero tensed.

Then Abrik unclenched them, let out a long breath, and almost seemed to deflate. His posture went out the window, and he all but slumped over his punch, staring at the liquid for several seconds.

When he looked back up at Piñiero, he looked defeated. "You mind telling me something, Esperanza?"

Encouraged by the sudden familiarity, she said, "Don't mind a bit, Jas."

"Where the hell did you *find* that woman?"

Piñiero couldn't help but laugh. "I didn't need to find her. My parents were two of the governor's closest friends, so I've literally known her all my life."

Shaking his head, Abrik said, "She's quite a woman. I figured she'd give us a good run for our money, but that she'd never be able to play on the big stage. I couldn't have been more wrong. Fel's still in shock from the first debate."

"She really did kick his ass all over the moon, didn't she?"

"Not at first." He picked up the glass and started whirling the punch around in it. "He had it pretty much in the bag, and then—I don't know what happened, it's like she threw a switch, and we've been on the defensive ever since."

"That's what she does," Piñiero said. "She adapts. No matter what life has thrown at her, she's faced it head-on. Sometimes it takes her a little while to readjust, but she does it, and comes out swinging."

That elicited a snort. "I see she's got you doing those sports metaphors, too."

"Occupational hazard." Piñiero took another sip of her soda, and decided to confide a bit in him. "Honestly, I misuse the references around her, just to get her goat."

"That's good—I mean, it's good that you have that kind of relationship. Builds trust."

Piñiero took that to mean that Abrik and Pagro *didn't* have that kind of relationship. *Then again, it's not like it's necessary to do the job.*

He went on. "And she's certainly had her share of adversity—the refugees, the war." Then he gave her a significant look. "Her ex-husband."

Letting out a sigh, Piñiero said, "I was wondering if you knew about that."

"I didn't just fall out of the cargo ship, Esperanza—of *course* I knew about it."

"We were really worried about whether or not you'd use it against us."

Abrik winced. "We thought about it, honestly, but—" He hesitated. "Well, in the beginning, we didn't think you were a big enough threat to warrant it. Later, we just figured it would come across as petty and irrelevant. And it is. I don't like to run that kind of campaign if I can avoid it, and we wouldn't have scored enough points with it to be worth it."

"Speaking of things that are worth it, I need to ask you something you haven't answered yet." Piñiero took a sip of her soda by way of strengthening her resolve. "Do you intend to reveal what you know about Tezwa?"

"I still haven't decided yet. I don't think this is something that should remain a secret."

Piñiero cursed to herself. *Just as I was starting to like the guy.* "Even though it will guarantee a war?"

Abrik's glower returned full force. "A hundred and forty-seven years ago, a Tholian vessel and a Starfleet ship got into a firefight in the Corwin system. That guaranteed a war, but the Tholians retreated into their territory. A hundred and thirteen years ago, a Romulan bird-of-prey destroyed half a dozen outposts along the Neutral Zone. That guaranteed a war, but cooler heads prevailed once the Romulan ship was destroyed. That same year, the Federation and the Klingon Empire had half a dozen border disputes. That guaranteed a war, but the Organians intervened. Fifteen years later, a Klingon captain tried to steal the Genesis device. That guaranteed a war, yet, once again, cooler heads prevailed. Eighty-six years ago, Starfleet personnel assassinated Chancellor Gorkon. That guaranteed a war, but we signed the Khitomer Accords instead. Sixty-eight years ago, the Tomed incident claimed thousands of lives. That guaranteed a war, but we signed the Treaty of Algeron instead."

Before Abrik could pull out another example of averted warfare, Piñiero said, "Seven years ago, the Klingons invaded Cardassia and pulled out of the Khitomer Accords. *That* guaranteed a war too, and you know what? We fought it, for over a year, and the only reason we stopped is because Cardassia joined the Dominion. And *that* just led to a much bigger war, one we're *still* trying to recover from. How about the Cardassian War, which happened despite the best efforts of the Diplomatic Corps to normalize relations with them? How about the Tzenkethi War?"

Abrik continued to glower, but said nothing.

Neither did Piñiero. *He's not going to back off on this unless I give him something,* she thought. She had been afraid that it would come to this, but she was truly hoping it wouldn't, especially since she hadn't discussed this with the governor or anyone else yet. *Helga will have a fit, especially since she wants Ross for this. For that matter, so does the governor.*

She took a sip of her soda. *Well, tough. Desperate times call for doing something really crazy.*

Finally, she said, "Tell me something, Jas—let's say Pagro wins. What's next for you?"

"A position on his staff, of course," Abrik said as if it was the most obvious thing in the world. "I got into this thing so I could help shape policy."

"All right, then, how'd you like to have that chance regardless of the outcome?"

Frowning, Abrik asked, "What do you mean?"

"Don't play dumb with me," Piñiero said. "You know as well as I do what I mean. If you and I keep Tezwa to ourselves, I'll make you the next security advisor to the president."

Giving Piñiero a dubious look, Abrik asked, "You're authorized to do that?"

"You're not the only one who got into this to form policy. You, Jas, are sitting across the table from President Bacco's chief of staff."

"Assuming there *is* a President Bacco."

Nodding, Piñiero said, "Assuming, yes. And if that comes to pass, you'll be security advisor."

"Not Ross?"

Piñiero almost sputtered her soda, thinking of what Helga was grooming the admiral for. "If Admiral Ross wanted to get into the political arena, he would have just run and had done with it," she said, hoping to hell it was true.

"And if the FNS is wrong and President Pagro is the one making decisions?" Abrik said with a smile.

Piñiero smiled right back. "Then you can do whatever the hell you want, and this conversation will be meaningless."

"Fair enough." Abrik grabbed his punch glass and leaned back. Again, he started whirling the drink around, staring at the liquid as it splashed against the sides of the glass. Then he looked back at Piñiero. "The FNS isn't wrong, is it?"

"Hasn't been yet." She leaned forward. "Look, Jas, this is your chance to make sure that Pagro's agenda will still at least have a voice in the administration. We both want the same things, it's just a question of how we go about it. You're right, we do need to defend people who can't defend themselves, but a kamikaze run at the

Klingon Defense Force won't do anything to help the *jeghpu'wI'.*"

Abrik's mouth fell open for a moment. "The what?"

"That's what the Klingons call their subject species. The point is, we can work to effect those changes through peaceful means. And you can help us do that—keep us on the right track. You're the right man for the job, Jas."

He smiled. "That, and I can screw your administration before it starts."

"Which," she said quickly, "doesn't do anyone any good, unless you're just in this to be a bastard."

"Don't underestimate the considerable drawing power of being a bastard, Esperanza. It can be very satisfying."

Piñiero refused to rise to the bait. "Not nearly as satisfying as doing the job right."

He set the glass down. "Let me ask you something. You joined Bacco's staff after you resigned your commission, right?"

Piñiero nodded.

"Funny—before that, she was a good, solid planetary governor who never showed any inclination to be anything but that until the day she died or retired. Then, suddenly, a little while after her good friends' daughter joins up, she decided to expand her profile." He picked up the glass again. "I'm guessing you were the one who put the idea in her head to run for president, and that you didn't let up until she agreed."

"You have every reason to guess that," Piñiero said neutrally.

Abrik chuckled. "All right, then. You, Esperanza, have

yourself a deal—and a security advisor." He moved his glass toward her in a gesture of toasting.

Picking up her cobalt soda, she did likewise. The clink of their glasses touching echoed off the wall next to them. "To the future," she said.

"I'll drink to that," he replied as he gulped the last of his *allira* punch.

Chapter 14
U.S.S. Enterprise

As he entered Ten-Forward, Geordi La Forge felt as if a giant weight had been lifted off his shoulders.

He'd been agonizing over what answer to give Riker regarding the position of first officer on the *Titan,* to the point where it was seriously interfering with his ability to do his job. Taurik had been taking up the slack, at least, and it wasn't as if engineering had a huge number of responsibilities while they remained in orbit of Qo'noS, but La Forge hated being too distracted to perform his duties properly—especially in the middle of an inspection. *Thank God Scotty's the one keeping an eye on me—if I got this flaky while someone like Go or Genestra was standing over my shoulder, I'd be busted back to ensign so fast . . .*

In addition to his talk with Scotty, La Forge had discussed the possible promotion with Data and with Troi. Both listened to him go on about the pros and cons, both agreed that it was a difficult decision, both said that either choice would be a good choice.

In practical terms, that meant they were both absolutely no help at all.

Then last night, he watched the feed from the Federation News Service, and saw Nan Bacco being declared the new president of the United Federation of Planets, winning sixty-one percent of the vote. La Forge watched as Bacco stood there with her entire campign staff, including Admiral Ross, all around her as she gave a speech about the need for change and to move forward instead of backward. And seeing that, he made his decision. It was the only one he could make.

Riker was sitting at a table with Troi, the pair of them sharing a large drink called a frozen hot chocolate. From what La Forge recalled, it included chocolate ice cream, hot chocolate, whipped cream, and chocolate shavings, and as he approached their table, he saw that those were, in fact, the ingredients, along with hot fudge poured over the top. *Talk about gilding the lily,* he thought.

Upon seeing the chief engineer, Riker said, "Geordi! Good to see you. Can I interest you in some of our frozen hot chocolate?"

With mock petulance, Troi said, "I never said we could share this. You're lucky I'm even sharing it with *you.*"

Holding up a hand, La Forge said, "Don't worry about it—I know better than to come between the counselor and her chocolate."

"You're wise beyond your years," Riker said gravely, then spoke in a more relaxed tone. "What can I do for you?"

Sitting in the seat next to Troi and opposite Riker, La

Forge said, "I'm afraid I'm gonna have to say no to the first officer job."

To La Forge's chagrin, Riker looked crestfallen. "Why?"

Quickly, La Forge said, "It's not that I'm not flattered by the offer, believe me. I've been turning this over in my head since you first mentioned it."

"I thought you wanted a ship of your own someday," Riker said. "That won't happen unless you put in some more time on the bridge."

At that, La Forge smiled. "I have my own ship—you're sitting in it."

Troi chuckled. "Captain Picard might have something to say about that."

"Look," La Forge said, "I'm sure I'd be a perfectly fine first officer—"

Riker put in, "I think you'd be better than that."

"Maybe—maybe not. The thing is, I already know I'm a good chief engineer. And I *like* being a good chief engineer. And not many people can do what I do. That may sound egotistical, but it's also the truth." He folded his hands in front of himself the way the captain and Data always did when they wanted to look authoritative. "Remember last month when we were all talking about the presidential race, and the captain said that Admiral Ross wasn't foolish enough to run?"

Both Riker and Troi nodded.

"I think the admiral knows that he's a good admiral, and he doesn't want to do anything to mess that up. Well, I'm not foolish enough to become a first officer for the same reason."

Troi and Riker exchanged glances. With his implants, La Forge could see that Riker's pulse had quickened a hair. Troi, though, was at her norm. *She probably senses how right this feels for me. Come on, Commander, pick up on that, please. I don't want you disappointed in me.*

Then Riker looked at La Forge and sighed. "Well, much as I'd have liked to have you on board, I'm not gonna stand in the way of your cavalier insistence on being happy with your career. Besides," he added with a grin, "I think I've proved over the last fifteen years or so that any idiot can be a first officer. But a good chief engineer is too valuable to lose."

Relief washed over La Forge, and he laughed, Riker and Troi joining in.

"I believe," Troi said to Riker with a certain pomp, "that this calls for special dispensation." She grabbed one of the spoons, scooped out some ice cream, with whipped cream and chocolate shavings on top of it and hot fudge dripping off it, and handed it to La Forge. "Commander La Forge, I hereby authorize you to partake of my frozen hot chocolate."

"I'm honored, Counselor." He put the contents of the spoon into his mouth. At once, he shivered from the ice cream and recoiled from the burning sensation of the hot fudge on his tongue. The whipped cream softened the blow, at least. *Yeah, that's* definitely *gilding the lily.*

As La Forge swallowed the dessert—followed by a glass of water that an alert Jordan provided moments later—Troi turned to her fiancé and asked, "So who's your next choice?"

* * *

"Me?"

Riker tried not to laugh at the person sitting across from him in the observation lounge. He had to admit that he had been hoping for a surprised reaction just for the facial expression it engendered.

"I won't lie to you," Riker said, "you're my second choice."

"I know, sir. Commander La Forge was your first. Hell, the whole ship knows that."

This didn't surprise Riker. It was hard to keep a secret on a starship, and neither he nor La Forge had made much of an effort to keep it quiet in any case. "You don't need to make a decision right away," he said. "The sooner I have a first officer in place the better, but I'd rather have the right person late in the game than the wrong person too soon."

Christine Vale shook her head. "I don't know, sir— I'm still getting used to the promotion, and now this . . ."

"The promotion," Riker said, "is part of why you're being made the offer. Lieutenant commander means you're up for new responsibilities—including that of a first officer. You've done stellar work these last four years in general and this last year in particular. More to the point, you've shown excellent leadership abilities."

"Thank you, sir." Vale absently fingered the hollow pip on her collar, something Riker noticed that she'd been doing since her promotion. Then she smiled. "Sir, this isn't because I've been beating you at poker and you want a chance to get your own back?"

"Not at all," Riker said seriously. Then with a smile of his own, he added, "That's just a fortuitous side effect."

She chuckled. "It's just that I've never even *consid-*

ered the command track. I went to the Academy later than usual. I was a peace officer on Izar—latest in a long line, in fact. After something happened—" Vale shifted uncomfortably in her chair. "Well, let's just say that there was a situation that Starfleet got involved in, and one of the security officers—a lieutenant on the *Roosevelt* named Corsi—inspired me to join Starfleet. I didn't start at the Academy until I was twenty-three, and all I wanted to do was security. I was bound and determined to make chief as fast as possible. Now—it never even occurred to me that I might do something beyond being a security chief, to be honest."

Riker shook his head. "First Geordi, then you."

"Commander La Forge said he wanted to stay in engineering?"

"Yup. It's kind of ironic, if you think about it."

"How so, sir?"

"Well, I turned down three commands over the years because I thought it would be better to stay on the *Enterprise*. Now, I've got two straight first officer candidates who feel the same way."

Vale pointed a finger at Riker. "Hey, don't count me out yet, sir. I just need some time to think about it, is all."

"Take all the time you need." He sighed. "Besides, it's not like I should expect anything to go smoothly in my life right now."

"Yeah, I noticed that you're still getting hourly updates on your new wedding plans. Sir," she added quickly.

"You don't know the half of it," Riker said. Now that he knew he would be having the ceremony on Earth, his *agita* about the ever-expanding Betazoid ceremony had diminished, but he still was wondering just what he was going to be in for when they got to whatever it was Lwaxana was planning.

"Picard to Riker."

Tapping his combadge, Riker said, "Go ahead, sir."

"I need you and Commander Vale on the bridge, Number One."

Both Riker and Vale were already moving toward the bridge entrance. "We're on our way."

They walked onto the bridge together, and were greeted by two familiar faces: Ambassador Worf and Alexander Rozhenko.

As he stepped up to his chair next to Picard, Riker asked, "What brings the ambassador and his son to our hallowed halls?"

Vale tried and failed to hold in a snort as she moved to the tactical station, relieving Almonte.

Worf replied, "It is traditional for ambassadors to resign when a new president takes office. The embassy communications systems are being upgraded at the moment, so I thought it best to conduct the ritual from the *Enterprise*."

Nodding, Riker said, "Makes sense."

Alexander smiled. "I'm just along for the ride."

"Well, it's good to see you again, Alexander—we didn't get much chance to talk in the Great Hall. Have you listened to those new jazz recordings I sent?"

Shifting his feet and looking down at the deck, Alexander said, "Not all of them, sir. It's kind of difficult on the *Ya'Vang* to get time to listen to music privately."

"Dixieland," Worf added, "is not commonly heard on Defense Force vessels."

"I imagine not." What little music Riker heard on the *I.K.S. Pagh* during his brief tenure as first officer of that ship fourteen years earlier was not remotely compatible with Earth jazz. *For that matter, I'm not entirely sure it was compatible with anything other than the mating cry of a hoarse moose.*

"In any event," Picard said from his chair, "I did not just summon you and Commander Vale to see old friends." The captain pointed at the viewscreen.

Taking his seat to Picard's left, Riker followed the gesture to see that a *Prometheus*-class ship had joined them in orbit of Qo'noS.

From behind him, Vale said, "That's the *U.S.S. Cerberus*—Admiral Ross's ship. And he's requested permission to beam over."

"Grant that permission please, Commander, and please meet him in the transporter room," Picard said.

"On my way, sir," Vale said. Almonte returned to the tactical station at her departure. Watching Almonte reminded Riker that they had yet to assign a new deputy chief of security to replace Jim Peart. Peart and the alpha-shift conn officer, Kell Perim, had resigned together after Tezwa to go off and be a happy couple. Thinking over the crew roster, Riker also recalled that Almonte was due to rotate off the ship to a new posting at Starfleet Headquarters as soon as they returned to Earth. *And here I am, trying to poach the chief, too. Well, that's Data's problem now, not mine,* he thought with amusement.

Picard said, "It appears that Emperor Kahless's departure has been delayed a bit longer, and we still have to be back on Earth for a certain major event."

Putting both hands on his chest, Riker said, "You mean there's a major event happening on Earth at the same time as Deanna's and my wedding?"

From behind him, Worf muttered, "I had hoped, Commander, that your sense of humor would have improved by the time you received your own command."

Before Riker could defend his wounded pride, Picard said, "Hope, Mr. Ambassador, springs eternal. In any case," the captain added, cutting off Riker's second attempt to speak, "Admiral Ross will join the *Ditagh* in conveying Emperor Kahless back to Cygnet IV, where, it is hoped, he will have the chance to finish the landscape he started."

From the ops console, Data turned and said, "I believe that such an effort would not be worthwhile, sir. Based on the emperor's style, his attempts at realism are sorely lacking, and he would be better off adapting a more pointillist style—or perhaps a neo-Vadrian mode."

This, Riker thought, *is your fault, Geordi—you're the one who encouraged him to start painting all those years ago.* Aloud, he said, "I'm gonna miss you, Data."

"I will miss you as well, sir."

A few moments later, Ross came onto the bridge, escorted by Vale, and also accompanied by Go, Genestra, Russell, and Scott.

Picard and Riker both stood, the former saying, "Welcome aboard, Admiral." For his part, Riker wondered why Go and her team were on the bridge. The four of them stood in front of the environmental control console. Go and Genestra were as inscrutable as ever, Russell looked almost constipated, and Scotty had the same genial expression he always seemed to carry. *I hope that means good news,* Riker thought. *After everything we've been through, it'll be a nice change.*

"Thank you, Captain. Good to see you all." Turning to Worf, Ross added, "And you too, Mr. Ambassador."

Worf simply inclined his head.

As Ross stepped down into the command well, standing between Data and Picard, the captain asked, "To what do we owe the privilege, Admiral?"

"I came on board for two reasons, actually. The first is to congratulate you all on passing the inspection with flying colors."

Several whoops and cheers broke out among the bridge crew, led, Riker noted, by Vale.

Go stepped forward. "You're running a fine ship, Captain. The *Enterprise* has always been the home of Starfleet's finest. Everyone who has served on this ship—including the new arrivals over the past year—has excelled beyond expectations. And I know that expectations on some of those new arrivals were fairly low. But this ship has its reputation for a reason, and you've spent the last year proving it. You should be proud. I know *I'm* proud to serve in the same fleet as you—and I'm sure Jill was proud to, also."

Riker couldn't help but smile at that. *Nice to know you can count on professionalism when it matters.*

"Thank you, Captain," Picard said. "I can assure you that I have been proud of this crew since we embarked for Farpoint Station fifteen years ago, and they have *never* given me reason to waver in that pride."

Unbidden, Riker's thoughts went back to his arrival on the *Enterprise*-D at that selfsame station, right after the ship's first—but sadly, nowhere near its last—encounter with Q. La Forge and Worf were just junior-grade lieutenants then, serving as bridge officers. Data was still early in his examination of the human condition. O'Brien was still on board, then serving as the battle-bridge conn officer, Sarah MacDougal was the chief engineer, and Tasha Yar the security chief. Wesley was just the doctor's precocious teenage son.

Now Tasha's dead, MacDougal's long retired, Wes is a Traveler, Worf's an ambassador, Geordi's chief engineer, Data's about to be first officer, and O'Brien's with the S.C.E. With him and Troi about to go off to the *Titan* and Crusher likely to be taking over Starfleet Medical, that meant that the only constant after fifteen years was Picard himself.

How appropriate.

Ross then said, "The other reason I'm here is a bit more selfish. I was the one who first suggested Worf for his current position, so I want to be here when he's given the job again by our new president."

Riker gave Ross a knowing look. "I understand you had a bit of a hand in the selection of that president, Admiral."

Shrugging modestly, Ross said, "I just saw the same thing the voters saw. President Bacco will do a fine job, I'm sure of that."

"Speaking of which, Commander Vale, open a channel to the presidential office on Earth." Picard took his seat as he spoke, straightening his uniform jacket. Riker followed suit a moment later.

It took almost a full minute for Vale to set up the communication. Any direct line to the Federation's seat of government in Paris had to go through several levels of security, and also passed through dozens of com beacons to boost the strength and speed of the transmission. Those two factors allowed both for near-instantaneous conversation as well as a pretty strong guarantee that the conversation wouldn't be overheard, but also meant it took extra time to set everything up.

Finally, the pleasant face of President Nan Bacco appeared on the *Enterprise* viewscreen.

"Madam President," Picard said, "this is indeed an honor."

"So they keep telling me, Captain. It's good to see you again."

"Likewise. However, I believe you're here to speak to my erstwhile chief of security."

"Yes, I am. Mr. Ambassador."

Worf stepped up to the tactical console next to Vale. Riker was amused at the picture they presented, the tall, intimidating Klingon male standing next to the petite human female. *Hard to believe they're both equally adept at the same job.*

"Madam President," Worf said. "I have my resignation ready to be transmitted." He turned to Vale. "May I?"

Vale indicated the console with a gesture. "You're probably the only person in the Diplomatic Corps I'd let touch the controls, Mr. Ambassador."

"Thank you." Worf entered several commands into the console.

Bacco looked down at a terminal on her desk. *"Receiving now."* She read the screen for a moment, then said, *"Your resignation is accepted and noted. I now hereby rein—"*

Worf held up a hand. "Madam President, please—with all due respect, if you are about to reinstate me, I must decline."

Riker turned around in shock. Most everyone on the bridge did likewise. "Worf?" Riker asked.

"Mind if I ask why, Mr. Ambassador?"

"I have—served the Federation in this post for almost four years. I believe that it is time for the position to be occupied by someone more—temperamentally suited to the task than I."

"Mr. Ambassador, I've been reading up on the job you've done for the past four years, and if you ask me, you're selling yourself and your temperament short."

"That may be, Madam President. However, I do have an alternative suggestion in mind. Someone who has proven himself capable of handling the diplomatic tasks necessary to be the Federation's ambassador to the empire. Someone who, like me, is immersed in the cultures of both nations." He stepped back and indicated his son. "I recommend Alexander Rozhenko—my son—for the job."

"What!?" Alexander said, his eyes growing wide, his jaw dropping. "Me? You want *me* to be ambassador?"

Worf looked down at his son, putting his hand on Alexander's shoulder. "Years ago, I received a—vision of your possible future. You were a skilled diplomat, one whose service to the galaxy was worthy of song."

"When was this?" Alexander asked.

Riker knew the answer, though he did not say so out loud. Worf had sworn Riker to secrecy on the subject, as he did not want it known that a future iteration of

Alexander, who was indeed a politician, had traveled back in time to prevent a future tragedy.

"That is not important. What *is* important is that I can think of no one better suited to the role than you, Alexander."

"I—I don't know what to say."

"You don't say anything yet." Bacco folded her arms and stared at the two Klingons. *"There's no way I can talk you into staying on, Worf?"*

His hand still on his son's shoulder, Worf said, "My mind is made up."

Picard put in, "It has been my experience, Madam President, that Klingons can be quite stubborn when they've set their mind to something."

Riker thought he heard Scotty mutter, "That's for bloody well sure," but he couldn't be certain.

"So I've gathered," Bacco said. She unfolded her arms. *"All right, then. Mr. Ambass— Sorry, Mr. Worf, please submit a formal report with your son's qualifications by the end of the day, and I'll review it. Mr. Rozhenko, we'll speak again in a day or two."*

Alexander still looked stunned. "Of—of course, Madam President. And thank you."

"Thank your father, it was his cockamamie idea." Again, she folded her arms. *"I think that's all. Oh—Mr. Riker, congratulations on your impending nuptials and your equally impending command. They're both well deserved. And sympathies on your loss—your father was a good man."*

"Thank you, Madam President," Riker said, surprised and flattered that the president was aware of his recent fortunes, good and bad.

"Best wishes to you all."

Picard inclined his head. "Thank you, Madam President."

After Bacco's face was replaced on the viewer with the image of Qo'noS slowly rotating below them, Riker turned to the prospective ambassador and said, "I guess now you'll have the chance to play those jazz recordings."

Grinning, Alexander said, "Yeah, I guess I will. Assuming the president accepts me, anyhow." He turned to his father. "I hope I can live up to the example you've set, Father."

"Of that, I have no doubt," Worf said in an unusually quiet tone. "And I have no doubt of something else: Your mother would be proud."

In an equally quiet tone, Alexander said, "I hope so."

Riker then looked at his old friend. "Worf, I have to ask—why?"

"I was wondering that myself," Ross said. Riker wondered if he heard a bit of menace—or at least confusion—in the admiral's tone, since he had indeed been the one to recommend Worf for the post in the first place.

After a moment, Worf said, "Alexander asked Kahless the same question. That is appropriate—for my answer is the same. All my life, every action I have taken has been out of a sense of duty to others. I joined Starfleet in gratitude for rescuing me from Khitomer. I became security chief in part to honor the memory of Lieutenant Yar. I twice allowed myself to be exiled from the empire in order to preserve it. I became ambassador to honor the memories of both Jadzia and K'Ehleyr."

At the mention of his mother, Alexander smiled. So did Riker, who had fond memories of the brief time he'd known the woman.

Worf continued. "When I look back on what has happened in the past month, I find that the only action I have taken in that entire time that I truly view with pride was when I was able to stop the *Klahb* takeover of the Federation embassy. Yet that was the only thing I have done in that time that was *not* diplomatic in nature. The rest of that time was spent in meetings. I was briefed, I was instructed, I gave instructions, I politicked, I negotiated, I—compromised. While it is true that I have served the greater good of both the Federation and the empire, it is also true that I have had my fill of serving the greater good. As with Kahless, so too is it with me—it is past time that I did something for myself. It is time for me to be selfish."

Ross walked up to him. Riker didn't know Ross well enough to predict how he'd react to this, so he braced himself for a chewing-out that only a person with flag rank could dish out.

However, to Riker's relief, all he said was: "Mr. Worf—I can't think of anybody I know who deserves a little selfishness more than you. Assuming it's what you want, you can consider your rank officially reinstated. You're back on active duty as soon as you give the word—Lieutenant Commander."

Worf's eyes widened in that way they did whenever he was excited. "The word, Admiral, is given."

"Good—as it happens, I know for a fact that there's a first officer position on the *Titan* available. It's yours if you want it."

Before Riker could say anything, Worf turned to look at Riker. "I would be honored to be your first officer."

Stricken, Riker shot a look at Vale.

"Is something wrong?" Ross asked.

However, Vale just gave Riker a smile and a quick nod.

"Nothing's wrong," Riker said quickly to Ross, then to Worf: "The honor would be mine, Commander."

And in truth, it would be. Worf had been a bridge officer for two years on the *U.S.S. Aldrin* and another one on the *Enterprise*-D before being promoted to security chief, where he remained for seven years. Then he became strategic operations officer on Deep Space 9, during which his duties included supervision of the powerful warship *U.S.S. Defiant*. He also served as fleet liaison between Starfleet and the Klingon Defense Force throughout most of the war. In many ways, in terms of variety of experience, he was a better candidate for the job than either La Forge or Vale, even with the four-year gap in his service record. More important, Riker and Worf had served together on several missions during their time on the *Enterprise*-D— and even served as commanding officer and executive officer during a harrowing battle simulation on the ancient *U.S.S. Hathaway*—and he was one of the few people Riker knew he could completely trust as his second-in-command.

But that doesn't make it any fairer to Vale. She should've had the chance to refuse it before Ross cut me off at the knees.

Admiral Ross departed the bridge to return to the *Cerberus* and prepare to ferry the Klingon emperor. Alexander returned to Qo'noS to begin his orientation. Worf commented that Giancarlo Wu "will make an excellent teacher." While he had not received the position yet, Worf wanted Alexander to be ready for when he did. Worf himself was remaining on board, to accompany the *Enterprise* back to Earth for the first of two wedding ceremonies.

Normally, that thought would lift Riker's spirits, but his heart was still heavy. Once the *Enterprise* broke orbit of Qo'noS and began the journey back to Earth, Riker asked Vale if they could speak in private.

The moment they entered the observation lounge, before Riker could say anything, Vale said, "Sir, before you even try to apologize, don't bother. It's all right, really. Honestly, if I were you and the ambassador—sorry, Commander Worf—became available, I'd snap him up in a minute."

"That's not fair to you, Commander. If you want the job, I can talk to Worf, see if—"

"Sir, like I said, it's all right. I wasn't entirely sure I wanted the job, and I'm happy where I am. Worf's on the command track, he's got the experience, and you two already know you click."

"Everything you say is true, but—" Riker let out a breath. "To be honest, Christine, I didn't want you to think you were getting squeezed out by the D guys."

At that, Vale laughed. "Honestly, sir, I hadn't even thought of it that way. Look, it's *really* not a problem. So stop worrying about it, and go get ready for your wedding."

Laughing, Riker saluted. "Aye, aye, Lieutenant Commander Vale, ma'am." Dropping his hand, he added, "Seriously, Christine, if there's anything I can do to make up for this, name it. I *know* it's not a problem," he said before she could say once again that it wasn't, "but I still feel I owe you something."

Vale considered that for a moment. "Actually, sir, there is. I've got a little bit of leave time due, and I have some relatives on Earth that I haven't seen since I was at the Academy. With your permission, I'd like to remain on Earth after your wedding and take some of that leave."

"It means you'll miss the Betazoid wedding."

She smiled. "I've seen the com traffic from your future mother-in-law, sir. I doubt one less person will even be noticed."

"Good point. All right then, as one of my few remaining acts as first officer of this ship, I hereby grant your leave, effective as soon as we achieve orbit of Earth."

"Thank you, sir."

Vale departed for the bridge. Riker remained behind as his earlier thoughts regarding the security staff came back to him. *With Peart gone, Almonte transferring, and Vale on leave, there won't be anyone to take over tactical for alpha shift.* True, it was just a run from Earth to Betazed and back, but with those three gone and with the casualties they'd suffered at Tezwa, the only people left on board rated to run tactical were Keru and Wriede, who were already assigned to beta and gamma shift, respectively. *Even for a milk run, we don't want to get caught with an inexperienced hand at weapons and communications.*

Then Riker realized with amusement that he had the perfect man for the job right on the ship.

Tapping his combadge, he said, "Riker to Worf."

Chapter 15
Earth

BEVERLY CRUSHER STARED at herself in the mirror of the anteroom. The small room was one of several set aside in the large pavilion that Riker had set up in the Denali Mountains for his and Troi's wedding.

God, I hate these dress uniforms.

Crusher had never had a problem with Starfleet's day-to-day uniforms, which had changed several times over the course of her career. That was in inverse proportion to the fiery passion with which she loathed all their choices in dress uniforms, whether the long tarpaulin-like skirt thing they had fifteen years ago to this white monstrosity that managed to add two kilos to the apparent weight of whoever wore it.

I should've insisted to Jean-Luc that we wear dressy civilian clothes. If nothing else, it would put Will in a suit or a tuxedo, which would be a big improvement on this thing.

She let out a long sigh. *The clothes are not what you're cranky about, Beverly, and you know it.*

Straightening the folds of the hated uniform, Crusher stared at her reflection. She saw a fifty-five-year-old woman with lovely red hair, more lines on her face than she wanted to see, in excellent shape for someone half her age (an opinion she could back up with medical data), and with the galaxy at her fingertips. She single-handedly raised a son who grew up to be a higher being—*and what mother wouldn't be proud of that?* She had just passed a medical inspection conducted by a woman for whom she had no professional respect, she had the opportunity to run Starfleet Medical, and only a few weeks earlier she had a wonderful short-term relationship with a young man who thought she was worth pursuing.

Crusher saw all that—and also saw a woman who was still doing the same job she was doing fifteen years ago under a man for whom she had had strong feelings for more than thirty years, and with whom she was no closer to having a real relationship than she was back when she signed on at Farpoint Station.

This is ridiculous. I need to get on with my life.

Just then, the door opened behind her to reveal Picard. Until this moment, Crusher had never believed in fate.

"Jean-Luc," she said, turning around.

Picard was yanking at his collar. "I swear, they make these dress uniforms more uncomfortable with each version."

"I'm sure they do it just to annoy you."

"Well, obviously." Picard stopped pulling at his neck and smiled at Crusher. "You look divine, Beverly."

"I look like a meringue." She hesitated. "Jean-Luc, there's something I need to say to you."

The smile fell from Picard's face. It looked like he knew what was coming.

Good. That'll make it easier.

"I've decided to take Yerbi's offer. It's just too good an opportunity." She put both hands on his chest. Owing to his rank, the middle of his uniform shirt was the same white as the sleeves and sides, as opposed to the gray everyone else had. "Seeing Will finally taking his own command, Worf leaving his ambassadorship—even seeing Wesley decide to stick with being a Traveler—it's made me realize that I need a change. Honestly, Jean-Luc, I'm tired of the front lines. Helping the Dokaalan, curing the Bader and the Dorset—with something that wasn't even a proper cure—and all those bodies on Tezwa. I've had enough." *And I'm tired of waiting for you to notice what's right under your face.* She couldn't bring herself to say those words.

But the question was whether or not he would say the words she wanted to hear, the words that would make her turn down Yerbi's offer and stay on the *Enterprise* for as long as he commanded it.

In all the years she'd known Jean-Luc Picard, she'd gotten fairly good at reading his facial expressions. She'd been with him through so much, from his brutal mind-meld with Sarek of Vulcan to his assimilation by the Borg to his torture by Gul Madred.

Therefore, she recognized his *I'm-suffering-for-the-greater-good* look. And was fairly peeved that that was the look she saw.

"In that case, Beverly, I wish you the best of luck. We'll miss you—but I can't think of a better person to succeed Dr. Fandau."

You couldn't do it, could you? Damn you, Jean-Luc.
"Good. Honestly, this is a big weight off my mind," she lied. "I've been thinking about this since Rashanar." She smiled. "Yerbi will be relieved, too—now he can have his retirement party."

"Beverly, I—"

Before Picard could continue, Crusher felt a cold wind in the room. Wrapping her arms around herself, she wondered if the pavilion's environmental system was breaking down and letting the cool Alaskan air in.

Then the wind died down, and the room started to warm again.

"Hi, Mom—Captain Picard."

Whirling around, Crusher cried, "Wesley!"

"Hey, I wasn't gonna miss this for the world."

Crusher ran to her son and embraced him with all her enthusiasm. Suddenly, nothing mattered, except for the fact that she was going to share this union of her two good friends with her son.

Picard frowned. "Er, Wesley—"

"Hey, why're you guys in dress uniforms? Isn't this a Betazoid wedding?"

Breaking the embrace, Crusher looked at her son. "Uh, Wes—this isn't the Betazoid wedding. We're having that on Betazed."

"However, since we're on Earth . . ." Picard said slowly.

Wesley winced. "I guess walking out that door naked probably wouldn't be such a hot idea."

Crusher smiled. "Well, some of the women on the guest list might not object too much."

"Mom!"

Picard tapped his combadge. "Picard to *Enterprise*."

"Wriede here, sir."

"Lieutenant, have the quartermaster beam down a dress uniform."

"Er, okay, sir. Ah, what size?"

"I believe the measurements of Wesley Crusher are on file."

"Yes, sir."

To Crusher's embarrassment, she hadn't even noticed Wesley's unclad state, so happy was she to see him. She noticed now that he was completely unself-conscious about it. *I guess Travelers aren't big on modesty.* After a moment's thought: *And why should they be?*

"I'm sorry, sir," Wesley said. "I was—well, elsewhere. I've been checking back up on you guys as much as I can, but I've been busy helping train Korgan and—well, traveling. I didn't want to miss the wedding, though. I mean, let's face it, those two should've gotten together *years* ago."

Crusher glanced at Picard. "Well, Wes, sometimes it takes people a while to realize how they actually feel."

Wriede came back on the line. *"Uh, sir, quartermaster says he only has a lieutenant's uniform in that size. The replicators are under maintenance right now, but he can make a new one for Mr. Crusher within the hour."*

"I'm afraid the need is immediate, Mr. Wriede. Have the lieutenant's uniform beamed down."

"Aye, sir."

Grinning sheepishly, Wesley said, "Thank you, sir. For the uniform *and* the promotion."

"Don't let it go to your head, young man." Picard wagged his finger in mock rebuke. "This is a temporary promotion for the express purpose of saving all of us some embarrassment."

"I'm not really embarrassed, sir," Wesley said matter-of-factly. Then, at Picard's aghast expression, he added, "But I don't want to embarrass Commander Riker or Counselor Troi, either, sir. Sorry, it's just that—well, I've come to look at the galaxy a lot differently."

Picard recovered. Crusher almost sprained her lips holding in a giggle.

"Understandable," the captain said. "I don't think I ever thanked you properly for what you did for us at Rashanar."

"Happy to do it, sir. It was good to have one last chance to save the *Enterprise*."

Riker pulled the curtain that separated the hallway from the main pavilion aside and looked out at the guests who were milling about, most of them holding drinks and some finger food. The latter smelled wonderful, and Riker's stomach rumbled a reminder that he hadn't eaten all day. *Only a little bit longer,* he thought.

He saw plenty of familiar faces, some old friends, some relatives of Troi's he didn't recognize—relations on her father's side—and even a few members of Starfleet brass, including Admiral Vance Haden. The serious-minded old admiral had been Ian Troi's commanding officer on the *U.S.S. Carthage* when Troi's father died, thirty-six years earlier.

A familiar voice from behind him said, "Don't worry, I've done this twenty-three times—it's a piece of cake."

Turning, Riker saw two old friends. One was a short woman wearing a lovely gold knit vest over a loose-fitting silvery-green shirt, long golden earrings, and a green hat that looked like a plate with a pituitary problem balanced on her head.

"Guinan! Glad you could make it." He turned to the woman standing next to the *Enterprise*-D's erstwhile bartender. "You too, Katherine."

Clad in a Starfleet dress uniform, Katherine Pulaski's eyes twinkled. "I wouldn't miss it." Her face soured a bit. "Especially after I heard about Kyle. I couldn't make the funeral, so I thought I should be here for this, at least."

Pulling each woman into an embrace, he said, "Thank you," to each of them.

"Nervous?" Pulaski asked.

"Surprisingly—no. Then again, there really isn't anything to be nervous about. Honestly, this is the first thing that's gone *right* since Rashanar." Again, thoughts of Tezwa returned, the remembered stench of the pit Kinchawn had thrown him in overpowering the existing smell of the finger food. Shaking the thoughts out of his head, he said, "I'm glad you two could make it. We've almost got all the D guys back."

" 'D guys'?" Pulaski parroted with a snort.

Guinan asked, "Almost?"

"The O'Briens couldn't make it, unfortunately." Riker shook his head. "Do you know that Molly's eleven now?"

"She's only eleven?" Guinan frowned. "I would've sworn she was older." At Riker's shocked look, Guinan said, "When you think of your own age in terms of centuries, eleven years really doesn't mean much."

"I guess not."

"Well, I sympathize with the chief and Keiko," Pulaski

said. "It wasn't easy for me to get away, either. The work we're doing at the Phlox Institute is at a critical stage—I'm afraid I won't be able to make the ceremony on Betazed."

"Speaking of which," Guinan said, "where *is* the mother of the bride, anyhow?"

With a knowing smirk, Riker said, "Back on Betazed, leaving no part of the ceremony unmicromanaged. There was no chance she would leave off planning the biggest social event on Betazed since the war just to attend some silly ceremony in the mountains."

Pulaski shook her head. "Somehow that doesn't surprise me."

"I see you talked Worf into coming back into the fold," Guinan said.

"I didn't talk him into anything—it was his own choice. I have to admit, I'm still surprised. Despite appearances, he made a damn fine ambassador."

Nodding, Guinan said, "He also looked like he was hitting the prune juice a little hard."

Pulaski shot Guinan a look. "What?"

"Long story," Riker said quickly. From what Riker understood, Guinan's introducing Worf to prune juice had eventually led to the beverage becoming a major export to the empire. "We were having a bit of a celebration last night, and Worf—well, let's just say he didn't stick with synthehol the way the rest of us did."

"Katherine!"

Riker turned at the voice of his captain, who was exiting the anteroom along with Crusher—

—and Wesley, wearing a Starfleet dress uniform.

"Wes! You made it!" Riker walked up to the young

Traveler and hugged him as well. Then he looked down at the collar on the uniform he was wearing. "Lieutenant Crusher? Let me guess, the Travelers kicked you out, and you've been finishing your time at the Academy for the last year in secret, and they made you a lieutenant because you already had a commission before you were a cadet."

Wesley blinked. "Hey, that's not a bad story. I oughtta try that one. But, no, I just—well, let's just say I was inappropriately dressed when I arrived."

The next several moments were filled with reunions, as Wesley, Pulaski, and Guinan talked about what they'd been doing in the years since their respectives times on the *Enterprise*-D. Without Riker realizing it, La Forge, Data, Vale, and Worf had joined them. Worf still looked fairly unsteady from his guzzling of Romulan ale the night before.

At one point, Pulaski said, "I hear you're going back to Starfleet Medical, Beverly."

"Yes," Crusher said. "I'm sorry Yerbi's retiring, but I'm thrilled at the opportunity."

Taking on a philosophical air, Picard said, "You know, the last time Beverly took over Starfleet Medical, I was given a stubborn, acerbic, cantankerous replacement who I firmly believed was sent specifically to drive me mad." He then looked at Pulaski. "And I'd love to have her back, if she's interested."

Pulaski, who looked like she had swallowed live *gagh* when Picard started talking, then broke into a laugh. "I'll pass, thanks, Captain. My days of starship medicine are long behind me."

A voice from beyond the curtain said, "Where *is* everyone?" The curtain parted to reveal Troi in her pink dress.

Riker first met Troi at a wedding on Betazed, so his first look at her was quite complete. Back then, he thought she was the most beautiful sight he'd ever seen. He thought that again now as she entered the hallway, and he was at once thrilled to be marrying this woman and annoyed that it took him this long to get up off his ass and do this.

"What are you all doing in here?" Troi asked.

Crusher smiled. "Just catching up on old times, Deanna."

"Without me? I'm hurt." She pouted, but her black eyes were dancing. Riker grabbed her and kissed her.

Then he looked around at his friends, who were starting to move toward the curtain. He held up a hand, "Wait, one second—I need to say something."

They all stopped and looked at him expectantly. Beverly, who looked content and happy for the first time in months, though whether from her son's arrival, her decision to take the Starfleet Medical job, or both, Riker couldn't say. Katherine, looking older and softer yet still as tough and hard as she was fourteen years earlier on the *Enterprise*-D. Geordi and Data, still best friends, still the most rock-steady reliable officers Riker had ever served with. Wes, with the same baby face he had as a teenager, yet who now carried a wisdom beyond all of them. Worf and Christine, like the good security chiefs they were, making everyone feel comforted by their very presence. Guinan, centuries of placid, philosophical wisdom in the galaxy's most garish outfits.

Deanna, his *Imzadi*, looking as radiant and beautiful as ever.

And at the center of it all, as he had been for fifteen years, Captain Jean-Luc Picard.

"This," he finally said, "may be the last time all of us are together. We've been through a lot." He looked at Picard. "Q. Borg invasions. The Romulans coming out of their shell." To Worf: "A Klingon civil war. The return of Kahless." To La Forge: "The *Phoenix* flight. First contact with the Vulcans." Back to Picard: "And a terrible, terrible war. We've seen friends die; we've seen *legends* die." To Vale and Pulaski: "We've let friends go and seen new friends arrive." To the two Crushers: "We've welcomed children into the world and we've let them go." Finally, he looked at his *Imzadi.* "And now we're all together one last time. A month from now, Worf, Deanna, and I will be on the *Titan,* Beverly will be frightening interns at Starfleet Medical, Wes will be traveling again. We'll be moving on."

He looked at each of them now in turn. "But for fifteen years on two starships, we got to make history. And I just want to tell you all here and now that it has been the pleasure of my life to make that history with all of you." Looking at the woman he loved more than anything in the galaxy, he said, "Now we get to make one last bit of history together."

Everyone clapped and cheered, except for Worf—who looked like someone had driven a spike into his head—and Picard, who stepped forward and put one hand on Riker's arm, and the other on Troi's.

"You know," he said, "one of the hallmarks of a good captain is the ability to make pretentious speeches at the drop of a hat. I always knew you'd make a good captain, Will, and you just proved it."

Everyone laughed at that—again, except Worf, who winced.

Picard looked at all of them. "Now come, friends, colleagues—family. Let's get these two married."

Epilogue

THE HEAT OF THE SUN warmed Christine Vale's skin as she lay napping on the beach of her aunt and uncle's house, making her feel as if she were glowing. A sudden wind wafted over her, then, cooling the skin down, and even causing a goose bump or two to pop up on her bare arms.

She lay parallel to the coastline of Rarotonga, the capital of the Cook Islands in the Pacific Ocean on Earth. If she opened her eyes, she could see the mountain at the island's center to her right and the gently lapping waves of the Pacific on her left. But she had no interest in opening her eyes, content to nap, with the sun's heat on her eyelids causing bursts of color in her vision. She had enjoyed the time spent with her aunt and uncle, whom she hadn't seen since graduation day. Her mother's sister met her future husband on Izar, but they moved to Earth shortly after they got married, since her uncle had this beautiful beachfront property.

Most of Vale's leave had been spent lying on this beach wearing a bathing suit, the sun shining brightly on

her while she thought about nothing. It was something—
or, rather, nothing—she hadn't done in far too long

The sound of footfalls on the nearby back porch of the
house interrupted her nap. The tread was too heavy to be
either of her relatives—who, like Vale, were rather petite, and unlike Vale, were also very slight—especially
since they never wore the Starfleet-issue boots that were
making the steps. Vale recognized whose boots they
were within a moment.

Without bothering to open her eyes, she said, "I was
wondering when you'd get here, sir."

She finally did open her eyes to see Captain William T.
Riker standing on the deck. He looked—confused. *Then
again, given what they all went through, it's not surprising.*

"You knew I was coming?" As Riker spoke, he bent
down to take off his footwear before coming onto the
beach. *Smart man,* Vale thought. Navigating the shifting
sands in anything but bare feet was just asking for trouble.

"I had a hunch. We may be in the middle of nowhere,
sir, but news still makes it here." She propped herself up
by her elbows on the beach chair. "I heard the basics of
what happened with the Romulans, and I heard who
died—including Data."

Riker rolled up the pants of his uniform and then
walked over to where Vale's beach chair sat. "Not exactly the milk run to Betazed we were expecting."

"What's the whole story? I heard the reports, but
that's not really the same thing."

Taking a seat on the end of Vale's beach chair, Riker
did as she asked. He spoke of positronic emissions detected on a planet near the Romulan border, and the sub-

sequent discovery on that planet of a prototype android that, like Data, was designed by Noonien Soong and that the eccentric old roboticist had named B-4. Immediately afterward came the part Vale knew from the Federation News Service: there was a coup d'état on Romulus, with a Reman named Shinzon now ruling the Romulan Star Empire. This was major news, given that the Remans had, up until now, been a slave race within the empire.

What the FNS didn't mention was that the Reman wasn't really a Reman—he was a human clone of Jean-Luc Picard. Part of a since-abandoned plot by the Tal Shiar, the Romulans' secret police, to replace high-ranking Starfleet officers with their own agents, Shinzon was raised in the Reman mines, eventually rising to prominence as a centurion during the Dominion War.

To make matters worse, Shinzon needed Picard—something in the captain's blood would save the clone from an early grave—and he used whatever means he could to get it. In the end, the *Enterprise* crew triumphed, but not before suffering heavy losses in battle to Shinzon's powerful ship, the *Scimitar.*

Among those losses: Lieutenant Commander Data, who sacrificed his life to stop Shinzon once and for all.

"It should've been me."

Riker shot Vale a look. "What was that, Commander?"

"I said it should've been me. I'm chief of security, it's *my* job to do what Data did."

"Nobody could've done what Data did. And if you were on board, you'd have been doing what Worf was doing in your place: repelling the Reman boarders."

Vale didn't accept that. Her job was to keep the rest of

the ship safe—that's what security did. That's what Domenica Corsi did for her when she shot Dar back on Izar, and that's what Vale swore to do every day of her life since then. That's what she'd been doing for four years on the *Enterprise*.

She sat up all the way, as regulation as she could be while sitting in a beach chair and wearing only a bathing suit. "I'm sorry I let you down, sir."

Riker looked at her as if she'd grown a second head. "You didn't let anybody down, Commander. You took a vacation—"

"When I should've been doing my job. I took advantage of your offer, and—"

"Did what every officer's entitled to. I checked, by the way—you didn't just have 'a little bit' of leave time coming, you had as much as possible without getting a formal reprimand on your record. Commander, you are entitled to the occasional break. We all are. And I think, particularly after what you've done for the past year, you earned the right to some time for yourself." He leaned forward. "Duty doesn't mean you're on every hour of every day, Christine."

"If you say so, sir." Intellectually, she knew the captain was right. But thinking about the fact that Data, who was functionally immortal, was dead, it still didn't *feel* right in her gut.

It should've been me.

She got up from the beach chair. The sunbaked sand flowed around and between her toes, sending a warm feeling through her feet.

Dammit, maybe Genestra was right about the guilt.

Then she realized just what she was thinking. *Am I*

*going to believe the smug manipulative bastard who was
sent to the ship to give us a hard time by an admiral with
an agenda? Or am I going to believe William Riker?*

It wasn't even a contest.

"You're probably right, sir," she finally said, favoring
Riker with a small smile.

"I'm the captain now, Commander Vale—I'm *always*
right."

Running a hand through her auburn hair, she said,
"Very good point, sir, I should've remembered that. My
apologies."

"I'll forgive it this time," Riker said with mock gravity.

She thought back over what Riker told her about the
battle against this Reman, or human clone, or whatever
he was. "Can I ask you a question, sir?"

"Name it."

"What would this Shinzon guy have done if Starfleet
sent a different ship? Or if someone else found that prototype android?"

Riker blinked. "I don't know, Commander. To be honest, that really wasn't our primary concern."

"Yeah, I can understand that. So this android—what's
it called, B-4?—is still around?"

Nodding, Riker said, "Yes, and he's got all of Data's
memories." Suddenly, Riker squinted, as if he realized
something. "Come to think of it, that also means he has
Lore's memories, Lal's memories, and the personal di-
aries of the entire Omicron Theta colony where Data
was created." He shook his head and chuckled. "All in a
brain that's barely at the level of a four-year-old. That
android's gonna have an interesting life."

"I'll bet."

With that, Riker stood up, and walked over to where Vale was standing. A gust of wind blew through, ruffling his hair and making the strands of gray stand out. "In any case, I didn't just come here to give you the inside scoop. I came to make you an offer."

This time, Vale blinked. "Huh?"

Grinning, Riker said, "The first officer position on the *Titan* is yours if you want it."

Shaking her head a few times, Vale said, "But—what about Commander Worf?"

Riker hesitated. "After—after what happened to Data, Captain Picard requested to have him back on the *Enterprise.* On top of everything else, Worf's star is pretty high right now, especially after single-handedly rescuing the embassy. It'll be good PR for the *Enterprise* to have him on board after everything we've been through this past year."

Vale nodded. "Can't argue with that."

"Besides," Riker added, "you look much better in a bathing suit than Worf."

Despite herself, Vale laughed. "Sir, you *are* a married man."

"Yes, and my wife would rather Worf was in the bathing suit. But I'm the captain, so I get to make those determinations."

"Lucky you."

Vale looked up at Riker's pleasant, bearded face. She liked the man, admired him, thought he'd make an excellent captain.

But will I make a deserving first officer? Or do I want to go on protecting the people on the Enterprise?

"What do you say, Christine?"

Vale made her decision.

The Traveler watched as a galaxy died.

Remnants of stars, fragments of planets, gases and particulate matter, energy of all kinds, it swirled toward the center like water flowing down a drain.

How many people lived there? the Traveler wondered. *How many trillions of creatures lived and died in that galaxy? Who will remember them now that they're gone?*

"You shall," said a voice that was both right next to him and across the universe. "That is why we travel—to witness the glory that is the cosmos."

The Traveler let out a very long sigh. It was an affectation from his time as a human being named Wesley Crusher that he had never been able to shake. "I know," he said. "And I wouldn't give it up for anything."

His fellow Traveler spoke in a teasing voice. "You almost did."

"I know. When I went to save the *Enterprise* at Rashanar, it was really tempting to go back." Thoughts of Colleen Cabot filled the Traveler's mind, the scent of her hair, the taste of her lips—and the sound of the Orion disruptor blast that killed her.

He looked back out over the galaxy going through its death throes. "But then I wouldn't have been able to see this. Or that stellar nursery. Or those spacesingers. Or—" He smiled. "Well, you get the idea. I couldn't go back to a life where I'd be restricted to one corner of one galaxy when I've got the whole universe to explore."

"So what brought you to this place?"

The Traveler paused and reflected on the question his fellow Traveler posed to him. Finally, he answered in one word: "Data."

"The android you served with on the *Enterprise?*"

"Yeah. He died right after I saw him on Earth—and I knew when I saw him that he was going to die, but I couldn't do anything about it."

"You could have."

"No. I learned my lesson on that score after Rashanar, *believe* me. But that's why I made sure I was at the wedding. I wanted a chance to see him—and everyone else— one last time, before . . ." He trailed off. "It's the cycle, I know that—life, death, rebirth. This galaxy will eventually be reborn. By the time that happens, the galaxy I'm from will be doing what this one's doing now."

The other Traveler prompted him. "And yet?"

"There's an old human saying that one death is a tragedy and a million deaths is a statistic." He pointed at the dying galaxy. "Trillions of trillions of life-forms are dying or have died because this galaxy is collapsing. But I can't make myself feel that the same way I feel about Data. He was one of my best friends, and he should've been able to outlive all of us." He smiled. "Well, except me, now, but you know what I mean." Then, for the first time, he looked at his fellow Traveler, the one whom he first met on the *Enterprise*-D in the company of a small-minded fool named Kozinski, the one who later welcomed him into the Travelers' ranks on Dorvan V. "There's so much more I understand now, so many new ways of looking at the universe. That's the other reason why I couldn't go back—it'd be like living in a box to just be a regular human again. But if I'm so much more, then why can't I—"

The other Traveler shook his head. "Ah, Wesley—don't you see? When you became one of us, you became more than human, it's true—but you didn't become *less* human. You still love your friends, and you still care when they die. Even though you've expanded the nature of who you are, that doesn't change the core. And at your core, you are still Wesley Eugene Crusher, son of Jack and Beverly Crusher, and friend to an android who is now gone."

The Traveler turned back to the galaxy. He squinted, and could see the singularity at its center, pulling all matter and energy into its vortex.

After several moments, during which he saw three suns disappear into the singularity's maw, he asked, "Does it ever make sense?"

"No. But we're working on it."

"I guess that'll have to do. But you know what?" He turned back to the other Traveler. "I'm tired of dead things. Let's go look at something living."

Together, the two Travelers left the distant galaxy. One thought of how proud he was of his protégé, and how far he was progressing.

The other thought about how much he would miss his friend.

Sunrise on Qo'noS was beautiful.

Alexander had never really seen the sunrise over the Klingon Homeworld before. Watching it paint its fiery yellows and oranges across the First City filled Alexander with a sense of pride and accomplishment.

Today, finally, I'm home.

He had been Alexander, the son of K'Ehleyr. Then he was Alexander Rozhenko, after Father's foster parents took him in. Then he joined the Klingon Defense Force, was made a part of Martok's House as his father was, and he was Alexander, son of Worf.

Now he was Ambassador Rozhenko. Father had written a glowing recommendation, and President Bacco had formally appointed him to the post.

It was his first day on the job, and he was looking forward to it. The second-floor office had been stripped of all personal items, save one: a picture of Alexander as a mere babe with his mother and father, taken back on the *Enterprise*-D not long before Mother died. *Father must have left it behind for me.*

The picture hung on the wall, looking rather overwhelmed by the blank space around it. *I'll have to do something about that.*

Moving over to the large wooden desk, Alexander stared down at the scattered mosaic of padds that covered the desktop, broken only by a com terminal. The padds' displays were full of words like "resolution," "request," "meeting," "extradition," "High Council," "Federation Council," "legality," "treaty," and so on. He had no idea where to start.

Then he sat at the desk. He felt almost lost in the large leather chair, which had obviously been designed for his much larger father, and made a mental note to ask for a smaller one. "Computer, call up the day's correspondences for Ambassador Rozhenko."

The computer obligingly did as he said, and listed all seven hundred and ninety-four correspondences.

Alexander felt the blood drain from his face. "C-c-computer? Are these just today's correspondences?"

"Results match search criteria. Messages displayed are those addressed to Ambassador Rozhenko since 2400 hours."

Clutching the arms of his chair, Alexander asked, "What am I supposed to do with seven hundred and ninety-four messages? I mean, I'm not gonna have time to read them all. And then there's all these padds." He picked one up at random. It was ostensibly written in English, but Alexander found he couldn't make heads or tails of what it actually *said.* "How can I—"

A voice from behind him said, "Computer, delete correspondences from this station."

The screen went blank.

Alexander whirled around to see Giancarlo Wu standing in the doorway, wearing a blue shirt, matching pants, and a yellow vest.

The aide added, "Computer, *raktajino.*"

With a hum, the replicator provided the beverage. Wu removed it from the slot and handed it to Alexander, who grabbed it hungrily. His mouth had gone completely dry, and he needed something to calm his nerves. *Okay, a stimulant may not be the best way to do that, but any port in a storm . . .*

"I'm sorry I didn't get here sooner, sir." Wu pulled a padd out of his vest pocket. "You don't need to view all those correspondences. That's what the staff is for."

Alexander felt fourteen kinds of stupid. "Oh."

"If there's anything that requires your personal attention, I or one of the other staff members will bring it to you."

His heart rate starting to approach normal again, Alexander indicated all the padds. "What about all this?"

"I intended to clean this up before you got here, sir, but other matters distracted me. We're still recovering from the takeover, plus there were several items that required my attention while you were getting settled in, so I haven't had time—"

Holding up a hand, Alexander said, "It's all right. You don't need to explain yourself to me, Mr. Wu. I'm the new guy in town, and you've been doing this a long time. Just tell me what I need to do."

Wu smiled and made a note on his padd. "Very good, sir."

"One question—is that normal?"

Frowning, Wu asked, "Is what normal, sir?"

"That many messages—I mean, seven hundred and ninety-four just in one morning?"

Wu nodded. "That is unusual, sir."

"That's what I thought." Alexander picked up his *raktajino.*

"It's usually much more than that."

Alexander almost broke his arm stopping himself from sipping the *raktajino* as he sputtered in shock. "You're kidding, right?"

"I'm afraid not, sir. That's why the staff goes through the correspondences."

This time he sipped the coffee, then muttered, "Let's hear it for the staff."

As Wu started to go over the day's agenda, Alexander finally let himself relax. *Okay, a few bumps in the road, but this is definitely a good thing. It feels right. The*

Enterprise, *Minsk, the Defense Force—I never fit in any- where. But here—here I can really make a difference. Here I can be somebody.*

He looked up at the picture sitting alone in the middle of an empty wall, and cast a thought at his parents: *I'll do you both proud, I promise you that.*

Worf was mildly apprehensive concerning what he was about to do. However, Geordi La Forge had asked Worf to accompany him to clean out Data's quarters, and the Klingon could think of no good reason to refuse him.

When Captain Picard had asked Worf to remain on the *Enterprise* following their mission to Romulus, Worf found himself unable to refuse that, either. He owed Picard a great deal, and as much as he looked forward to serving with Riker on the *Titan,* to be back on the *Enterprise* was the greater honor.

But this was not his *Enterprise.*

The vessel on which he had served proudly for eight years was long gone, and—though he had been on its successor several times, against the Borg, in the Briar Patch, during the gateways crisis, and any number of other occasions including this latest battle against Shin- zon—he was never truly a part of this ship.

Until now. Worf was finally doing what he wished. Of his four years as an ambassador, he had no regrets, but he also knew that the best years of his life were in the service of Starfleet, whether on the bridge of the *Enterprise*-D or in Deep Space 9's operations center or in the command chair of the *Defiant* or by Martok's side on the *Rotarran.*

None of that, though, made what he and La Forge had to do any easier.

"Thanks, Worf," La Forge said as they approached the door to Data's cabin, each of them holding a small plasti-form container. "I feel better having someone else along."

"Of course." If nothing else, La Forge was a good comrade of many years' standing—as was Data.

They entered the darkened cabin. Data had decorated his quarters on this ship in a similar fashion to the way it was on the *Enterprise*-D. The walls were lined with paintings—Data's own work—and a full computer station had been installed to allow the android a greater range of work functions.

Worf had never thought much of Data's paintings, though he had never said so. One of his regrets about the destruction of the *Enterprise*-D was that the hideous painting Data had given him as a birthday present, *The Battle of HarOs,* had survived the ship's crash landing intact, thus forcing Worf to keep the work. It was currently hanging in the Rozhenkos' living room, where Worf had sent it prior to his posting to Deep Space 9. He briefly considered sending for it to keep as a tribute to his fallen comrade, before Klingon aesthetics triumphed over human sentimentalism.

La Forge went over to the desk where Data kept his violin, then proceeded to where he kept the pipe and deerstalker hat that went with a literary holodeck program that the two of them indulged in fairly often.

I should not be here, Worf thought as he set the container down on the floor. This was La Forge's time to grieve. Data had started painting in part because La Forge encouraged him. The Sherlock Holmes program was something the two of them shared. The music Data played on his violin was human music that to Worf was just painful noise, but which La Forge genuinely appreciated. Worf had many fond memories of Data, but none of the items in this room prompted them.

"Geordi—"

"It's weird. You know that they took his emotion chip out last year after Rashanar, right?"

Worf nodded.

"I was really worried there for a while. At first, he wasn't interested in doing any of this." La Forge gestured at the paintings on the walls and to the items on the desk. "I felt like I lost my friend. But after the Dokaalan mission, he started to act like himself again. Maybe not the same as he was with the chip, but he was definitely more than he was before he put it in. Now—" He shook his head. "Now I've lost him all over again."

La Forge's voice was shaking, and Worf wondered if he was going to cry. *Can he even cry with his optical implants?* Realizing that his friend needed some kind of response, and not wanting to deal with the spectacle of human tears, Worf said, "When Kahless appeared on Boreth, Data questioned me about the nature of my faith. He was—curious."

Smiling, La Forge said, "That was Data all over."

"When Kahless was exposed as a clone, Data remarked on the Klingons who still believed in him despite his origins in a laboratory. They had made a leap of faith, trusting that the clone was the true reincarnation of Kahless. Data told me of his own leap of faith after he was discovered on Omicron Theta."

Looking at Worf quizzically, La Forge asked, "What do you mean?"

"He said that he was told that he was an android—a machine—and that he could not accept that he would be nothing more than an automaton. So *he* made a leap of faith that he could grow as a sentient being." Worf moved closer to La Forge, and spoke in a softer tone. "Everything he did after that was an attempt to become more than what he was programmed to be—including his sacrifice to save the captain. It was a very Klingon gesture—and a very human one."

La Forge took a long breath. "Yeah, you're right." Then he smiled. "Being an ambassador definitely had an effect on you, Worf—you never used to be this eloquent."

Worf straightened. "Perhaps. Or perhaps I merely did not have anything eloquent to say."

Chuckling, La Forge said, "Right. C'mon, let's get this stuff—"

A meow interrupted La Forge's sentence.

Oh no.

Spot ambled in from the bedroom. The cat, who was now well over ten years old, leapt onto the table, right next to the deerstalker.

The last thing Worf wanted to deal with was Data's pet, so he reached to move the creature out of the way. Before he could do so, however, Spot leapt into the Klingon's arms. Instinctively, Worf caught the animal.

The cat then seemed to almost burrow into Worf's chest, making a noise like the one a tribble made when it was near humans. Worf found it nauseating—yet also oddly soothing.

"I think she likes you," La Forge said with a grin.

"I am *not* a—cat person." Even as Worf spoke, Spot started to close her eyes and fall asleep. *This is a nightmare.*

La Forge was still grinning. "Looks like you are now. Hey, look, she never liked me—remember what happened when I tried to take care of her? And as I recall, when Data was having those problems with his dream program, *you* were the one who took her in and did just fine."

Worf sighed. La Forge's words were true, but he was not sure he would be able to tame the animal a second time. Absently, he started to stroke the cat's fur as La Forge continued gathering Data's personal items, from the volume of William Shakespeare's works that Picard had given him to the handkerchief with the "D" monogram Riker had given him shortly after getting his emotion chip ("for the next time you start crying," Riker had said).

Perhaps once again attempting to tame Spot will be a proper tribute to Data's memory. It is certainly preferable to putting that painting back on my wall.

Bending over, Worf gently let the animal onto the floor. Spot woke up and ambulated toward her bowl of water, pausing for a moment to turn her head back toward Worf and meow at him.

Suppressing the urge to growl at the cat, Worf picked up the container and placed it on the desk.

Worf exchanged a nod with La Forge, and the two of them began gathering their friend's possessions.

"You know, if you'd told me when we started this whole shebang that the Romulan government was gonna fall five minutes after I took office, I would've stayed on Cestus III where it's safe."

Esperanza Piñiero sat in the guest chair of the presidential office in Paris, saying, "Yes, ma'am," in reply to President Nan Bacco's diatribe. Piñiero knew that, as long as she served as Bacco's chief of staff, she would have to listen to these diatribes. *Why stop now?* she thought. She had, after all, been listening to such diatribes all her life.

Piñiero looked around the office, and found it a bit too minimalist for her tastes. White carpet, a Federation flag on a pole, and a large metal desk. Piñiero suspected that Bacco would put at least some personal touches into the office—a picture of her daughter and her family, if nothing else.

Then again, there was always the spectacular view. Although not quite as exquisite as Venezia, Paris still had an unparalleled majesty to it.

Bacco was still carrying on. "I haven't even had a chance to figure out what height to put this chair at, and one of the major superpowers in the quadrant has its government literally fall apart. See, this is why I like baseball: It's predictable. There's an order to it."

Piñiero tried to hold back a smile and didn't entirely succeed. "Aren't you the one who's always telling me that what makes baseball a great game is that it's completely unpredictable?"

Bacco pointed at Piñiero and said, "Listen, you, I'm president now, and that means there are six security guards outside those doors who will kill you on my say-so, so kindly watch your mouth." She picked up the mug of coffee on her desk, started to sip, then stopped. "Dammit, they make these mugs too small."

The president started to get up, but Piñiero said, "Ma'am, the replicator's right there on the desk, remember?"

Sitting back down, Bacco said, "Of course I don't remember. I'm old and feeble, I haven't had enough coffee, and you're giving me nonsense about the Romulans." Looking at the desk, she asked, "So where is it?"

"Just tell the computer what you—"

"Computer, coffee, black, unsweetened."

A mug of coffee materialized in the center of the desk, right next to the com unit.

Taking the steaming mug in hand and smelling its contents, Bacco said, "I think I can get used to this." She took a quick sip, set the mug down, then said, "All right, what're we doing about the Romulans?"

Consulting the padd on her lap, Piñiero said, "You're meeting with their ambassador, as well as Ambassador Spock, at 1300."

Bacco frowned. "Spock? Does he know anything about Romulans?"

Panic gripped Piñiero. *Oh no, please, no, don't let this happen, not now.* "Uh, ma'am, Ambassador Spock has *lived* on Romulus, and—"

"Oh for heaven's sake, Esperanza, that was a *joke.*"

Piñiero tried to regulate her breathing. "Ma'am, you really can't do that as often as you used to."

"When it's just you and me in the room? Like hell, I can't. Don't forget, I changed your diapers."

"I couldn't possibly forget with you reminding me every five minutes, ma'am. In any case, there's another situation."

"Naturally."

"The Deltans' water reclamation system is horribly out of date and falling apart. They like the system on Gault and wish to utilize it."

"So let 'em."

Piñiero winced. "The problem is that the one on Gault is actually a Carreon design, and the Carreon refuse to allow the Deltans to use it."

Bacco rolled her eyes. "Of course they do. How can we talk the Carreon into it?"

"That's what I'm going to ask the Carreon ambassador when I meet with him this morning."

"Good. What's next?"

Piñiero went through the day's meetings and events and happenings. Most of the staff was in place now. Fred MacDougan had taken over as communications director, with Ashanté Phiri serving as Esperanza's deputy chief of staff. Jas Abrik had accepted the position as security advisor, a move that turned many heads. Kant Jorel, the Federation Council's press liaison, also worked for the president, so Bacco and Piñiero had both strongly recommended M'Tesint to now-Governor Gari on Cestus III to replace the woefully inadequate Piers Renault. Helga Fontaine had moved on, currently running the campaign of a minister on Kharzh'ulla.

When she was finished, Bacco said, "Good. I've got my security briefing, where I'm sure I'll get an earful from Abrik about the Romulans. We really had to take him on?"

Nodding, Piñiero said, "Yes. And you know why."

"Know, yes. Like, no. Go on, get out of here and talk to the Carreon ambassador before they decide to go to war with the Deltans *again.*"

Rising from the guest chair, tucking her padd under her arm, Piñiero said, "Thank you, Madam President."

She turned to leave the office, her feet not making a sound as they pressed against the soft white carpet.

"Oh, Esperanza?"

Stopping and turning around just as the security guard opened the door for her, Piñiero said, "Ma'am?"

Bacco gave Piñiero a warm smile. Not the smile she used when she was giving people a hard time or when she was talking about baseball. This was a heartfelt smile that she usually saved only for family. "Thank you for talking me into doing this."

Piñiero gave her an equally warm smile in return— and for that moment, they weren't president and chief of staff, or even governor and campaign manager, but two old friends sharing a happy moment. "No need to thank me—just do the job right."

The red-hued river flowed down from the distant mountain, its current splashing regularly against the black rocks.

Kahless ran a brush over his canvas, transferring the black paint from the bristles onto its target. For this painting, he had decided to begin with the rocks. The *fortra* flowers were no longer in bloom—his "rescue" by the *Enterprise* meant that re-creating that particular vista was lost to him for at least a year—so he contented himself with simply painting the river. No trees, no bushes, very little of the sky, no mountain. He would simply convey the liquid-ruby nature of the water as it flowed downstream.

He had spoken briefly with the android on the *Enterprise* about his painting, and he had provided some good advice.

Kahless intended to take it at some point, but for now he simply wished to paint the river. If it was not the best work available, it would at least be a learning experience.

For many turns, he had been what he was programmed to be. He had done his duty, like any good Klingon, and he had made the world a better place than it was when he arrived in it. *What warrior could ask for more?*

As he put the finishing touches on the rock, the sun broke out through the clouds overhead, brightening the vista in front of him. It was just noontime, so he had the best light at the best time to have light. Any flaws in the work would be the result of his own shortcomings, not a lack of visibility.

Today, he thought with a smile, *is a good day to paint.*

He mixed in the bright red with the black paint he already had handy. It was time to start the river.

Jean-Luc Picard entered the bridge of the *Enterprise.*

He had not had this feeling in fifteen years, when he brought the *Enterprise*-D out of Farpoint Station. Then he was surrounded by a command crew he barely knew. Some he'd just met, some he knew primarily from their service record, some he knew only in passing—in truth, at the time only one person on the ship, Beverly Crusher, could be considered a friend of any standing. In the decade and a half since, on two different ships, the core had remained together. It was the second time he'd been so fortunate; the senior staff of the *Stargazer* had also stayed more or less intact for most of the two decades he'd commanded that vessel.

Now, he was once again entering a bridge that had more strangers than familiar faces. The first and second officers, counselor, and chief medical officer on whom he'd relied for so long that they were almost extensions of his very person, and who had been there from that beginning at Farpoint Station, were gone. Old faces had returned, new faces had come on board, but in truth the only constant was Picard himself.

Each station reported ready, all systems were functioning, and the crew awaited their captain's orders.

Picard sat in his command chair and looked forward at the new viewscreen, replacing the one that had been destroyed in the battle with Shinzon. Earth rotated beneath them, the blue gem of a planet visible through the structure of McKinley Station. He looked at ops, half-expecting the familiar black hair and opalescent skin of Data, and Picard experienced a pang of sadness in the knowledge that he was gone forever.

But we have had our time to mourn—now it is our time to dance. "Helm, set course for the Denab system, full impulse until we are clear of the solar system, then engage at warp seven."

The conn officer replied crisply. "Aye, sir."

Picard leaned forward in his chair, his hands gripping the armrests, and a smile playing across his lips.

"Let's see what's out there."

To everything there is a season, and a time to
*   every purpose under heaven;*
A time to be born, and a time to die; a time to sow,
*   and a time to harvest;*

*A time to kill, and a time to heal; a time to break
down, and a time to build up;*
*A time to weep, and a time to laugh; a time to
mourn, and a time to dance;*
*A time to cast away stones, and a time to gather
stones; a time to embrace, and a time to refrain
from embracing;*
*A time to get, and a time to lose; a time to keep,
and a time to throw away;*
*A time to rend, and a time to sew; a time to be
quiet, and a time to speak;*
*A time to love, and a time to hate; a time for war,
and a time for peace.*

—The Book of Ecclesiastes
Chapter 3, verses 1–8

Acknowledgments

Primary thanks go to my fellow *A Time . . .* authors (who are also good friends), Kevin "Bubba" Dilmore, Robert "Bob" Greenberger, David "Dave" Mack, John "John" Vornholt, and The Chosen One himself, Dayton "Ol' Jarhead" Ward, who were a joy to work with, and great fun to bounce ideas off of. We were all in constant contact during the writing process, and I think our communication made this series much stronger as a result. (Special kudos to Dave for all those instant-messenger conversations, which I think served to make each of the final three books in this series *much* stronger.)

Secondary thanks go to Pocket Books editor Ed Schlesinger, who kept the balls in the air regardless of the number of banana peels thrown under his feet. Thanks also to past and present Pocket Books folk John J. Ordover, Scott Shannon, Marco Palmieri, Margaret Clark, Jennifer Heddle, Jessica McGivney, John Perrella, and especially Elisa Kassin, as well as Paula M. Block and John Van Citters at Paramount Licensing, all of whom were tremendous, fantastic, and other superlatives.

Tertiary thanks go to my wonderful agent, Lucienne Diver, the acquisition of whose services has proven to be one of the smarter career moves I've made.

Additional thanks to:

Michael Jan Friedman, J.M. Dillard, and the writing team of Michael A. Martin & Andy Mangels. They've all got novels coming out in the next year or so—two post–*Nemesis* TNG hardcovers and the first *U.S.S. Titan* book, respectively—that you'll all want to read after perusing this volume, and they were good enough to let me help set them up.

Several writers (some of whom I've mentioned already) whose novels, eBooks, stories, and/or comic books provided useful background material: Kevin J. Anderson & Rebecca Moesta (*The Gorn Crisis*), Peter David (*Imzadi, Triangle: Imzadi II, Double Time, Stone and Anvil*), Charlotte Douglas & Susan Kearney (*The Battle of Betazed*), Christie Golden (*Homecoming, The Farther Shore,* and the forthcoming *Old Wounds* and *Enemy of My Enemy*), Robert Greenberger (*Doors Into Chaos, Past Life*), J.G. Hertzler & Jeffrey Lang (*The Left Hand of Destiny* Books 1–2), David Mack ("Twilight's Wrath" in *Tales of the Dominion War*), Michael A. Martin & Andy Mangels (the forthcoming *Worlds of Star Trek: Deep Space Nine: Trill*), Vonda N. McIntyre (the *Star Trek III: The Search for Spock* novelization), Terri Osborne (the forthcoming *Malefictorum*), S.D. Perry (*Unity*), Josepha Sherman & Susan Shwartz (the *Vulcan's*

Soul trilogy), Dean Wesley Smith (*The Belly of the Beast*), John Vornholt (*The Genesis Wave* Books 1–3, *Genesis Force*), Dayton Ward & Kevin Dilmore (*Interphase*), and Howard Weinstein ("Safe Harbors" in *Tales of the Dominion War*).

Amusingly enough, my own name probably belongs in the above two paragraphs. I've got a forthcoming novel that will also spin out of this book (focusing on the Federation government in the first year of the Bacco presidency), and I built on material from my previous novels *Diplomatic Implausibility, Demons of Air and Darkness, The Brave and the Bold* Books 1–2, *The Art of the Impossible, A Good Day to Die,* and *Honor Bound;* my upcoming novel *Enemy Territory;* my comic book miniseries *Perchance to Dream;* and my *Tales of the Dominion War* short story "The Ceremony of Innocence Is Drowned." But it's silly to acknowledge oneself, and I endeavor never to be silly. And if you believe *that . . .*

The actors provide face, voice, body language, texture, and so much more that give authors like me a blueprint from which to write: Majel Barrett (Lwaxana), LeVar Burton (La Forge), Kevin Conway (Kahless), James Doohan (Scotty), Michael Dorn (Worf), Jonathan Frakes (Riker), Bruce French (Genestra), Whoopi Goldberg (Guinan), J.G. Hertzler (Martok), Barry Jenner (Ross), Caroline Kava (Russell), Clyde Kusatsu (Nakamura), Gates McFadden (Crusher), Erik Menyuk (the Traveler), Diana Muldaur (Pulaski), Kate Mulgrew (Janeway), Suzie Plakson (K'Ehleyr), Marina Sirtis (Troi), Brent Spiner (Data), Patrick Stewart (Picard), Wil Wheaton (Wesley), and the quartet of Marc Worden,

James Sloyan, Brian Bonsall, and Jon Steuer (who played Alexander at different ages). Also, John Logan, Rick Berman, and the aforementioned Brent Spiner, the minds behind *Star Trek Nemesis,* who provided me with my end point.

The usual reference sources: *Star Charts* by Geoffrey Mandel, *Star Trek Encyclopedia* and *Star Trek Chronology* by Mike & Denise Okuda, *The Klingon Dictionary* by Marc Okrand, *The Star Trek: The Next Generation Companion* by Larry Nemecek, and *The Star Trek: Deep Space Nine Companion* by Terry J. Erdmann & Paula M. Block. Also Paramount Pictures for releasing *TNG* and *DS9* on DVD, which sure made checking back on episodes a lot easier. . . .

Dean Wesley Smith—who, in addition to his skills as author and editor, is also a damn fine card player—for vetting the poker scene in Chapter 2; and Dr. Lawrence Schoen—who, in addition to *his* skills as author and linguist, is also head of the Klingon Language Institute—for providing helpful Klingon language stuff to supplement the dictionary.

The usual gangs of idiots: the Malibu crowd, CITH, the Geek Patrol, and the Forebearance (especially The Mom, GraceAnne Andreassi DeCandido). Also, the regulars at the *Star Trek* Books BBS (www.psiphi.org), the TrekBBS Literature board (www.trekbbs.com), the *Star Trek* Books Yahoo!Group (groups.yahoo.com), the *Trek* books board at Simon & Schuster's Web site (www.startrekbooks.com), and the Federation Library at *Star Trek* Now (www.startreknow.com).

For inspiration and assistance they probably didn't

even know they provided: James A. Hartley, Peter Liver-akos, Glenn Hauman, David Honigsberg, Alexandra Elizabeth Honigsberg, Peter Wheeler, Tynan Wheeler, Julienne Lee, Esther M. Friesner, Jacqueline Bundy, Paul T. Semones, Killian Melloy, Tom Holt, Tim Lynch, Bill Williams, Aaron Sorkin, and especially my bestest buddy Laura Anne Gilman.

Last but never ever least, the love of my life, Terri Osborne, who was not only her usual supportive self, but also made one particular suggestion that made the whole book come together.

About the Author

Keith R.A. DeCandido was once described as a "veritable engine of *Trek* tale-telling" by the book review Web site wigglefish.com, which explains why he hasn't gotten much sleep lately. His output in the *Star Trek* universe since 1999 has included the novels *Diplomatic Implausibility, Demons of Air and Darkness,* and *The Art of the Impossible;* the cross-series duology *The Brave and the Bold;* the comic-book miniseries *Perchance to Dream;* short fiction in *Tales of the Dominion War* (which he also edited), *No Limits, Prophecy and Change,* and *What Lay Beyond;* eight eBooks in the monthly *Star Trek: S.C.E.* series (which he also co-developed); and the first two novels in the *Star Trek: I.K.S. Gorkon* series, which chronicles the adventures of a vessel in the Klingon Defense Force. Among his many forthcoming *Trek* projects are the *Tales from the Captain's Table* anthology, the Ferenginar story in *Worlds of Star Trek: Deep Space Nine* Volume 3, more *I.K.S.*

Gorkon books, and a book that will chronicle the first year of the President Bacco administration following this novel.

Keith has written novels, short fiction, and nonfiction in other universes as well, including *Gene Roddenberry's Andromeda, Resident Evil, Farscape, Buffy the Vampire Slayer,* Marvel Comics, *Xena, Doctor Who,* and more. His original fantasy novel *Dragon Precinct* is on sale now, and he also edited the groundbreaking anthology *Imaginings.* He lives in the Bronx with his wonderful girlfriend, their adorable cats, and way too much stuff. Learn more than you really need to know about Keith at his official Web site at DeCandido.net, or e-mail him directly at keith@decandido.net and let him know *just* what you think of him.

What began in *A Time to . . .* and *Nemesis*
continues in

STAR TREK®

TITAN

TAKING WING

by
Michael A. Martin and Andy Mangels

**Turn the page
for a preview of *Taking Wing*. . . .**

Among stars his kind had not yet traveled, Will Riker soared.

Scarcely feeling the observation platform of *Titan*'s stellar cartography lab beneath his feet, Riker let go, surrendering to the illusion of gliding swiftly "upstream" along the galaxy's Orion Arm. Buoyed on the strains of Louis Armstrong's 1928 recording of "West End Blues," Riker seemed to move far faster than even his ship's great engines could propel him. The familiar stars of home had long since fallen away. What lay ahead and all around him was an unknown expanse whose mysteries he, his crew, and their young vessel were meant to discover.

So much to explore, he thought, at once humbled and exhilarated by the realization. *Who's out here? What will we find waiting for us? And what'll we learn along the way?* These were the same questions that had led him to join Starfleet years ago. Now, as then, he could think of only one certain way to unveil the answers.

Soon, he told himself. *Soon . . .*

"Will?"

Deanna. He was suddenly grounded again, the solidity of his starship sure and tangible once more, though the rushing star clusters and nebulae remained. Standing in the center of the spherical holotank, he'd been so immersed in the simulation that he hadn't noticed her entering the cartography lab.

"Computer, deactivate audio," Riker said, abruptly silencing the music of the immortal Satchmo.

Deanna came up alongside him, her eyes searching his as they met. "Are you all right?" she asked.

He nodded and wrapped an arm around her shoulders; she slipped one of her arms around his waist. "Just looking over the road ahead," he said quietly.

"And how does it look to you?"

The question took him off guard, forcing him to grope blindly for an answer. "Big," he said finally, unable to keep a slight laugh out his voice.

"Then maybe you shouldn't take such a long view," she said lightly. "Just take it a step at a time."

Grinning, he asked, "Is that my counselor talking, or my wife?"

Deanna shrugged. "Does it matter? It's good advice either way."

His brow furrowed; he could read her emotions as clearly as she could anyone else's. "Is something wrong?"

She hesitated, then said, "I know what this assignment means to you, what you think it represents. I know you take it very seriously—"

"Well, shouldn't I take it seriously?" he asked, interrupting her, his words coming out more sharply than he had intended.

Deanna let it pass. "It shouldn't be a burden, Will. That's all I meant."

Riker sighed, leaning forward on the railing and looking

down into the void, watching the stars as they continued to stream by below him. "I know. It's just hard not to think that there's a lot at stake. I look back on the last decade and I wonder how so much could have happened, how so much could have changed. Sometimes I felt like we were speeding through a dark tunnel, with no way to turn, and no idea what we'd hit next. The Borg, the Klingons, the Dominion . . . We spent most of those years preparing for the next fight, the next war." He didn't bother to mention this last difficult year aboard the *Enterprise;* he didn't need to. She knew as well as he what they had endured.

He turned to her again, and saw that she was watching him carefully. "Now we've come out the other side, and for the first time in nearly a decade, it feels like we have a chance to get back some of what we lost during those years. We can do the things we set out to do when we joined Starfleet in the first place—the things I grew up believing Starfleet was primarily about. The Federation's finally at the point of putting ten years of near-constant strife behind it. This mission, this ship, is my chance—*our* chance—to help. That burden is real, *Imzadi*. I'm not going to pretend it doesn't exist."

Deanna smiled gently at him, then reached up to touch the side of his face. "You shouldn't. But you can share it. That's why you have a wife, and a crew. So you don't have to shoulder it alone."

He took her hand, kissed the palm of it, and nodded. "You're right. And I won't. I promise."

"Bridge to Captain Riker."

Still holding his wife's hand, Riker tapped his combadge. "Go ahead, Mr. Jaza."

"Sir, the U.S.S. Seyetik *has docked at Utopia Station One. They report that Dr. Ree is preparing to beam over. We have transporter room four standing by."*

A small, puzzling smile tugged at the corners of Deanna's mouth. "Acknowledged," Riker said. "Tell the transporter room that Commander Troi and I are on our way. Riker out." Turning away from the railing, Riker reached out to the platform's interface console and deactivated the Orion Arm simulation.

He turned back toward her. "What's that smile for?"

"I'll tell you later," Deanna said, brushing the question aside.

Riker's eyes narrowed with good-natured suspicion, but he decided to let the matter drop. As the captain and counselor walked together toward the exit, the walls of the lab shifted, returning to their usual standby display of the visible universe surrounding *Titan*. Beyond the gridwork of the ship's drydock, the orange sunlit face of Mars dominated the space to starboard, the flat, smooth lowlands that were home to Utopia Planitia's ground installations obliquely visible to the extreme north; at *Titan*'s port side, the stations and maintenance scaffolds of Utopia's orbital complex stood out starkly against the yellow-white brilliance of Sol.

"Has the rest of the senior staff come aboard?" Riker asked Deanna as they exited the lab and strode into the corridor. He nodded at two of the ship's biologists as they passed, an Arkenite whose name he couldn't recall at the moment, followed by a lumbering Chelon of the palest green Riker had ever seen on a member of that species. The scientists nodded back.

"Almost," Deanna answered. "Dr. Ree is the last. Well, except for the first officer, of course. But assuming nothing goes wrong there, you'll be able to hold your staff meeting on schedule, and with everybody present."

Riker tried to keep his expression steady as they passed an exposed length of the corridor wall, where several techs from the Corps of Engineers were still working at replacing a faulty ODN relay in a replicator network that crossed half the corridor. The work looked considerably more complicated than it had half an hour ago, when Riker last passed through this section.

"I'm less worried about having a quorum at the staff meeting than I am about launching on schedule."

"Don't be such a worrier, Will," Deanna said. "A few bumps along the way are natural. We still have two weeks. She'll be ready."

"Any new bumps I should know about?"

"Not really. Just the challenges you'd expect from trying to accommodate a crew this biologically diverse aboard a single starship. I was on deck seven while the construction team was putting the final section of Ensign Lavena's quarters into place. I must say it's a little unnerving to see a wall of Pacifican ocean water that extends from floor to ceiling. If we ever have a forcefield problem, her quarters will have to stay sealed; otherwise the rest of that deck will have a huge flood on its hands."

Riker smiled. *Titan*'s distinction as having the most varied multispecies crew in Starfleet history was one in which he took great pride. He was convinced it set the right tone, for the right mission, at just the right time in the Federation's history. Small wonder, then, that it was also an engineering and environmental nightmare—at least until all the kinks were finally worked out.

"You're right," Riker said. "I'm not going to worry about it. Besides, it wasn't all that long ago when we had to deal with ships that took on a lot more water than that." *Our honeymoon on the Opal Sea,* he thought. *Quite an adventure that was.*

They reached a turbolift and stepped inside. "Transporter

room four," Riker instructed it. The doors closed, and the lift started to move.

"There's something I do need to bring up," Deanna said. "It's Dr. Ra-Havreii."

"What about him?"

"He's asked to remain aboard *Titan* during its shakedown."

Riker frowned. "Did he say why?"

Deanna shook her head. "He wasn't specific, but I could tell he was troubled about something."

"A problem with the ship?"

"No, I asked him that immediately. He said he has no concerns about how *Titan* will perform, and his emotions bear that out. This is a personal request."

Riker nodded, considering the matter for a moment. "All right. Let him know he's welcome to remain aboard during the shakedown. No, wait, belay that. *I'll* tell him. A personal invitation from the captain is the least of the courtesies I can extend to *Titan*'s designer. And while he's with us, see if you can probe a bit deeper about his reasons for staying aboard—without offending him, of course. Maybe after Dr. Ree is settled."

"Understood," Deanna said, and there it was again—that small, restrained smile, the same one she had nearly released when Jaza had informed him of Ree's imminent arrival.

The lift halted, depositing them outside the transporter room. Riker stopped. "All right, Deanna, what is it?"

Her smile finally broke loose entirely, spreading across her face until it became a grin. It was almost as though she was trying to keep herself from laughing. *Not a good sign.*

"You never read that file I left you on the Pahkwa-thanh, did you?" she said.

The Pahkwa-thanh, Riker thought. *Dr. Ree's species.* "I didn't see the hurry," he said aloud. "What's important to me about Dr. Ree are his talents and his record as a Starfleet physician, not where he comes from. I care about *who* he is, not *what* he is."

"But you've never met him," Deanna said, still smiling enigmatically. "Nor any other Pahkwa-thanh."

"Deanna," Riker said, then lowered his voice upon noticing a passing crewman. "If there's something about Ree I should know before I meet him, what is it?"

Troi straightened his combadge as though preparing him for an admiral's inspection, her demeanor suddenly innocence itself. "As you said, it's probably not important. So let's just go meet him." Doing a quick about-face, Deanna marched into the transporter room before Riker could stop her. Now more than ever, he questioned the wisdom of captaining a ship whose crew included his wife as a senior officer and advisor. He knew he could trust whatever decisions Deanna might make on his behalf to be in the best interests of both himself and *Titan*'s crew. But he was also well aware that she wasn't above having a bit of fun at his expense in the process.

Riker sighed and followed her inside.

"Good evening, sir," said the young lieutenant who was standing behind the transporter console.

"Good evening, Lieutenant." Riker searched his mind, but still didn't remember the young man's name. "I'm sorry, but what was your name again?"

"Radowski. Lieutenant Bowan Radowski," the dark-complected technician said. "And no apology is necessary, sir. We all know who *we're* serving under, but I'm sure it's difficult learning so many new crew members' names."

Riker tried not to smile. He wasn't certain if the transporter chief belatedly realized that he had just insulted his captain's intelligence, but Riker knew no offense was meant.

Kind of reminds me of something I might have done in my *younger days,* he thought.

A beep sounded from the console, and Radowski quickly ran his fingers over the controls. "Dr. Ree is standing by, ready to beam over."

"Energize, Mr. Radowski," Riker said.

On the transporter pad, the familiar luminal effect grew and coalesced into a solid being. As it materialized, Riker finally understood why Deanna had been so amused by his casual ignorance of Dr. Ree's species.

He had known from the head shot in Ree's personnel file that the doctor was quasireptilian. But he saw now that the little two-dee image, taken head-on, had been misleading. At his full height, Ree must have been over two meters tall, and built like a running dinosaur. His scaly, vivid yellow hide was accented by jagged stripes of black and red, and partially covered by an oddly configured Starfleet medical uniform designed to fit his unusual frame. A thick tail snaked behind two powerful legs, which had clearly evolved to chase down prey, and whose feet ended in talons and rear dewclaws. Ree's upper limbs more closely resembled humanoid arms, though it was hard to gauge their length because he kept them bent at the elbows, folding them close to his upper chest. His iguana-like head held a mouth full of sharp, finger-length teeth that glistened wetly.

Ree stepped off the transporter pad and approached Riker, staring at the captain with large, vertical-pupiled eyes that made him feel like a field mouse caught in the basilisk stare of a barn owl. "I am Dr. Shenti Yisec Eres Ree. Permission to come aboard?" the Pahkwa-thanh said. His diction was nearly flawless, though Riker saw that a forked tongue, as well as twin frontal pairs of upper and lower fangs—barely visible amid the rest of his formidable-looking dentition—

were the likely source of the overly sibilant esses in his speech. Riker also noticed that the doctor was emitting a strange odor, something vaguely akin to burnt toast.

Not wanting to appear put off in the least by the doctor's appearance, Riker stepped forward and extended his right hand in greeting. "Permission granted. I'm Captain William T. Riker. Welcome aboard *Titan*, Doctor."

Ree extended one of his own hands and grasped Riker's with surprising gentleness. "A pleasure to meet you, Captain. I'm eager to get to know you better."

As Ree made contact, Riker almost flinched reflexively. Ree's manus was cold, with long, nimble digits that wrapped almost entirely around Riker's hand. The hard claws tipping the Pahkwa-thanh's fingers were, thankfully, filed down, but the overall experience of shaking Ree's hand raised the hair on the back of Riker's neck.

I'll get you for this, he projected toward Deanna, carefully schooling his features into poker-tournament mode and focusing his attention on *Titan*'s chief medical officer.

To his surprise, Deanna acknowledged having "heard" him. That seldom happened, except when they were in close proximity or during times of exceptional emotional stress. The instinctive unease he had experienced at his first sight of Ree—perhaps an atavistic human fear—certainly qualified as the latter, Riker thought.

What's important is who *he is, not* what *he is,* Troi quoted.

All right, lesson learned, he shot back. Clearly, despite his high-minded ideals and enlightened self-image, Riker could still be caught off guard by the unexpected, and by what he didn't yet understand. He realized now that Deanna had set him up in order to give him a wake-up call about the challenges that *Titan*'s crew—including her captain—would have to face in learning to live and work together. Riker resolved to read Deanna's files on the Pahkwa-thanh as soon as possible—as well as those of any other species represented among his crew about which he had a less than thorough familiarity.

Mastering his revulsion by sheer force of will, Riker withdrew his hand and gestured with it toward his wife. "This is *Titan*'s diplomatic officer and senior counselor, Commander Deanna Troi."

Ree bowed slightly, though he did not offer his hand. "A pleasure." He peered at Deanna more directly. "I look forward to discussing empathic theory with you, Counselor. Some of us Pahkwa-thanh possess empathic sensitivities similar to those of some Betazoids. While I have no measurable degree of this talent, I still like to think it is my empathy that makes me such a good surgeon." He paused, then added, "It certainly isn't my humility." A dry laugh followed, sounding not unlike maracas being shaken.

Troi beamed at him. "May I escort you to sickbay, Doctor?"

"That would be delightful," Ree said, somehow hissing and clicking simultaneously as he spoke. Riker thought of drawers full of steak knives when Ree's top and bottom teeth came into contact. "Since that is where I'll be spending half of each ship's day, I hope that I will bond with it immediately."

Deanna led the way out of the transporter room, with Ree walking directly behind her, his head dipping to avoid hitting the doorframe, his claws clacking loudly across the deck as he moved. Out of Ree's line of sight, Riker started rubbing his right hand—which he imagined felt strangely clammy in the wake of Dr. Ree's handshake—when he "heard" Deanna in his thoughts again: *Just deal with it, Will.*

As he stepped into the corridor, a voice once again issued over the comm system. *"Bridge to Captain Riker."*

Watching Deanna and Ree disappear around a curve in the corridor, the captain tapped his combadge. "Go ahead."

"Sir, we've just been hailed by the runabout Irrawaddy, *on approach from Earth. She's requesting priority clearance to land in the main shuttlebay. Admirals Ross and Akaar are on board."*

"Thank you, Mr. Jaza. I'll be right there," Riker said as he headed for the turbolift, his poker face suddenly inadequate to the task of suppressing the frown that was creeping across his features.

A surprise visit from two of the most influential admirals in the fleet. This can't *be good news.*

To be continued in

STAR TREK®

TITAN

TAKING WING

Coming in 2005

KNOW NO BOUNDARIES

Explore the Star Trek™ Universe with Star Trek™ Communicator, The Magazine of the Official Star Trek Fan Club.

Subscription to Communicator is only $29.95 per year (plus shipping and handling) and entitles you to:

- **6 issues of STAR TREK Communicator**

- **Membership in the official STAR TREK™ Fan Club**

- **An exclusive full-color lithograph**

- **10% discount on all merchandise purchased at www.startrekfanclub.com**

- **Advance purchase preference on select items exclusive to the fan club**

- **...and more benefits to come!**

So don't get left behind! Subscribe to STAR TREK™ Communicator now at www.startrekfanclub.com

www.decipher.com

DECIPHER®
The Art of Great Games®

A VIACOM COMPANY
www.startrek.com
STFC